THE GREY AREA

ALSO BY KEN EDWARDS

THE
GREY
AREA

A MYSTERY

KEN EDWARDS

grand
IOTA

Published by
grand**IOTA**

2 Shoreline, St Margaret's Rd, St Leonards TN37 6FB
&
37 Downsway, North Woodingdean, Brighton BN2 6BD

www.grandiota.co.uk

First edition 2020
Copyright © Ken Edwards, 2020. All rights reserved.

Typesetting & book design by Reality Street

A catalogue record for this book is available from the British Library

ISBN: 978-1-874400-76-9

Excerpts from this have appeared in *Golden Handcuffs Review*.
My thanks to Lou Rowan, the editor, for help and encouragement.
And to Brian Marley for his support and editorial nous.

I

The sum of human knowledge is far from complete. We arrived here, without quite knowing why or how. Consciousness – some might venture to say collective consciousness – is an emergent property of our condition. Consciousness at any rate of phantasies as reflected socially; all we can say in this case is that there were evident possibilities, but also circumstances that would have negated these.

We had been driven by market opportunities, or their lack. That has to be admitted. If you spend, you have to get. You have to crunch the numbers. Everyone in a partnership is a potential divorcee. It's that simple, that brutal. That was always known; it went, as they say, with the territory. But it became particularly brutal. The metropolis offered too much risk. Complications led to extreme danger; led to exit.

There was a parting of the ways, and it was acrimonious.

We had had enough; it was time to begin again. Our work has of course always taken place in an age of mechanical reproduction, but has it ever been a work of art? We think it could be argued as such. It could also be viewed as a narrative, that's to say, that which keeps one going; that which retains the attention. But there are countervailing arguments. Thus we are always confronted with dilemmas. Our condition is dilemmatic – to coin a fanciful word – and the work reflects that. We cannot say it is a science either. Or can we?

What was this place at which we arrived? Dead Level Business Park, formerly the All Saints Industrial Estate. A world away from the metropolis. Would the winter ever end? There *was* pollen in the air. The signatures of disengagement were everywhere evident, but they were unreadable. There was no back-story here; that, at least, was encouraging. And there were security cameras installed at strategic points around the premises: a comfort. It was time for a pause. Perhaps for a pill to purge melancholy. Onward. There were transitions to supervise, alignments to check, documents to process, possibilities to investigate, crises to contend with if not to overcome, bullets to avoid. (We speak metaphorically, of course; this was, after all, still England.) At least there was internet access. But then, a work of faith, maybe? No, emphatically not. We knew what was in those buildings, behind that signage. There was painted, corrugated iron in every horizontal direction, and above us a sky that foreboded.

What happened was that the sale fell through, so a rough Plan B had to be brought into operation. Strictly speaking, this was not legally watertight, but who was going to monitor it? And it would only be temporary. Things had not gone as expected. Despite generally depressed market conditions, the weatherboarded cottage in snug Deadhurst – two bedrooms, delightful walled garden in the back – had been highly sought after, and we were no match for the competition. So the dream of the secluded village had to be abandoned, and we were now in unmapped territory. There was an unmitigated horizontality about it, and the usual aura of uncertainty: that which was seen serving as an armature for that which remained unseen. Everywhere was evidence of solid materiality. The garage for the heavy plant, for the machinery. The meat locker. Treated and untreated timber. Sundry signage.

Industrial unit 13 was vacant for our operation at an affordable price; and was situated right next to unit 12, Dead Level Self Storage, where a sub-unit, one of 169 advertised, could be rented to contain the unmanageable library. All well and good, and convenient, if not ideal.

The wider surrounding area had been deemed – internet searches confirmed this – to contain many pockets of deprivation, which was surely observable right from the off, and yet there had surprisingly been only one reply to the advertisement. Lucy White was the name of the sole applicant for the position. Perhaps the wording had been wrong? So: a business park in a rural setting; that is, after all, enough of a contradiction. But to be more accurate: in a hinterland, or an interland, which Tibetan Buddhists would have called a *bardo*, a site of transition. And that was always our lot, and our place, just as surely as a raptor's "place" is the highest point of its range. In the one direction, Deadhurst, the "quintessentially" (how restrictively may that adverb be deployed!) English village, where money shouted quietly and politely from the other side of lace curtains, where rooks nested in tall trees sheltering the half-ruined Norman church (All Saints), the four spires of whose square tower were impressive outlines against a silvery-grey early evening sky; where artisan loaves might be obtained from a beautiful but blank-eyed girl in the half-timbered delicatessen/teashop. And in the other direction – two miles away, hugging the coast – Deadmans Beach, with its faint scent of rotting fish, its abandoned playing fields, its beach-launched fleet of clinker-built vessels and its miniature township of mobile homes. Deadhurst was to have been our home, and perhaps ultimately the site of our retirement; but it was not to be.

Two youths – the one, a hoodie, the other, a beanie – were observed at 10:57 sharing a plastic bottle of cider behind the electricity pylons. White Lightning. They moved hardly at all. They occasioned a shudder, for their presence was for a brief moment a reminder of our nemeses – those who were even now searching and would eventually track us down. Yet their harmlessness prevailed for now.

The weather was clement, if still chilly. At the road junction for Deadmans Beach, just beyond the Barbican Gate, was an abandoned pub (the Barbican Inn in fact, the faded sign said), half-timbered and lead-latticed, advertised as being for sale, with temporary wire mesh fencing mounted on breeze blocks barring access to the rutted car park at the side of the premises. How much was being asked for *this* property? But clearly there had been no interest for a very long while. Through the windowpanes, condiment bottles and salt and pepper shakers could be observed on the tables within, but the estate agent's board affixed to one of the timbers was already weathered. Pieces of concrete had been dumped against a wall. On a window ledge, a dented cola can. Further along, at the road junction, bunches of wilting flowers were seen tied to a roadside fence, clearly to mark the spot where a fatal accident had occurred. A pause, a shudder. But it was an urge to explore, as well as to escape, temporarily, the self-imposed drudgery of administration, that led us here, and once here it was natural to go past, and on. Pleasant, even. So then, at 11:21, the road was quitted and the Old Canal followed, on the right. It extended, straight as a die, to both horizons, a dead glint under the white sky, bordered with reeds, interrupted only by plank footbridges. A direction having been chosen, there was then a further interruption, a tumble and splash in the water, quiet but distinctive; and in the murk below could now be glimpsed a moving body, scaly, fringed, that was there, gone, there again, gone. Unquestionably some species of catfish – more than one specimen – though surely not native – and how on earth had they got there? But there was no present answer to this, and the creatures had now vanished without return, so (interrupted only by a necessary comfort break in a hollow behind some shrubbery) the itinerary recommenced.

On the far side of the canal, facing the long, flat plain, now loomed the head of the escarpment upon which the village of Deadhurst sat: a steep, wooded bank where the money spiders roosted and also the many varieties of beetle, preyed upon by rooks that set up an immense cawing in those high trees. But this was not our destination; turning left on reaching the next plank bridge, skirting the churned-up mud and proceeding away from the canal across the plain that spread to the sea and was once (mere thousands, not millions of years ago) part of it (the escarpment forming the ancient sandstone sea-cliff), the flat, bumpy, excrement-dotted pastures of the Dead Level were next encountered. Here, sheep accompanied by sullen lambs lifted their heads and stared for a few moments, as though astonished by our presence, before moving out of the way; and, further off in the more waterlogged regions, a pair of swans, spaced far apart, sat mutely, one carefully opening and closing its wings. In the extreme distance to the east, against the sky, where the marshes began, could be perceived a line of wind turbines, their blades slowly revolving.

On regaining the coast road after the long interval required to cross this sheep pasture, concrete steps were to be found, furnished with hollow steel handrails, and on mounting these one was confronted finally with the immense expanse of the sea. At the top of the sea wall a walkway was provided alongside the wide shingle beach. The rhythmic, swishing sound of the waves could now be heard. The tide was out; the sea was grey, but not too troubled, given the stiffish onshore breeze. Swifts darted around, and on the shining sand flats beyond were groups of herring gulls and lesser black-backed gulls, sampling the wares on offer. The tang of fish and salt was present. Occasionally a person and a dog might be observed. A man with long white hair obsessively rode a bicycle too small for him up and down this flanking footpath, and it was necessary to step aside more than once to accommodate him. He made no acknowledgement. Below, to the left, in the lee of the sea wall, was the Sanctuary caravan site, where the only activity was that of a family packing their belongings away into a camper van. They were surrounded by an army of fixed caravans or mobile homes in rank and file formation, but these were apparently deserted. Would this have been an option? Not an attractive one. By now it was 14:20. At the adjoining café a number of bikers were observed to be disembarking, removing their helmets outside before entering.

At Deadmans Beach itself, just before the fishing boats came into view, hauled up high on the shingle, another shanty-town consisting of numerous bungalows fringed the original settlement of traditional houses (the Old Town) above which the gulls circled and shouted. Many of these bungalows had been de-anonymised by being given names and/or makeovers to suggest ranches, Irish rural cottages, an Italianate residence, a Mexican hacienda. A Mr Whippy ice cream van was parked in the driveway of this last one. Horseshoes were nailed to its gate. Further along: a stone heron on the front lawn. And then, abruptly, the bungalows came to an end. After this, a thicket of notices. No turning. No parking. Area under surveillance. Heavy plant crossing. Beach Community Association Bingo.

Sounds of human voices began to drift on the breeze. On the other side of the road, playing fields and a pavilion building were visible. The fields hosted two or three boys' football matches, taking place simultaneously, with parents, relatives and teachers howling on the touchlines; in one game, the tiniest boys ran around clad in red or yellow bibs obviously intended for adults, so that it looked as though they were playing in long dresses.

But one cannot stand and watch strange children for very long these days without drawing attention to oneself. In any case, rain clouds began to gather. So, on the way back to the business park a small farm shop (set back from the road in what had evidently once been a garage) tempted with its high-priced products; a jar of French fish soup was purchased to be heated up for the evening meal, as well as jars of garlic and curry sauce and sun-dried tomatoes. It was 14:55, and the shadow was already on the land.

•

George was difficult yesterday. Unsettled. It's always the same when he sees his father, but there is nothing I can do. And Dave himself is no help. No help at all. Dropped him back here quite late, having filled him up with fizzy drinks and whatnot, got him hyper, and this after a problem day at school. Then turns and gets back in the car with barely a word to me and off he goes, so rude he is these days. Not that I want to talk to him. We have nothing to say. We have nothing to talk about any more.

But George was jumping up and down, very excited, firing questions at me. When is Daddy coming back to live with us? We'll see, I said. I was finally able to persuade him to go to bed, but then he called me twice before 10pm. First he wanted juice, then, the second time, inevitably, the toilet. Just go, I called up, you're not a baby any more. He does start reverting to babyishness after he spends time with Dave, why is that?

Well, I'm a bit exhausted. Don't know how I can manage

the transition back to work. Don't know whether I want a job, even. But needs must. First I have to collect my thoughts. That interview tomorrow at Peralta Associates, Private Investigation Agency. Nine o'clock it's scheduled for, after I drop George off at school. What to think about that? I still have no clear idea what the job involves. Very vaguely-worded advert. It's at 13 Dead Level Business Park, so not too far from here. Mornings only. That's pretty convenient, but we shall see. Experience of investigative work an asset? An asset? Intriguing. What does that mean? Do I have that? And why a clean driving licence?

But I need the money, and to be honest I also need something to distract me. When I picked George up after school yesterday Mrs Darling, who I chanced to meet, said he had been "fractious". There had been a disciplinary "issue".

Then this morning, that letter arrives from the school. I can't believe it. Climbing the school flagpole at break, I ask you. Why had he done that? I phoned Mrs Darling and when I finally got through to her she said he was trying to frighten the seagulls. Perhaps we'll talk about him some time, Mrs Darling said. He's a good child, Lucy, she said, his heart is in the right place. Well, I know, his little heart is ticking away reliably in his chest, but it's like a madness enters him sometimes. The last thing I want to do right now, though, is talk about it endlessly with Mrs Darling.

I asked George, and all he said was that a seagull had stolen part of his lunch and he had been trying to retrieve it. Very hard to get any more out of him.

Anyway, back to school again tomorrow. After the job interview, I shall need to do some shopping in town. It would be good to have an income again, that's the truth. I wonder if I should have rewritten the CV. Does it give a good impression, I fear not. Too much clutter. There is noise upstairs. Only the windowpanes rattling, the wind is getting up again.

•

When one is a prisoner of one's memories, the aim must be to get rid of them. But their mechanisms are obscure; to understand them, it's necessary first to examine their effects and thence reverse-engineer them to understand how they obtain the results they do.

Midnight approached, and still distressingly few inroads had been made into sorting and classifying the clutter that emerged from the boxes. (Even taking the library out of account – and that loomed, waiting to be unloaded from its temporary tower of cardboard.) A wire mesh cylinder intended for containing pens and pencils. A cutting board. A draining rack. Souvenir mugs. A chrome and glass cafetière, faintly stained brown. Stacks of old Chinese notebooks with black and red bindings, some full of jottings, some still relatively pristine. Microphones. Cables, colour-coded. Remote bugs, with their receiving stations. Rush matting, rolled. A china pig with an insane grin on its humanoid face. Sundry, dusty computer kit, much of it obsolete. Headphones. A small tower half full of CD-Rs. Stacks of black bin-liners packed with clothing, shoes, towels. An easel, and A2 chart paper. A fly-swatter, a chipped biscuit tin. Assorted pairs of binoculars. An oscilloscope. An electric drill. Toolboxes. A small, soft bag containing dice.

Isolated from their familiar context, outlined and shadowed in the light of the anglepoise lamp, all these items seemed now mysterious, alien, threatening even.

They represented memories. If they could be made to speak, they would say: one day we shall all be gone. But for the present they were mute.

The site manager had been affable, one might say jocular. In his early sixties perhaps, he had a pronounced dent in the middle of his denuded forehead, while stringy, greying hair was stacked mostly in wings or curtains on either side, above the ears and overflowing them – and he wore a yellow pencil tucked above the right ear. His name was Trevor Tanner. Industrial unit 13, ah yes, I take it you're not superstitious, Mr Peralta? Not in the slightest? That's good. It has traditionally been our least popular unit, ha ha. But very compact and convenient. Right next to the self-storage facility, which is number 12. Dead Level Self Storage. So it's doubly convenient for you. Yes of course, the library can be deposited in there, for a monthly charge.

That was indeed handy. It was noted that the facility offered 169 storage rooms on three floors – an odd number. Storage units in a range of different sizes, to suit the customer's requirements, Trevor Tanner asserted.

On being asked if his brains could be picked concerning a certain technical issue, he replied, reasonably enough: I ain't got none, but you can have a go. And laughed good-humouredly at his own joke. The impression gained was that any client, in the present economic climate, was to be nurtured proactively. The unspoken truth was that few of the units were currently occupied. So, continued Trevor, it was a question concerning legal wording in the contract, here, and here. His uneven brow furrowed as he studied the page. Coming over the speakers in his cramped office, The Israelites by Desmond Dekker. He confirmed that the contract did not indeed permit residential use. But as to the definition of "residential" ... well, hours of business were not actually stipulated. Suppose that late-night working, or indeed early-morning working, was called for, and suppose late-night merged into early-morning, well then, it would be a matter for security, not for himself, Trevor Tanner. It would be a question of liaison with the security officer. Gordon was his name, Gordon Prescott. Gordon would be on duty later. The segue was imperceptible. Exodus, exhorted Bob Marley, movement of Jah people.

So, to reiterate, late-night working, or even all-night working, would not invalidate the contract, *per se*? Because there were special circumstances. Unfortunate circumstances, but of a temporary nature only. Gazumped, is what we call it. When property is the question, people are vicious. Trevor was most solicitous about our homeless state. But we're always anxious to be flexible, Mr Peralta, he said; for example, take the self-storage rooms, he explained, one had been hired by a local pub band, not for storage as such but for weekly rehearsals. Unusual, very unusual! But it had been felt they were not after all violating their contract. Even use of the power supply, that was allowable. If that was what they wanted to do, and no-one else objected, indeed, if there was nobody *to* object, even though the room was not sound-insulated (in fact, the reverse, the reverberations were if anything amplified by the steel partitions), well then, in the absence of complaints, it could be permitted. Folk metal, they called their music, ha ha. What was the name of the band? He couldn't recollect it. Something to do with hedges. Or hedgehogs. The Hedgehogs? No, that wasn't quite it. Three boys they were, lovely boys, very polite. People commented that it was very unusual, but there had been no complaints at all. So it had been allowed.

Trevor Tanner tended to repeat himself a great deal, using only slight variations in wording, to make his points. About this matter you raised, you want to talk to Gordon, he deals with security. Just let Gordon know, so he's in the picture, in regard to *de facto* residence. On being thanked for his help, he exclaimed: No problem! No problem at all! Just have a word with Gordon. He's the security officer. Gordon has been here on site for over ten years, even before the business park took its present form. Lovely bloke, Gordon, loves nothing better than the fishing. There's good fishing round here. I'm talking about freshwater angling, obviously, not the sea fishing at Deadmans Beach, that's a different scenario altogether. But

Gordon, he's the guy, you just put him in the picture, Mr Peralta, and everything will be fine. Any other problem, just ask me, any time, OK, cheers.

The music abruptly faded, and so did the daylight. It was still officially winter, according to the meteorologists. Sea temperatures remained cold, and ambient temperatures on the estate could plunge to a degree or two above zero at night. Gordon, a heavy-set, completely bald male in his forties wearing rimless spectacles, was located in his tiny office, where a bank of video screens showed live CCTV feeds in saturated colour, with a bias toward purple, mauve, magenta, from various locations within the site; this variegated light glancing off his smooth pate. His greeting was warm. The formalities having been complied with, beckoning, he walked quickly out of his room, chatting the while, and along multiple corridors. White painted brick, a maze made of it. He pointed to the fire extinguishers, snapped lights on and off. His head gleamed again in the creamy light. He entered one room, picked up a cardboard box full of documents, and minutes later deposited it in another. He agreed that security, including data security, was paramount.

Back in his office: photos of large freshwater fish were evident, tacked up on the wall. Are you interested in angling, Mr Peralta? No? Wildlife? Ah, yes. How did the catfish come to be in the canal? Ah, you noticed that? he observed approvingly. Beats me, it really does. Well, you know them catfish, people buy them as pets, they don't know they grow to great sizes. When they're too big to manage, too big for them tanks, they dump them. Maybe put them in the canal, or even flush them down the toilet, and they find their way through the sewerage system to the Industrial Ponds. Years later, they're multiplying, migrating. Unbelievable. Not the only alien species around here, he went on, you might want to check out the Marsh Frog, for example. There's a lot going on that's not what it seems, he added again, mysteriously, after another pause. But (regaining his enthusiasm) there's good fishing in the Industrial Ponds these days: tench, bream, roach, very good pike in the winter, and you might catch the odd catfish, obviously. And very odd catfish they were.

And as regards "all-night working", just so long as I know you're there, Mr Peralta. Just so long as I know you're there. So that was clear enough.

The light went out. Number thirteen. One of the smaller units.

The air had been moving outside, brushing the trees, but it had long stopped and such sustained environmental noises as there were, including the buzz of a power saw, had died. Isolated sound events still occurred. They could have included the hooting of owls. Yet this was inconclusive. Inside the unit, the air was warm and still. It was quite snug here. Remarkable how the piece of carpentry fitted so neatly into the alcove, as though it were prepared for it, that is, the space prepared for the object and the object prepared for the space. A mutual accommodation. "You have made your bed, and now you must lie in it." And so it happened. One can lie tucked into a wooden bunk or casket and dream the entire universe; one can imagine being safe in one's grave.

However, for now sleep was not an option, comfortable enough though the bunk was. The ticking of a wristwatch was exposed, reverberant. And there seemed to be uncanny moans from other rooms – but there were no other rooms.

The rumble that could just be perceived in the distance was a train. Deadhurst station, situated on the far side of the village, received an hourly passenger service in either direction throughout the day, but the last one was no later than 22:15. Freight and engineering works took over after that. It would be well past midnight when the gypsum train was released from the exchange sidings at the mouth of the mine, deep in the woods, and this is what could be heard, when all else was still, heading with its lengthy load for the Moorish tunnel, thence to Moorshurst and the long haul to the metropolis beyond. It was a melancholy sound.

By now the radio was on, softly, a local station, because it was a comfort in those dead hours, even though its content was meaningless. The balm of melody! In time the Rockies may crumble, Gibraltar may tumble, the song went, softly, they're only made of clay. But Gibraltar is actually made of limestone. As for the composition of the Rockies, it is complex: both metamorphic and sedimentary deposits, laid down in different eras. But our love is here to stay. When the tune faded, the DJ uttered, again softly, his consoling inanities. The local news on the hour. A 70-year-old man had volunteered a statement to police that in the course of a vigorous discussion with his partner concerning her children he had placed his hands around her neck while explaining his argument. Two climbers whose bodies were found "roped together" in the sea by search crews were a teacher and former pupil at a local independent school. Love is strange. On the anniversary of his great-aunt's disappearance a man had posted a new plea online for any information that might lead to a resolution of the case. A bounce of static, and Julie was on the line. She appeared to be trapped in a phantasy of transcendence, but the DJ made no effort to disabuse her. There were too many stories to be indexed. When the DJ, the king of metaphor, announced that it was time for a little jazz, what was it he actually meant?

The rumble was that of monstrous, unseen creatures, the size of Indian elephants, never revealing themselves but felt to be always in the rear in steady pursuit along the forking railway lines; urgently to seek the refuge of the units in time, while negotiating that labyrinth of options, became a priority.

This treacly easy-listening was never jazz. But by now, the complex chatter of finches outside was beginning to proclaim the advent of dawn, the palest of light accompanying it from the unseen direction of the beach and entering through the window.

•

Hello, I'm Lucy White.

Ah, good morning, please do come straight through. I'm Phidias Peralta. Sorry about all the mess here – still settling in. As you can see.

That's all right.

Please, take a seat. Sorry, I'll take the papers from that chair.

Thank you. So you haven't been here long?

No, no, just moved in three days ago. The business relocated. There were teething problems, shall we say, but I think they are on the way to being resolved now.

You moved – from where?

Relocated to this part of the world from the great metropolis. The Great Wen, as someone once called it. Oh, by the way, I am being very rude, would you like any refreshment, some tea or coffee, perhaps...?

No, I'm fine, thanks.

Actually, that's as well. Just remembered – no milk. And no refrigerator to put it in. But all these things will be fixed in time. When I get some help, obviously.

So there are no other staff?

I beg your pardon?

Nobody else working here?

No, no ... just myself. And yourself, or ... whoever, whoever takes this position.

So, sorry if I'm speaking out of turn, so there are no associates?

Associates?

As in Peralta Associates? Peralta Associates, Private Investigation Agency?

Ah, no, I see what you mean, the associates long disassociated themselves. The business, in effect, is no longer a partnership. I am now a sole trader, technically, despite the historical, um, baggage, the persisting documentation. As a matter of fact, the business was to have moved to a property in Deadhurst which would have provided living accommodation upstairs, but that regrettably all fell through. It was a very attractive property. Weatherboarded, with rambling and standard roses in the garden. It had a plaque designating it as the home of a famous writer of the early twentieth century, though I know for a fact he was only in residence a matter of months. Never mind.

So where are you living now, Mr Peralta?

Please, call me Phidias.

Sorry ... Phidias ... I seem to be asking all the questions, which is not how it's supposed to happen is it? I do apologise.

(Laughter.)

No need to. Actually, I am – unofficially, you understand – living here for now, here in the office. A nod and a wink secured the situation. Purely temporary, of course. Until other arrangements can be made. I don't find it too bad, in fact. It suits me. It's a blank canvas, you see, or a bare stage, whichever metaphor you wish to choose. There's no back-story here. I like that. I have a bunk and a toilet, and this little shower cubicle you observe there, and the kitchen area, with a hob, even a baby oven. Admittedly, you could not cram a fowl of any reasonable size into it, but it will do for now. Yes, temporary, you understand. We are in a state of temporariness, or temporaneity, or ... what's the word? But we had better get to business, hadn't we?

I really do apologise, Phidias.

No, no, it's entirely my fault. Lucy – if I may call you that – please tell me about yourself.

Well ... I'm separated from my husband, with one small son, seven years old. His name is George. I've got quite extensive admin background, as you probably saw from my CV, but I'm particularly looking for interesting part-time work. Can't do full-time because of the childcare.

Where does your son go to school?

All Saints Primary in Deadhurst. We were very lucky to get him in there, because I live just outside Deadmans Beach.

Where the junior school has a very poor reputation.

That's right. You knew about that?

I make it my business to find out all relevant facts. And your separation from your husband has been ... moderately difficult?

Well, yes.

I don't mean to pry. But I'm experienced in these matters, I suppose. Your husband no longer lives in the area?

That's right, he doesn't. He visits from time to time. Takes George out for the day regularly, or for an hour or two to free me up. But George mostly lives with me.

So you will need to deliver and pick up your child daily during the school term. I can see how the hours would suit you. Now you have a clean driving licence, you said.

That's right.

Part of the work would entail transporting me, you see. I am unable to drive. It was never a problem in London. Here, we are in a different ... kettle of fish, you might say. Let's see, what else? Would you say you are observant?

Observant?

What colour are the door and window frames of this building we are in, did you notice?

Goodness ... a sort of greeny-blue.

Excellent. Teal, I think it's called. How many industrial units are there on this estate?

Trying to think. Oh yes, the board on the front said twenty-one.

Very good, well observed and remembered. How are you with technology?

(Laughter.)

I can just about cope with my mobile phone.

Are you willing to learn new technologies, surveillance technologies for example?

Wow. I'm ready for anything.

Can you lipread?

Lipread?

A very useful skill. And not too hard to learn.

I'd be happy to learn. If it was useful.

Good. Well, I think that will do, don't you?

We are always beginning again, it seems. Continuity of consciousness is an illusion, but one that persists. Who is writing this, that's always a relevant question. Who knows? Our method must always conform to the forensic norms and ethics required, in order to glean the necessary data without too much social cost. Nevertheless, it was to be hoped that on this occasion it wasn't excessively like an interrogation for the poor woman. And so what was the conclusion? There were glimmers. Sometimes she definitely glimmered. Sometimes not so much, it had to be said. But then a glimmer – or even a flash – which gave encouragement. A pleasant enough woman, anyway, in her mid-thirties (check her birthdate, yes, 34), thin fair hair, glasses, around 60 kilograms, had been to college, clearly a very capable administrator, but with the potential for other responsibilities. Clean driving licence, yes. So was Lucy White the answer – or Lucy White even the question? Was Lucy Black or White? What was the question to be answered, anyway? That was too murky. The answer: neither Black nor White. The truth is rarely pure and never simple, as Oscar Wilde once remarked. But sometimes was lucid, actually. Well, we were committed, in any case. We did not know how this was going to work out. Somehow, though, things were becoming clearer, or at any rate more settled. There was hope that the past could be left behind. That figures would become more palpable against the ground. There were pieces on a chessboard, but with the board blurred. There were no other viable alternatives present. With suitable training? The right move. White to play.

Hello?

Is that Lucy White?

Speaking.

This is Phidias. From Peralta Associates.

Oh, yes, hello. How are you?

Very well, thanks. Where might we best purchase a small refrigerator locally?

Beg your pardon?

A fridge. You may recall we were lacking this convenience.

There's a very good white goods store in Moorshurst ... oh, I can't remember what it's called, but I could look it up and call you back. If that's OK?

A thousand apologies, I should have anticipated you'd be busy. I was thinking hours of nine-thirty to one-thirty might suit.

Suit?

Yes.

Suit me, do you mean?

Yes.

Well, yes, that would be ideal, but ...

Good. Well, may we take that as read, then?

Phidias?

Yes?

So you're offering me the job?

Oh, I'm sorry, Lucy, perhaps I hadn't made myself clear. I've had a lot on my mind. I had a kind of epiphany yesterday which confused me. I was under the impression I had.

Not in so many words. In fact, you ended the interview so abruptly I thought I'd said something wrong.

Not at all, not at all, Lucy. A thousand apologies if I gave the wrong impression. But setting that aside, I'm sure you'd be excellent. Yes, I intended to offer you the job if you would like it.

Thank you, er, Phidias. It's just you didn't say.

Then consider it offered. Starting next Monday?

Can I consider whether to accept?

By all means.

So can I call you back?

The case continued. It was built sentence by sentence. And so we were sentenced to death. The sea was lucid. The sea was impossible. How could we proceed? One plus one is two, but one times one is one. The story so far: still a south-westerly, with gulls wheeling in it. No further, then. But all these manila folders had re-emerged, bulging with cases, past and indeed ongoing. There were stacks of them. Now there was a new one. A disappearance. And these cases, closed or still open, were all in the end sub-sets of the case that continues: the case of all cases, in which we reside, and maybe have traction or maybe not, but figure in some way. The case of all cases. All that is the case. That which we are all inside of – the events we mark, notate, report on – but do we imagine only that we are inside of this, this case of all cases, or in reality is the distinction between outside and inside illusory? What would be the boundary – the container? But if there is no boundary, it isn't infinite either: perhaps finite yet unbounded, as in Einstein's formulation. And the reports. The reports conflicted, or were full of internal contradictions; while they were being considered, even as the sentences they were composed of were built, they were already decaying slowly in their manila folders, or if not so palpable no less real the sequences of zeros and ones in

which they were encoded decayed. The logic gates corrode.
One times one times one is one.

2

First day in the new job. I don't know what to say about it. It isn't like anything I've done before. I'm not sure how long I'll be able to stick it, but I suppose it will do for now.

Having said which....

He seems extraordinarily disorganised. No, that's not correct, he's got an organised mind, no question, but his attention to the practical details of life or is it the details of practical life, well, that is deficient. He needs help.

He's homeless, really – he's living in the office, which he's not supposed to do, but is as comfortable as he wants to be, and appears to like it. He says he had put an offer on a cottage in Deadhurst, but at the last moment he'd been beaten to it by another buyer. His intention had been to run the business from there (he said the previous owner of the house was a psychotherapist – you can't trust them, he commented acidly). So anyway, now he's rented this space, the smallest unit in the business park, and he's actually proposing to live there too, for now. Well, he *is* living there. Says the security manager is turning a blind eye. It's not really very adequate, but he appears happy enough with it. For now, he says. I don't know how long "now" will last. Not bothered, anyway. There's a tiny kitchenette with a hob, and a cupboard of a shower-room and a toilet. It's clean enough. Also a narrow bunk bed, like a coffin (said that himself), which has been shoved into a convenient alcove. He told me he had built that bunk out of railway sleepers, many years ago – in a temporary spirit of enthusiasm for carpentry, is what he said. And it fits that space perfectly – it's a miracle, he says, with a little smile. So he has some practical skills, then. But it's a bit monastic.

No room for the Associates there, he said, meaning the bed. His idea of a joke.

We got the front office sorted. That's the priority, I suggested, and he agreed. Clients need to get a good impression. A desk. We need better chairs, I said, where they can be comfy while waiting, maybe a coffee table with magazines. He looked puzzled at that, but shrugged his shoulders. He has an odd sideways look. Put all that on the list, he said. What about plants, I suggested. Potted plants, that's good, put that down. The back office. We need to clear this mullocks, he said. Mullocks, that's the word he used, which is new to me. He meant the huge pile of stuff that is slowly being burrowed into and sorted. And the majority of it is a mountain of cardboard boxes containing books. The library, he calls it. Well, that will be unpacked and moved to a space in the self-storage facility next door, because there really isn't room for it in the office. I envisaged walls of oaken shelving, he said mournfully. Gave me that crooked grin again.

But what a job! We can't let anybody in here until it's done, I suggested. Sorry, no, that's not an option, he said. Turns out there's a client coming tomorrow, a new case. Well, we'll have to do the best we can, and hope they're not put off.

So who's the client?

Do you recall Edith Watkins?

Should I?

No reason why you should.

So she's coming tomorrow?

No, no, he said. No, no, no. She disappeared.

So we won't be seeing her, then?

Ah, no. She famously – or not so famously, since you don't seem to remember – disappeared over a year ago, and has not been found. A lady in her late eighties.

Now I did remember. The story made the regional TV news, I think. A local elderly lady wandered, and went missing. I remember for example there was some CCTV footage that was shown. Then after a while, like everything on the media, the story, too, disappeared. I suppose if I thought about it at all I would have assumed she had been found eventually and I had missed the story.

When I explained this, he replied: That's absolutely right – no, you didn't miss anything – and well put. The woman disappeared, and then after a while the story disappeared. Because it didn't have what they call closure, so there was no use for it.

I imagine her family are upset, I said.

That is what I imagine too, but we shall find out tomorrow at 10am. Her nephew has made an appointment.

That was all he knew. He assumed, he said, that the family were unhappy with the way the police had handled the case in the year since Mrs or Miss Watkins had gone missing.

Now ... any other suggestions for the present time? he asked me.

Air freshener?

Can't abide it. Don't, he said. But a refrigerator.

So I suggested doing an initial shop at Blackwater's in Moorshurst, and he agreed readily. Now this is another thing. I'm to drive him everywhere. He had seen my car where I parked. A Peugeot four-door hatchback, perfect, he said, with a look of satisfaction on his face. Let's go.

On the way, I said: Isn't it funny, how you never hear the end of these stories that run on the news?

Not funny, he replied. Endemic to that mode of discourse.

That's the word he used, endemic. He uses a lot of fancy words.

Good morning. Appointment to see Mr Peralta.

Ah yes, you're Mr ...

I knew quite well what his name was, for heaven's sake. It was my first morning in the front office, and we were expecting only the one client. No doubt he saw through my lame pretence of riffling through the diary to remind myself.

Watkins is my name.

Kieran Watkins was a man in late middle age, of an exceptionally neat appearance, a little tending towards plumpness, short, sandy greying hair, what else can I say? Dark, open-collared shirt, tweed jacket. He jingled his car keys in his hand as he spoke.

Of course, Mr Watkins. Please take a seat and I'll let Mr Peralta know you're here....

Tell him to step in, Lucy, said Phidias.

Mr Watkins, would you go through?

Ah, hello, I'm Phidias Peralta, pleased to meet you – do call me Phidias.

Hello, it's Kieran, Kieran Watkins.

Do sit down. Can we get you some tea or coffee?

No, I'm all right, thanks.

I do apologise, we're still in a state of, um, transition here, I think you'd call it, so do bear with us.

You've not been based here long?

A matter of at most three weeks, and trading for less than that. We were previously based in London.

Ah, down from London, ha ha.

Like so many!

DFL, they call us.

I believe that's the acronym.

We're DFL too, my wife and I. We moved to Deadhurst more than twenty years ago when we had the opportunity. Twenty-odd years, it makes no difference, you're still DFL, especially if you venture out into Deadmans Beach. But Deadhurst itself: a beautiful village, beautiful.

Ah yes, rambling roses at the door, the sweep of the downs behind ... Do you know, I put in an offer on a house in the village, but I regret to say I wasn't successful, so the hunt for a home goes on.

I'm sorry to hear that. Property is always in high demand there, despite the hard times we are experiencing.

Indeed. So you're happy with that move of twenty years ago?

Never regretted it. Especially now that I'm taking a back seat in the business.

Which is?

I'm a partner in a firm I co-founded, based in London. I used to commute every day. That wasn't always so much fun. An hour and a half, maybe two hours each way, even in optimum conditions. Train from Deadhurst, changing at Moorshurst, or alternatively driving to Moorshurst, parking there and getting on the direct train. But now I've taken on a new role, I've become a consultant to the firm, I only need to travel to London once a week.

And what does your firm do?

We're a leading chemical manufacturer, specialising in innovative food preservatives and flavour enhancers. I helped to found the company after I achieved my doctorate in chemistry some decades ago, and we're an international business now. You'll find our ingredients in many household name food products.

That's very impressive, Kieran. And the company is currently prospering?

We've been hit by the recession like everyone else. These are challenging times.

I fully sympathise.

But we have to keep on keeping on, as the song says, ha ha.

Good. Now, um, Kieran, you're here to talk about your aunt, I believe?

Yes, that's right, Edith Watkins. Are you at all familiar with the case?

I've acquainted myself somewhat with it, yes. Although so far I can only go with the information freely available on the internet. She went missing, let's see, on March fifteenth a year ago, and has not been heard from since?

That's correct, Mr Peralta.

Phidias.

That's right, Phidias.

And your aunt is a single lady in her late eighties?

Is or was. This is what's distressing to our family, you know, the uncertainty. And it continues, because the police have come up with nothing. She was 89 when she disappeared, a year's gone by and she would have turned 90 by now.

Well, well, that's a fair old age. And she was suffering from dementia to some degree?

We were pretty certain she had Alzheimer's. But the doctor had not given a diagnosis.

How did you assess her condition, I mean what did the family think?

So she got a bit confused at times, but she was living on her own, and up to recently had been coping quite well. Living in Moorshurst, little semi-detached house, been there a number of years. Refused to move to a sheltered flat, which she could have purchased at a very reasonable price, but that was her decision. Bright as a button, she used to be, in her prime. But we began to notice things.

Things?

Well, one time, this is going back a few years now, we motored over to see her, she seemed rather anxious and distressed. Couldn't find the remote for her television. In the end, we discovered it by chance in the garden, in a flowerbed. How it got there, heaven knows. Well then, when we took our leave she asked us particularly, as she often did, to phone her as soon as we got back, so that she would know we'd got home safely, so I did, I phoned her and said, Aunt Edith, we're back home, and she said, why, where've you been? We laughed about that later, but ...

What else?

It started getting worse. We began to notice the house wasn't always as clean as it once was. She used to be extremely house-proud. We tried to hint tactfully that she might want to get someone in to do the housework she could no longer manage, but she went up the wall at that. Can't manage? I've always managed, and I always will manage. That's what she told me. In no uncertain terms. But she was getting really muddled and contradictory, was forgetting things.

Had she ever previously wandered off and got lost?

No, never. She was actually used to going for long walks and long bus rides, but there had never been a problem.

Until that time.

Until that time – over twelve months ago.

Please tell me in your own words how you discovered she was missing.

Well, then. I've told this so often.

To the police?

Exactly. The same story, over and over again, every time a new officer takes over, or whatever. Every time there is a "new development". (And he made the sign for inverted commas with crooked fingers of both hands.) But there never are developments. Well, what can I say? The reason I've come to you, you see...

You're disappointed in the police?

I'll say so. They appear to have dropped the case. They won't tell us that, they claim they always keep such cases open, but they have. A year has gone by, they've made no progress, despite our prompting, and now they've just dropped it.

Why doesn't that surprise me?

My son Robin urged me to come and consult you, actually. That website about my aunt Edith that was set up – you've seen it, I think – that was all my son's doing. Robin put it together, did all the technical stuff. And all the social media online, you know. We got dozens of responses to all that, and we passed on any leads to the police. They thanked us for them, but I know they failed to follow up most of them, and any they did follow up they took weeks to do it.

I understand. Look, it's frustrating and upsetting to go over the same ground again, I know, but if I'm to help you I've got to hear it from you. So, how you discovered she was missing, tell me, Kieran. In your own words.

I'd phoned her a couple of days in a row, but she didn't answer.

This was, what, around March fifteenth?

Sixteenth and seventeenth. The fifteenth is when she actually vanished, they reckon, but we didn't know at the time. We had asked her to come over for Sunday lunch previously, but she never replied. I mean, despite her age and beginnings of confusion, she was usually very good about returning phone messages. So we thought, hey, something funny here.

You were worried she had never replied to your invitation?

We were worried because of her increasing memory loss, you see. We did have her round regularly for Sunday lunch. Usually we'd fetch her. Anyway, after a couple of days I got in the car, I had to go into Moorshurst anyway, I said to Anna, my wife, I'll drop in and see how she is.

And she wasn't home?

That's right, she didn't answer the bell. I wasn't too bothered at first, because she did go out for walks. But I noticed there were three milk bottles on the doorstep. And then her next door neighbour, nice young woman, Sharon her name is, came out into her front garden, and she said, I'm a bit worried. She said she hadn't seen her for three days. Well, that gave me a bit of concern.

A bit?

Quite a lot.

And you entered the house?

Yes, I had a key. First thing, you know, there's a bunch of mail on the doormat, just fliers and junk mail you know, but still. So we pop up the stairs to the bedroom, heart in mouth. But it was empty. The bed had been made. Everything in order. No sign of her anywhere. And the neighbour, who came up with me, said, She's gone for one of her walks and not come back.

Very distressing.

You know, when you have an elderly relative you don't expect them to be around forever. It's quite natural for them to go. But this way ... all we want is, you know, what's it called ...

Closure?

Yes, that's it, closure.

I understand. I understand perfectly. Everybody seems to want that. It would appear to be part of the human condition. And yet, so often – in fact, almost invariably – it doesn't happen. It's a comforting illusion.

Well, there we are. We just want to know what happened to her. That's all we hope for now.

I will do my best to help you. But lack of closure is also part of the human condition. Lack of closure defines the onward process that we call living. And closure, which we claim to want so much, is actually death. That's a paradox, isn't it?

•

Towards dawn, the rattle of rain on the windowpane ceased, and all became still. A dim, milky light was beginning to fill the pane. The unit had the aura of an eternal waiting room. But soon the end of night would be present; we were just about coming up to it, dawn on earth. Still dark, but the dim light from outside percolated. It was an out-of-body experience. It was the moment of creation.

In the distance could be heard, faintly, laughter. Or what seemed like laughter: brief peals spaced by silence.

Ha-ha-ha-ha-ha.

Sleep had been abolished some time before. The crossword had yielded but fitful solace. We had learned that the author of the metamorphoses with a zero at his heart is egg-shaped, but there was little more to glean here. So nothing to be done but succumb; get up, put on clothes.

Now the hands were being washed; now the teeth were being scrubbed.

Ha-ha-ha-ha-ha.

That is what it sounded like. It was coming from somewhere outside, somewhere in the middle distance.

In the alcove kitchen, the blue light of the kettle's on-switch glowed. The kettle began to rumble. It was still cold in here; the radiators had not yet come on. Coffee was spooned into a jug. Light spilled briefly from the newly purchased refrigerator, then was shut off again with a soft thud. The kettle shuddered, coming to a boil.

The clouds were at last parting, and there would perhaps be some moonlight before dawn.

The coffee poured from the cafetière, and was hot and welcome.

Exit from Unit 13.

Tall depot lamps at each corner suffused the site with an even glow. A quilt-coated figure would have been picked up by the CCTV cameras, departing the Dead Level Business Park, Unit 13, and heading for the perimeter and exit at 05:35. Dawn was due at 06:01. Isolated in the flat surrounding countryside, the site would have resembled a fortress or maybe a fortified homestead on the pampas of Argentina; beyond it, the silver moonlight was only fitful and there would have been barely any hint of lightening yet in the rapidly moving clouds on the eastern horizon.

Ha-ha-ha-ha-ha.

The Old Canal was quickly reached. A distorted mirror in darkness, slipped between rush banks. But now there was little or no sound; perhaps the odd tiny splash, or a soft rustle in the undergrowth. Moonlight was inadequate, and a torch therefore essential to enable one to pick a way safely along the uneven and potentially treacherous footpath, mud-swollen by the rain of the night. The patch of light bobbed. But the laughter had stopped for the while. The question was, where was it coming from? Was it best to keep to the canal, or to follow one of the back drains?

The torch was switched off.

Silence and darkness were everywhere, cloud cover having again hidden the moon, but now there was more than a trace of that eastern promise.

A certain splash again, and then: Ha-ha-ha-ha-ha. The same five-fold peal, more distinct than before, and a good deal louder. Probably coming from the bank opposite. The suspicion was close to being confirmed. Almost certainly then *Pelophylax ridibundus*, the Marsh Frog, also known as the Laughing Frog, with its distinctive quintuple call. Not native to this part of the world – they were introduced to this country as garden pets in the 1930s from Eastern Europe – but known to have colonised ditches and streams extensively. Their existence had first been brought to our attention by security officer Gordon Prescott. Clearly, there was now a thriving population in the Old Canal, and perhaps further afield. Was it possible to discern a tiny dark shape, of amphibian provenance, moving at the foot of the reeds? And another? One could not be certain.

But what then were those larger shadows?

For, as the light grew, two tall dark figures had emerged on the far bank upstream, like sentinels watching, spaced apart. They loomed as dark shapes against the faint background of incipient dawn. It was uncertain how long they had been there. They were seemingly motionless, and yet it was undeniable that they were living, and watching. One on the left, larger, but the other, too, of a considerable size, spaced by possibly four or five metres' distance from the first. They presented as sentinels or, if one were being fanciful, angels or harbingers, their message inscrutable, their portent unknowable.

The apparition caused palpitation of the heart, constriction of breathing.

The figures remained in place, quite still, but no, not perfectly still, and therefore undoubtedly alive. Why did they seem to be watching, and to what purpose?

It seemed now that an eternity was encapsulated or fixed in what can only, in retrospect, have been a few brief moments. What sinister avatars were these, of what provenance? Multiple possibilities raced through the brain. There are phenomena, and there are human descriptions of such phenomena. How these match up – how truth-value can be assigned to such matchings – is the question. Two observable entities. Observable, but for a period non-explicable. Is it too fanciful to suppose that during that period, however brief it might be, all possibilities were equally valid? A coalescence of energies occurred, concentrated in two locations, identified as being on the bank of the Old Canal of the Dead Level, and these coalescences might be representable as anything that could be imagined – ghosts, for instance, unwelcome memories, perhaps, of enemies from the past – messengers carrying as yet unknown information; or else, random accumulations of non-being, cosmic junk, meaningless patterns. And might all of these possibilities for that infinitesimal instant be equally "true"? And when they arrived at the point of observation, let us suppose, might these wave-functions of infinite possibilities immediately collapse into that which we term "reality"?

It cannot be denied that the thought of old enemies was the first to spring to mind. Idiocy it now seems in retrospect, but that first thought was: surely Borg and his cohorts had not tracked us down yet? But why would Borg, if it was he, and whichever henchman he now hung out with, be perched on the canal bank just before dawn? That thought froze the blood. To say that sanity prevailed is to say that such bizarre possibilities – ghosts and angels too – were eliminated in favour of the one selected.

There was a soft, croaking roar, crescendo.

The figure on the left lifted its wings, and began to rise. A dark angel? Yes, it had wings, powerful ones, which it beat as it rose into the air, gathering itself for flight, long legs packed together, the distinctive s-crooked neck now visible.

They were two grey herons, *Ardea cinerea*: very likely from their appearance an adult and a yearling. The first was soon in the air. And the other on the right, the juvenile, now followed, and as they gained height, both started to head separately for the light in the east, which now had some rosy-pink to it, ponderously lifting their weight with rhythmic movement of their wings as they made their deliberate way towards the distance. In that immense silence, in which the heartbeat was actually heard, the blood pumping through the system at an increasing rate, the rhythmic swish of their wings formed a counterpoint as they departed into the horizon of the Dead Level, where they quickly vanished from sight.

A frog again made its five-fold song ring out over the cold water.

Heartbeat slowed, and there was more light.

06:15. Dawn was well underway.

Tough night, couldn't sleep. Kept waking from dreams. Dreamt all the fish in George's aquarium were dead – eaten or horribly maimed by ghastly spider-like creatures with rubbery flesh that had invaded the tank. Some of them raced around at high speed. Black, they were. And in the dream I fretted about how I was going to break the news to George. So I woke, and heard rain and wind outside, rattling the panes and shaking the house. But despite the conditions, and the central heating having gone off, I felt strangely hot, I had to throw off the covers. Then I heard mutterings from the next room. Please, no. Mummy, Mummy, I heard him shout. George, I called, it's not morning yet. Go to sleep. He was grumbling and muttering. I glanced at the green LCD of the radio alarm. Just gone four o'clock. Eventually, thankfully, I managed to drop off for a while before, all too soon, the alarm went.

The light level slowly increased over the business park and the Dead Level beyond. It became pearly – if that is not too fanciful, too poetic. For a long time it had seemed poetry offered what the business people call a "solution" – not just as consolation in times of sleeplessness, but as a way of being in the world – but that was before disappointment set in. As for pearly.... It no longer appeared relevant. To what? It was the metaphorical dimension that niggled. A pearl of great price. Clarity is important. To the continual, and neverending investigative project. The case of all cases. Investigation is an art, but a science also. Science can suggest techniques, but has limitations too. The Dead Level presented, in all its complexity, as an environment: the shaggy shapes, dotting the distances, of lumbersome sheep, attended by their recent offspring; the unseen life-forms and ditches; the discarded human detritus; the mud pools with the imprints of birds' feet; and at the very horizon the stately wind turbines, twenty-six in number, their rotor blades turning slowly, not entirely in synchrony. A poet might have suggested these elegant structures marked the border between the known and the unknown. But it was all unknown: the fantasy that one might comprehend every molecule of that landscape – every anomaly it might give rise to – does not bear very much scrutiny. Poetry or science – it is all a question of managing the unknown, extending to the limits of knowability.

One might research quantum mechanics, for example, insofar as one could understand the subject, which was not very far at all. Quantum theory applied to real-world (macro) investigation projects? (Thinking of the collapse of the wave function.) And probability theory. For example, the probability of finding a particular object, or a particular event (which amounts to the same thing), or even a missing person, in a particular location at a particular time. Throw a grid over the area. Actually, it would have to be a four-dimensional grid, the passing of time having to be taken into account. But you could model it in three dimensions. Then compute the probabilities for each cell of the structure. And focus the work on the high-probability regions. It was a hard problem, certainly.

Equally, a predator might use such procedures to find and remorselessly close in on its prey.

The quiet was disturbed by the crescendo hum of a vehicle passing on the road outside, reaching a brief apogee before the decrescendo back to silence.

And it is understood that the macro and the micro, the "real" world and the "subatomic" world, are two separate, irreconcilable realms. But this is nonsense: reality is plainly a continuum. So the limitations – it would be too much to say the failure – of science were evident here. Somehow, science, or shall we say computation, needed to be supplemented or countered by intuition. Or the aesthetic, even. A synthesis. So, then: poetry reconciles the macro and the micro in ways that science cannot. This is the function of poetry. Discuss. Well, the conclusion was that there was nothing really to discuss there. That was a meaningless statement. Because one suspects that, just as there is said to be a black hole at the centre of every galaxy, so irrationality is at the core of every apparently rational system.

If there's an answer, a poet once said, there must be a question – but if there's no answer then, it follows, there is no question, that is to say no meaningful question. So we understand.

In the distance could be discerned the glitter of water.

First thing this morning, after a dreadful night when neither of us could sleep, George said he wasn't very well. Didn't make clear exactly what was the matter, but that's often the way. I took his temperature – normal. But he wouldn't have breakfast. Didn't want to feed the fish either, which was unusual. He was so enthusiastic when we first bought the aquarium, he's gone off it a bit, but even so, he's always wanted to give them their breakfast before having his. So I can't find anything physically wrong. Generally a bit listless, though, which is not his normal demeanour.

I rang the school to say he wouldn't be in, left a message for Mrs Darling. Then I rang work, explained the problem, said I'd be in when I could. Phidias was very nice about it, said he'd see me when he saw me, but it isn't too good to do this on your second week in the job.

Who are you calling? asked George. I explained to him I would have to stay in until I could get someone to look after him, so I needed to call Mr Peralta to tell him that.

Who's Mr Peralta?

He's my employer, he's in charge at work, I said.

Is he the detective?

That's right, I said.

He could look after me, was George's bright suggestion.

Sorry, darling, Mr Peralta can't look after you, don't be silly.

But he could teach me how to be a detective, George said, suddenly a little more animated than he had been.

I don't think he has time for that, I replied, but then I thought, well, if he doesn't have a temperature, I don't know, I could take him in, assuming Phidias was agreeable to that, so I said: If I take you into work, would you behave yourself, do some drawing and painting quietly?

And his eyes lit up, yes yes, the first signs of animation this morning. I'm not promising, I said, it depends on Mr Peralta, I said. Oh, please, he said. Please, please.

Sorry, I'm not at my best this morning. I slept badly. By the way, are you sure it's all right about George coming in with me this morning?

That's perfectly in order. I too had difficulties last night. I heard sounds, which penetrated my dreams and interrupted my sleep.

I did too! What kind of sounds did you hear, Phidias?

Oh, laughter in the night, which was most disturbing. Having established that I was no longer dreaming, I went out before dawn in pursuit of these sounds, which kept coming and going, and reached the canal, where I experienced, what shall we say, apparitions that unnerved me. I had an atavistic shock. But the least said about that the better.

Apparitions?

They were hallucinations. They weren't real. Or rather, they were real creatures – herons – I had mistaken for phantasms.

And they were laughing?

No, no, that was the laughing frogs.

Oh.

They were real. The sounds were therefore explained.

I see. I also had bad dreams.

Well, it must be something in the air. Is your son all right in the reception room?

He's got his drawing stuff. He likes drawing, he can be occupied in it for hours.

Well, that's good. Shall we resume where we left off yesterday? Or did we cover it all?

I believe we did, Phidias.

OK, so that concludes the roundup of cases that are still live. Have I forgotten anything?

I don't know. Have you?

I hope not, Lucy. We're still working through the blip of post-Christmas divorce cases. Usually quite dull and sordid. But nothing very out of the ordinary.

What about this one, Edith Watkins?

Ah yes, I was coming to that, the one new case, the missing octogenarian. Or presumed octogenarian, were she still living. Or she might possibly even be a nonagenarian by now, in that unlikely event.

You don't think there's any chance she is?

Obviously quite improbable. However, there are some things we can do immediately to pick things up from where the police have clearly abandoned the trail.

What would they be?

First thing is to retrace, as exactly as possible, her last known movements. I know the police will have done some of that, but in my experience they miss a lot. Their approach is commonly shoddy, I'm sorry to say. They blame the cuts in public expenditure. But be that as it may, let's get that going in the next few days.

It's very distressing, isn't it?

This one is, certainly.

Aren't all disappearances distressing?

Some cause more distress than others.

Do you, have you had a lot of disappearance cases?

Oh my word, yes, they're very common. Very common. I'm afraid they're more or less our bread and butter. Second only to the divorces, of course.

And how many of them are solved?

How many? Well, usually if there are people wanting to find an individual who has disappeared they will be found, or what happened will be discovered. In many cases, however, nobody cares about the disappeared individual. In those cases, the chances of a conclusion are much more remote. Particularly because such cases don't hit the media.

What about this one?

A child, or a young, attractive woman – those are the dis-appeared the media are interested in. Particularly white and middle-class individuals. An elderly person, well, there is a novelty value – though more elderly people unaccountably disappear than you would think – and this one, Ms Watkins, I believe featured as a story in the local and regional media but not much further, as far as I am aware; and the lack of devel-opment in the story means that it has tailed off to nothing. I assure you the police take their cue from that.

What, you mean the police don't put so much effort in –

Oh, there are cynical calculations there. No doubt about it. To be fair, their resources *are* constrained, so they have to make decisions on that basis. A high-profile case will attract more police resources, whereas one where the interest is not there, or has tailed off ... well, the profit margin, if we can use such crude terms, declines sharply. So resources will be switched to where they can have more impact.

That does sound very cynical.

It's as it is, not as we would wish it to be.

(Pause.)

But Lucy, I do assure you, disappearance is common. Indeed, you could say it's universal. We are all scheduled to disappear.

To die, you mean?

To disappear. One day, the perceived entities that are you or me will have vanished, irrevocably. That is certain. It's also banal. Let's put it this way: the universe has existed for billions of years, this earth has existed for four and a half billion, without any trace of you or me. Then, we appear. An entity appears, struggling into life. A few years later, a few moments later in cosmic terms, the entity disappears again, and is forgotten. Was it ever there? What does appearance signify?

But when we die ... people will at least know what happened.

Normally there is evidence, yes. To wit, a corpse. But even that does not persist for very long. It is a piece of evidence, it is *in* evidence for only a short period of time, a tiny fraction even of our brief lifetimes, before it, too, vanishes, is put out of sight, to decay, to be consumed by flames. As Hemingway once wrote: Life is much shorter than death.

But, Phidias, this is a disappearance without *any* evidence about what happened!

True, and in this case this is what we have been engaged to seek. But disappearance ... you must understand, it is commonplace, it is banal, in and of itself, it is a necessary condition of existence. Even in the cosmic void, physicists tell us virtual particles are appearing and being annihilated all the time. As in the micro world, so in the macro: human beings, stars, galaxies. Just on different time scales. In the city, we were dealing with unexplained human disappearance on a daily basis. London is, as you know, famed as a city of disappearances. The phenomenon even directly affected our practice. A colleague had staff who disappeared.

The *staff* disappeared?

A woman who worked as my associate's assistant for a

while – well, she wasn't the first one, but was perhaps the most notable and perplexing case. Not that this ever became a "case", if you see what I mean. She was a woman he had hired about six months previously, basically doing what is now your job.

Oh my god.

I didn't mean to worry you, Lucy, sorry. This was a one-off. I was called in to help solve the problem. I was unable to do so.

She disappeared?

Quite suddenly. She had been doing her job quietly, well if not outstandingly. She was hard to get to know, but pleasant enough. Efficient. A woman in her late thirties, a bit older than you. Unmarried. Apart from that, she revealed little about her private life. We were just closing a case that had been concluded more or less satisfactorily; the client had paid his bill, and there was no more to be done. My associate asked her to return some documents that belonged to the client, and she said that, by coincidence, the address was just a block away from where she lived, so she offered to save postage by delivering the package in person on her way home at the end of the day. And that was the last we saw of her. The following morning she didn't show up to work. Very unlike her. There was no reply to a telephone call. The same again the following day. We contacted the client, who confirmed the package had never arrived, and as a matter of fact this was corroborated when it was later retrieved from her home. The police were contacted, her landlord was contacted. He said she had absconded, owing him rent. The police, with our help, managed to find an ex-boyfriend. They questioned him, but he said he had not seen her for months, and his story seemed sound. They had only met in a bar and gone out for a few months before she had cut off the relationship. In truth, he didn't seem to know much about her.

That's spooky.

But not unprecedented. That was the city. A place of millions of anonymous comings and goings. Another statistic, no more.

Didn't she have family?

The boyfriend said he thought she had a father, and possibly a sister or a stepsister, somewhere up north. That's all he knew. They were never traced. She was never reported.

What happened in the end?

There was no end. My colleague hired another assistant.

Mummy, look.

George, I thought I told you to stay in the front office and do your drawing there.

I *am* drawing, I wanted to show you. It's a spy plane, I call it the Flying Cat.

George, Mr Peralta and I are trying to work.

Can I see that, George?... Very good, excellent draughtsmanship.

What's that mean?

It means you're good at drawing.

George, go and do another one.

I was just showing Mr Peralta. Mr Peralta, are you doing detective work?

That's right.

Could I be a detective?

George, don't bother Mr Peralta, he's busy.

That's all right, Lucy. Could you be a detective, George? Well, anyone could. If I were to give you some advice, well, I'd say three words first of all.

What's that?

Observation, observation, observation.

That's funny! That's only one word. But you said it three times!

That is correct. Because it's an important word. Do you know what it means?

No.

It means looking at things very closely and noticing every-thing you can and remembering it. That's what you have to do to be a detective.

Cool.

OK, George, will you go back in the other room and do another drawing for Mr Peralta?

All right, Mummy. Mr Peralta?

Yes?

What's that?

It's a digital recorder, or you could call it a dictaphone.

A dictaphone?

Don't touch it, George.

It's perfectly all right, he won't damage it.

How does it work?

You can record sound. You press this to turn it on. Then you press this button to start it, and speak into the microphone there. When you've finished, press the button again to stop.

You've got a lot of cool stuff, Mr Peralta.

Listen, why don't you take this into the other room and use it to report on your Flying Cat? I want to hear the report.

OK. Thank you.

(Pause.)

Sorry about that, Phidias. George sometimes gets over-excited. Where were we?

No problem. I have too many gadgets here. Most of them have been rendered obsolete by technological developments. Most surveillance now can be accomplished by hacking into voicemail or intercepting texts or email. Not that we would condone such methods, you understand. So, Edith Watkins. Would you open a new case file, Lucy, the way I showed you, and start filling in the details from here?

But this assistant to your associate, I don't understand. Did the firm not have a duty of care to her as an employee?

I believe so, which is why we worked with the police to do what we could to locate her. But we came to a dead end, and it was not justifiable to devote the resources of the firm to do more than we did.

Did she leave behind any possessions, were there any clues there?

Only clothes and some other bits and pieces. She had not left a phone, or money or documents or anything else of value. Which suggested she wanted to disappear, for whatever reason. And the subsequent silence implied either that there was no-one to care about her, or that she had disappeared into the care of those who did. We observed and took note of what had happened, or at least the evidence for what had happened – which is never quite the same thing – but in the end we ran out of observations and came to the end of the trail. The trail petered out on the brink of the usual abyss. So it goes.

There was no conclusion?

Sometimes we have to accept that. You know, Robert Frost – a poet I am not particularly keen on, as it happens, but never mind – said free verse was like tennis without the net. I paraphrase. But what we are attempting in the field of investigation sometimes seems to be tennis without net, racket or ball.

That's pretty tough!

We have to persist. You see, humans have an insatiable need for narrative, a need to know what happens next. To construct meaning. That's part of it. But what if the meaning we construct is an unreliable fiction? What if it doesn't correspond to anything in what we are pleased to call the objective world, or to anything that may enlighten us? Or what if it just doesn't resolve? What if what happens next in the story is just another sentence?

So you have to just go on, until it makes sense?

That could work.

You think so?

That's one way. It's about pattern recognition.

George seems to have enjoyed his morning in the office, and took pains to tell me so, repeatedly. And continued to talk excitedly about being a detective, last night and again first thing this morning, when once again he showed interest in feeding the fish that we have named together: Cat, the bristle-nosed plec, the two algae eaters Big and Little Al, and the sail-fin mollies, seven in number now, Blackie, Whitey, Bruiser, Orpheus, Eurydice, Sunset – and Little Bro, the latest addition, with the spectacular lyre tail. But no further sign of any illness, real or imaginary, that's for sure. On the other hand, school will become twice as difficult. He's still moaning about it. So I have to make it clear it's not a precedent. I mean, he's advanced for his age in so many ways, but he does need to attend, he needs to avoid falling behind.

Phidias was fine about it. Well, I think he was fine. It's so hard to make him out. That conversation about disappearances unnerved me. He said, very nonchalantly, it wasn't the first disappearance, and "won't be the last". I made a joke about where all my pens go to, and he laughed at that, the short laugh he has. But it upset me, that, gave me goosebumps.

And meanwhile George going: "The Flying Cat is a spy plane with a number of interesting feechers, it has two engines, one is a spare in case the main engine gets shot, and there is space for two people, one is the pilot and the other one is the spy, who is like a detective but he can see all the observations from the air." Et cetera et cetera. All recorded on Phidias's dictaphone.

So anyway, Phidias has entrusted me with research for one of the cases we've got on, which I am quite excited about. This is the case of Edith Watkins, who went missing a year ago. Where the police seem to have given up. So Phidias wants me to do a number of things: first, start to compile a dossier about her life, for which I am to begin with any online sources, including the website the great-nephew put up; then, find out and collect some facts about the day she went missing, such as weather reports, local bus timetables, any other regional or local news that was reported on that day or immediately thereafter; and also he wants a map of the area, so we can plot her last known movements. Well, I hope I repay the trust he's put in me. I've never done anything quite like this.

•

Union flags and flags of St George were flying (lazily and intermittently in the fitful south-westerly breeze) from several masts outside the bungalows and mobile homes in the environs of Deadmans Beach – a development extending almost as far as the canal's long loop. A white plaster tiger stalked the neat garden of a newly built bungalow, to the front wall of which was affixed a pot-holder fashioned out of a cast-iron treble clef. Next door, an elaborately carved wooden notice on a post proclaimed this to be the domain of a "ship-faced aquaholic". Model boats could be observed crammed into the window beyond.

Gulls (as usual, mainly herring gulls interspersed with the occasional lesser black-backed gull) were dotted around the town's playing fields, and also in the farmer's fields beyond, between the sacred white goats that could be espied with the aid of binoculars. Closer up, it was noted that several long greenhouses with missing or broken glass panes sat empty in a wild sea of overgrown vegetation. In a front garden could be observed a dilapidated telephone kiosk, some glass panes missing, its red paint considerably faded to a shade of pink, its interior denuded of telephone equipment. A ruined bird table lay on its side, almost hidden by the undergrowth. There were low buildings of concrete and corrugated iron. Further along, a new estate of identical houses with hanging-tiled walls had been thrown up. Also, more bungalows, and then the beginnings of a farm. On further approach, a dog barked from within the farm buildings as soon as the binoculars were deployed. Flashing bird scarers, apparently repurposed CDs, dangled from telephone wires. Red and white traffic cones marked out a line across the far field. A foal lay there with its legs furled. A conservation notice affixed to chain-link fencing explained basic facts for the benefit of visitors about the varieties of wildlife to be found in the area.

Closer to the coast, amid puddles the colour of milk, the disused lifeboat station stood abandoned, its great wooden doors bolted, heavily weathered and disfigured by graffiti. By the side of the approach road a lengthy wall of caged pebbles was ready to hold back a storm surge from the sea.

Over the ridge, the sea itself: grey and white rollers moving in relentlessly from the south-west. And a prominent notice: BEACH LEVELS MAY CHANGE – *For your safety keep off groynes and other structures.* The mainly shingled beach stretched for miles in either direction, a wide expanse of it: the part furthest from our vantage point, beyond a ridge, sloping gently towards the shoreline; the nearer part flattened and showing the rutted track marks of bulldozers and other heavy plant that were accustomed to pass along here from time to time. Deadmans Beach and its fishing fleet would be situated a good way to the west of this location, out of present sight, and the only person to be observed on the entire beach was, at some distance, a solitary sea angler in a woolly hat, casting his line again and again. And for a long time the rhythmical rasp of the waves was all there was to be heard.

3

Our work is difficult and frequently beset with disappointment. We are perennially engaged in trying to map something that is essentially unmappable.

The case continued. A new file had been opened. Pencils were sharpened; metaphorical ones, at any rate. One had to say that Lucy White was now learning fast. Quite impressive, and surprising. Gratifying, too. And a relief.

She arrived promptly this morning, ready for the half-hour drive to the 10am appointment at Edith Watkins' residence in Moorshurst. A sharp fall in temperature was again predicted, as were high winds, and sure enough there was a light dusting of snow first thing this morning on the roofs of the units opposite; but within minutes the sun had melted it away. The basic temperature was not that low, but there was a slight, icy breeze. Flurries of temporary snow would have occurred during the night, but the morning was for now reasonably clear if overcast.

The route was eastward; on leaving the business park, we turned left at the Barbican Gate (the right turn leading to Deadmans Beach) and skirted on our far left the forested escarpment above which could be glimpsed some of Dead-hurst village's rooftops and the tip of the Norman tower of All Saints, masked by tall beeches, leafless now, with their freight of rooks, and, we noticed, evidence of heronries; then headed for the bleak open spaces of the Dead Level. At the round-about, the sign to Moorshurst was to be followed. The railway line was now visible, emerging from the woods at the far side of a great sheep pasture on the left; at one point, the faint rumble of a train could be heard and its distinctive livery briefly glimpsed then, bright against the gloom: a two-car diesel multiple unit, a Turbostar Class 171, on the down line approaching Deadhurst.

At the following junction there was a hold-up in the traffic: the number 201 double-decker bus directly ahead slowed to a halt, but there was no bus stop here. A police car had been parked diagonally in the centre of the junction so as to block access to the right fork, our intended route. A woman police officer in uniform with short blond pigtails protruding from her chequered hat emerged from it and approached the bus. The driver leaned from his cab, and there was a brief, ener-getic exchange between them, but it seemed good humoured. There had clearly been an incident. She returned to her car and reversed it a little way and to the side of the road, thus leaving space for access. The bus restarted, and our vehicle followed, edging past the police car, out of which the police-woman had re-emerged to wave us on.

A quarter of a mile further up the road a male police officer stood by a dark grey, unmarked car, parked with its boot wide open. He too waved the traffic on with slow, careful gestures. There was no further evidence of the incident.

Onward past marsh and field, through edge and hinterland, where the wind pulled, where the sun withdrew, across boundaries, transgressing frontiers and ditches, fences and hedges, under sullen air, through water meadow, through dead ground. And the distant glitter of drinks cans. And the sandpits. And noticing how the ground dipped to a body of water, a flat sheet dully shining, and an oil drum left there. The spells, the routes, the forking paths. Animals ruminating. A solitary kestrel appeared, still as though painted into the air it hovered within, the head absolutely motionless pointing down to its unknowing quarry. Then it was gone. And once more marsh and field, the vacuum of it reaching to the horizon, to the flat limit, the turbines. Rooks and jackdaws dotted around the fields, feeding on hard ground. And then the industrial plants coming into view off the horizon and the sun appearing but almost immediately beginning to vanish again. Glitter on the ponds fading, waterfowl glimpsed. Enigmatic, derelict buildings flashed past. They were shadows. Following them, a function hall, a row of houses, dismal front gardens, some overgrown some denuded. Road furniture looming up and rushing ever closer, to left and right, painted white lines zigzagging within an immensity of uncertain time, and then receding into the background, into the past, still unfathomed.

So, Lucy, let's recap. What have we learned so far?

Well, Edith Watkins was last seen a year ago, to be specific, fifteenth of March.

An inauspicious date.

Yes. She was reported missing on the eighteenth, and the police issued a statement and a photo of her, which reached the news – the local newspapers and regional TV, anyway. The officer in charge was a Detective Chief Inspector Green, from Moorshurst Police.

They put out a statement, or an appeal to the public, then, what did it say?

Just that they were hoping to find her safe, and they were appealing to anyone who knew her or had seen her recently. Edith Watkins, 89, five foot two inches, white hair, blue eyes, last seen wearing a red coat and a black hat. There was some reference to her having possibly become confused.

Yes, her nephew said they suspected dementia. But her physical health?

Pretty good, I think, she got about on her own quite a bit, apparently.

So any comeback from that public appeal?

I spoke to the police, and they said they had had a few people contacting them, but there wasn't anything much conclusive. They said they would be happy to meet you and discuss it.

OK, if you would make an appointment with DCI Green I'd be grateful.

I'll do that tomorrow.

So what sightings were there on the fifteenth?

Her next door neighbour had seen her briefly in the morning. She'd seemed normal. Also the owner of her local corner shop said he thought he'd seen her early that morning. And apparently a few members of the public rang up saying they might have seen her, but it seems rather vague. Apart from that, there was some CCTV footage from the Sanctuary Café.

In Deadmans Beach, right?

That's right, it appears she liked to take the bus to Deadmans Beach sometimes and walk along the front, and then she would go into the café for a cup of tea before catching the bus back home. Anyway, there is some brief footage of her possibly arriving and leaving that afternoon.

You've seen it?

Yes, there's a link to it on the website the great-nephew put up, you know, Mr Watkins' son. You can see an elderly woman in a dark red coat and a black hat and black handbag, walking with a stick. But it's not very distinct, I have to say.

That's good, well, maybe that's something to talk to the

police about. Any information from bus drivers or passengers?

I don't know. Again, you'll have to ask the police.

So did anything more come of that in the following few weeks?

Four months later there was another public appeal from the police. They went round parts of Deadmans Beach, including the seafront, and the outskirts of Moorshurst also, asking people in the area to check their gardens and outbuildings again.

And nothing?

No outcome that I can find. And apparently they started scaling down the search soon after that.

What was the weather like on that March day or the day after?

I thought you'd ask that. Windy.

I'm thinking of the possibility of her going onto the beach, maybe being caught up by a wave, being swept out, something like that?

Oh, that was mentioned, and I think the coastguards were alerted, but nothing was reported. We're coming close now, I think?

Yes, it should be next right. And what was this lady like?

Bit of a character, it appears. Unmarried, no children or living siblings, but knew a lot of people. She would talk to anyone, apparently, and she wouldn't mince her words.

Not the shy and retiring type, then?

Not at all, she had a lot to say for herself, but she seemed well liked, eccentric some people called her. But anyway it seems her disappearance caused a lot of sadness. Here we are.

That's right, this is it, Meeting Place Avenue. Number 104, it should be on the left, right at the end of the road.

The Watkins residence was to be found in the suburbs of

Moorshurst, a drab location close to a complex of retail warehouses. The street was long and straight, saplings having been planted at intervals along the pavement on either side, enclosed in their tubular cages of wire mesh. The house itself formed the end of a row consisting of small 1930s-built Elizabethan-themed semi-detached homes – many now grubby and some with inappropriate 20th and 21st century adaptations – and was situated around fifty metres from a bus stop. A modern corner shop occupied the end of terrace on the opposite side. The front door was approached by a short path traversing a tiny front garden dominated by flower beds, now presenting a bedraggled appearance. The door was painted white and had a pebbled glass panel below which 104 stood out in raised black italic numbers.

Kieran Watkins, the nephew, was waiting by the front door; evidently it was his black Range Rover parked outside, ahead of where Lucy had drawn up her Peugeot. His greeting was courteous and civil, though he seemed slightly nervous. For the record: of medium height and build, somewhat fleshy of face, jowls with the faint dark sheen characteristic of men who need to shave often, brown eyes, receding hair going speckled-grey. He wore a dark overcoat, white shirt and sober tie, as though dressed for a formal and perhaps unwelcome event; contrasting with the casual jacket and open-necked navy shirt of the previous meeting.

It's got a bit colder, hasn't it? he said.

Lucy volunteered to reply in the affirmative.

Kieran produced a key to the front door, and entrance was effected, whereupon he immediately adopted the manner of an estate agent.

So this is the entrance hall, normal end of row house, as you can see.

Indeed. Are you OK with this, Kieran?

Yes, of course.

Only it must be a bit traumatic, reliving this unhappy occasion once again?

You suggested it had to be done, Phidias.

Quite so. I'm glad you understand. I see a coat stand there, which presently has a couple of light coats on it, but you saw no sign, did you, of that distinctive dark red overcoat, or her handbag?

I think it was later we noted her winter coat was missing.

And you concluded from this that she must have gone out?

In discussion with the police, yes.

OK, let's backtrack. So then, when you entered the house, March fifteenth last year...

Eighteenth. Fifteenth is when she was last seen alive.

Ah yes, I beg your pardon. Of course, it was not you who saw her on the fifteenth. Morning of the eighteenth, was it?

Yes.

So when you entered the house, what did you do then?

I called my aunt's name. A couple of times, I think. No response.

And this neighbour, Sharon I believe is her name, came in with you?

That's correct.

Can we talk to her?

Is that necessary?

It would be good to obtain any insights from her, particularly about when she last saw your aunt alive and how she found her then.

Yes, of course. Let's see if she's in.

It can wait until we've had a brief look round the house. Lucy, would you mind making some notes as we go along? We shall need to speak with the neighbour. And also, by the by, Kieran, it might be helpful to talk to your son, who made that website, and also your wife, if she's willing.

I'm sure Robin would be more than happy to help you by

answering any questions you may have. But as for Anna, she really is very upset about all this, and I don't see the need for her to be troubled any further, so if you don't mind –

I understand. Let's get back to the matter at hand, then. Please remind me, you had previously found three milk bottles on the doorstep? And your aunt had a pint of milk delivered every morning, so from this you concluded she had not collected her milk for three consecutive mornings?

Yes.

Despite there being a convenience store opposite, she still had milk delivered in the traditional way?

Yes, she was quite modern in many of her outlooks, but she stuck to some old-fashioned habits. She was an old lady.

So, three pints on the doorstep. And, this being the eighteenth of the month, this information tallied with her neighbour's assertion that she had last seen her on the fifteenth?

Correct.

So, not having had a response to your calling her name, what did you do next?

I checked the front room – here – then went on to the dining room and kitchen at the back.

No sign of her?

No.

Could we draw open the curtains here? It's a little dark. So then you went upstairs?

Yes, we ascended the stairs, I think I may have called out again.

You were in some trepidation, I imagine.

Yes, I was.

So nothing. She had no pets? I see the –

Cat flap? Used to have a cat, it recently died. Would you like to have a look upstairs?

Please. Lead the way. Did she have any difficulty with the stairs?

We were starting to worry. But she strenuously denied

there was any problem. So, up we go. Here's the landing. There's nothing much to see. There are two bedrooms, the large one which she used, here, and a smaller one, over there, which is for, as you can see, for storing stuff. Bathroom and toilet back there.

So the bed is made, everything seems intact. Is this how it was, or has it been tidied up?

We haven't touched a thing. It's been like this for a year.

So you checked the rooms, then, no sign of your aunt?

No sign at all.

You looked for her handbag, her coat?

I can't remember. There was a search. The police searched thoroughly. That was later. And they asked me a lot of questions.

Is that what you did, then, phone the police?

I had a discussion with Sharon, and we decided to call the police. There was a wait ... they didn't come at once. Sharon put the kettle on downstairs and we had a cup of tea.

You looked in the back garden?

Sharon did. And in the shed too. I was a bit ... I called my wife.

Are you all right, Kieran?

Yes, just a little overcome right now. I'll be OK.

Take your time. That's the loft, up there?

Yes. Do you want to look?

First impression of Edith Watkins' house, on entering: that faint scent, a mingling of musty air, trapped for too long behind glass and curtains, with hints of dust, dead flowers, artificial perfume, air freshener and distant rot – the oddly familiar sensation typically associated with an old person's dwelling, still present here even after a year's non-residence. It presented as a typical English suburban home, with front and back rooms and a kitchen on the ground floor. There was, it was ascertained, no cellar. A coat stand in the narrow hallway still bore two or three coats or rain jackets – but missing, we were told, was the heavy winter coat Edith normally wore at this time of year, and in which she was pictured in that fleeting CCTV footage. Beside the stand was an umbrella holder, a ceramic cylinder with a willow pattern containing no umbrella but two walking sticks: a traditional wooden one with a shepherd's crook and a mauve one with a pink floral pattern. Kieran Watkins asserted that a third walking stick was missing. In the front room, the curtains were closed; even after they had been drawn back, at our request, the light on the furniture and artifacts came in milky and indistinct through the net curtains. An oval table of inlaid walnut was revealed, crammed with photographs in glinting frames. Observable among these were distinct likenesses of younger versions of Kieran Watkins: with more hair, with discreet facial hair, with a pleasant-faced woman, evidently his wife, with her and a boy (the son, clearly). And the same woman beaming and striding past a farm gate, the same boy rather older, pictured with a young woman, the family in Christmas hats by the tree, a dog, a cat, sundry children, all these in more or less faded colour, and then, dissolving to mono-chrome, a woman in a cloche hat (ascertained to be a portrait of a very young Edith), a stately couple captured in the studio in formal attire, the same couple with two solemn children; and a handsome young man with a pencil-thin moustache, in a Navy officer's uniform, this portrait bearing a handwritten message, "Edith – with all my love, Derek."

In a corner was a small, old-fashioned mahogany roll-top desk, on which sat a green-shaded lamp. The cover was closed, and there was no sign of a key, but the lock showed evidence of damage, and the cover was easily rolled back to reveal a modest clutter of papers and pens. Kieran was unable to answer whether it was the police who had forced the lock, but confirmed they had searched the desk for evidence. And the remaining space in the room was dominated by a huge three-piece suite of velour with lace antimacassars in place, grouped around a newish flat-screen television.

If evidence of life was already fading in this room, the back dining room, also accessed from the entrance hall, showed none at all. A polished mahogany table claimed this space for its own, six chairs ranged around it, with a matching sideboard freighted with silverware, and more family portraits on the dark green wallpaper. A faint scent of furniture polish added to the ambience. Off-white net curtains veiled the French windows giving onto the back garden. This was a room for show, a formality, little used.

The fourth doorway off the hall (the third belonging to a cupboard-sized toilet, fragrant with blue toilet cleaner) led to a narrow kitchen, also with access to the garden – unexceptional, some of the original wooden built-in cupboards, painted white, containing crockery and utensils but emptied of food products, as had been the tall fridge. There were traces of damp near the ceiling, and evidence of staining on the linoleum floor. The part-glazed garden door incorporated a cat flap.

The unexceptional back garden consisted mainly of a modest square of lawn, in transition to meadow, having evidently not been mown for at least a year. Damp shrubs and weed-ridden flowerbeds surrounded it. A wooden shed at the bottom contained rusting garden tools, sacks of compost, small towers of plastic pots, and little else.

And so up the carpeted stairs to a landing leading to a diminutive second bedroom used as storage space for boxes, a chest full of blankets, piles of jigsaw puzzles, a set of encyclopaedias, hillocks of unshelved, assorted mass-market paperback thrillers, a pair of old-fashioned wooden tennis rackets, a tea set still in its cardboard and cellophane box. And next door to it, the shrine that was Edith's bedroom, illuminated by slatted light from a Venetian blind. The single bed was covered by a patterned eiderdown, the white sheets neatly tucked in, the pillows plumped and set against the padded headrest; this, we ascertained, was how it had been found. A telephone extension and a reading light next to it, and a pair of reading glasses with tortoiseshell frames, lacking its case. Two chests of drawers, heavy pieces of furniture in solid wood, the one topped by a formidable iconostasis of portraits continuing the themes of the living room below, the other bearing an ormolu-framed mirror. The wardrobe, facing the bed, was still full of clothes, hung or neatly folded and stacked on shelves, many unworn in unopened boxes.

In the bathroom, at the back of the landing, rubberised handles had been affixed to the tiled wall behind the bath. The toilet was surmounted by an elevated plastic seat, part of a wheeled contraption with a tubular metal frame and high handles on either side. A barcode sticker was observed to be still affixed to part of the frame. These disability aids had, we were told, been installed at the suggestion of the family two years previously, after Ms Watkins had "had a fall" here in the bathroom – fortunately, without serious consequences. The solitary cabinet on the wall, mirror-fronted, had been entirely cleared. The floor was covered with vinyl, and again, although everything was spotlessly clean, there was old staining visible here.

So to the loft, reached from the landing by an aluminium extending ladder, unclipped from its cradle on the wall. Kieran assured us he had never known his aunt to venture up there in all the time he could remember, and there was nothing much to observe. It was necessary to borrow a torch, as no electric light could be found. Rafters impeded the search. Foam insulation tucked between the joists had been installed in the past two or three years, we were told. There were present here two or three old-fashioned suitcases, all without contents, and various cardboard boxes – likewise. Though empty of remains, this space was as silent as any grave.

It remained to be seen to what extent any clues harvested here might help in solving the mystery of Edith Watkins' disappearance. As to her life up to that point, the evidence was supplemented by her nephew.

She had been born in the village of Needless, a few miles from here across the county border. Her father had been a market gardener, her mother a part-time domestic servant. One elder brother (Kieran Watkins' father), deceased twenty years ago. By her own account, her childhood had been a happy one. She had been bright at school. On several occasions she had related her frustration at being prevented from going on to higher education – a thing presumably unheard of for a young lady of her class at that time. At any rate, she went on to become a telephonist, working for the War Office during the 1940s and in civilian telecoms in London thereafter. She had never married, but had been engaged to a young naval officer – clearly Derek, the man pictured in at least one of her photographs on display – who had been lost at sea during the war. She spoke infrequently of this young man, and according to Kieran "quickly changed the subject" when questioned about him.

She had purchased 104 Meeting Place Avenue, Moorshurst, with the residue of a legacy following her brother's death. By then, she had been retired from her job for five years.

What of her thenceforth? Edith Watkins' nephew sketched an impression of a woman who, until the first shadows of dementia began to appear, was very much of her own mind. Feisty, he said she was. We didn't agree about politics, for example, he added. After she'd passed a certain age, "feisty" would have been replaced as an adjective with "fiercely independent" – meaning, in short, refusal to be patronised. She took nothing for granted, argued a great deal, but seemed on the face of it to have been gregarious and generally popular in the neighbourhood. She even – her nephew stressed the *even*

– befriended some of the fishermen at Deadmans Beach. He related a story of some years back when she had persuaded the crew of one boat to take her out on a fishing trip overnight, an episode which he said had passed into local folk-lore – she was already in her late sixties at this time. It had shocked the family, clearly.

And so the habit had developed in the following years of regularly visiting the fishing beach. One favourite routine became invariable, and well known. She would take the 201 bus from Moorshurst to Deadmans Beach. At the waterfront, she might hobnob with any of the fisherfolk who were around, or just gaze at the boats. Then she would walk the length of the front, past the caravan park, until she reached the Sanctuary Café, where she was accustomed to call in for a cup of tea and a bun. She would then catch the bus back home from the stop just outside the café.

That's where the CCTV footage comes from, explained Kieran Watkins. You can just make her out leaving the café and heading to where the bus stop is. Apparently it was timed at just before 2:30 on that day, the fifteenth of March, which would have fitted in with the bus timetable.

Lucy confirmed this: the timetable showed the 201 service, hourly at this point, leaving the Sanctuary Café stop at 14:35.

So how had this footage been acquired?

That's about the only piece of initiative the police showed, said Kieran. We told them about her habitual walks and they investigated and that's what they came up with. I was gob-smacked.

Gobsmacked?

I didn't expect it, I suppose. It was a shock … stroke of luck. There she was on video. Maybe the last we'll ever see of her. But if you ask me, he added, they could have done more. A lot more.

Such as?

They questioned the Deadmans Beach fishermen, but they

drew a blank there, said Kieran. They know a lot more than they're letting on, the fishing community. They knew my aunt. I'm not saying they had anything to do with it, I'm not saying that at all. But they keep themselves to themselves. They won't co-operate with the police, and the police know that and don't bother much.

It appeared therefore that the description of Edith Watkins' final journey had been backfilled from those CCTV images and the bus timetables. And if the footage identified her correctly, and half-past two on 15 March at the Sanctuary Café was indeed the last time she was observed alive, then somewhere and somewhen, between that place and time and the bus's arrival in Moorshurst without her, a terrible thing was likely to have happened.

These, therefore, were the leads to follow, to re-investigate. It was now 11:10, and there was no reason why a start could not be made there and then.

•

The Sanctuary Café, Deadmans Beach, had previously been noted, appended as it was to the Sanctuary Caravan Park ("where holiday memories begin"), and so was easy to find. The caravan site clearly provided much of its clientele, though possibly not to such a great extent at this time of the year. A single-storey, breeze-block-built structure of moderately shabby appearance, it stood next to a small car park (presently containing only Lucy's Peugeot, though three picnic benches, padlocked to stakes in the ground, also took up part of this space), and faced onto the main road, opposite the bus stop for the number 201 in the direction of Moorshurst.

The CCTV camera was noted, positioned outside on the wall close to the entrance, a glass double door to which was affixed a neon sign indicating OPEN/CLOSED (OPEN being currently illuminated in green) – giving onto an L-shaped dining area furnished with eight melamine-faced tables of two sizes, four-seat and six-seat, the chairs being of tubular metal. Illumination was provided by overhead strip lighting. In the crook of the L, opposite the door, was the serving counter, presumably forming the frontage for a kitchen area that occupied the hidden quarter completing the building layout. Featured prominently in the space above the counter as well as being attached to various walls and windows were notices, some printed (for instance, a menu including faded colour photographs of selected dishes), others computer-generated on white or fluorescent green or orange A4 paper in several different fonts, and one or two handwritten in black felt-tip pen. For example:

Breakfast served until 12.00 noon only. Fish & chips on Friday between 12-3pm.

We don't give a refund on food.

Do not open or touch please.

Please please all rubbish in the bin provided thank you.

Please can you dress appropriate on entering the café thank you.

SORRY no dogs.

Toilets for customer use ONLY.

And the most eloquent, next to a microwave oven positioned on a small side table:

This microwave is for CUSTOMER USE. It may only be used for heating baby food/milk. The Sanctuary Café accept no liability for your use of this microwave whatsoever.

A nice touch. Whatsoever.

A wave of warm air from an unseen convection heater hit one immediately on entry. An unsmiling, open-mouthed girl with heavy eye make-up, blond hair in a tight bun, served customers from a narrow serving hatch.

Yeah? she enquired.

The possibility of an English breakfast for one was mooted.

(Lucy had said she did not want anything to eat, just a coffee.)

Sorry, breakfast is finished, said the girl.

This seemed a puzzle, if not an outright contradiction, in that it was now 11:45 and a cooked breakfast was promised, according to the notice, until noon. In answer to the query, the girl replied, jabbing her finger at the notice: Yeah, it says breakfast is *served* until 12. But if you order now, it will be after 12 by the time it's served, you know what I mean?

I know exactly what you mean. Just two white coffees, then, please.

'Mericano?

If that's what's on offer, yes, please.

You want milk?

I did say white, yes, please.

Take a seat.

Whatsoever.

Pardon?

Never mind.

Lucy, removing her coat, suggested a table on the left and places were taken.

The only other customers were two men in their forties, both wearing woollen hats, sitting at a table in the corner nearest the entrance. They were both tucking into the full English breakfast – clearly the last two servings of the morning. They looked like fishermen. One of them was heard to say: I was in Dover, at least that's where I thought I was. To this, the other made no reply, but merely forked a small, neatly layered bundle of bacon and egg smeared with ketchup into his mouth.

The girl emerged from behind the counter bearing aloft two plates each containing twin slices of white bread and butter. She went over to the fishermen and slammed the plates on their table with some force.

Thanks, sweetheart, said the first man. The other continued to eat silently, with single-minded application.

Two white 'Mericanos!

Over here, thanks. Oh, I see, you want us to come up to the counter to collect them.

(She placed the white china mugs without saucers on the counter, their handles facing towards her, in a way that made it necessary to lean over merchandise to turn them around and take them.)

All right? Sugar's over there. Thank you.

Thanks.

So, Phidias, this is where Edith Watkins used to come. It's a bit –

I know. Shall we try and put together what we've found out?

Yes, let's.

The problem as always is the quantity of banal detail that mounts up. The more it does, the more…. Well, we have to sift. And reflect. There is an absence here that we have to account for, somehow…. This is never Americano, Lucy. Is it? Nescafé, at best. Never mind. I need the caffeine. Where was I? Yes, the detail, the banality. The mystery is in the banality. And you can never, in such cases, say: this is what happened, definitively, this is what has been, what is.

I've never been in this café before, in all the time I've lived here. I thought it was just part of the caravan park.

I noticed it previously in my perambulations, though it didn't attract me at the time. But Edith must have seen something in it. At any rate, we appear to have a final definitive sighting of her here, or more particularly, a non-human sighting, an image captured on video.

It's interesting that she used to walk along the front from the fishing beach up to here, isn't it?

And used to befriend the fishermen. But no definitive statements from that quarter about that fateful day?

That doesn't surprise me, Phidias. (Keeping her voice low.) I mean, it doesn't surprise me the police got nothing from the fishing community.

There is antagonism?

Historic antagonism, I'd say. Perhaps with some reason, I don't know. But they would tend to clam up if any detectives were snooping around.

I think you're probably right, Lucy. Perhaps we should do some snooping ourselves and try and make a better job of it.

That would be interesting.

But the first priority must be to contact this, what's his name, Detective Chief Inspector Green?

Yes, I'll make an appointment, Phidias.

And it would be imperative to talk to the owners of this café too, and I'd like to inspect that CCTV footage more closely. I'll see if I can do that. Did you want another coffee?

No, thanks, Phidias, I'm done. I'm sorry you didn't get your breakfast.

Despite its poor quality, I think I might order another coffee for myself, if you don't mind. The fix was not sufficient for my need. Are you all right, do you need to pick up your boy from school?

Oh, heavens, no, not for another couple of hours.

I don't want to rush you. I can easily walk back to the office.

No, that's fine.

(The men at the table at the other end of the restaurant had finished their breakfast and left. The sullen girl emerged from her lair again to collect the used crockery and cutlery from their table.)

Oh, hello. Miss? Miss?

Yeah?

I hope you don't mind my enquiring – we're investigating the disappearance of an old lady, a Ms Watkins, I believe she used to come in here regularly?

Dunno about that.

Do you recall the police coming in here to ask questions about her?

Don't remember, the police, they come in here all the time.

How long have you been working here?

'Bout a year.

Yes, it would have been just under a year ago, but perhaps you weren't around.

Dunno.

Could I speak to the owner or the manager?

Mrs Hastings, she's the proprietor.

Could I speak to her?

She ain't here today.

Well, could we make an appointment?

You'll have to ring up.

We will do so. Meanwhile, I think I'd like another Americano, please. You sure you don't want another, Lucy? No? Just the one, then. With milk.

Yeah, I'll bring it. Sugar's over there. Thank you.

I'm much obliged.

Phidias, shall I phone Mrs Hastings here, then, and make an appointment for you?

Please, that would be helpful. Meanwhile, let us set out the probabilities as starkly as we can. Least probable: that Edith Watkins is still alive. Most probable: if the CCTV footage is verified, and she did indeed leave this establishment at 2:30 in the afternoon of the fifteenth of March last year, which we shall check, with the intention of returning home to Moorshurst, that somewhere between here and her home something bad happened to her. The evidence suggests that she boarded or intended to board that bus, the number 201, which stops right outside this place, although it's unclear whether there is any corroborating evidence for that. But if she did do that, it's at least a possibility that she became confused as to her whereabouts; she may have alighted from the bus at the wrong stop, before reaching home, and wandered off. Though I'm bound to say I would be surprised in that eventuality if the bus driver had failed to remember an elderly lady descending from the bus at an inappropriate location, so we shall have to double check the police investigation of this point. We have now covered most of that bus route by car, and as you will have seen it traverses some quite desolate and uninhabited spaces, specifically the many square kilometres of the Dead Level, and, beyond that, extensive areas of marshland. So if she did do this, who knows then where she might have ended up. Where is she now, or if she died, where are her mortal remains?

I can't bear to think of the poor lady getting off the bus where she thought she was near home and getting more and more lost as she wanders on.

Quite so; it's distressing.

What must have been going through her head? I can't bear to think of her getting lost, getting colder and more upset as night comes on....

Though perhaps even more distressing is the thought that someone may have done her harm. But there is as yet no direct evidence for that. Where's that coffee?

The police did say that the evidence for her being on that bus was inconclusive. Shouldn't they have been able to pinpoint the bus driver? I mean, there's only one bus an hour, for heaven's sake.

Well, we shall determine that after I've had a chance to speak with the detective chief inspector. But you would not believe how shoddy the police can be in their routine investigations.

Your coffee is taking its time.

Yes, where is that girl? I'm concerned that you will be needing to move on.

Oh, don't mind about me.

Nevertheless ... this is most annoying. It's not as though

that coffee is worth waiting for. Listen, shall we get going?

If that's all right with you, Phidias, but it's really up to you. We shall leave the money on the table. Let's go.

One white 'Mericano!

(The girl, mug in hand, stared vacantly around the empty café, trying to take in this new situation. She called back to her unseen colleague in the kitchen:)

The bloke's gone!

I'm beginning to see more clearly what my part in this is.

Today, Phidias was quite obviously starting to get up the nose of Kieran Watkins. I mean, seriously. I could see Mr Watkins was already distressed, or ill at ease anyway, to begin with. It's not surprising. This meeting must have stirred up memories. And then I think he couldn't quite see the point of going through his aunt's house again in such exhaustive detail. I had to apologise to him when Phidias was out of earshot, and explain that the re-investigation necessitated going through all the ground the police had already covered – or maybe not covered properly – and that I hoped he understood that. I think he did.

So my role, or a good part of my role (apart from doing all the driving), would seem to be customer relations. Maybe Phidias's people skills are a little lacking there.

The day started, after I'd dropped George off at school, with the drive from the Dead Level Business Park to Meeting Place Avenue, Moorshurst, which took about half an hour. We saw Kieran Watkins' black 4x4 parked there, and he was waiting for us anxiously on the doorstep. He was stamping his feet and blowing into his hands, though I don't think it's that cold. Phidias flew into action straight away, asking for curtains to be drawn, doors to be unlocked. On his hands and knees, he looked under furniture. He stood on a chair, precariously at times, to investigate the tops of cupboards, occasionally shining a small LED torch attached to his keyring. Mr Watkins, who'd already shown many signs of unease, asked abruptly "Do you have to do that?" when he opened the desk and started riffling through – I was astonished too! – but he took no notice and continued. We had to look for a bigger torch when he insisted on searching the loft, and we found one in a kitchen drawer.

Having been told that Edith Watkins was starting to neglect the housework, triggering alarms about dementia, and also that everything had been left "exactly as it was", I was quite surprised how relatively spruce and tidy the house was. I think there has been some cleaning done. Mr Watkins implied that Sharon, the next door neighbour, who he said must be at work, had had something to do with this. I will have to arrange a meeting with Sharon, as Phidias would like to talk with her.

I asked Mr Watkins before we left if we could borrow a rather good recent photograph of his aunt that we noticed, which was better than the blurry ones we've seen online.

In all the time I've been living in Deadmans Beach I have never actually been before to the Sanctuary Café, which was our next port of call, and to be truthful I don't know that I would care to go there again. It must have had some attraction for Edith Watkins, but maybe that was just convenience.

George was in a bad mood when I picked him up from school.

Where in the world was a particular individual at a particular time, alive or dead? That was the question we were being posed. Quantum physicists now tell us that locality may be a chimera, that there may be no such thing as place or distance. Particles may discontinuously appear in distant parts of the universe even when deeply entangled with other particles nearby. Well, that may be so in the sub-atomic world. But in the real world? Has nonlocality a practical meaning?

There is no geography! That was the message posted by the adversary with whom we had parted company. He was going by another name then, not Borg, but his identity could not be doubted. He claimed by then to be living on a remote Western Canadian island; then drew attention to the non-verifiability of his claim. It was an act of aggression. It meant: you do not know where I am, and so there is no escape from me.

He might have considered the vulnerability of the predator. Every predator will, in the end, itself become prey. And all debts shall be cancelled.

Nevertheless it is all real. And locality *has* meaning for us. This world, the one we can touch, in all its errant spookiness, sparkles with phenomena we cannot decipher. We have to solve our problems, in the best way we can, in a way that makes sense to us.

4

The tide was in at Deadmans Beach, and the wind was up. The fishing fleet was ranged on the banks of shingle being encroached by rushing and receding waves: an impressive if heterogeneous collection of chiefly traditionally clinker-built vessels (but some of fibreglass), both larger trawlers and also punts, that's to say, undecked boats, all with diesel engines, sitting on their greased hardwood blocks or planks, awaiting favourable conditions. Linseed oil dully gleamed and colours faded against the whitening sky. Winch engines and their cables, some apparently half consumed by corrosion, also lay dormant, and among them the detritus of a fishing beach: walls and labyrinths of creels, plastic and wooden boxes or their fragments, piles of greasy nets. Two or three men wandered between the huts; one called briefly to another – but this was all the human life that could be observed. A crushed, stained white latex glove and a dirty, crumpled T-shirt with the Superman logo that had evidently been employed as a rag lay discarded on the intervening gravel. Used plastic bottles were scattered here and there. On the casing of a winch, a hand-painted notice in white lettering on a black ground: KEEP OFF. On the shingle banks, eviscerated fish corpses and emptied skulls stank and were disdained by the ragged flocks of gulls, terns and plovers that edged the moving foam. From the sterns of various boats fluttered black flags on tall poles. Some vessels had names painted on their bows or sterns, for example: *Moonshine, Candice Marie, Zelda, The Brothers Grim, David Bowie, Blackbeard, Our Dot & Danny, Little Mayflower, King Hell, Safe Return*. Their registration numbers were prominently displayed in most cases, and the following were noted: DB11, DB16 (etc, all the way up to...) DB590 – DB signifying that the boats were registered in the port of Deadmans Beach. All in all, including small row boats and others whose registration numbers were obscured or not present, a total of twenty-eight vessels were counted.

A huge volume of water appeared to be driven repeatedly and relentlessly by the strong breeze – verging on gale – onto the beach. The line of undulations could be tracked like a moving graph against the concrete groyne that marked the southwestern boundary of the fishing beach, in the lee of which was suddenly observed a shining black creature – at first glance a seal, but quickly revealed to be a solitary surfer in black wetsuit, crouching, waiting for the right wave to arrive. And so this mysterious being watched the approach of a tall one with rippling white foam at its rim; the foam starting to glitter, for the sun only then began to make its presence felt through the white banks of cloud, the shoreward wall of the wave now being in shadow, and darkening further as it rose.

But the wave seemed to pause. And at the last possible moment the surfer took advantage, and, embracing his electric blue board tightly as one would a newly re-found lover, launched himself into the van of the approaching current that swept him inexorably shoreward, showing only a flash of his orange flippers, before it broke over him in a white explosion. Then just as the figure seemed lost, he reappeared in the midst of the retreating water, struck out and began to swim back to where he'd come from, following the flowback to the lee of the groyne, where he would turn, shelter and repeat the experience.

The fishing community's favourite hostelry, enquiries quickly established, was the Richard the Lionheart Inn.

Set back from the front and faced by the fishermen's tar-black wooden sheds that flanked the shingle beach, it presented as an ancient inn that had seen better days and had somehow survived misjudged attempts at modernisation on the cheap: a tiled roof, tall chimneys, with weatherboarding at the front and hanging tiles on the sides filling the spaces between modern UPVC windows. Vertical rust-streaks down the wall bearded the cast iron brackets for hanging baskets that bore no blooms at this time of year. Pasted inside the front windows were posters for local bands: Monday nights were blues nights, Saturday nights featured a wider variety of genres, including a psychedelic option. Entry to the bar was via a short flight of stone steps flanked by railings.

Fluttering on high: the red-on-white cross, emblem of the Crusaders.

The south-westerly was beginning to pump up seriously now, and with it came flecks of rain, so entering the pub was a welcome relief, the more so as ale from a respected regional brewery was advertised. The interior was badly lit. The only other customers, seated on high stools at opposite ends of the long bar, were an elderly man with hair in long white ringlets descending to his shoulders, wearing a black jacket, khaki cargo pants and impeccably white trainers, slowly supping a pint; and an overweight woman, who was engaged in shouting at the barman. She too wore white trainers, but quite scuffed, and black trousers, and her anorak was open to reveal a pink poodle on her sweater. She cradled a glass of something with lemon in it.

The low ceiling, crisscrossed by beams, featured giant crabs and other marine creatures trapped there by netting; paddles, flags and lifebelts decorated the walls, also a dartboard, and a noticeboard pinned with photographs and advertisements for forthcoming events. At the far end, next to the toilets, a much scrubbed blackboard advertised the dishes *du jour*. These included soup, the idea of which appealed.

So what, then, was the soup of the day?

Vegetable.

A deal was struck with the young, monosyllabic barman: soup and a pint. A table in the corner was claimed.

Giles, cried the lady in the poodle sweater, addressing the ringleted elder from her end of the bar.

Closer observation now revealed that this snowy-haired gentleman was wearing makeup and eyeliner, and his fingernails were polished in a fetching shade of teal. What's that, my dear? he said.

Have you finished planning your funeral?

As a matter of fact, yes, Dodie, if you really want to know.

You going for burial at sea?

(Giles turned to our corner to acknowledge the presence of the outside world in this enclave.)

Highly irregular, of course. (Palm vertical on the side of his mouth, he continued in a stage whisper with a wink for our benefit:) Mum's the word.

So you going to be dumped over the side, then?

Dodie, there will be more to it than that. You make me sound like an illegal catch.

I always thought you were! And Dodie, spectacles glinting, laughed uproariously at her own witticism.

The padre has agreed to be involved, just between us, you

understand. There'll be a ceremony, of sorts. Prayers will be said. I *am* a man of faith, you know.

I knew you were, Giles, said Dodie, you believe in God, don't ya.

I prefer to speak about the Author of everything in this world, both seen and unseen.

But you believe in Him.

I don't know so much about that, but I trust that *He* believes in *us*. You understand what I'm saying?

You're a one, Giles.

If the Author doesn't believe in us, who else is going to?

I dunno.

The Author of all things knows where we're going.

And He believes in us?

It could be a She, conceded Giles.

Maybe He or She hasn't got a clue, was the poodle lady's suggestion.

Well, you've got to trust they do. It's trust more than belief, you know what I mean? That's what you call faith.

And you think you're going to Heaven?

We are, said Giles solemnly, already living in Paradise.

Could've fooled me, said the poodle lady.

Deadmans Beach. Every morning when the light comes up here in Deadmans Beach I give thanks for another day that's been given me. It is fucking Paradise, is it not, excuse my language, mister.

(He received an assurance from our quarter that no offence was taken at bad language.)

Yeah, it is nice here, admitted Dodie. I wouldn't live nowhere else now.

We all drank.

Are you down from London, then? inquired Giles of us.

In a manner of speaking. And you?

Born and bred in Deadmans Beach, myself. Proud of it. *She's* from London, she's a bloody DFL, he added, pointing with his pint mug at Dodie, who burst into another loud cackle of laughter.

I've only been here thirty years, Giles!

You've served your apprenticeship then.

I'll say. And don't call me *she*. You're a very rude man, Giles, I don't care if God believes in you or not, it's a fact. Me old man it was (Dodie went on for our benefit), who brought me here when we got married. He was in the fishing trade all his life. But he passed on, what is it, two year ago.

We expressed our sorrow at her loss, and there was a brief silence to mark it.

You down on business then, or holiday-making or what? continued Giles politely.

Our assurance that there was no holiday-making involved met with general approval.

A private investigator? Blimey, that's something new, ain't it, Dodie? We haven't had one of them down here before. But you're not with the police then?

By no means. And your secret is safe.

Secret?

The burial at sea.

It was Giles' turn to laugh, which he did quite lustily.

Of course, scattering ashes at sea is perfectly legal, we pointed out. But an intact, unburnt body, that's quite a different matter.

You are correct, sir, it is against the law, but it happens all the time in the fishing community, explained Giles. Quite regularly you get a church funeral, somebody local, and the bearers may notice the casket is unusually light. You follow my drift? Everybody knows what that means.

The body is not there?

Exactly. The real funeral occurs under cover of darkness. Boat pulls out to sea as per usual a day or so later, when the tide and weather conditions are right – maybe more than one boat, depends on how many mourners, you see. Out a couple of miles, then ... well, I don't need to spell it out.

Understood.

It's important to us. Well, I was in the fishing for many years. Can't say I chose it, but I was brought up to it, like. It's a hard life, but it's still in my blood, even though I've been retired for longer than I care to remember. And so I want to go back to the bosom of the sea when my time comes.

It seemed an apt moment to bring up, discreetly, the subject of our investigation.

Edith Watkins? Giles frowned into his drink.

I remember her, volunteered Dodie. Lady what disappeared.

She wasn't the one who – ?

She used to go for her walks along here, Giles, you remember, she talked to everybody? Edie, that's what we called her. Little Edie.

Did she come into the pub?

Not often. I seen her in here with a cup of coffee sometimes. Maybe once or twice. I don't think she drank.

She wasn't the one who wangled herself a trip on a fishing boat, was that the one, Dodie?

That is the one, Giles, that was, what, ten or twenty year ago, she was a brave lady. Getting on even then, a bit mad, you know, but anyway she disappeared last year, it was on the news. Come on, you must remember?

Yes, I recall Little Edie now. Haven't seen her for ... ooh, donkey's years. So is she dead?

The police, we explained, had not been able to determine this, and looked unlikely to, but it seemed that her last journey might have involved a visit to the waterfront.

So what do you think, she might have stowed away on a boat and fallen off the side? exclaimed Dodie with great excitement.

It was necessary to reassure the pair that this was not a leading theory, and that the task at hand was simply to establish her movements on the last day she had been seen alive. Neither, however, could recall when precisely they had last seen her. Nor could they remember any police inquiries last year, and the name of DCI Green meant nothing to them.

Who was it, Giles demanded of Dodie, who took her out on that fishing trip a few years ago, was it old Gallop, you know, Doc Gallop? I have a feeling now it was.

Yes, that's right, old Doc, bless him.

Would it be possible to speak to Mr Gallop? was our inquiry.

You'd have a job, said Giles.

Why so?

He died.

Buried at sea?

Who knows? Don't ask, don't tell.

But his son still runs the same boat, said Dodie, he'll have known her better than us. Darren Gallop, he's the president of the Fishermen's Association now.

So he should be easy to contact?

Comes in here a lot, said Giles. Partial to a pint in the old Dick, is the younger Gallop. Very eminent man these days, though. The *Jumpy Mary*, that's his boat. You'll find him in the book, or just call in here again. He'll be around anyway, nobody's going out fishing in this weather.

And as he drained his pint mug the fingernails flashed briefly like blue jewels.

How was your soup, sir? was everything all right? asked the quiet young barman, who had suddenly appeared with a wiping cloth.

He was reassured as to the quality of both the fare and the service.

Dodie stood down from the bar, zipped up her anorak, concealing the pink poodle from view.

Where you going now, my love? asked Giles.

Never you mind. Nice meeting you, mister.

And you.

I am going out for A Fag – *should* anyone inquire.

Ooh, lovely, my dear, I'm sure.

I didn't mean you, Giles. See ya.

Filthy habit, commented Giles when she'd gone. As filthy as the weather.

He motioned to the barman for another pint. We attempted to pay for this, but he would not hear of it.

•

Colourless green ideas sleep furiously. Why did this sentence come back to mind when thinking of Detective Chief Inspector Green?

It was a sentence devised by Noam Chomsky to illustrate ... what was it meant to illustrate? The possibility of grammatical correctness co-existing with semantic nonsense. That was it. Except that Chomsky did not, it appears, ever state explicitly the sentence was nonsensical, merely that it stood a good chance of never having been uttered before. In which case, the same would apply, for example, to most lines of poetry. Shall I compare thee to a summer's day, Thou art more lovely and more temperate, etc. Did anyone ever utter those precise words before it introduced a sonnet? Or A rose is a rose is a rose, whoever would have said that before?

We always come back to poetry.

Colourless green ideas sleep furiously. That described exactly the Detective Chief Inspector when discovered in his office behind his nameplate: DCI Oliver Green, in plain sans-serif. That is to say, he appeared colourless, in the figurative sense, while simultaneously and contradictorily being branded with the livery of his name. And he represented a set of ideas, embodying perfectly the idea of a police officer, though actually seeming without body – an abstraction masquerading as a man. And somehow also uniting the qualities of somnolence and fury, a contained fury that sleeps. The impression of somnolence perhaps reinforced by awareness of the presence of the Happy Sleeper hotel next door. (The Happy Sleeper – the local branch of the well-known budget chain of hotels – that is how one found the headquarters of Moorshurst Police, next to which it was located, its distinctive logo overlooking the yard in which were parked in ranks dozens of police vehicles, their acid fluorescence – lemon and blue squares, vermilion and lemon chevrons – penetrating the gloom of a Monday morning. Next to the Happy Sleeper, you can't miss it, that is how it had been identified.)

But grammatically correct in all his utterances, this DCI, so far as we were able to tell.

He welcomed us into his sanctum.

Do enter, Mr Peralta – please take a seat.

This is my assistant, Lucy White. Do you mind if she joins us?

Of course, pleased to meet you.

And I hope you don't mind if we record our conversation on this device, just for our private use, you understand.

Agreed, and I should say that I too will be taking an audio recording on the police's behalf, if that is all right with you.

No problem.

Lucy had driven us to Moorshurst as usual – damp roads, dishwater sky. Is that accurate? Is that too poetic? The little light there was played on her face, which frowned as she drove, her eyes behind her spectacles darting occasionally to glance in the rear view mirror. She took care of all that very well. But it was necessary to be freed to pay attention to ironmongery as much as weather and landscape. The bus stops along the way were, for example, noted and enumerated.

Counting as the first the one at the Barbican Gate – where the road divided – there were thirteen before one reached Meeting Place Avenue, Moorshurst, which on this occasion we bypassed. As to the general forecast: stuck weather, Lucy commented, the same patterns repeating themselves over and over; all to do with the position of the jet stream apparently. Will this winter never end? she'd complained, and it was heartfelt, even though this was becoming a commonplace reaction in this neighbourhood. But we had arrived. A parking space not otherwise reserved for officers of the constabulary had eventually been found. We had been ushered to an anonymous waiting room, and thence to the office of the Detective Chief Inspector.

Let me note down some facts to begin with, he said, you have been engaged by the family of the disappeared lady ... (he consulted his computer screen to remind himself), Ms Watkins.

That is so. To be specific, Mr Kieran Watkins, the nephew.

Aha. And they have, he has, asked you to do what, precisely?

If I may be quite frank –

Please.

It is now a year since the lady disappeared. Mr Watkins is, shall we say, a little frustrated. He is disappointed your team has not made more progress in finding his aunt. I realise, of course, the enormous –

Mr Peralta, I assure you my officers have been doing everything in their power to bring this case to a conclusion.

I appreciate that. I completely appreciate that, Chief Inspector. But look at it from the family's point of view: months have gone by, there is a complete lack of new information, and, as they perceive it, the police have closed the case –

Mr Peralta, you have presumably been in the private investigation business for some years, and you must know the police never close such cases until such time as the missing individual is found, alive or deceased, or there is evidence that suggests decease.

Well – I apologise for any offence caused – in theory, technically, that is true. In practice, and I understand this, the general workload is overwhelming, resources are ever more stretched, and officers have to prioritise other investigations, is that not so?

I would say Mr Watkins is not being entirely fair to us. His son, I can't recall his name, was very helpful with the internet and social media and the like, and we have been working hard with the family to do the best we can to find the elderly lady. I hoped Mr Watkins would have appreciated that. I understand the whole affair has put a lot of pressure on his family and business life –

Be that as it may, Mr Watkins has hired us to do what we can do, so –

I fail to see what you can bring to the case that would have added value, but please enlighten me.

Mr Watkins has asked us to review the case, to go over all the facts and evidence in the manner and circumstances of his aunt's disappearance, in order to ascertain whether anything has been missed, or whether there might be any new leads. Now, I don't want to trespass on the force's territory, or indeed to reinvent the wheel, or whatever, but it seems to me there is no harm in this, and there may be some advantage to all of us.

I didn't say there wasn't.

Good, that's good. Then let's make some progress. Would you be able to share some results of your investigation with us?

What would you like to know, Mr Peralta?

It seems to have been established that the last day Edith Watkins was seen alive was March fifteenth last year, and that she was in Deadmans Beach, is that right?

So we believe.

Could we recap on the evidence for this?

You've seen the CCTV video?

We have seen a not particularly good resolution twelve-second clip online – haven't we Lucy? – of Ms Watkins leaving the Sanctuary Café on the day in question. She seems to be wearing the dark red overcoat and black hat described in the public notice that was put out, but it's hard to make out much else. Is there a better version of that video available?

I'll see if I can call it up on my computer right here, Mr Peralta.

That would be wonderful. While you're doing that, is there any other evidence that the old lady was in that vicinity that afternoon?

As I understand it, the principal evidence is the testimony of her next-door neighbour.

That would be Sharon?

I'll double-check the name. Yes, the witness stated that Ms Watkins had told her on the morning in question she was intending to take her usual bus trip to the fishing beach, Deadmans Beach that is, prior to walking along the front. Witness said the disappeared lady was accustomed to have a cup of tea at the Sanctuary Café while waiting for the bus back home. Now, according to the notes here – you'll have to bear with me, I'm still trying to retrieve that video file from the computer archives – my officers ascertained the times of the buses and asked the café owners to provide video clips from their CCTV system, timed to coincide with bus departures from the nearby stop. And we were fortunate in obtaining that footage. I believe there is some of her arriving at the café too, but ... I'm sorry, I'm having difficulty here, it says "file not found". There seems to be some retrieval problem ... and the only person who can understand this system and sort it is my PA, but unfortunately she's off today. Look, I can arrange to have that video file forwarded to you if you like, if you give us your email.

That would be very helpful, Chief Inspector. And were there any other witnesses?

We had our officers check the local area thoroughly, but no witnesses came forward to give positive sightings for that day.

Including the café staff?

Including the café staff. It appears they identified her from photographs as a customer who came in from time to time, but were reluctant to say definitively she was in the establishment that day. However, the CCTV footage speaks for itself.

What about the fishing community?

Yes, as I recall, Mr Watkins put some pressure on us to investigate that angle. He seemed convinced they would know something about it. However, we got nothing from there, as I understand it. But then, that community is very protective and suspicious of outsiders, including, if I may say so, representatives of the law. According to the reports I have here from my officers, again, there was some positive identification of the lady from one or two individuals, but they denied having seen her on the day of her disappearance.

What about the driver of the Moorshurst bus that left Deadmans Beach at 14:35 that afternoon?

Now you have me. Let's see ... bus driver, bus driver ... ah yes, here it is on the record, my officer reports the bus driver thought he recognised the lady from her photograph, wasn't sure, couldn't definitely say she had been on the bus that day, however, but stated it was possible she had been.

No CCTV on the bus?

The report I have here is that there is no other conclusive footage.

That's odd.

I have a note here, it's unclear – apparently the CCTV on the bus may not have been working that day.

So, do you have any theories as to how she may have vanished?

Unless Ms Watkins did not after all catch that bus after

having left the café and disappearing out of the frame of the CCTV camera – in which case, where would she have gone? – and I should add that we did also put out a public appeal asking residents in the area to check their gardens and outbuildings, and so on – I think the leading theory is that she must have indeed boarded the bus but did not reach her destination of Moorshurst.

You think she might have become confused and alighted at the wrong stop?

That is a strong possibility. According to her nephew, she had been diagnosed with Alzheimer's and had manifested episodes of confusion in the recent past.

We were told no diagnosis had actually been made.

Be that as it may – there is evidence of episodes of confusion.

In which case?

In which case there would have been multiple opportunities for her to become lost in the countryside between Deadmans Beach and Moorshurst. As you know there are some desolate and treacherous spots, particularly as you get past the Dead Level and into the marshlands.

She wouldn't have, I don't know, fallen or thrown herself off a cliff into the sea?

The nearest cliff would be at the coastguard station, actually –

I believe so.

– three or four miles off the bus route. Unlikely she could have walked that far. And incidentally, no coastguard reports of a body in the sea or washed up or whatever.

You went through her papers? Any sign of distress, a suicide note or similar?

We have no record of such.

Had she made a will?

I would have to re-check that, but I have no record of such here.

Well, you've been really helpful, Chief Inspector, I appreciate that. I would be grateful if you could forward that CCTV video file when you retrieve it, so we can look at it in a bit better detail. One last question, if I may.

Go on.

If we fail to make progress and her disappearance remains unresolved, we are looking at, what, declared death in absentia?

Yes, Mr Peralta, that would be the legal term.

And how long are we talking about before such a court ruling comes into effect? Would it be the statutory –

In the absence of any positive evidence that the individual is deceased, it would normally be a term of seven years.

Seven years before she is presumed dead?

About seven years, that's correct. Unless there is some evidence before then that establishes her death, which need not be a body as such. If you can come up with any evidence of this kind, Mr Peralta, do let us know.

Of course.

•

So Mrs Darling, the head teacher at All Saints Primary School, wanted to meet with me, that's what the message said. And after all this time trying to get to talk to her because of my worries about George, finally she popped up on my mobile and it only stirred terror in my heart. How is that?

All right, "terror" is hyping it a little. But nervousness, yes.

I have been pressing for a meeting, it was me who started it. But when she came back to me I realised I wasn't at all sure.

I was thinking about this all through the interview with DCI Green, trying to sort through in my head what I was going to say to her, what she had to say to me, instead of concentrating on the interview. But Phidias's voice was calm, soothing even. I did try to concentrate.

Once we'd got back from Moorshurst, I parked in the tree-lined road outside the school, just down from All Saints Church, which is usually chock-a-block with parents' cars, picking up and dropping off. In the autumn, the pavement is thick with yellowed leaves, but now the tall trees are bare, there is no birdsong. And there were no kids about, because the school day was still in progress. But I could hear child-like chanting from far away, from inside one of the classrooms. They chanted, then there was silence, then I could hear faintly the teacher's voice, then the children again.

I locked the car.

Phidias had said, before I dropped him off: What did you make of that?

It was on the drive back from Moorshurst that he suddenly said it. I'd thought he was distracted, staring at the landscape as it slipped by, but he was thinking hard all the time, I suppose.

I got the impression DCI Green's attitude changed as the interview went on, I suggested tentatively.

Yes it did.

He looked like a man under pressure, I said.

From above and below and from all sides, Phidias said slowly, still staring out into the landscape. It goes with the role of senior police officer, he added.

A rather colourless man, I thought.

My goodness, Lucy, we are of one mind there, said Phidias.

At first he was hostile to us, I sensed. And then maybe he realised we could be an opportunity rather than a threat. Do you know, Phidias, I went on, by the end I thought he was starting to become keen to outsource this investigation.

And Phidias said: That's very good, Lucy, I like that. "Keen to outsource the investigation." That's about it.

Emboldened somewhat, I said: It sounded to me like he has been getting it in the neck from Kieran Watkins. And so if we can take over, it lets him off the hook.

That's what I'd been thinking, and Phidias nodded very hard. Because there is no way, he said, the police are going to put any more resources into this one. An old lady disappears. There are other priorities. The story barely makes the local or regional news, and is quickly dropped by the media. It's not as though we are talking about the disappearance of a child or an attractive teenager. Still less a celebrity. So this could be a way out for him.

I said: It was like, by the end, the chief inspector was almost telling us, just take over, guys, it's all yours.

Absolutely, Phidias said, you've got it. It's down to us. So I hope that at least means the police will co-operate with us.

I suggested we were a sort of privatisation solution, and he chuckled in a deep rumbling way.

Do you know, I said, if I were asked to describe DCI Green, well, I'd say he reminded me of a Photofit picture.

And Phidias laughed out loud at that. And was still chuckling as we entered the Dead Level Business Park car park, where I left him and continued onward to Deadhurst.

I walked up to the school gate and pressed the security buzzer. I spoke into the grill.

So he really is a delightful little boy, Lucy.

But?

I beg your pardon?

I can hear a but coming, Mrs Darling.

Would you like some tea or coffee? I can get our admin assistant to make some.

No thanks, I'm all right.

You see, we like to think we're a caring and tolerant school. All our children are important to us. We all need to get on with each other, no matter what our background.

I understand.

We have children from different backgrounds here, and they all need to learn how to get on together. I am glad to say our recent inspection resulted in an assessment in this respect of "excellent".

About this flagpole business.

Yes?

I received a letter.

I believe you did.

Well, you signed it, Mrs Darling, so I assume it came from you. Anyway, according to that letter, George had been punished for breaking school rules, to wit, and I quote here, by "climbing the school flagpole".

U-huh.

Now, Mrs Darling, I have to say my first reaction was amusement. My second reaction, based on having had a look at that flagpole, is, well, incredulity. I'm not sure how it is possible for a boy of seven who hasn't had circus training to do that.

Well, you have to understand –

I asked George, and according to him it was all the fault of the seagulls. He said a gull had swooped down in the playground at break, and taken the bit of sandwich he had in his hands, just snatched it away, and then had flown up to the top of the flagpole with it.

There has indeed been an increasing issue with seagulls gathering at breaktime when the children are having their lunch. I assure you we're trying to address that.

Anyway, according to my son, he was merely, and I quote him, "jumping up and trying to frighten it". Upon which he says he was hauled off and made to stay in a classroom on his own, which he was very upset about.

Well, and according to his year teacher he was halfway up the pole, to the great amusement of his classmates, and did not offer any explanation for this.

George says he tried to explain. Also he was upset because his classmates were laughing at him.

His teacher reports that he was cheeky to her when she tried to reprimand him.

Mrs Darling, I really really think this was an overreaction by the school.

I assure you, Lucy, we are careful to ensure that our sanctions are at all times appropriate.

Well, we may never get to the bottom of this, but I have to say my son is in my opinion a very normal little boy, and this does seem to me rather a storm in a teacup.

And I have to say to you that we have George's best interests at heart, as we do all the children in this school, and we are keen to work with parents, whatever the difficulties, for the best possible outcomes both at school and at home.

Bloody woman. I sat in the car for a while afterwards thinking about everything. I was on the verge of tears.

The sun was trying to break through the cloud, without a lot of success. I could hear the rooks cawing in the tall bare trees surrounding Deadhurst. But the children could not be heard now. What a beautiful, peaceful village this is.

There are things that could have been different.

"Whatever the difficulties." Was that a coded message?

Yes, it would have been better had they been different.

Or would it have been the same?

•

So – uncertainty.

It is where we dwell. In the heart of it, that's where we live.

At the sub-atomic level it rules absolutely. There is complete indeterminacy. It is inherently impossible to predict the outcome for any known particle: crudely, where it will go next. Heisenberg teaches us that. If the position is known, the momentum (direction and speed) cannot be known, and vice versa.

And then there is all that business about the observer necessarily interfering with what is being observed. How observation cannot but change the path of the particle being observed, so what is observed is not what was there before the observation.

Yet the world seems to us to be stable, to be there, unshakeably, independently.

At the quantum level, randomness. At the scale at which we imagine we live, a measure of predictability.

But surely we live in one unified world. How is it possible that uncertainties can be resolved into predictable patterns? At what point does that resolution take place?

Or does it not? Do we then live in a world of infinitely forking paths, every single indeterminate movement of the particles of our bodies and all the matter we interact with giving birth to alternative worlds, endlessly multiplying at every point in time, and therefore existing simultaneously?

And can there then be no communication between these diverging worlds – between our diverging selves – so that we drift into a multitude of different futures, each possible future entailing complete ignorance of the alternative path taken?

Or is there leakage? Can it be that mistakes occur in a tiny proportion of those divergences, as they do in genetic reproduction – for mistakes drive the world – and that these mutations cause leakages resulting in mysterious anomalies, insoluble conundrums?

It's inconceivable.

We have to fill in the lights. Someone on the water at once is at sea.

In the Dead Level Business Park, at 17:15 in early spring, as the light dimmed once again, we were discovered in the heart of the quantum void. Which teemed with every possibility.

•

If my life had turned out different, but it didn't. It turned out this way and it had to be this way. It had to be this way because it *is* this way. And no other. Or is there another way, might there have been? And if I had taken a different turning, gone down a different pathway? Suppose, just supposing? If I hadn't got married, for example. Let's take that as an example. We're going back eight years, what happened? A decision you took, Lucy. Pay attention. "She thought too late and spoke too soon", as the song said, who was that? Elvis Costello I think. But the outcome would have been different and would it have been better, not necessarily. No, not necessarily. There would have been no George, for example. No George, the thought of it! Poor little man. He makes his own universe, and finds it hard to fit into someone else's, he doesn't understand it. That's the heart of it. He means well. That woman blathered on, about his "hidden potential" and this that and the other, but all it really was about was normalisation. Though she pretended it wasn't. She talked the talk, I'll say she did. Potential, she said, but no. It wasn't about potential really. It was about control. It was secretly about control and conformity. Covered up in the appropriate language, the language of appropriateness. How it could be, or would be, or might be or might have been, but it isn't, that's who *he* is. If he had turned out different, but he didn't, he turned out exactly how he is. He is who he is and what he is. And he will be who he is. Whoever *that* is. If he is helped to be that. But I didn't have the words to explain this to her. All I could do was stare at her, at her own grim-faced photograph on her identity badge, swinging on its lanyard round her neck. I mean, I might have done had I taken that different path, or one of those many different paths, mightn't I, a million of them to choose from, I might have had more confidence then, or more knowledge anyway, but then I would be in some other place, with some other people. That situation wouldn't then arise. It wouldn't have arisen. I wouldn't be here, we wouldn't be. It would be a different we. And I would have been a different me, and I would be a different me now. How many times must I turn that round in my head without coming to any sensible answer? How many times, stupid woman? I wish, I wish. I wish I had a pound for every time I said I wish. But all I can do is the best I can do. There is somebody there who makes all the decisions, somebody resembling me, but I can never find her. Somebody in there. She is below the radar. She is under the enamel. Stop it, stop it. Stop it, Lucy. How much more time must I spend chipping away at that veneer, inch by inch, before somebody resembling me emerges?

5

Ah, Gordon, have you got a moment?

(Gordon Prescott, Dead Level Business Park security officer, was discovered in a fluorescently lit intersection within the labyrinth of corridors that was his domain.)

Phidias, my man. What can I do for you?

I wanted to ask you about closed circuit television for security purposes.

Fire away.

If the police were investigating an incident here and asked you for CCTV evidence, how would you proceed?

Here in the business park? Depends when the incident took place. We have fifteen days' continuous storage here which I can retrieve immediately.

And after that?

All footage is transferred to external digital video storage. Our policy is to keep it for a year. I can show you, if you like.

•

I told Dave about my meeting with Mrs Darling when he brought George round from his overnight stay. He said, Ah, don't pay any attention to the old bat.

But it's not as simple as that.

Dave was actually not paying much attention to me. His manner was distracted, there was something peculiar in his eyes. I don't mean wrong, I mean unusual. He seemed to want to talk, and then he didn't.

How has George been this weekend? I asked, by way of drawing him out, and he said: Oh, George has been great.

No climbing up flagpoles?

He laughed.

No, nothing like that.

I noticed when Dave turned his head that the small bald patch on his crown was just that wee bit bigger. The sun was trying to come through the window, then giving up. His coffee mug cooled on the table. I suddenly started noticing all the clutter in the kitchen. How did it get that way? I have to do something about this. Maybe when Dave has gone I'll have a clear-up, I told myself. But he showed no signs of going, although he wasn't drinking his coffee either. He suddenly said:

Maybe we should ... maybe you should move somewhere else.

What do you mean, move?

Out of Deadmans Beach.

What are you talking about, I said to him, how can we afford to move, and where would we go?

I'm all right lodging, he said. Just worried about you and George.

I said there wasn't anything to worry about.

Maybe, he said, this isn't the right environment for you.

Puzzled, I didn't know how to reply.

I said it wasn't too bad. I said we had to make the best of it. I reminded him what a triumph it had been getting a place in All Saints school in Deadhurst. I pointed out it was a great opportunity, no matter what the problems might be.

I know, he said.

Then he said, What about that job of yours?

What about it? I asked.

Working for that weird guy.

He's not weird, I said .

Sounds weird to me. You could do better. Elsewhere.

I didn't know what to say to this.

Then he blurted suddenly: He likes the beach, doesn't he?

Who?

George.

Yes, he does, he loves it. That's one reason to stay.

When Dave turned round to face me I saw he had a little sparkle in his eye. Surely not a tear? But he looked quickly away again, and I believe it was gone, if ever it had been there.

I am a deluded woman.

I'd better go, he said.

I imagined that sparkle, of course I did. Trick of the light. Stupid woman.

We're all right, I said in what I hoped was my kindest voice, trying to sound reassuring. We're all right.

That's good then, he said.

Now George said he was not feeling very well this Monday morning. Surprise, surprise.

So what's the matter? I asked.

I'm just not very well.

You're repeating yourself, love, I said. But I knew what was next.

Can I come to work with you instead of going to school?

So you're not feeling well enough for school, but you are well enough to go into the office and pester Mr Peralta?

No, I'm going to peralta Mr Pester! exclaimed George with great glee.

Oh, very clever, I said sarcastically – but sarcasm is wasted on George, and he merely beamed with pride.

Number one, I told him, you're going to get into serious trouble if you keep taking days off school, quite apart from the effect it will have on your education. Number two, I have lots of work to do at Mr Peralta's office, and I can't be distracted looking after you.

George said that he wouldn't need looking after, that he had plenty to do himself, thank you very much – that was the gist of his argument.

There is plenty for you to do at school, I reminded him, and there'll be more to do for every day you've missed and have to make up for. Now do you want to feed the fish and get ready for school?

He sulked.

I don't want you sulking, I told him.

But I'm not well, and you don't care about me.

That made me angry and I let him know it. He sulked some more. How did I get into this mothering lark? I'm not cut out for it. I could read Mrs Darling's thoughts as if they were words printed in a book: Bad Parent. And she's right, I'm piss poor, I suppose. But then again … I watched as George got up on his little stool and started to sprinkle flakes on the surface of the water, and the fish shoaled upward eagerly to greet him. How would I be, how was I at his age? I haven't done too badly, surely? Come on, this isn't the Mothering Olympics.

His small intent face studied the mollies with the utmost concentration as they greedily consumed the flakes – the cat-fish and algae eaters meanwhile waiting at the bottom for those fragments that had been missed to glide gently down.

•

Gordon Prescott's sanctum – his office at the centre of the
labyrinth – was, as described earlier, dominated by a bank of
video screens relaying the changing views from around and
about and within the complex; the pictures alternating auto-
matically or at the flick of a pointing device.

Gordon was in affable mood.

So how are you getting on here, Phidias? he enquired, and
was reassured that all was well in Unit 13 and that the business of Peralta Associates was thriving.

Well, we're watching you all the time, he remarked jovially.

The constant surveillance has been noted.

Seen any more of them marsh frogs?

They were most unnerving. Particularly their call.

Yeah, spooky, that laughing. But they're not the only alien
species around here, in the Dead Level and the marshes.

Is that so?

You should see some of the catches my angling mates come
up with from time to time. Weird stuff.

Creatures that should not be here?

Mutations, mate. Mutants.

I should like to meet some of them.

Ha ha, laughed Gordon shortly, making a sound not dis-
similar to that of the marsh frog. But anyway, Phidias, he continued, what was it you wanted to know?

About retrieving security video clips.

Ah yes, you're dealing with the police about an inquiry?

Not here – a case in Deadmans Beach. But what can you
tell me about your setup?

So, we have sixteen analogue cameras here in Dead Level
BP, said Gordon with great gusto, positioned at various places

internally and externally, feeding into DVR via an analogue to digital converter. They are a mix of wired and wireless cameras, depending on location. The cameras are capable of HD video, or we have the option of lower resolution if storage space is an issue. The system could be adapted to cope with additional cameras if required.

Very impressive. And you say you maintain fifteen days' continuous storage? from all sixteen cameras?

Yes, and as you can see, I have four monitors here in the control room, each of which can be switched to any of the cameras, and I can replay footage instantly from any time and date reference within that period.

And so after that period –

There is automatic backup to our external hard disks.

That must represent an awful lot of storage capability.

Yeah, it's an ongoing conversation I have with Trevor, know what I'm saying? I mean, there are affordability issues.

No kidding.

I would like more cameras and better continuous monitoring. But hey, Trevor's the boss, so we have to make do.

So if the police came to you and said there was an incident they were investigating on such and such a date and time –

We could retrieve the footage. All footage carries a time and date stamp and is searchable by that.

Understood. That's pretty high-quality video you have there. What we're dealing with in our case is a fairly low-grade clip, further degraded when you view online.

Well, the standard is high-def, 30 frames per second, but – what's the establishment your video comes from?

The Sanctuary Café.

In Deadmans Beach? Yeah, I know the place. They'll probably be using a fairly entry-level system. Just the one camera, maybe. Possibly VHS videotape storage even. Won't be HD. Could be a frame rate as low as six fps, or even down to one, to save storage space. Might also be set to record only when motion is detected. That's what Trevor wants me to do here. What's the point of hours and hours of static video of the outside of buildings, he says.

He may have some reason on his side.

He's all right, old Trev. We go back a long way, him and me. We both worked on the railways back in the day.

Oh yes?

He's an old railwayman from way back. Dyed in the wool. I was on the security team at Moorshurst station. He was a train driver, you know. Railwayman through and through. What he doesn't know about the railways –

Must have a chat with him about that some day.

Don't. It will never stop. You know his house is entirely filled up by a giant train set?

Is that right?

Yeah, it broke up his marriage. Wife couldn't stand it. Trev would come in here and say, Gordon, I'm in the doghouse again. And I'd say, what's been going on, Trev? And he'd say, I want to extend the model railway layout into another room and she won't let me. And this happened several times.

He was in the doghouse repeatedly?

La maison des chiens, said Gordon, unexpectedly breaking into French.

Bien sur.

But he'd get his way and extend the train set into another room, and then another and another. She couldn't stand it, I tell you. Fair play to her. Anyway, eventually she gets the hump big time and moves out. So that's how it is, he's on his own.

And now it's *la maison des trains*?

Gordon laughed.

That's right, mate. Get him to show you, it's amazing.

•

Mr Peralta?

Yes, George?

Mummy says is it OK if I play here this morning? She says to say please.

Yes, that's perfectly all right, George.

I'm really sorry, Phidias, said Lucy, he just would not go to school and I gave up. But I told him it's a one-off. Say thank you, George.

Thank you, Mr Peralta.

Well, George, this morning we're going to be sorting out the library. You see all those cardboard boxes? They are full of books. We're going to transport them next door to the self-storage warehouse, and put them in order on the shelves I've set up in the room we've rented, which is Room 248. So the first thing to do will be to find Room 248. If you have time to spare from your play schedule, perhaps you could help us find it?

Oh yes, Mr Peralta!

Let's do it in a minute. But first I need to discuss something with your mother. Meanwhile, are you good at maths?

Pretty good. I can count up to a thousand.

Really?

Well, I nearly did the other day, but I got a bit mixed up around eight hundred and something.

Maybe you can have another go at that, but first can you help me solve a problem?

What's that?

The self-storage warehouse is a four-storey building. The ground floor consists of offices and general storage. The storage units you can rent start on the next floor up, which is floor 1, and then there are two floors above that, floor 2 and floor 3. Are you with me?

Yes, Mr Peralta.

Now, the rooms on floor 1 are all numbered 101, 102, 103, 104 and so on, all the way up to 156. So there are 56 units or rooms altogether. Then there are another 56 on the second floor, numbered 201, 202, and so on. And the same on the third floor, 301, 302, all the way up to 356. So there are 56 rooms on each floor. Can you tell me how many there are altogether in the building?

Hmm.

Here's a notebook and a pen if you want to work it out.

All right.

While George is doing that, Lucy, did you make any progress on finding out more about the Sanctuary Café?

Yes, I did, Phidias, though the owner is not returning phone calls. But as a matter of fact, it has a bit of a sorry history. Do you know, the council closed it down for a while? It had only recently re-opened about a month or two before Edith Watkins' last visit.

So what was that about?

Environmental health concerns. I've got the report here, it's from the local press, dated last July.

What does it say?

On 25th June Moorshurst and District Magistrates imposed a total of £10,000 fines on Mrs Deirdre Hastings of the Sanctuary Café, Dead Level Road, Deadmans Beach, for food hygiene and safety offences. Environmental Health Officers from Moorshurst District Council carried out a full inspection of the café on the previous 10th November following a complaint from a member of the public. Officers found a filthy, greasy kitchen with flies throughout. The fridges were disorganised, with defrosting foods dripping onto other foods. Officers found out-of-date food on the shelves and an out-of-date tub of mayonnaise propping open the kitchen door. The refuse area was dirty, with loose refuse in the bottom of bins. And so on and so forth.

Say no more. So had environmental health closed the café?

Yes, it was closed immediately for a period, apparently, and it looks like it re-opened at the beginning of February. It says here: Mrs Hastings accepted the kitchen was filthy and pleaded guilty to sixteen breaches of food hygiene and safety regulations. The chair of the magistrates accepted Mrs Hastings' timely guilty plea but said, I quote, that there is no excuse for filth as it could lead to other issues.

Well, I look forward to talking with Mrs Hastings eventually.

Mr Peralta?

Have you got an answer for me, George?

I think there's a hundred and sixty-eight rooms.

Good man, I think you've got it right. That's what I make it. The only problem is they advertise 169 rooms on the board outside. So there's one extra room which is not accounted for.

Maybe it's a mystery room.

Possibly. So now you're going to help us find Room 248, on the second floor, which is our room, and then help us move the books in there.

OK, cool. Can I keep this notebook?

George!

That's all right, Lucy. Yes, you can, George, keep it handy.

Say thank you, George.

Thank you, Mr Peralta.

The fortress had (we had established) 168 rooms and one which was undefined – which eluded our perception. It is possible, of course, that the advertised total was a simple mistake that has gone uncorrected; otherwise, the elusive, missing unit was the "mystery room" whose existence was so cogently posited by the young man, its location yet to be determined.

Entry was via a front office not unlike that of Peralta Associates' next door, staffed by a bored teenager behind a desk who indicated languidly the register we must sign, and this is what then ensued. A key, with the number 248, was issued, and entrance to the premises obtained.

Beyond the door was another labyrinth of airless passages, the one ahead leading to the loading yard and goods lift; but it was first necessary to turn right for the stairs to take us up to the next level, level 1. Our young man correctly identified the need to go up another flight to level 2, where his search on our behalf began.

The layout appeared to be uniform on each of the three floors: on entry from the stairwell, one was confronted with a corridor straight ahead leading to an emergency exit just visible on the far side in the dim fluorescent overhead lighting. There were three intersections along this, with corridors at right angles to left and right. These were themselves interrupted at two regular intervals each by right-angled intersections. All corridors were flanked equally by grey steel walls with doors at intervals, and there was no natural lighting. The symmetrical grid framed eight blocks, each containing either four or six storage rooms, with a row of further rooms on three sides of the perimeter. The central lateral corridor, intersecting at right angles in the dead centre with the corridor leading from the entrance door, led on the far right to a second emergency exit, and on the far left to the service lift.

The only way to identify the storage rooms, which were of four different standard sizes, was by the number stencilled on each door – the numbers on this floor ranging from 201 to 256. The only feature therefore distinguishing the floor above and the floor below from the present one was that the numbers began with 3 on the former and 1 on the latter.

Our young guide's first task was to figure out the numbering system, and he quickly identified that numbers 201 to 216 ran anti-clockwise on the rooms of the outer perimeter, and the numbering then continued from 217 to 256 in a regular up-and-down pattern along the central blocks. He led us to our target, 248 – first right, first left, crossing the central corridor, last on the left – with impressive ease.

Footsteps rang out as progress was made. Somewhere in the complex, a steel door was heard to clang shut.

So that was, if I may say so, a job well done, Lucy.

It didn't take too long at all, did it?

Is your son all right – where is he?

Don't worry, he's in the outer office. He's counting up to a thousand. I'm timing him with the stopwatch on my phone.

I see. So, we're pretty well done for the morning. By the way, I've made an appointment tomorrow to see Darren Gallop in Deadmans Beach. He's the president of the Fishermen's Association. And I will also try and talk at some point to Deirdre Hastings at the Sanctuary Café if you'd like to attempt to call her again. I know it's a pain.

OK, Phidias. I'm seeing Sharon, Edith Watkins' next door neighbour, on Monday, as you asked me to. And hopefully calling in at the corner shop, too, to see if I can speak to the owner.

Excellent.

Mummy! A thousand! How long was that?

(Lucy consulted her phone.)

Seventeen minutes and ten seconds.

Well done, George.

Mr Peralta, a boy at my school said he could count to a million.

Did he now?

I don't believe him.

Neither do I.

Do you think I could try and count to a million?

I wouldn't advise it.

Why not?

Because if you count at the same rate as you've just

counted to a thousand – let's say, roughly one number each second, or sixty numbers per minute in other words, which is quite realistic – how long do you think you would then take?

I don't know.

About eleven and a half days.

Wow.

I think you have better things to do, George.

I could count a bit at a time.

I suppose you could if you really wanted to.

What about a billion, Mr Peralta, how long would that take me to count?

A billion? That's agreed these days to be a thousand million.

I know.

Well, that would mean a thousand times eleven and a half days. Do you know how long that is?

A long time.

Over thirty-one years.

Thirty-one years!

You'd be a grown man by the time you'd finished, said Lucy. Though there wouldn't be much time for the growing up. And I'd be an old woman.

And I probably wouldn't be around.

Where would you be, Mr Peralta?

Who knows? What about a trillion, would you like to tackle that?

How much is a trillion?

It's a thousand billion. So that would take a thousand times thirty-one years. That's thirty-one thousand years of counting.

Maybe I won't bother, said George.

•

Darren Gallop turned out to be a stocky, powerfully built man of under medium height, possibly in his late thirties. He entered the Richard the Lionheart Inn with something about his manner that might have been interpreted as a swagger – as an index of cultural ownership – were it not so subtly stated. Wintry light flashed briefly in the pub before the door banged shut again.

He pulled off his woollen beanie with the left hand – revealing thin, sandy hair – while he proffered the right. His smile was brief, but not unfriendly. Pleased to meet you, Phidias, he said. He accepted the offer of a drink: a sparkling mineral water. When he pulled off his anorak and draped it round the chair back, his forearms were instantly revealed to be thickly contused with tattoos.

Giles told me you preside over the Fishermen's Association.

Ah, you met Giles? The local legend. Legend in his own lunchtime, know what I mean?

Used to be a fisherman himself?

That's right, he was a tough old bird, back in the day.

Darren leaned back in his chair cradling against the wool on his stomach his glass of water, the tiny bubbles winking. His eyes were half closed.

You know, it's never been an easy life, he said. I been doing it twenty-odd year now, since me dad started taking me out. He didn't really want me to go into fishing, he wanted me to get a good education, he said you've got the brains for it, son, but I wouldn't. I fancied the free and easy life of the fishing, that's what I wanted. So he reluctantly took me on. But it ain't free and it ain't easy!

That was Doc Gallop?

Yeah, Doc, me dad was known as. Come from a long line of fisherfolk, we go back generations. He died a couple of years back. Bowel cancer. By then I'd taken over the boat and the business.

And how's the business?

Not too bad generally. But how long I want to keep going, I don't know. There's much more bureaucracy now, more regulations, than when I started. So it's more difficult in that sense. And it's all weighted against the little guy. You know the smaller boats, like what we've got here, we're up against the big boys, the big trawler fleets, and the way the quota system works favours them, and yet we're the ones what are fishing in a sustainable manner, so it don't make any sense. Ah, don't get me started on that.

You know we're investigating the disappearance of Edith Watkins, do you recall her?

Yeah, I remember Little Edie. That's what we used to call her.

Did you ever speak to her?

Oh yeah, many times. She used to know me dad. And she'd ask after him when we met on the shore from time to time, when she was going for her walks. Young Darren, she'd call me, young Darren, and how's your father, remember me to him. That was when Dad was ill.

I understand that a few years ago she actually went on a fishing trip on your father's boat, is that right? Were you on that trip?

Oh, that was famous. That went down in local folklore, like. She really, really wanted to go out to sea on a fishing boat. She was obsessed with it. She kept going on at Dad about it until he gave in and said, OK, I'll take you but you've got to muck in. But I wasn't on that trip, that would be a good twenty years ago, when I'd not long left school, I'd just been taken on by Dad as a boy-ashore.

A what?

A boy-ashore. You help push the boat down the beach to launch it. The boy-ashore's job is to lay down the trows, which is the planks of greased wood the boat goes on, and then collect them up afterwards, and then help haul the boat back up when it returns. And you have to do other odd jobs too. So I didn't go to sea that time, but I remember clearly Little Edie all wrapped up in the early morning, in her trousers and boots – we kitted her up in the smallest pair of yellow waterproofs we could find, which was the very pair I had when I was a child, but she was still lost in them – and she went on that trip with me dad and his then crewman, whose name I forget.

That was in your boat the *Jumpy Mary*?

That were a different boat we had then, the *Dead Level Boys*, an old clinker-built wooden boat. The *Jumpy Mary* is a modern fibreglass boat.

And what did your late father have to say about that?

When they came back? He said she was brilliant, very game lady, Edie. She would have been in her sixties even then. She was only little. But he never fathomed out why she wanted to go so badly.

Did he have any theories?

No, but he said there was a strange moment, when they was a couple of miles out to sea, it was very cold and calm that morning. He told this story ever so many times. Anyway, a bit before they was going to start to haul the nets in he said she was standing near the bow, looking over the side, staring very intently at the sea. He said she had a lost expression on her face, that's how he described it, a lost expression. She weren't saying anything, and normally she was very voluble, you know what I mean? And he said to me afterwards, I thought at first she was going to throw herself into the sea – he really had the jitters about that. It really came upon him, like a shadow, that she was going to do herself in, so then he called her name, Edie, he said, are you all right? or something like that. And then he said the shadow passed, and she turned and smiled and said she was OK, and after that she helped get the catch in, she did everything she was asked to do, he showed her how to gut a fish and she did it, she was brilliant he said. And afterwards nobody said nothing, but he never did figure out what that was all about.

So this must have run through your mind when the police were investigating a year ago?

Sure did. But the police didn't know nothing about that, and I didn't care to enlighten them.

Was it Detective Chief Inspector Green who questioned you?

Don't know him, it weren't no chief inspector. Just a couple of kids.

Kids?

Yeah, young police officers, a male and a female, wet behind the ears. Did you see Edith Watkins on such and such a date, March the something, and they showed me her photo, I thought oh no, please not Edie. I said I knew her, but I hadn't seen her for a while. I honestly said so. If I started talking about a twenty-year-old trip out to sea, and her possibly wanting to take her own life at that time they would have been all over me, and quite truthfully I don't think it was relevant. But no, all they wanted to know about was CCTV, who was in charge of the CCTV? They were obsessed with that. They'd seen the cameras on the floodlight poles along the beach. And I said, let me tell you something, officers. Them CCTV cameras, they're effectively dummies. Because we applied to the council for a grant to have them installed, as we'd had big problems for years with thieves breaking into our huts at night and stealing the fuel. Not to mention anti-social behaviour and that. Kids vandalising the boats. But that worked for a year and then the council said they'd run out of money, they couldn't operate the cameras no more. So having spent the money to have them installed, they're now fucking useless, excuse my language. So the police officers said, all right then, but check your buildings and your boats, let us know if perchance you find her or you find any clues or whatever. And that was that. Then afterwards I saw they had got some footage from the Sanctuary Café, so she must have been about that day, but we never saw her. We never. I'd have been

[116]

around, because I remember it was windy, we wouldn't have been out to sea, but I would have been busy, I was having a bit of trouble with the boat so I would have been fixing it. I'm really sorry about that, that she's gone, in fact, I beg your pardon, I'm starting to get a bit choked up about it again now.

(And Darren Gallop drained the remainder of his mineral water at a single gulp.)

Sorry to drag all this up. It's Edith's nephew who has asked us to re-investigate, so you must understand –

I know, I know.

Is there anything else you can tell us?

Just one thing I have to say, Phidias. Another matter I didn't mention to the police was that Edie kept telling me she wanted to make a big donation to the Fishermen's Association. Last time I spoke to her, which would have been some months before she disappeared, she even said she'd left us a sum of money in her will. I didn't want to mention it, otherwise we'd probably stand accused of doing her in for her money.

Well, the police have confirmed that no will has been found.

I just wanted to say that to you in confidence.

Your honesty is appreciated.

Can I buy you a drink in return, Phidias?

No, that's perfectly all right. Do you still make a practice of taking elderly landlubbers out on fishing trips?

Why, you wanna come on one?

It would be fascinating.

Yeah, I can take you out one day. Why not? Keep in touch. But for now, duty calls. Now that the wind's died down we need to go out fishing again. Tomorrow morning. Got to get ready. Yeah, give me a bell some time whenever you fancy doing that and we'll see what we can do.

Darren Gallop stood up, put his coat on, pulled the beanie out of the pocket. He looked about him; greeted the bartender; greeted another customer lurking in a corner of the bar. Wintry light from the window fell on him again; he seemed like a figure carved from granite. But moments later he was gone.

•

George had a great time. He led us through that grey steel labyrinth. He found the room, which Phidias unlocked.

There inside the 3m x 2m cell were the floor to ceiling constructions of Dexion shelving Phidias had previously assembled.

We found the service lift, a great discovery for George. He quickly discovered how to operate it, and even hauled the heavy latticed gate across on his own, his little muscles straining, shutting it with a satisfying clang that resonated throughout the complex. We found the trolley down in the yard and he rode it back with us to the office. Between us we loaded the cardboard boxes of books.

It took us three or four trips back and forth with the trolley to get all the books into Room 248. George insisted on operating the lift each time, pushing and pulling the gate, pressing the appropriate button. The boxes had each been carefully marked, and under Phidias's supervision we took the books out in order and gradually filled the shelving, from left to right, from top to bottom. The fit was good, the planning had been meticulous.

How many books do you think you have here? I asked Phidias, and he said he didn't know exactly but estimated around three thousand. I looked in a few, but there wasn't much time for that. Mainly philosophy, a lot of it, and scientific books, some popular some apparently quite abstruse, works on criminology, business, technical manuals, a lot of poetry, a few novels.

From time to time – but not often – we heard footsteps resonating somewhere in the maze of corridors, and then they faded and all was silent again. We didn't meet anyone.

Once, we were stopped in our tracks by what sounded like the distant but clear sound of a woman's voice calling out. It spooked me, because I was convinced I heard her call "Help!" We listened, but didn't hear it again. Just somebody outside in the yard, said Phidias with a shrug. I said it was my impression, on the contrary, that it was coming from somewhere within the building. But maybe I was mistaken.

I think, said George solemnly and portentously, it's coming from the mystery room.

Oh don't, you're giving me the willies, I told him. I looked round at Phidias for support, but he was already resuming the transfer of books to the shelves. So we continued.

The boxes were crushed and disposed of down in the yard, in the huge skip that was there.

George was jabbering excitedly all the way home. There was no sign of the illness he had previously complained of. My fear is that it will be hell getting him to return to school. I tried to explain to him how important that was, but he just changed the subject.

6

This was a world of meticulous realism. Except that it wasn't.

The railway theme was already evident on entering the front hall of this otherwise undistinguished modern terraced house in the suburbs of Deadmans Beach: an original oil painting of a train, identified as a Class 201 multiple-unit diesel in original British Railways green livery. Known colloquially as "Thumpers" because of their engine sound.

Trevor Tanner was pleased with this identification. He provided the further information that the particular train in question was depicted leaving Moorshurst station, and that he used to drive one.

But them days are in the past, he added. Lots of things have changed. Including in my life.

For example?

Trevor considered, and said: Never used to eat seafood before we moved here, me and the wife. She doesn't live here any more, by the way. Now I love it, seafood of all kinds. That's one example. I have fish nearly every day, I even cook it myself. I eat half a crab each morning for me breakfast. One time, Sonny, you know, the landlord of the Richard the Lionheart, he gives me a huge crab in return for a favour I done him. Huge it was. Well, it was still alive, so I couldn't eat it. There it was, waving its claws around. In the end I asked my nephew to throw it back, and he did, he took it down to the sea, you know that place where you can see the rocks sticking up when the tide is out, and chucked it in.

We were in his kitchen. The light was poor.

Tea with a drop of rum in it, that was the tipple.

This is what I regret, that I didn't do what I ought to have done, he said, standing in front of the door lifting his mug to his face. What I ought to have done earlier. His face looked somewhat battered in that light. It was the dent in the forehead that did it. This is what I regret, he said. I don't regret doing things, I regret not doing them. But it's an open question, mebbe.

The Catholic church distinguishes between sins of commission and sins of omission.

I dunno about that, he replied, I dunno. He frowned and grimaced, then his face lighted up again.

He said: I'll show you. I'll show you my train set, that's what the wife calls it. Yeah, I'll show you everything. Just bring your mug with you, we'll go upstairs. I hope you'll appreciate the detail. I reckon you're the kind of chap that does appreciate detail. Detail I think is most important, I mean actually it's everything. It's crucial. If you don't have that, forget it. If you don't put in the detail. You have to be convinced it's a railway. It is an actual railway. I suppose it's a world really. But does it exist? It might have done. That's the whole point of it, explained Trevor, it might have done.

You have to believe in it.

That's right.

It's a picture of the world as it might be.

That's it, that's it, he said excitedly.

Aside from the occasional visible items of memorabilia, the hall and kitchen, as already observed, gave little indication of or preparation for what would be revealed upstairs.

What once had been the spare bedroom ("It used to be my daughter's room," said Trevor) was entirely taken up by a model railway. It was constructed on a shelf ranging in depth from about a metre at its widest to a foot or so at its narrowest, supported consistently on a sturdy framework of one-inch by two-inch battens, running round all four walls of the room (the gap allowing the door to open was closed up, once entry had been effected, by means of folding up a hinged section forming a bridge). Running along the entire length of the far wall was an enormously detailed scale representation of Moorshurst railway station: the long platform accommodating eight-car trains, the retaining wall behind, the stairs up to the station building, all as remembered, with rows of houses built in low relief framing the whole composition. Trevor explained that the model was in OO scale, each foot being represented by four millimetres. The tracks emanating from the station merged in an elegant, sweeping system of curved pointwork, running round the corner of the room and under bridges at two locations, into a double main line threaded through a cutting dense with vegetation. After a space, this line then bifurcated again, the left fork leading, via the section that bridged the doorway through which we had entered, to a complex of parallel sidings thickly populated with stationary trains, parked ready for action; the right fork, meanwhile, disappeared into a tunnel mouth – apparently into the wall of the room itself.

A through line from the sidings joined up, via another tunnel, with the other end of the magnificently detailed station.

A four-carriage train, hauled by a model steam locomotive (4-4-0 Schools class, said Trevor), had been waiting on the station platform; Trevor switched on the current, set it on its way, and it pulled out, slowly at first, then gathering speed as it passed the signals, taking the left fork, passing the stationary trains (at the location he designated "the fiddle yard") and thereby eventually completing the circuit of the room.

Now I'll show you the next section, he said.

He pulled up the drawbridge, and before we left the room set the points to divert the train into the tunnel. Let's go next door, said Trevor.

The adjoining room, which was larger, would have been the master bedroom of the house – what had once presumably been the marital bedroom – and did still contain a bed that had evidently been recently slept in. But, as before, the room was encircled on all sides by a superfluity of model railway. On our entering, the same train that had previously been set in motion could now be observed emerging into this room from the other mouth of the tunnel, having traversed a gap in the wall into a whole new world. Recognisable here was an similarly detailed representation of Deadhurst station, set against a background of individually modelled houses and gardens and lush miniature woodland, the tunnel mouth being clearly a representation of the Moorish Tunnel. The train ran through this landscape for a short while before Trevor, wielding a wireless controller, stopped it at the station.

This new panorama was difficult for the observer to take in immediately; but attention was also distracted by an extraordinary towering construction in wood, built up from the baseboard level to the ceiling. And now it could be seen that approaching this point a single track started to climb an embankment, entering this construction, whereupon it continued its upward gradient in a long winding spiral heading towards the ceiling, where could be seen an open hatchway, and darkness above.

That, said, Trevor, is my helix. I'm very proud of that. Here we depart from our basic everyday reality.

He realised that his remark had caused puzzlement.

Look, he said, you see that station?

Deadhurst station. An admirably accurate model.

That's right, up to a point. But do you see something wrong with it?

It seemed immaculate.

Well, I'll tell you. It's a junction. You see that line branching off it? That has no counterpart in real life, if you see what I mean.

Trevor explained that he had become frustrated by his doomed project of modelling exactly the real life railway, a project which for logistical reasons, and given the actual limitations of time and space, had no chance and would never have any chance of complete success. And so one day he had had the inspiration to abandon this fruitless effort to achieve absolute realism, and model instead the railway that might have been.

That was the breakthrough, he said excitedly.

In the alternative reality he imagined, he would follow through with a plan which had in the actual history of the railway once been mooted but never achieved: the building of a branch line from Deadhurst to Deadmans Beach. He could barely contain himself as he described the dream he would now put into practice.

If it had happened in the nineteenth century as planned, if the railway had actually been built, the town of Deadmans Beach and its economy would have been transformed, he said. The local fishery would have had an outlet for its produce, with rapid transport of refrigerated vans directly by rail to London.

However, he had run out of space for this major extension to his model. The only location remaining was the attic. Building a model railway up there would pose no major problem: it was dry, it was spacious, there was already an electricity supply. But how to join the railway on this floor with that on the floor above? The answer, he said, had come to him in a flash one day. Thus was the helix born. Let me show you, he said.

He set the train on its way once again, this time diverting it to the junction. It started to climb the single-track gradient.

He led the way out of the room and back to the landing, and indicated a fixed loft ladder.

Revealed at the summit of this was a third model world, in darkness until the master of this domain flicked another switch and brought instant daylight to the scene. Bare beams and rafters framed it. Above, the underside of the roof of the house. A track wound its way along the perimeter of the attic, past model fields, farms and ditches, recognisable as a representation of the Dead Level, eventually arriving at a sea diorama, lit to suggest a vast expanse beyond, and in front of it, still under construction, but already familiar in parts, an immense representation of the town and port of Deadmans Beach; but here on the seafront, before the beach with its population of fishing boats, was an entire station and freight yard that had no counterpart in real life; and so this version of Deadmans Beach, more magnificent than the reality, was indeed a work of the imagination.

Can you hear the train coming? said Trevor.

There was a faint rumble, and out of the tunnel at the far side now emerged once more our model train, which had spent the past two minutes slowly climbing the spiral track that had taken it from the main bedroom below, at a manageable gradient, all the way up to the attic – and here it came, through the hatch and into its new space.

This is it, said Trevor, this is the railway that might have been. His voice was full of emotion.

The train slowed as it pulled into the terminus, and was brought to a halt at the platform by Trevor's wireless controller.

•

Once I was. I was and I was single. I didn't have anything to fear.

Then there were two. There were two of us. We went everywhere. We felt we could do everything, and anything. The two of us. There were so many horizons to explore.

That was so beautiful.

And he was inside me, and then the third that was inside me. That was inside me. The third came then. Inside me waiting to come out. And he came out.

Then there were three.

Oh, so good with the three of us.

It was so good. I have to remember that.

But it didn't last. I truly wish it had lasted. Something went very wrong. Whose fault was that? Was it my fault? There was fault. Whose it was, who can say? And so then there were two, we were back to two – two of us. But a different two. Two and two. Or two and one and one and two.

I wish, I wish.

I said to him, I think ... something's happening.

We were parked at the side of the road. Just beyond that fence the marshes started, you could see them stretched out, in the twilight, because the last of the pink light in the western sky had gone, and evening was coming on. That was one horizon. Nothing much to disturb it. Just one or two trees, in clumps. Nothing else. Not even sheep. There were no street-lamps here, of course. And the two of us – standing on the verge.

He waited patiently, he was smoking a cigarette. He hadn't yet given up then. I could see the glow as he put it to his lips. What is it? he asked.

I could see his face still, I mean *can* see his face still.

What is it, Luce? And I could hear concern in his voice.

I've missed two in a row now.

No kidding?

Things are going to change, I said, I didn't know what I was saying, I'm scared, I'm suddenly scared.

No need to be, he said. Is there? He meant to be reassuring, but he seemed more like a little boy, the little boy that was being left behind.

It's good, I decided to say. It's all good.

That's good, he said, and he threw the stub on the muddy ground and stepped on it, squelch.

Let's get back in the car, it's getting cold, he said.

There was a movement in the darkness of one of those trees. And all of a sudden a pale shape emerged from it. Silently, it flew straight as an arrow, towards us it seemed, but then actually over our heads, becoming darker against the paler sky, crossing the road, and still silently, completely silently, descending on a fence-post in the field on the opposite side. There it stopped, and settled, motionless once more, a pale, compact bag of feathers.

It's a barn owl, I said, laughing, relieved.

I think maybe he was watching us? Or maybe he was oblivious to us.

It was very quiet and peaceful there, I remember. It seems a long time ago now.

Let's go home, Luce, said Dave.

•

The installation, unfinished as it was, and maybe unfinishable, was clearly on an epic scale, partaking of the quality that in former ages might have been designated as the sublime.

That is to say, stupendous and not a little frightening in its cancerous beauty.

The master, Trevor Tanner, seemed lost in contemplation: no longer a man approaching his middle sixties with a failed marriage to his deficit, no longer the manager of a business park in a remote and obscure location, but a secular saint – a god.

What had possessed him?

He had only meant to build a model of Moorshurst train station, he said, a modest proposal conceived while his daughter still occupied the second bedroom. For years he had taken photographs of the prototypical location, made draw-ings, formulated plans. The only question in his mind had been whether to model the station as it was now, in its depleted state, its freight yard demolished to make way for car parking, or to restore it in model form to its former glory. Then the daughter had departed the nest to go to college, and the plan had been put into action. That would have been twenty or so years ago. Seven years in, he had run out of space. He had pleaded with his wife to be allowed to bore a hole in the dividing wall between the rooms and introduce a spur, an extension, into the marital bedroom. That had hap-pened. But the "spur" grew by subtle increments over the next couple of years. By the time his wife had moved out, it was already encroaching on three sides of the room. A year or two later, and already the "helix" was being contemplated. By now, he was devoting every minute not occupied with the day job – he'd left the real railways and taken up the post at the Dead Level Business Park – to the construction of his model empire. The attic was prepared – that alone took a year – and the bare structure of the imaginary Deadmans Beach branch laid down, before, only twelve months ago, work on the helix was finished and the two railways were finally joined together. The elation he'd felt when the first train successfully climbed from the first floor to the attic and arrived at the terminus was, he said, the greatest emotion he had ever experienced in his life.

But was his an experience he could share? By its very nature, this was not a construction that lent itself to being exhibited in the various model railway shows around the country. It was not, for sure, portable. But it had been photographed copiously and repeatedly, with all the sophisticated lighting otherwise traditionally lavished on high-end pornography or food; it had featured more than once in the top trade magazines – he proudly showed copies and cuttings – and visitors arrived regularly from all over the nation, and indeed occasionally from overseas, anxious to view close up for themselves this legendary creation.

Yet the impression remained that as his project developed over the years he was slowly, inexorably, barricading himself in. The model itself, in its various sections, with the attendant infrastructure of timber and electrical wiring in all its complexity, seemed to be forming a carapace around him, a system of defences against the world outside his world, that year by year was extended in ever newer and more ingenious ways, that would eventually seal him in permanently; in other words, he was constructing his own sarcophagus, or even his pyramid, like the kings of Egypt – except that he commanded no slaves and had to do all the work himself.

There could be no other epithet for this but heroic.

And so when do you think this project will be completed?

A model railway is always complete but never finished. That's what they say.

So let me ask a different question then: what next?

There's still a huge amount to do in the attic, as you can see. The detail in what I've done so far is still inadequate. And a lot of it hasn't even come into existence yet. Proper signalling, there ain't none yet up here. And I want to model the town, not just as it is but as it might have been. If the railway had actually come to the town, is what I'm saying. Only a quarter of it's been done. And that requires a lot of thought, Phidias. A lot of thought and planning, never mind the actual modelling and construction work. But I also have further plans.

What may those be?

I'm thinking about downstairs.

The ground floor?

Yeah.

I imagined you would be thinking along those lines.

I was thinking – the living room, for example, I never use that. And in parallel with that – well, I was thinking, the other end of the line, from Moorshurst. From Moorshurst on to London.

You're planning to build a model of the line to London?

Well, not the whole of it, obviously. That would be impossible. I'd need a much bigger house. I mean, I'd need a blooming mansion, it's beyond my resources, totally. But a representation of it.

So that's what's coming, then – drilling down to the ground floor?

I've already made a start on that. I don't mean the drilling, there are huge engineering problems there, it would need a massively more complex helix to build a link line between those two floors. But on the railway side, yeah, I've got a small baseboard already in the living room, and a test track. And I'm drawing plans all the time.

How do you find the time?

Well, I'm due for retirement next year. I shall be saying goodbye to the Dead Level BP. I'll get a good pay-off, and I've also got my railway pension, but the main thing is I shall be able to devote myself full-time to the project. But you say time – yeah, it does bring it home to you when you get to my age how little time there is. I mean, I've spent a good twenty years on the project. Maybe twenty years before that thinking about it and planning it. And for a man of my age, do you know what the average life expectancy is?

About another twenty?

Close. Nineteen years, actually, that's the average. So I'm over halfway in time, but not halfway through the possibilities. On the plus side, as I said, I'll be through with the job, so I'll be able to work full-time on the model. On the minus side, well, my health and strength might deteriorate.

Well, good luck with that. And – I don't want to pry, but – you said your wife couldn't cope with it, she moved out?

Yeah, we came to an amicable agreement, you might say.

Do you still see her?

Oh, yeah, of course, the wife comes round quite regular, like. She brings me food she's cooked sometimes. She's living in a mobile home in the Sanctuary Caravan Park.

And she doesn't mind that?

Oh, she loves it. Absolutely loves it. She's on her own, she's got peace and quiet, she's got everything she wants, she's got two cats, which I can't stand, I wouldn't allow them here because they used to jump up on the layout, she's got a lot of friends about, and she doesn't have to put up with me and my schemes.

And you will spend the rest of your life here?

Yeah.

What will happen to it – the layout – when you're gone?

I dunno. I ain't given it too much thought, to be honest with you. It'll probably all get trashed and thrown out. It'll probably end up in landfill eventually. Otherwise –

Si monumentum requiris, circumspice.

I beg your pardon?

If you need a monument, look around you. St Paul's Cathedral.

Oh yeah, I get your drift. I have to admit, sometimes it scares me.

It scares you?

Yeah, I wake up in the early hours of the morning, three, four o'clock, with nightmares, where the model is growing out of control, I can't stop it, it's already taken over, it's creeping into places I haven't even thought of yet, the garden, the garden shed. I mean, it's not just my monument, as you put it, it's actually living, you know what I'm saying, it's a living thing that is slowly killing me. Then that scares the daylights out of me.

But you still continue.

Yeah, what can I do? Listen, do you want some more tea and rum? Let's go back downstairs.

On closer inspection, there were definite indications of further metastasis on the ground floor. Boards, track, wiring. A row of three small paint cans, encrusted, and a white-spirit-scented jam jar crammed with paintbrushes, on the dining room mantel shelf. A circular burn mark on a coaster. Many sheets of A3 graph paper, the pale green squares covered in immensely complex pencil drawings, strewn next to the computer on a table – further sheets crumpled into balls half-filling the plastic wastepaper bin next to it.

The case continued.

•

After that it all went wrong. After he was born, that's when things started to change. But no, that's not right, they had already been changing. They had already been changing for a long time. It was a long time, a long decline. I had never ever dreamed he might be violent. And I did dream. There were all sorts of things I dreamed. To have a little boy of my own, that was a miracle. But I'm not thinking straight today. There's a mist coming in off the sea, I think it's gone into my brain. I can't remember what I said to him that day when he hit me. Perhaps it was what I said. But there was no excuse for it, was there? Something was said, anyway. And then he came after me, it was in the kitchen that time. It was only a glancing blow, but he caught me unawares and I went flying to the floor. It was a terrific shock and a surprise, finding myself on the floor, for a moment I didn't have a clue where I was or what had happened. Here was the floor, right next to me all of a sudden – and far above me, too far, the ceiling, the ceiling lamp like a distant sun. That was all wrong. What I think was he didn't know his own strength. He stood towering over me, but it looked like he just didn't know what to do next, like he was appalled by what he had done, and then I was up and screaming at him, get out, get out of this house. And the worst thing was when little George appeared in the doorway – he was only tiny then – and he was running from one of us to the other, bawling his eyes out, he was too young at the time to have any idea what was happening. And I remember Dave started crying too – I'd never seen him cry before. They were both crying, and I was shouting. The injury was the least of it. A bruise came out later, just a small one on my right cheekbone. It didn't hurt that much. He went, anyway. He went. I don't know what he did with himself that night, where he slept. And that one didn't blow over, and I still flinch. Just once, he kept on at me, much later with attempts at remorse, just once, I've never done it before, I'm so sorry, I shan't do it again, why am I being punished for just one slip? But it wasn't just that incident, obviously. A slip, he called it. A mistake, what is it they say, an error of judgement. I hate it when they say that. No, what it was was that after all these years we had run out of things to talk about, at least that is from my perspective, his might be different.

•

Realities that might have been. The world as it might be. Many interacting worlds. All possible alternative histories and futures are real. Such musing led back to the library in Room 248. A comfortable chair and a standard lamp had been set up in that metal cradle.

Hear that train coming.

Not a ghost train – but a train travelling on a track that was never built in our version of history.

In the distance, it rumbled. The rumbling continued, a slow, subtle crescendo. But the rumbling was not coming from outside; it was generated within the complex.

It was like a drum roll.

And then, out of nowhere, an immense, dissonant chord, a great and formidable clanging, an explosive event that rang out once and reverberated, and then echoed again and again through the storage room corridors.

The door of Room 248 was opened. The echoes could better be detected now, passing away gradually down the corridors in the direction of oblivion, a long dying without end.

But now there were also the unmistakable sounds of human voices.

Sorry, we didn't mean to disturb you, mate.

(There were three of them: young, angular, dark. One bespectacled, one hirsute, one tall and lugubrious. They were gathered in Room 210, one of the larger units at the corner of the perimeter of the complex. They had amplifiers, guitars, percussion items, other unknown instruments.)

So you're the band that regularly rehearses here.

Yeah, every Tuesday at this time, but if that's a problem –

No, not at all. The manager of the business park forewarned me, and it's not an issue for me in any way. He said he thought you were called the Hedgehogs.

(General laughter.)

No, we're called Hedgemonicker.

Hedgemonicker?

Hedge as in hedge, and monicker as in someone's name.

I see.

It was Pete's idea. He's the intellectual of the band. The future Sir Peter.

I write the words. They mistake that for intellect.

And you play –?

Guitar, sometimes bass guitar. This is Geezer, he's the hairy drummer. And that's Lurch, our multi-instrumental virtuoso. He don't say much.

I speak when I'm spoken to, asserted the tall, lugubrious one.

And what kind of music do you play?

Folk metal.

Folk metal?

Yeah. Medium heavy, with gothic tendencies.

I thought we were more, like, sleazepunk? With a bit of dark throat-singing. Also very poetic.

Quite poetic. We're poets really.

I'm pleased to know that. Some of my best friends in the past have been poets. Sorry, I should have introduced myself. My name is Phidias, I'm a private detective.

No kidding?

What are you detecting?

Well, I'm detecting an abundance of musical talent right now.

Hey, that's a nice thing to say.

But I really do not wish to hinder you.

It's OK, man, we were just waiting for Geezer to set up his kit, he takes fucking forever.

Pete, I'll have you know I'm a serious creative artist – I need plenty of time and space if I'm to give of my best.

Serious creative artist? You're a drummer! Reality check, man.

You defo take up a lot of space, that's for sure.

Thank you, guys. You sure know how to hurt a sensitive fellow.

Seriously, Phidias, what does a private detective do?

Well, we have an office right here on the estate, Peralta Associates. And the answer to your question is very boring things mostly. A child has run away and the parents want to trace her. She's gone to London, and she soon turns up. We identify the location and inform the child protection authorities. A wife wants to ascertain what her husband is up to, prior to divorce proceedings. Can be pretty sordid, as well as tedious. Industrial espionage is another one, that can be more exciting. Or not. Sometimes more intractable problems turn up.

Like what?

One of the cases we're dealing with right now is an elderly lady who's been missing for over a year. There are very few clues as to what's happened to her. So we have to piece together the history, the last sightings.

I think I remember there was something on the news about that.

Well, without breaching the confidentiality of my client, the facts in the public domain are that she was believed to have been on the 201 bus to Moorshurst, but was not seen subsequently.

Well, if she disappeared between here and Moorshurst you'll never have an end to it.

Why is that?

You're talking about the Grey Area.

What do you mean by that?

That's a load of old cobblers, Geezer.

It's true, Pete, I tell you. There are loads of stories.

Fairy stories.

Ask my uncle, he manages Manor Farm out on the edge of the Dead Level, just where the marshes begin. He's a sheep farmer, they're into the lambing season at the moment, I'm helping him out. Anyway, we're going back a few years here, he had a mate who lost an entire flock overnight. He's told me the story many times, he wouldn't lie.

The sheep disappeared?

Oh, they came back. What happened was he left the flock in a field, went in to have his tea, when he came back out an hour later, the entire flock, maybe fifty or sixty sheep, had completely vanished. They were nowhere to be seen. He's doing his nut. He's looking in the adjoining fields, checking the fences and the gate and the road outside in case they slipped through, nothing, everything's fastened, and no sheep. Then he gets a phone call from a neighbouring farmer, what are your sheep doing in my field? What do you mean, he says, I've just lost an entire flock, well they're here, says his mate, I recognise the marks, they're in my field. So he drives over, it's about a mile or more, and there they all were, a bit nervous and frightened, but all accounted for. Well, how was that possible? Not only was it a long way away, too far for the sheep to have made it on their own in the time, but there were ditches and fences and bolted gates in the way. It was a hell of a job to get them back. And according to my uncle it turns out there have been lots of similar stories of miraculously transported animals, going back hundreds of years. There was that horse –

Oh yeah, you wrote a song about that, didn't you –

What happened to the horse?

This was meant to have occurred nearly a hundred years ago – near Thieves Bridge, do you know it? on the road to Moorshurst. So there was a haunted house in the village where there'd been a lot of weird happenings reported, and the weirdest one was one night when a horse disappeared from the barn and was discovered the next morning up in a hay-loft, although how it came to be there was a mystery. And in fact apparently they had to knock down a partition and then lower it with a crane through the hay-hole to get it out.

And have there been any human disappearances?

There have been quite a few, yeah. There was a craze for alien abductions out on the marshes a few years ago. Though you don't hear so much about that now.

People disappeared?

Yes, people disappeared, and sometimes people came back, or they never actually disappeared but claimed to have been abducted. And lights in the sky, what was said to be UFOs, and all that. Years before that it would have been fairies, and ghosts with lanterns.

Most of it is bollocks.

Not all.

It's true that the marshland, what some people locally call the Grey Area, is a pretty treacherous place. You wouldn't go out there lightly. There are paths going nowhere –

Paths that change and are no longer there when you try and find them again –

It's mind-boggling, it's an area where the rules keep changing, or there are no rules as to what's normal. One moment there's a field, the next it's a bog – you've got to be very careful, there's no consistency, there are a lot of – what's the word I'm looking for?

Anomalies?

Yeah, that's a good word, Phidias, anomalies. It's a place full of anomalies. You can feel it even here.

What do you mean, here in the self-storage depot?

Yeah, have you heard the voices?

Ah, come on, Geezer –

You've heard them, Pete.

I dunno that I have, actually.

I have myself heard some phenomena. But one has to investigate rational explanations first before exploring more exotic scenarios, and almost always the rational explanations have the required validity, and the fanciful ones are therefore rendered redundant.

But there you are, *almost* always!

So we are left with anomalies, phenomena that do not make absolute sense, or are contradictory, that we cannot explain at this time, with the resources available to us. Lost locations. Old ladies who unaccountably disappear, even. On the whole, then, we must remain in a state of profound unknowing; we must retain our humility in the face of our ignorance. There are, however, quasi-rational theories to explain away otherwise inexplicable anomalies. I have just been reading about quantum leakage, for example.

What's that?

You are familiar with the many-worlds interpretation of quantum theory?

Yeah.

No.

I think so, I'm not sure.

Well, this all arises from the fact that indeterminacy is built into our reality at the atomic level. It isn't possible to predict what an atomic particle will do next. Quantum mechanics teaches us that particles do not have a definite locality, they can equally be described as waves as well as particles, they don't behave like discrete objects in what we like to call the real world. Where they are and where they go is governed by probability. Some scientists have postulated that it is the observer that decides what will happen, that as soon as you observe the atomic interaction, then the wave function collapses, as they say, and the position of the particle is fixed. Others say that this is not so, that at every point in time particles find themselves in more than one place, and so history multiplies and different universes evolve. That's the many-worlds interpretation.

Wow, mindfuck.

But if this is so, how is it possible to test this, since by definition we continue to inhabit only one of those possible worlds? Well now, quantum leakage suggests that diverging worlds close to each other are still capable of interacting, or interfering. In other words, some of those parallel realities are in principle observable, even though they conflict with the coherence we like to ascribe to our world. Hence, anomalies. But this is an extremely speculative, exotic, possibly absurd theory.

So how does it explain why these anomalies, as you call, them, seem to happen especially in zones like the Grey Area?

An excellent question, Geezer. It's possible that anomalies occur all the time everywhere yet in most cases remain largely unnoticed. It's possible that ... but forgive me, I'm trespassing on your rehearsal time. I had better leave you to yourselves and to your music.

That's OK, man. If you're sure we're not disturbing you?

Not at all, it's about time I hauled myself back next door. I hope to catch you guys some time in performance. Do you have any gigs coming up?

We're about to go on a little tour. Nothing locally until, when is it, Lurch, October?

Yeah, that's right, not till October, at the old Dick.

The Richard the Lionheart?

Yeah.

An admirable establishment. Well, I shall have to wait until then, if I'm still around.

Interesting talking to you, man.

•

Dave has George this weekend, so I met up with Kitty at Buddies wine bar in Moorshurst and we had a good old natter over a bottle of white wine.

Kitty was full of it and I wasn't at first but she eventually cheered me up, and that's how it goes sometimes. Her face was shiny and her hair was done in a very nice new style.

And she said I shouldn't put up with it, I should insist the school meets George's needs and my needs as a parent instead of forcing him to conform to their protocols because that's what suits them, and I agree with her, though it's so easy to say. It's easy for her to say, and also it's easy for me to nod my agreement, and I do, repeatedly. You want to do this, you don't want to do that, and I'm nodding and nodding because she's nodding, but I'm thinking what is it I *want* to do, actually?

But she is so entertaining and bright, you have to give her that.

And she said, and she said, and sometimes I was listening and sometimes I wasn't. She changed tack.

So what about this new job of yours, you say you're now a *detective*?

Well, we both roared with laughter, then I said, it's true.

So what's he like, this, what's his name, Peralta? she demanded.

I had to reply, truthfully, it was hard to say what Phidias was like because he wasn't like anybody or any thing, his attributes were his own and no one else's (but I put it very badly – that's to say, less eloquently than that). But I did try to impress upon her that I was learning on the job, and it was very interesting.

What are you learning, she wanted to know.

I said Phidias had taught me some things about observation, about paying attention to detail, and I told her how I'd had some interesting discussions with him about what was relevant detail and what was not, and how he'd once said all detail was relevant, and I'd said you can't possibly take in all detail, at least my brain can't, and he'd countered that when you feel your mind can't cope any more, can't continue any longer, that's exactly when you have to go that bit further.

That's funny, she said, and laughed. Did he really say that?

He says a lot of stuff like that, I told her.

What other examples, she begged me.

For example, I said, trying to recall, he once said to me: What is is clothed in what is not.

Say that again, she said.

What *is* is clothed in what is not.

Wow, that's pretty enigmatic, said Kitty, what did he mean by that? and I said I wasn't sure. But then she interrupted me, I bet he's Catholic, I bet he was brought up Catholic.

I don't know, I said, he doesn't talk about his background. Why?

Oh, she said airily, they all say that kind of thing. The world is not what it seems. There's a hidden world beyond this world, and all that.

I don't know if that's specifically Catholic. But I didn't actually say this, I let it pass.

Then the food arrived. I had a very nice bowl of seafood linguine and a salad, and Kitty had the vegan risotto. The talk turned to this and that, it petered out somewhat.

•

The Dead Level Business Park is normally as serene as is the proverbial grave during the hours of nightfall. However, the keen listener might just hear the faint sounds of revelry, as though a lively party was going on, but immensely far away, possibly on a different planet. Then again, even closer listening might suggest a null-signal, the alleged sounds now to be reinterpreted as artifacts, noise to be discounted, and therefore neither really nor officially present.

And then there was that rumble again, in the dead of night. And the setting was the labyrinth of the self-storage warehouse. Two shadows emerged at the far end of a transverse corridor, dimly delineated in the low-level security lighting: two pursuers patiently negotiating their way through the labyrinth. No matter which decision one might take at each intersection, which corridor one went down, the pursuers were never far behind, could not be shaken off. Their appearance: the angular shapes of grey herons, *Ardea cinerea*. Their names: yet to be revealed. If the unknown room, the room with no number, could be reached, then safety might be attained.

The voice of a small child, crying out, perhaps from the unknown room: "Mummy!"

No it wasn't; it was the hooting of a tawny owl outside, and now it was just before dawn.

7

It's coming up to May. There are buds on the twigs in our garden. Perhaps the stuck weather is showing signs of coming unstuck or something. Monday morning. I was late for work.

Just as I was about to set off for Moorshurst from the office a call came through for Phidias. It was Robin Watkins, Kieran Watkins' son and the great-nephew of the vanished lady. Phidias was grumpy. Apparently, he had not had a great night in his bunk. He grunted, Are you all right interviewing the neighbour? I said I was. He grunted again. Off you go then, I'll deal with the younger Watkins.

Maybe he's rethinking options, but I don't know what those are. Anyway, I put him through.

Robin, this is Phidias Peralta here, many thanks for calling back. Is it convenient to talk?

Yes, certainly.

As you know, I'm investigating the disappearance of your great-aunt, at the behest of your father. I just wanted to have your take on this rather tragic business if I may.

OK, go ahead, ask any questions you like.

I believe it was you who set up the social media and web sites appealing to the public for information about your great-aunt's disappearance, is that right?

Yes, my dad asked me to do that, because he knew I had the skill set for that kind of thing, so I was happy to help.

I've had a look online, and I see you have photographs of her and a link to that CCTV footage at the Sanctuary Café. I believe the police have more of that, but they haven't sent it to us yet. So what sort of response have you had?

At the beginning, lots of visits, lots of likes and sympathy messages. A few reminiscences posted up, which is very nice and heartwarming, you know. And I put the police contact info on there, as you probably saw, and I understand the police have had a few contacts as a result.

But not a lot of new information?

No, sad to say, not as far as I know. And there hasn't been anything for months now.

Do you have any personal opinion as to what may have happened to your great-aunt?

Well, Mr Peralta, you know, I cling to the belief she may still be alive somewhere. But I know that's unlikely. If we never get to know what happened to her that will be very sad. That's what I said to my dad, that's why I suggested he contact you guys, which he did, but all the same he says very bluntly she's dead. And he's probably right. It's been over a year now.

Your father said he asked me to intervene because of frustration with the lack of progress in the police investigation. So I'm sorry to go over old ground, but we have to make every effort to ensure nothing's been missed.

I understand that.

What was your own recollection of your great-aunt, what was she like?

Aunt Edith? She was great, I loved being taken to visit her as a child. She used to bake cakes for us, I remember. And she was quite funny. Joked with me when I was little, told me stories. Very talkative, nineteen to the dozen. Very independent. And she would talk to anyone, whoever they were, regardless of class, colour or creed. My father said of her what she lacks in height she certainly makes up for with her voice.

Did you see much of her after you'd grown up?

Usually only at family occasions. My mum would regularly tell me about her, when they visited, or she visited them. That was only very occasionally, but I think there was a bit of an increase in that over the past couple of years, because according to my mum Aunt Edith was getting a bit, you know ...

Frail? Forgetful?

Yes, that's right.

What was your father's relationship with her like?

Dad? I think he was fond enough of her. But my dad's never worn his heart on his sleeve, like. I think the relationship got a bit strained in recent years, because he was worried about her, I guess. He wanted her to move to sheltered accommodation, but she wouldn't, and then there was a big row because he thought if she stayed in her house she should have a carer, as her memory was deteriorating, but she resisted that, well, quite fiercely, actually.

And how do you think all this has affected him?

I think badly.

Can you say a bit more?

Well, I have to say Dad is not an easy person to get close to. He doesn't say much about his feelings, and that. But it's affected him, definitely. One thing, the relationship between my parents has taken a turn for the worse, and maybe the stress of this has contributed – well, I would say it has.

Ah, that may explain why your father has taken pains to keep your mother out of this.

Yes, they've not been on speaking terms really, in the past year or so.

Is she still living with your father in Deadhurst?

No, she's just moved out, actually, about three or four months ago, to live with her sister.

I'm sorry to hear that, I didn't know.

Yes, there's been a lot of stress. Not just Aunt Edith's disappearance, but even before that, things going wrong at work, all of that's maybe contributed.

Things are not good with your father's firm? I thought he had semi-retired?

Yes, he came to an agreement that he'd take a back seat. It hit him badly, you know, because this was a firm he'd co-founded, and still has a major share in. He's not used to taking a back seat, my dad, he likes to be in control.

But there were financial problems?

I don't want to go into all that.

I understand, I don't mean to pry into matters that are of no concern to me. Do you get on well with your father?

Let's say we get on.

But the relationship is not warm?

We get on.

Has it always been the same?

I think he was more relaxed years ago, when I was growing up. I remember he used to come home from work with all these strange experimental concoctions developed by his firm. One time he put this food colouring into the pasta as a joke. We had blue spaghetti. My mum was maybe not so amused, but as a child I thought it was hilarious. Also he'd play these games – he'd have my mum and me taste something the company was experimenting on and ask what flavour we thought it was. Sometimes we'd get it right, sometimes spectacularly wrong. One time it did actually go wrong – the whole family became ill as a result of ingesting one of these experimental products – I mean, not badly ill, but anyway – he was mortified when that happened. Actually, I think he stopped doing that from then on.

It wasn't so much fun any more?

That's right, I think he became aware of the dangers.

So basically he's quite a serious person?

Well, as I said, my dad's not touchy-feely. Actually, I'm concerned about both my mum and dad.

And how is your mother?

Calmer, now they've had this trial separation. Happier, I would say. But she doesn't say much either.

But getting back to your great-aunt, you think your father was indeed badly affected by this terrible business, even though he maybe doesn't express his emotions directly?

Yes, I believe so. Actually, I think when it really hit him was when he first saw that CCTV footage from the café. I was with him when we first watched it, and he went very pale, as white as a sheet, actually, and said something like, my god, I can't believe this. And I said, I hope to god that's not the last time we see her alive.

What did he reply?

He went very quiet for a while, then he said: It might be. It was way out of character for him, I've never seen him so badly shaken. Maybe it was the first time it had hit home, I don't know.

So your father believes your great-aunt is dead. But you cling to the belief we may be able to locate her somewhere?

Well, Mr Peralta, that's a very forlorn hope, I must admit. In my heart of hearts I may have to accept that my dad is right, and we shall never see her again.

What do you personally hope to achieve by engaging us?

Actually, it was my mum first suggested calling in a private investigator, I think. I supported my mum, I said we had to do something. My dad was reluctant at first, but he came round to it. If you ask me what *he* wants to achieve, I don't know, you'll have to ask him. Some kind of closure.

That's what everybody hopes for. But also dreads.

No sooner had that phone conversation ended than a call came through on the mobile.

Phidias, this is Darren Gallop, of the Fishermen's Association.

Hello there, Darren.

Fancy going fishing tomorrow morning?

I beg your pardon?

The weather is holding, so we're off at five in the morning. You did say you had an interest in seeing what we do at first hand.

Of course I did, and indeed I do.

Well, meet us at the *Jumpy Mary* on the beach at four-thirty and we'll kit you out. Only, my second man isn't able to make it.

I can't say I would be all that much use to you.

You won't have to do nothing you can't handle.

In that case, I'm very grateful to you for asking. I shall be there promptly.

•

I did think at the time it might have been a mistake to give the fish names. Well, it was done. The thing is that Bruiser was now dead, and it was George who found him, first thing in the morning. He'd been feeding normally the night before. Now there he was, semi-floating near the surface of the aquarium, barely recognisable through having lost most of his colour, but George had gone through the process of elimination and identified him exactly. Well, he was upset, to put it mildly. I tried to soothe him, these things happen, I said. Fish don't live very long, not compared with human beings. But he only got more uptight, on the verge of tears, wanted to know if I was going to die, and if so, when. Nobody's going to die any time soon, I assured him.

But what to do about the fish corpse? The breakfast routine was completely upturned.

I thought it was better if he fished the thing out, so handed him the little net, and he did so, very carefully.

What shall I do with him? he asked me, rather piteously.

So I said, Just chuck him in the bin. And he was aghast.

I can't do that!

What do you mean?

I can't put Bruiser in the dustbin!

George, I said, it's a dead fish. When we eat fish, we put the remains in the dustbin, don't we?

He wasn't having that. But it's Bruiser!

So I asked him what he wanted to do, and he said he would like to bury the corpse. And in the kitchen I found a large box of matches which was almost empty and transferred the remaining matches to a new box, and then found some cotton wool in the bathroom, which we used for padding around the tiny body, and then George was happy with that. So we went down to the bottom of our little garden, George with his trowel. I told him where to dig a hole in a flowerbed, and he grumbled because it was hard work, but I pointed out if he didn't dig it deep enough the local cats would come round and disinter poor Bruiser. Eventually (I had to help him) we had an adequate grave. After one last, solemn look at the ex-Bruiser, George closed the matchbox and reverently deposited the improvised coffin in the bottom of the hole, and together we trowelled back the earth on top and stamped it down. It was a ceremony of a sort, I suppose.

Now we need a gravestone, insisted George, but I reminded

him it was way past time to go to school, and he reluctantly agreed when I said we could look for a suitable stone later on the beach and inscribe it with a message in magic marker.

That is why I was late for work.

I drove to Moorshurst. It was a morning suitable for a funeral. Meeting Place Avenue looked exactly the same as we had left it three or four weeks ago, when we had spotted Mr Watkins' black 4x4. There were plenty of parking places.

I rang the doorbell of number 106, adjoining Edith Watkins' house. It was answered by an overweight, pleasant-faced young woman with short, dark, bobbed hair.

Hello, I said, you must be Sharon. I'm Lucy White, Mr Peralta's assistant.

Ah, you're the detective, she said brightly. Do come in.

So let's get this right, Sharon – you were actually away during the time Mrs Watkins disappeared?

That's right. I was on a city break with my boyfriend. Three nights in Paris.

Oh, nice.

We enjoyed it very much.

Because we had the impression you were there from March fifteenth, and you started to get worried when you didn't see her –

No, that's not correct. I saw her March fifteen in the morning, just before I went off on holiday. Then when I returned three days later I noticed the milk-bottles on the doorstep. And I called her nephew.

You did? Mr Watkins didn't mention that.

I left a voicemail message. Anyway, it doesn't matter, I caught him when he arrived. I was worried.

Had you tried ringing the doorbell?

Oh yes of course, I did, there was no reply.

You didn't have a key to her house, by any chance?

No, funnily enough, I'd been talking about that with her not so long previously, about getting a duplicate key cut, just in case of emergencies you know, and she was keen on that, but we just never got round to it.

So you were worried. What did you think might have happened?

Obviously that she was ill in the house, or ... worse. She was very old and getting quite frail, you know. I never expected she'd be found missing.

So let's get back to the morning of the fifteenth, then – how was she when you saw her?

I wanted to let her know I would be away a few days, so I called round, about nine or nine-thirty in the morning, I think. She was in her dressing-gown. We chatted about the weather and that. She wanted to know how it was out. I said it seemed a little blowy. She said she thought she might go for one of her walks. I knew what she meant, because she'd often talked about how she would take the bus to Deadmans Beach, look at the fishing boats, have tea in the café. Actually, I tried to put her off, I said the wind was brewing up, it wasn't a good day to go, and I thought she'd agreed, she said maybe I'll go another day. You know, she was very physically frail indeed by then. And rather dithery.

Dithery?

Yes, kept forgetting things that had been said, seemed a bit bemused at times. I mean, she was in her ninetieth year. Also, to be honest, she didn't look very well.

What do you mean by that, do you think she was seriously ill?

No ... well, I don't know. Her colour wasn't good, I'd noticed that before, not just that morning, but for a few weeks previously. Maybe she wasn't eating properly. That's part of why we were all rather worried about her.

Well, Sharon, you did the best you could for her.

I hope so. Anyway, that was how we left it, I advised her to stay indoors that day, for all the good it did, and a bit later my boyfriend picked me up in the car and we went off to the airport.

So you didn't actually see her set off on that trip to Deadmans Beach?

No. I'm surprised she did, because she did say she probably wouldn't. But on the other hand, as I've said, she often forgot conversations directly after they'd happened. And anyway that CCTV definitely showed her at the café on the day, didn't it?

That's right. When had she previously gone on one of those trips, do you remember?

Oh, she did it regularly. Sometimes I'd see her walking back home from the bus stop. The previous time ... I don't remember, maybe three or four weeks back.

And her mobility was –

She walked quite slowly and carefully, with that stick of hers. She didn't use a walking frame or nothing. Many's the time I'd see her go across to the corner shop, leaning on that brightly patterned flowery stick.

Oh, I saw a walking stick with a pink floral pattern on it in the house, in that umbrella stand. Is that the one?

Sounds like it.

Well, that's funny, why would that still be there in the house?

I don't know. She had two or three sticks, I think. There was a traditional wooden one with a crook, which had been given to her and she said she didn't like very much, and also a black one, I remember.

Don't think I saw a black one in the umbrella stand. That must have been the one she took that day, then.

Probably. The flowery one was her favourite, I suppose.

Leaving aside all that ... you say she was very frail?

Oh, getting worse. She didn't like to admit it. There was the time she had that fall.

When was that, can you tell me about it?

Oh, she'd fallen down in her bathroom, that was about a year or so before her disappearance. It's a miracle she didn't break a limb. She actually got herself up, came downstairs, and round to my front door. There she was on my doorstep, her head bleeding. I said, Oh my god, Edith, what have you been doing to yourself? Said she thought she'd banged her head on the wall or on the floor when she went down. I took her in, cleaned her up, gave her a cup of tea. Fortunately, it wasn't very bad, but she was a bit shaken up. I said, Shall we phone your nephew? But she wouldn't have it, oh, don't bother Kieran, she said, but in the end I did, and he came round the next day. We both went in to hers. We saw the bathroom, there was still dried bloodstains on the floor, and I tried to clean it up as best I could. And she was like, what's all this about, as if she'd forgotten what had happened.

Was that when the handles and disability aids in the bathroom were installed?

Yes, that's right, Kieran arranged all that. She didn't want it, said it was an unnecessary expense.

But he persuaded her?

Yes, I suppose he did. I didn't know him at all previously, but in the last two or three years, as she was declining, he came over more and more frequently. He'd pop in to have a cup of tea with her.

Just him, not his wife?

Usually just him. Well, I suppose she *was* his aunt, and there was no-one else. He gave me his telephone number in case of emergencies. I was increasingly worried about her, as I said, she looked ill sometimes, just getting weaker physically. That's why I tried to persuade her not to go on her walk that windy morning.

And so, apart from being physically frail, you think her dementia was advancing as well?

Oh god, yes. She would regularly knock on my front door, maybe late at night, ask me what time is it, Sharon? And I'd say, maybe, ten-thirty. And she'd go, oh, is that ten-thirty in the morning? Because it's ever so dark. No, evening. Oh my goodness, I was just going to the corner shop to buy the morning paper, she'd say, I'm ever so sorry, I'm getting a bit old. And to be honest, the few times I was in the house, well, I couldn't help seeing it was going to rack and ruin. I've tidied it up now, because her nephew asked me if I would. But she'd previously been a very fastidious woman –

How long had you known her?

Well, I've been living here, what is it, nearly fifteen years, so I've been a neighbour of hers that long. She used to keep the house spick and span, but no longer. And I don't know if she was eating properly any more. But she'd tell me her nephew's family were trying to get carers in, and she'd go up the wall about that, she couldn't bear the thought. Actually, she was a very feesty woman, is that how you say it, feesty?

What do you think has happened to her?

I don't know. All I can think is that she lost her bearings and wandered off.

Got off at the wrong bus stop, maybe?

Very likely. Goodness knows where she ended up. I don't like to think about it, Lucy, I really don't. It's very distressing.

I understand.

After saying goodbye to Sharon I went across the road to the shop. It was a normal corner shop, stocking everything from newspapers to vegetables to mops. I wondered why Edith had not simply bought her milk there and had stuck with an old-fashioned doorstep milk delivery. But there we are, she was an old lady. A very smiley man behind the counter greeted me. I asked if he was the proprietor, and he said he was. I asked about Edith. Oh my goodness, poor Edie, he said. He had a very strong Indian accent. Yes, he remembered her very well. And yes, the police had come round asking him questions. Was it really a year ago? Oh, my, he said. And there is no more news of her? he enquired. Such a tragedy, such a tragedy. He had told the police he recalled her coming into the shop for her newspaper on that fateful morning. At what time? He thought it would have been around nine-thirty or ten. So perhaps soon after she had been talking to Sharon. How had she seemed? Just normal, he said. Just normal? Well, a bit under the weather maybe, you know, he said. I think maybe she was not very well. I been a bit worried about her for a while, I used to say are you looking after yourself, Edie? Very nice lady. Such a tragedy.

You know, Mummy, George said, you know.

What, dear? I said.

When you and Daddy decided to move to Deadmans Beach, he continued, well, that was the *best* decision you ever made.

I had to laugh at this. His face was so earnestly pleased-looking, the little love.

We were on the beach. He adores the beach. Afternoon, after school, dusk now approaching, but still a bland light. I was walking on the path above the shingle and George was trampling his way through the shingle itself. Far down the beach the shushing of the grey waves came to our ears, and far to the left I could see the fishing boat fleet pulled well up out of the tide's way.

We were looking for a pebble.

George wanted to find a suitable stone to inscribe and place upon Bruiser's grave. He was fastidious about it. Nothing but the best would do. A stone of a suitable size and colour and roundness, and he alone was the person to take the decision. He had already picked up, inspected and rejected several candidates.

We passed a row of wooden memorial benches the local council had erected along the seafront path. The first one was inscribed on the backrest: *In memory of Stephen Davies, fisherman. May those who rest awhile find peace.*

George asked: What does that mean, Mummy?

I told him that when someone died, sometimes his or her family and friends paid to have an inscription on a bench to remember them by. It's a lovely idea, I said.

Can we have one for Bruiser? George asked eagerly.

No, you can't have a bench for a molly.

Why not? he pleaded.

We couldn't afford it. Especially as you've got to get used to the fact that the fish don't live that long, and we could be bankrupt soon if we have to remember them all that way. And there'd be no room on the seafront for benches.

But a bench for Bruiser would be really cool.

I think a stone will be more appropriate.

All right.

George went back to his pebble hunt on the beach, and I walked on.

I could see a small band of gulls floating, rocking up and down on the swell inshore. It seemed a long way off. Here was another group of benches. They looked quite new. And then this:

Please rest and enjoy the view as did Edith Watkins.

And following that, in brackets, her birth and death dates. The date of death given as 15 March last year.

I stared at it in disbelief. I read it again. And again.

Mummy, I think I've found the stone! I heard George cry out.

The words were etched, or incised, or whatever the term is, into the dark, weatherproofed wood of the bench backrest. And they tried to be etched in my mind, but they would not stay.

Mummy! Mummy!

Sorry, George, I had a bit of shock. That's a lovely stone.

Can we go home now and put a *scription* on it?

In a minute, I said to him. I pulled out my mobile phone and pointed it as closely as I could, framing the inscription that was on this bench. The light was not good; it was failing fast. I touched the camera button.

Nothing happened.

A message flashed onto the screen: *Insufficient power for this operation.*

I swore under my breath, and George heard me and chided me for it. I apologised.

Indeed the battery level was well into the red. There was not enough juice.

Please rest and enjoy the view as did Edith Watkins.

The sky overhead was now slate-grey. I could see a man in a dark polo shirt carrying a litre of milk up the steps onto the sea embankment. The only patch of sunlight was focused on the line of wind rotors so that they gleamed on the far-off headland beyond the fishing boats. Elsewhere, there was gloom now. On the horizon just ahead, the complicated grey outline, a bit faint, of some ship or dredging machinery. It looked like that little group of birds that floated on the sea near the beach were not gulls but ducks. A dog yapped in the distance.

I tried again. But as before, no dice.

I switched to phone mode and called Phidias on his mobile.

But the phone went completely dead and the screen completely black as the last of the juice leaked out of it.

•

It was an hour before dawn on the beach. The debris began to accumulate. Visible on the shingle under a solitary arc-light mounted on its tall post were: a white upturned plastic café chair, the rear left leg missing; the skeleton of a skate; coils of rope; stacked lobster pots. Scents conveyed on the breeze – of which there was, actually, very little – included those of salt, and of decayed fish.

Against the dark background of the sea, which was at high tide, a still darker figure emerged. Or to be more precise, two: an upright figure and a smaller one beside. As the resolution improved, it was possible to observe that this was a human with long hair that glistened in that inadequate light, in a windcheater and shorts revealing grizzled and gnarled legs, towing, by means of a long lead, a portly dog. It was an old person and his hair was long and white. He was unmistakable.

Hello, Giles.

Good heavens, it's Mr Detective.

How are you?

I am as well as can be expected, given the situation and the prognosis and so on and so forth.

The dog, some type of terrier breed, snuffled and investigated, its breath exceedingly wheezy. After an awkward pause, Giles said: What brings you here to the fishing beach at this hour of the morning?

I'm actually going fishing. With Darren Gallop.

Ah, son of the legendary Doc Gallop. So you're going out this morning?

Yes.

Blimey, mister.

His eyelashes fluttered – visibly, even in such poor light. He was being pulled hither and thither by the investigatory movements of his dog on its lead, but nevertheless stood firm on the shingle. His fingernails, dark on the lead, shone briefly.

It was explained to him that Mr Gallop had offered this trip, and that it formed part of the investigation into the disappearance of Edith Watkins – Little Edie, as she was known locally – and into her psychology when she herself had taken such a trip twenty years previously.

Blimey, he repeated. And then, unexpectedly: I wish I was going with you.

You do? I thought you were done with all that, with the hard life of the fishing.

I am. But it don't mean I ain't nostalgic.

I am apprehensive about it.

You'll be all right, Mr Detective. Good luck to you, and good fishing.

And with that he turned and, led by the urgent dog, slowly left the shore, to disappear eventually into the darkness of the pre-dawn Old Town district of Deadmans Beach.

The eastern sky grew paler by the minute. Ahead, among a group of smaller boats pulled up on the shingle, could be seen the bulky form of the *Jumpy Mary*, surrounded by three silhouetted human figures, being readied for launch.

The *Jumpy Mary*, DB104, was a fibreglass-built boat of over seven metres in length and with a beam of just under three metres. Her wheelhouse was set forward and she was equipped with radar and with a hydraulic net-hauling facility. Her engine power was up to 120kw and her cruising speed around 14.5kph or 7.5 knots. Her purpose was inshore fishing (that is to say, within three miles of the coast), by means of trammelling.

The trammel net system consists of three parallel nets that are run out and left anchored to the sea-bed overnight; then hauled back in bearing the day's catch.

Darren Gallop, in woollen beanie and waterproof trousers, stood by the bow in the pre-dawn darkness. From time to time he murmured his skipper's orders, but little needed to be said. He introduced his crewman, Bob, a thin, wiry man in a bobble hat whose age was impossible to tell in that light, and who kept up a stream of unreturned volleys of wisecracks as he worked. Once or twice, a gull cried from afar. The third figure was the boy, who was not introduced, and who remained silent.

Here, put on this gear, Darren abruptly barked, throwing down with a thump onto the shingle objects that turned out to be a waterproof set of overalls and a pair of rubber boots. They were capacious – over-capacious by some way. We had a lot of problems with fitting out Little Edie, because of her size, continued Darren, waiting patiently. And I remember my dad had the bright idea of fetching the waterproofs I wore as a child, and that did the trick. I remember everyone but me being very amused about that.

He went on: This morning we'll be running out one net and hauling in another. At the present time, we're fishing mainly for sole, but we're hoping there'll be plenty of plaice and dabs as well. Maybe other stuff. We're missing our third crew member, John, because he's unwell this morning, so that's where you come in, Phidias. The boy is needed onshore. Don't worry, as I said before, we won't ask you to do nothing you can't manage. You'll be all right. Fleet off in twenty minutes. Firstly, can you help the boy with the trows?

The boy silently indicated a quantity of greased blocks that required placing and replacing on the shore in a line to ease the *Jumpy Mary*'s path down the shingle to the water. This was done. The boy ambled towards the rusty machinery of the tractor, and moments later its engine coughed and rumbled. The boy steered the tractor towards the bow of the boat, its bulldozer blade engaging.

It was cool: an ambient temperature of maybe seven or

eight degrees. Shingle was stamped upon. The eastern sky continued to brighten. All breath of wind had subsided, and the sea was like glass.

Slowly, the boat was pushed and pulled over the greasy trows towards the gently breaking waves that began to lick at her hull. The three crew members jumped aboard; the boy remained at the wheel of the tractor.

She bobbed in the dark shallows. Her engine came to life and purred now, in reverse. Darren Gallop turned her, and set course for the brighter horizon.

Tubby and flat-bottomed, the *Jumpy Mary* creaked softly on the tide, and Bob kept up his stream of witticisms. Darren meanwhile sat silent at the helm. The engine rumbled continuously. In the boat were stacked plastic boxes, buoys, flags. The grey of the dawn sky lightened considerably, while the grey of the sea remained smooth so far as could be observed, ahead and to port and starboard. And visibility was fair. Imperceptibly, the distance from shore lengthened; the shore was still dark, and the lights of the Deadmans Beach settlement shone within that darkness, spread out from side to side of the field of view. And within a very few minutes the boat was beyond the headland and had entered open sea.

The sun was not visible, but an eastern luminosity picked out the contours of cloud and touched the gentle yet constantly changing crests of the swell. The line of the horizon was indistinct, darker grey abutting lighter, but it was not possible to determine exactly where the darker ended and the lighter began. And inside of these divisions there were ever shifting bands of subsidiary dark and light. For one instant, the water froze into an image of a ploughed field or perhaps a meadow – then reverted. But behind the boat, the wake tumbled and roared, a chaotic white turbulence without cease, occasionally throwing spray onto cold human faces. Further out to sea, close to that horizontal distance, the shapes and lights of vast freighters could be discerned, plying continuously on their trade routes, but our vessel would stay well clear of those dangerous shipping lanes.

An hour out – 06:07 – and Darren powered down the engine. The wake subsided, and the silence around the vessel, suddenly, was palpable. We drifted, as rubber-aproned Bob shouted that he had seen the first floating marker: a black flag fluttering above a dull orange buoy. His face was contorted with unreasonable happiness. It's the best time, this, he stated firmly. It was unclear what he meant by this: that the early morning was the best time for sole fishing, or the early spring, or that the moment of anticipation before the nets were hauled in was the most enjoyable part of the whole process; or that this was the prime of his life personally, or that this era now being experienced was the greatest of all possible times. He reached over the side, grasped the flag and hitched it out of the water, guiding the trailing rope through the machinery. Darren, who mostly seemed to ignore him while working in absolute synchrony with him, promptly set the hydraulics in motion to retrieve the first of the trammel nets that had been set the day before; and a new roar now joined the muted sound of the boat's engine.

The net-hauling machinery consisted of twin revolving drums, in the shape of two cones joined together at their points; they settled into a constant rumble as the fishing apparatus surfaced and began to run through.

Back in the day we used to do the net hauling completely by hand, said Darren – back-breaking work.

He supervised the operation from start to finish. First it was rope and chain that emerged from the sea, then the anchor appeared and came through. And finally the dripping nets began coming in, sea water blowing off them, and were coiled in a box on the deck, but there was at first no sign of any fish. Watch Bob, keep watching, do what he does, called

Darren, who continued to guide the nets between the drums. Then came a silver flash as the first of the catch appeared over the side: a medium-sized sole that flopped onto the deck, whereupon Bob seized upon it, expertly unhooked the creature from the netting and flung it into the first of the plastic boxes. More and more began to come through, of a variety of sizes. Bob pounced on a creature of a different shape: We don't take them, he said gently, unclipped it, threw it back over the side into the sea. Crab, he said of another, intervening briskly, crabs we keep separate, see? Over there. His wiry, tattooed arms and hands were a blur as he worked. And eventually, the end marker came through, and Darren, turning off the net hauler, remarked laconically: That's the finish of it.

But though it may have been the finish of a task, it was by no means the finish of the operation. Darren, back in the wheelhouse, said: Next, we're going to set some new nets. You all right there, Phidias?

He gazed at the horizon: Do you see that, over yonder?

It was a grey shape on a grey ground, indistinct.

That there is the enemy. One of them big-beamed foreign trawlers that are taking our livelihood. They are allowed to within six miles of the coast. And they just scoop up all the fish stocks, they just hoover up everything. It's disgusting. And then we're told we're the ones that are unsustainable.

He spat over the side.

You know, Phidias, he went on, you know, you was asking me about Little Edie? How she was when she took a fishing trip? Well, I can't say I have first-hand knowledge, because, as I said to you, I was a kid, I was the boy-ashore on that occasion, so I didn't go out to sea then. But she made the trip on the *Dead Level Boys*, the boat my dad had then, and he said she were really game. Did I mention that? Really game, really up for it. Only, when we got up to around here, around where we are now, let's say up to three miles out, that's when she had that turn, what I told you about, which gave him the willies, he told me afterwards, he really thought that she was going to throw herself overboard. And another thing I remember now he told me, she said, I lost someone near to me, or dear to me, or something like that.

Did she mean lost someone at sea?

Yeah, I reckon that's what she meant. It was someone she was sweet on, like. I think it would have been during the war. A long time ago, anyway. But she told me herself many a time in years to come, even after my dad passed away, how much that trip had meant to her.

Darren frowned. He had revved up the engine, and the boat's wake began to churn again.

You sure you're all right, Phidias?

A breeze was now starting to be evident, stiffening by the minute, and the boat began to rock gently up and down in the swell as it progressed. The horizon was no longer uniformly horizontal.

We didn't bargain for that breeze, Phidias, said Darren, it weren't in the forecast. We'll be home soon, an hour and twenty minutes to shore. You're all right, you're all right.

Bob had already set to the gutting and cleaning. He was producing a great deal of perspiration. On board were boxes crammed and gleaming with ice and fish on the one side, and on the other, boxes of slimy brine, guts and diluted blood. The scent was powerful. At the stern, black flags fluttered hard.

Darren's verdict: Yeah, pretty reasonable catch. Mostly sole, plaice, whiting, we've got some brown and spider crabs, a couple of turbot and john dory. Well done, guys.

We were not done yet. The boat was heaving regularly, rhythmically, its engines working hard the while. Sky and sea began changing places. Clouds of a milky whiteness spread. Boxes slid across the deck. The conversation ceased. It seemed no progress was being made, but the coast now appeared in the distance, blurred and indistinct, and inch by inch – it seemed – it came closer. An hour went past; another hour. The position was checked every few minutes, and every few minutes a small advantage accrued; the shore had increased in apparent size, but not by much. And so it went on, repeated vertical movement, incremental lateral movement.

It was past midday, blustery and dull. Overhead, gulls were present in large numbers, circling the vessel, the dynamic level and urgency of their calls increasing rapidly. Knuckles rested on the gunwale, surf stung the face. The shore approached. It was very close now. Darren was on the radio. Visible on the beach was the solemn boy, ready with the winch, his eyes fixed exclusively and calmly on the *Jumpy Mary* as she neared the end of another journey.

8

A coin is tossed in an empty room. It clatters to the floor. Heads.

There is no-one in the room.

•

The stone George had selected from all the stones on the beach was almost perfectly round, smooth, a uniform greyish-white and about the size of a cricket ball.

It was, I have to say, a great selection.

In black indelible marker, he had written on it:

Bruiser
a good fish

And at my suggestion the date of demise of the unfortunate little creature was added below.

He carried it solemnly as we walked to the bottom of the garden. There, he set it on the flower-bed, in roughly the position where the fish had been buried, and on his hands and knees bedded it in as best he could. Then he stood up and looked at me.

Perhaps you'd like to say a few words, I suggested.

He looked nonplussed at first. Then he said, slowly and deliberately: Bruiser was a fish who always tried his best. So ... all credit to him.

He paused. Then continued: He will always be remembered ... so long as this stone is there.

Another pause. Then added, for clarification: In the ground.

He looked up at me. I can't think of anything else, he said.

That's absolutely lovely, I assured him. Shall we go in for our tea now?

He nodded his sturdy little head.

So, Lucy, this business of the memorial bench.

Yes, do you know, I think I'm going mad. Am I?

Probably not. But you're sure you saw it?

I'm beginning to doubt it now, but I was.

And it definitely cited Edith Watkins?

Yes. I wrote down the inscription in my notebook when the phone camera didn't work. Here it is: Please rest and enjoy the view as did Edith Watkins.

And the date of death was fifteenth of March last year?

That's what it said.

Well, Lucy, I have to say that since you told me about it I have been all the way up and down that seafront and observed a number of memorial benches, but for the life of me I cannot find that one.

Me too, Phidias, I went back later when I'd charged my phone, but couldn't see it.

And the other thing is, I just rang Kieran Watkins, who was very surprised, and confirmed that no such memorial bench had been ordered.

Well, that confirms it, either I'm crazy or –

Or?

Or we're living in a parallel universe.

A remote possibility.

Maybe the fishermen clubbed together to put up the bench. And then they changed their mind and took it away again. Which reminds me – how was your fishing trip?

Oh, fascinating, fascinating. I learned a great deal. Darren Gallop was most kind and helpful. The return journey was … challenging. The wind got up, you see. I was glad to see the shore, and to step upon it.

I understand, Phidias. I'm not much of a sailor myself. Did you get your share of the proceeds?

My share?

You know, I think the custom is the skipper shares out the earnings with the crew and the boy-ashore?

Oh no, no, I was merely an observer. Although I did do some cutting and gutting. And hauling. And fetching and carrying.

And did you learn anything about the case?

I attained some insight into the mindset of Edith Watkins, yes. And I gained a new respect for her, having done that trip when she was already in her late sixties. Quite remarkable. I think Mr Gallop has considerable respect for her too. He was only a boy at the time, working for his father.

Did they … do they –?

You mean, do the fishing community, or some of them, know more about her disappearance than they're letting on?

I just wondered.

It's a relevant question, and one I cannot answer definitively.

But in my dealings with Mr Gallop I found him to be straight-forward. That's all I can say. I did not get the impression he for one was hiding anything. So we still have a conundrum.

We do.

A conundrum laid upon a conundrum.

Oh, I nearly forgot, Phidias, speaking of the case, the police finally emailed those video files. It's only taken them six weeks.

Files, plural?

Yes, there are two short clips from the CCTV at the Sanctuary Café. The one we haven't seen before is one of the lady entering the café.

Well, thanks for badgering the police on that. Let's have a look at them.

So this is the one we've already seen online, Phidias.

Resolution is no better than before.

That's her all right.

And of course it's one frame per second, so it presents as just a jerky series of stills. Twelve seconds, twelve images. Let's run it again.

Here we go.

She exits the café, walks down that path to the pavement. Quite steady gait, actually, nothing looks wrong there. The date is correct, the time shows 14:30 and some, absolutely right for catching that bus to Moorshurst. So she's aware of the timetable. And disappears to the right in the direction of the bus stop as soon as she reaches the road, and that's the end of that. Obviously the bus stop itself is not visible from this angle.

Shall I play the other one?

Please, Lucy.

Right, so this is one of her arriving at the café, which we haven't seen before. Here she comes.

The time shows, what, 13:55 and counting. So she has spent thirty-five minutes in the café.

Definitely her, you get a good look at her face there as she approaches, Phidias.

Indeed. And she's approaching from the other direction, which tallies with her arriving from the seashore. Also exactly twelve seconds, this one. Interesting.

She does depend on that walking stick, but she's all right. What do you think?

Lucy, there's just one small thing that bothers me somewhat.

Oh, do you know, I was bothered by something too. What's worrying you, Phidias? I wonder if it's the same thing.

OK, let me tell you. Do you see the background there? It's the same in both videos. I mean, the mobile homes.

Yes, that's right, there's a couple of mobile homes visible, they're part of the Sanctuary caravan park, aren't they?

Correct. Now, look at the flagpole outside the one on the left.

That's not what I was thinking about. What about it?

The flag is hanging limp. If I recall from our visit, it was a St George cross, and you can see a hint of it there. Now, do you recall the weather conditions reported that day?

Yes, I know, it was windy. Wow, I didn't notice that.

It's the same in both videos.

Yes, it is.

It's possible there was a lull in the wind in that half hour. What was worrying *you*, then, Lucy?

Well, Phidias, this is probably nothing –

Nothing is nothing.

The earlier video, the one where you see her approaching.

Yes.

You can see a better view of her walking stick. Can you see, there? It's really a very poor video, so it's hard to see, it's very blurry. But look ... a flash of pink.

Ah, interesting. Well observed, Lucy.

There were two walking sticks in that umbrella stand in her house –

That's correct, a plain wooden one and a mauve one with a pink flowery pattern, as I recall.

But Sharon, the next door neighbour, said she thought the only other one she had seen, which was missing, was a black one.

Could that be the black one? Could that pink flash be just an artifact of the video?

I don't know. Do you want to see that video again?

Yes, please, Lucy.

Here we go. Here she comes.

Inconclusive still. Can we freeze it there? That looks like pink on the walking stick. But it's terribly pixellated.

You can't really tell. Sharon did say the pink flowery one was her favourite.

So she would likely have taken it on her walk. But it remains in her house. So, unless she had two identical ones ... but then, where's the black one?

So what's the weather going to do today, Lucy?

Dry. Cloudy. Do you have any plans?

I may do.

Do you still want me to set up a meeting with Mrs Hastings, the owner of the Sanctuary Café?

Is she still being recalcitrant?

She's hard to get hold of.

Well, I would like to talk to her.

OK, I'll try again.

Are we ever going to solve this mystery?

I would hope identifiable so-called "mysteries" are always capable in principle of being solved. But it does depend how you define "mystery". Questions are always nested within larger questions.

So the answers –

Always beg further questions. That's my opinion.

Didn't Kieran Watkins say he was after closure?

There is no closure.

That sounds cynical, Phidias.

It's not meant to be. But we solve a problem, there is pay-off, which is never more than partial, and we go on to the next problem. That's all we can do. Meanwhile we are in the midst of a bigger mystery.

What mystery is that?

The mystery of banality.

I don't know what you mean.

The mystery of why everything is as it is and not otherwise.

We're not being paid to unravel that.

Exactly, Lucy. Well put.

All right. Is there anything else?

I think we're done for this morning. I have plans for the afternoon, as I intimated.

What do you plan to do?

I think I might take the bus.

The bus?

The bus that our client's aunt is supposed to have taken, approximately fifty-eight weeks ago, from Deadmans Beach to Moorshurst. I want to have that experience. Maybe to follow in her footsteps.

We don't know what her footsteps are.

Very true. Where determinism fails, we may have to resort to randomising techniques. Or, shall we say, chance procedures.

You mean, guesswork?

That, if I may say so, is a rather crude and not entirely accurate way of putting it. But I suppose I shall have to concede the point.

So where will you get off the bus?

Chance will determine that.

Really?

Where we lack firm knowledge, we have to trust to rule and method.

Take care.

I shall.

Take your phone, Phidias. And make sure it's charged, unlike mine!

I will ensure that.

•

The bus stop at the Barbican Gate, five minutes' walk from the Dead Level Business Park, and just past the fork in the road by the abandoned Barbican Inn, was deserted. The glass of the panel on the stop sign where the timetable should have been affixed was missing – indecipherable, faded graffiti occupying that space – but undoubtedly the bus departing the Sanctuary Café, Deadmans Beach, at 16:35 – that is to say, two hours later than the service that might have been caught by Edith Watkins on that fateful March day a year and six weeks previously – was due any minute.

The time difference was intended to allow for the change in sunset time, including the introduction of daylight saving, since then. Sunset would have taken place around six o'clock then, and soon after eight now.

But the weather was overcast.

A small velvet bag containing two dice was extracted from a left-hand pocket. The dice were rolled on the low brick wall that bounded the narrow pavement.

The dice showed five (two and three).

The double-decker bus could now be observed, approaching from the direction of Deadmans Beach, its destination board indicating: 201 Moorshurst. It came to a halt, the door folded silently open, the driver waited. Few passengers were on board.

The top deck was selected. Clearly, it was not where Edith Watkins would have ventured – she would probably have chosen one of the seats near the driver designated for those with mobility difficulties – but it afforded a better view of the surrounding environment.

So stop number five was the destination, selected by the dice. The bus slowed, and stopped. It waited for the solitary passenger to descend, then went on its way, and eventually disappeared from view. The sign above the bus service emblem showed that this was the stop for Thieves Bridge. Another sign pointed the way: to Thieves Bridge Village, and to the Industrial Ponds.

The weather was not only overcast, but breezy, as it would have been, insofar as we can tell, on that inauspicious day. A nearby row of trees waved, and it was cold for the time of year. Yet beyond it seemed peaceful. There was no sound of birdsong or bird calling. An engine of some sort could be heard coughing in the far distance.

And there were fields visible to the west, grey fields where daisies and buttercups were present abundantly, and where one or two horses grazed among them. Patchworked among these, the brilliant lemon-yellow shapes of fields of oilseed rape, now come to flower, stood out, hard-edged against the steel-grey sky. Closer at hand was a meadow of a uniform but stippled white, resembling nothing so much as a shingle beach; but its constituents, on closer examination, proved to be not stones but an excess of daisies, so tightly and densely packed that no greenery was visible between the individual plants, this growth only petering out at the far right edge, where a small yellow patch of buttercups was cornered. This yellow was of a softer hue than the acid tone of the oilseed rape flower. The fields formed non-symmetrical patterns of quadrilateral forms, their boundaries sometimes marked by ditches radiating from the Old Canal, but the watercourses themselves were rarely visible. All those edges seemed to be going into the ground. The location of the Old Canal itself, to the north (beyond the road), was marked by a line of birches, and beyond that could be seen the distant hills where the presently invisible village of Deadhurst would be concealed behind thickets of tall trees with their freight of rookeries and heronries.

And then to the east, the direction of travel, all was flat and open, as the Dead Level gave way to marshland beyond. On the horizon could be seen the row of wind turbines, their vanes slowly turning. It seemed as though, whatever the vantage point, these structures would always appear to be at the same distance, like the rainbow.

The community of Thieves Bridge appeared to consist of a row of perhaps a dozen custom-built houses and bungalows of all forms and sizes, presenting as an isolated outpost of the Deadmans Beach sprawl. The most modest was a converted railway carriage, painted Brunswick green, to which a timber verandah had been attached; the most ambitious, a two-storey construction of modernist flavour, its plate-glass windows impervious to inspection, a car port embedded at ground level. Next door to this, a bungalow offered a window display of tightly packed cacti and succulents in pots. One or two of the dwellings were in a poor state of repair and were adjacent to ramshackle outhouses. All homes had front gardens of various sizes and scope, planted with hardy vegetation adapted to withstand the salt breezes coming in along the flats from the coast, and incorporating areas of pebbles and gravel. No inhabitants were visible.

The houses lined one side only of the unmade road, facing the west, a broken hedge marking the other perimeter, and here occasional vehicles were parked on the verge, where there were small masses of white narcissi. At the far end, a footpath intersected this road, and along it a young woman could be observed sedately leading two ponies, chestnut intermingled with white and grey, away into the distance.

Then, from the far end of the row, approached a group of people and dogs.

On closer approach, this group resolved into eight or nine individuals, with a dozen or more dogs circling them, all of the same breed: grey, black or peppery in colour, with white socks, shaggy moustaches and sharp pricked ears. The individuals talked and laughed among themselves while their animals darted from side to side, investigated the verges or trotted back to look quizzically at their owners, who were mostly of late middle age or older, evenly balanced as to sex, and of generally jovial disposition. They were dressed principally in fawn, with some exceptions and eccentricities.

Greetings were exchanged. One or two of the dogs approached and greeted in their own fashion.

In response to enquiry, one man, in his seventies perhaps, sporting a heavy salt-and-pepper moustache that lent him an uncanny resemblance to his dog, explained: We're the Schnauzer Walking Club.

Had they been out on the marshes?

Oh yes, interrupted a corpulent woman with a smiling face, in a baseball cap, the dogs love it out there.

But you have to be careful, the moustached man warned, it's treacherous in places.

Yes, treacherous.

The dogs know their way.

Just follow the designated paths, advised the moustached man (who, despite the chill, was wearing shorts, bare below the knee, with hairy shins disappearing into yellow Crocs), and you'll be all right.

The *designated* paths, echoed another, a cerise-faced woman, before wandering off to attend to an errant dog.

The Schnauzers, they're very intelligent.

They know the ways.

It was helpful to be reassured on these points. Further questioning elicited the information that this outing took place every month, regardless of the weather. Had they, then, recently observed anything of a disturbing nature: lost individuals, persons in distress, evidence of trauma?

Oh, said the woman in the baseball cap, fending off a Schnauzer puppy that had suddenly decided to distract her attention by leaping up at her repeatedly, oh, there's always weird things going on out there. People do get into trouble.

But no dead bodies, we haven't seen any dead bodies recently, if that's what you mean, interrupted another man, in a sleeveless puffer jacket. At least, nothing human. And he roared with laughter, as though he had just cracked a joke. And his partner, who walked with the help of a single crutch, a dog lead in her other hand, joined in the merriment, their dog meanwhile reaching eagerly on its leash to sniff another. And all the dogs leapt and trotted.

The party started to move off. Two couples were beginning to load their pets onto parked vehicles. Others moved in the direction of the bus stop.

The Schnauzer Walking Club members were left behind, and so, eventually, was the settlement of Thieves Bridge. A look at our position on the GPS-generated map on the phone screen revealed a blue dot on the threshold of a great nothingness. Ahead, in the real world, could be observed sodden fields dotted with sheep each accompanied by lambs, and then empty fields criss-crossed by ditches, and then, far beyond, the grey shimmer of the Industrial Ponds.

A solitary woman approached down the designated path.

She was perhaps in her sixties, of medium height, had short, dark, greying hair fringing a woollen hat, and wore a navy anorak over a green jumper, jeans and walking boots.

Hello there.

But she did not respond to the greeting. Close up, it was observable that her eyes were large and lustrous; they looked in our direction but they saw no-one. In her hands she held a dog lead, and kept twisting it round repetitively.

Hello, are you with the Schnauzer Walking Club?

She had stopped in her tracks. It was as though she had heard the greeting, but either did not understand it or did not know where it was coming from. She still did not appear to see anyone in her path. She looked from side to side, then her gaze returned. She continued to twist the strap.

Have you lost your dog?

She looked around her, as if this idea might just have been put into her head, and the dog might reappear at any instant, from any direction.

They went that way. The Schnauzer Walking Club. If you're with them.

She continued to stand there, apparently uncomprehending. The fingers of her hand went on turning the dog lead over and over, and then a curious fact became evident. She had six fingers on each hand. It was necessary to count them and count again, just to make sure, but when the hands remained still for a moment or two, the number became incontrovertible and the fact was established.

A smile of encouragement was offered to her, and a pointing hand.

That way.

Without warning, she smiled back, as though with thanks, her face transformed for an instant.

And then her smile faded and, still silent, she resumed her silent walk, past our position, in the direction of Thieves Bridge. And was lost to view.

A little further on, in a hollow just off the path, was encountered what appeared to be a research station, a small compound nestled within the adjacent banks studded with patches of marram grass, encircled by chain-link fencing topped with barbed wire. The compound contained several ranks of wooden frames, each holding rows of samples of metal tiles in a variety of different colours and finishes, deliberately exposed to the sun and wind in what was clearly a scientific experiment. Some of these tiles had already experienced considerable weathering, others had evidently been more recently installed, or were less susceptible to adverse local conditions. There was no information provided about it other than three KEEP OUT notices, spaced regularly.

Beyond that was the shimmer, suggesting the presence of the Industrial Ponds. So it turned out. They were tranquil, with not an angler or any other human in sight. The path went right round the grey trembling water. Once it would have been toxic, but no longer. We had been assured – by Gordon Prescott, among others – that it had been restored to full health, that fish stocks had recovered. The occasional discontinuous ripple, running counter to the prevailing wind, would be evidence of this.

Near the right bank, a pair of mute swans could be seen sailing slowly. There was some observable bird life beyond them; binoculars revealed possibly greenshank, possibly plover. Beyond the far bank, a rook suddenly dived with a rough croak and was lost in undergrowth between some trees. To the south, a double V suggested a pair of herring gulls catching the breeze.

Ha-ha-ha-ha-ha. The familiar five-fold peal.

So there were marsh frogs in these waters.

Silence descended, and weighed heavily. But not completely, as was soon evident. A muted hum could now be detected rising and falling, and also, far off, the intermittent call of a ewe.

Then again: Ha-ha-ha-ha-ha.

And an echo across the lake.

There was no visible sign of the amphibians. Possibly they were dwelling in the reeds close to the near bank. This region had been described as uninhabited. Clearly, of habitation there was an abundance – but not of the human kind.

The water closest to our position was almost black. There was an object stuck in it – in the shallows. With the naked eye, it was hard to discern detail, but binoculars revealed it to be the wrecked remains of a baby buggy, half-submerged. Of the child, there was no sign.

Without warning, a sudden turbulence broke the surface near the shore. For the briefest of instants, a shiny, mottled dorsal fin was visible before plunging back into the depth. It was undoubtedly a monstrous catfish. It did not return.

And now the perspective started to become unstable. There were density changes in the air, between those distant objects on the opposite bank and the observer; these changes possibly being caused by heat from sources far from this present location: chimneys, vehicle exhaust, roofs or roads. The path encircled the ponds, then led away into poorly mapped areas. A thicket was encountered – the cold wind blowing softly through dwarfed willows – and then terrain that might be described as willow carr, that is to say in transition between marsh and meadow. Marsh frogs were no longer audible. In the open country now visible, tall wooden poles, eight in number, the height of telegraph poles but bare of any encumbrance or detail, were observed to be grouped together; to be more specific, five in one group, three in another. Their purpose was unknown. The spacing between objects increased. From time to time, a plank bridge had to be negotiated over a ditch running between fields.

A sudden movement interrupted the stillness: a hare. The animal leapt from cover and bounded away from our position, being eventually lost from sight in the adjacent field.

And then inaccessible across another ditch, some fifty metres distant, a hoarding came into view, weather-battered, its wooden frame corrupted by rot. In block capitals, it proclaimed:

DÉJÀ VU

The lettering was sans-serif, a very much faded tan in colour, shadowed to the bottom and left in a slightly deeper colour, the background creamy but rough. If this was an advertisement of some kind, there was no clue as to what it might be promoting. Its enigma as an object of religious contemplation was satisfyingly complete.

The global positioning system had failed. There was no electronic signal discernible. The path forked; then forked again. There was no basis for any decision as to which fork to take. Therefore this had to be taken randomly. A field was skirted. The oceanic marshland continued ahead for mile upon mile.

A sheep called nearby. After a few moments the call was repeated, sounding closer. On mounting the shallow crest of a small dyke, the animal became visible, a lost ewe sheltering by the ditch in the lee of the slope with its single half-grown lamb. The rumps of both animals, the older and the younger, were caked with dirt. The ewe's eyes briefly turned in our direction; she called again. She seemed bewildered. The lamb staggered; it was possibly lame. The flock would be some distance away. A catastrophe had separated these two from it, and it was only to be hoped that the shepherd would eventually locate them. There was, in any event, nothing to be done.

It was no longer clear what manner of path this was. A step to either left or right resulted in the foot sinking into soft mud; and on retreating, the former path was difficult to regain. Hillocks protruded. Animals would be burrowing here.

It could, however, be estimated that we were close to the point where, from the other side of the ponds, the rook had been observed to dive. At any rate, there were two of them now, to the right of the path, if path it was, loudly squabbling on an isolated tussock. One had a scrap of something in its beak which the other – its eye glinting, as could clearly be seen – coveted. And there was something bulky hidden in that undergrowth, something precious to them, something from which that disputed scrap may have been torn. As one moved sharply in the direction of their battleground, the sweet smell of decay became evident. The birds stopped their fight, froze in their positions, alert to the approach. A step nearer – and they instantly fled, flapping their wings rapidly until each settled on a bush, separated from each other and from the location that had been their battleground. The object in the undergrowth remained still. The scent increased in intensity. Further approach was difficult. It was constrained by vegetation.

The object could, however, now be glimpsed. It was pale, swollen. It appeared to be a torso, or part of a torso. It was difficult to make out its shape. It lay partly covered by the shrubbery. It had the stillness of death.

There were white feathers scattered around. That was a clue. Now it could be ascertained it was the carcass of a large bird, almost certainly a swan, badly decomposed and half sunk in mud. Part of its neck could be seen. We withdrew. No sooner had distance been re-established than one of the rooks walked back towards the location of the carcass, the other having flown off meanwhile. Then with jerky motions it recommenced pecking, extracting what looked like a jelly-like substance. A few feathers flickered in the breeze.

The paths re-forked. Decisions were now once again being taken using chance procedures. But at a further intersection a broken down sign pointed, its weathered lettering showing as "Marsh Farm". However, there was no sign of any farm. A second look at the sign produced uncertainty as to what its text established. Here, clearly or unclearly, words were beginning to lose their shape. The more one examined them, the less certainly did they signify. There were also no electronic signals discernible. The mobile phone was dead. It was almost as though – absurd thought! – the electro-magnetic spectrum was no longer present.

No buildings, no human-made structures of any size, were apparent. But those cathedrals of cloud, bearing down on this marshland! They made their own structures, changing by the minute, and their depth created the illusion of a mirror of the land below, which itself was an ancient sea, of course, the ghost of a shallow ocean that had retreated millennia ago, hiding beneath it, in the manner of a palimpsest, evidence of even older times, of unimagined undersea forests, now turned to coal and other sediments. Coal, no longer worth extracting, but buried there still.

And then, a minute later, there was a man-made structure up ahead, or the semblance of one. It seemed to be a barn, set on a slight rise, sheeted with rusting corrugated iron. Its distance from our position was uncertain, perhaps indeterminate. But if this was Marsh Farm – and how could it have been missing from view such a short time ago? – then there was the possibility of a farmer, who could give advice on our co-ordinates. If it could be reached.

There was now thunder in that sky; it was the colour of bruising. Isolated raindrops manifested.

The barn was reached, but at some cost. Although at times it appeared very close at hand, such that one could reach out and touch its side, the approach journey seemed to take the best part of an hour. On arrival, finally, it appeared vast in dimensions. But its wide interior space had been abandoned. There was an uneven dirt floor underfoot, littered here and there with the remains of straw bales, and on this floor our damp footprints appeared. It was reminiscent of a crime scene. But what crime might have been committed here? At least it offered shelter from the rain, which could be heard drumming softly on the roof far above. Wrecked wooden benches tilted. A faint scent of the animals that might have been housed here once – or that of their ghosts – still remained. An opening in the far wall offered a concrete path that led beyond. At the other end of this there appeared to be a farmhouse, but its windows gaped, revealing no content. It seemed as though centuries had gone by, and here with the passage of that time came unknown memories, arising out of their sediments. But the notion of the death of the electro-magnetic spectrum now appeared doubly absurd, for one could feel electricity and awe in abundance. The spectrum, of course, permeated everywhere, but was here simply beyond human vision. Volumes formed, and dispersed with inexorable movement. There were squares, quadrilaterals, multilateral shapes of various shades. Through this disorder, this cascade of consciousness, was it possible to regain some semblance of control? One shape, standing perhaps for human awareness, had to be moved to the "danger" area as though on a computer screen. One had to do this very slowly so that it entered the danger area only very gradually, for if it were to touch the edge too suddenly there would be a loud bang and everything would vanish, not just the computer screen, or even the computer itself, or whatever device it was that all this was mediated by, but the very world, so that nothing would exist except one's bare consciousness. The field would become a *tabula rasa*.

The presence of the observer interferes, as it always has done, and always will.

The farmhouse was a mere shell, as could be seen when it was approached, for daylight was observable through the broken glass and empty spaces of its upper floor windows – but its doors and ground floor windows were barricaded against entry. There was no shelter to be obtained here, and so it was necessary to retreat to the barn. And now the storm was fully raging. The lightning and its concomitant thunderclap must have been directly overhead, for there was barely a gap between them. There was a bang. Then there was nothing. And then something again.

It appeared there was a world – out there – that was not the real world. The storm flew overhead. And night was beginning to fall.

Hello! Is anybody there?
(There is no reply.)

The rain had stopped. The wind, too, had died. The thunderstorm had passed just as quickly as it arrived, leaving a great stillness behind. There was a hint of luminescence in the lighter cloud to the left, which would make that the west, for it was undoubtedly the faint and masked evidence of a sunset. And to the right, the outlines of the distant, easterly wind turbines could just be discerned on the darkening horizon. That meant the way ahead, northward, would surely lead back to the main road. It was only necessary to continue taking the fork in the path that kept the fading light to the left and the turbine silhouettes, insofar as they could be made out in the gathering dusk, on the right. With luck, it would surely be possible to arrive in time to pick up the last bus of the evening from Moorshurst to Deadmans Beach via the Barbican Gate, due at the Thieves Bridge stop at 21:15.

Domestic animals could now be heard again: the distant cries of sheep, the yelp of a dog. A human voice? Perhaps. Location was beginning to reassert itself, with greater strength every minute. The electronic device clicked into life; the time showed glowing in the dim light as 20:48. It was necessary to deploy a torch to guide the way now, to avoid a possibly catastrophic deviation from the path, whichever path was chosen. The world was made of flesh again. Currents flowed through it, and constituted it. Fields were skirted. Something scurried in a low hedge. There was a lingering scent of sewage. We were in open country, and car headlights and tail lights could be seen proceeding slowly in the distance.

With great difficulty, the road was reached, and the recognisable hamlet of Thieves Bridge, unfamiliarly approached from a different direction. There was nobody waiting at the bus stop. It was 21:11.

A single street lamp pooled the stop in light. Darkness was settling all about. In the rightward direction, the road to Moorshurst stretched to the bend; to the left, that to Deadmans Beach disappeared into the night. All was quiet. Presently, a low rumble could be heard. A faint light outlined the small grove of trees at the bend, and from here now approached the welcome sight of the illuminated double-decker bus, its destination board indicating in bright amber digits piercing the gloom: 201 Deadmans Beach.

The last bus of the evening was not uninhabited.

For on the top deck as the night greyed, as fields and ditches beyond the glass disappeared, briefly encountered human agencies flourished in their own individual ways, within their own consciousnesses.

The numbers on the bus varied slightly, perhaps two dozen on balance for the duration of the trip (at least as far as the Barbican Gate), plus or minus a few, evenly split between top and bottom decks.

There was muted chatter. Some were silent, even perhaps contemplative. At this hour the majority would have been workers at the end of a late shift. One appeared to be eating shrimps from a small cardboard container.

Car headlights approached from time to time, and in a rush were gone.

From one of the seats behind, there was a humming, or

maybe a whining. It came and went, rising and falling in volume, but never loud, never above p – eventually revealing itself to be a woman's voice continually essaying with varying success a hymn-like tune or dirge. And on occasion (but indistinctly) the tune may have been identifiable as that old favourite "Abide With Me"; but then receding in presence and definition, re-entering the category of indeterminate wail. The memory, the faint echo of the banshee.

At the third stop, a drunken man boarded the bus, ascended the stairs and lurched into a nearside seat. He laughed to himself from time to time. Where he had been, only he knew. He wore a gold lamé or gold-lamé-effect suit, crumpled, and a trilby hat of the same material. The outfit had probably been purchased at a novelty fancy dress store rather than a tailor's. His plastic spectacles looked fake too. He uttered vague imprecations to nobody in particular, and at one point attempted, but failed, to harmonise with the woman's hymn or dirge singing. Following this, he slumped back in his seat, but moments later revived to start a musical performance of his own. With spectacular lapses in intonation, he burst into folksong:

> How many gentle flow-ow-owers grow
> In an English country ... ga-arden?

The hymn-singing woman was momentarily silenced.

The drunk tipped his hat, and made his trick plastic spectacles light up, a bright lime green, presumably at the discreet push of a button in his pocket: a feature that, despite his looking around for approval, went largely unappreciated by the other passengers. He continued:

> How many songbirds ma-a-ake their nests
> In an English cunt ...

He paused here, and made the spectacles illuminate another four or five times. There was a brief moment of silence, then the woman resumed her murmured and dreamy rendition of "Abide With Me".

No more passengers got on.

Fast falls the eventide.

Darkness – and the road ahead. The Barbican Gate.

The voice of a child from the back: Mummy! Mummy!

Hello, is anybody there?

(There is no reply.)

Hello! Is anybody there?

(There is no reply.)

Who is it?

(There is no reply.)

I've got to go now. I'll be off in a minute. I have things to do, I have to move on. Now's the time, if you want anything. Is there anything you need?

(There is no reply.)

Who is that?

(There is no reply.)

9

Suspicious activity by two individuals in the vicinity of the Peralta Associates office. That is what Gordon Prescott reported. Essentially, there was no more to report. The office had been closed throughout. Gordon said: I had no means of contacting you, Phidias. Your mobile was offline.

I'm sorry. The device has been on the marshes, beyond all signals. What did these individuals look like?

Two males, of middle age, the one tall, dark, the other a little shorter, balding, and both of them in dark suits. Suits? Dark coats, possibly worn over suits and ties. Dark? How dark? Just dark. And what were they doing that was suspicious? They were observed outside Unit 13 on several separate occasions, passing and re-passing. One was observed trying to look through the window. They were caught on the security camera. You can come and have a look, Phidias, said Gordon.

Tall and dark, and the other shorter, balding. There surely

could be no question who these were. The heart began to sink, the palms to perspire a little.

Did they walk with any suspicious gait, did the shorter one perhaps limp a little, none too obviously?

Were they cadaverous in aspect, did they resemble birds?

Ancient birds, perhaps? Reptilian?

Were their voices heard?

How often did they return?

What was the last that was seen of them? In what direction did they disappear?

Did they co-ordinate their movements, did they anticipate each other, as twins might?

Were they jerky or sinuous in their movements? Or was one jerky and the other sinuous?

Were they apprehended? Is that why they slunk away?

I did try, said Gordon, to address them. The third time I spotted them, on camera four. I went out there, he added, it was already dusk, I called out to them.

You approached? What did you say?

Can I help you gentlemen? That's what I said, I think. Are you looking for something? But they just looked at me, I could see them looking at me.

They didn't speak?

They didn't say a word.

They didn't mention their names?

As I said – not a word.

And then they slunk away?

They left the premises quite smartly, yes.

They ran?

No, they didn't run, they turned and they walked off normally. I thought I should just let you know. Here they are, on camera. The resolution isn't great in that evening light.

It was hard to tell – but in one's heart it could not be escaped. Those were they, for certain. For almost certain. Two of them. One slightly taller than the other, both slim, or not running to fat too obviously at any rate, both soberly clad. They passed in front of the camera, there was a pause, then they passed in the opposite direction. And retraced their steps once more; and subsequently again. And one, the shorter one, strained to look inside the window, then reported something to the other. One could see his mouth moving, even though his face was indistinct.

Do you know them, then? asked Gordon, anxiously. He moved his hand over his bald pate as he waited for an answer, his rimless glasses glinting softly. He could recognise distress.

Possibly, was the answer. Possibly.

Do they in your opinion pose a threat?

A threat? Possibly. There is always that possibility.

So they walked, quite normally, Gordon asserted again, until they were finally out of sight, and did not return.

And left behind only pixels, dark pixels, suggesting a build, a demeanour, a way of moving, nothing more. But who else could they be?

Phidias, I could sense, was troubled. I asked him about last night's venture into the marshes, but he didn't answer at first. Instead, he hovered over the computer, humming and thinking. I let him be for a while. He had something going through his head, some jazz tune that he liked, maybe, and was almost inaudibly humming along with it, also imitating the drum kit by moving the saliva rhythmically around in his mouth in the way he does.

So then I asked again, how was your walk into the marshes? And he started, as if being woken out of a dream.

It was most interesting, Lucy, he said. Most interesting.

I mentioned that I had been a little worried about it. Why was that? he asked, apparently bewildered by the question.

I mentioned the thunderstorm that had passed overhead yesterday evening. George and I had heard it, and seen the rain pattering outside, and George had been a little scared. I wondered if the storm had reached him out there in the marshes.

Oh that, he said. Yes, it was moving eastwards.

Had he got soaked? Well, a little damp, he said. But apparently he had found an abandoned barn to shelter in until it passed. So the worst had not hit him.

Then I asked whether the experience had got him any further forward in his quest about the disappearance of our client's aunt. And he said: It depends how you define "forward".

Which is a typically irritating response, but that's how he is.

After a pause, he added: I discovered how one possibility may have played itself out. But we are still mired in a conflict of realities. If you mean, did I find the body – well, of course I didn't, though I found a corpse of sorts, not human. And it seems incontrovertible that venturing out there would be extremely dangerous for someone not of a robust constitution.

Easy to get lost?

Very easy to get lost, yes.

I said I was glad he got back safely, but he didn't answer.

Then he said, suddenly: You didn't see any strangers hanging around here yesterday morning, did you, Lucy?

Strangers?

Yes, he said, specifically two men. Two men in dark coats.

I said I had not. There had been no clients yesterday morning, and, besides, he had been around most of the morning so he should have known that. I inquired what was bothering him. I have to say that I started becoming a little concerned about his state of mind. But he seemed to brighten suddenly, perhaps too deliberately, perhaps trying to reassure me, and replied that it was probably nothing to worry about. Only Gordon Prescott, the security man, had caught two men on camera early evening yesterday, apparently, and they were wandering around looking a little suspicious.

I repeated that I had seen no-one, and it was indeed probably nothing.

Probably nothing, he agreed. And then abruptly went back to his marsh-walking activities. He had taken his binoculars. He had got down from the bus at Thieves Bridge, he said, and walked round the Industrial Ponds, and then headed out from there. He related a list of the bird and animal species he had observed on his walk.

And did you meet any people?

People, he said, yes, there were some dog walkers. Delightful people. And also a strange woman, who looked lost.

Not Edith Watkins, I joked, but he took it seriously.

Not her. But a lost soul. A woman younger than our client's aunt, perhaps in late middle age. I thought at first she had become separated from the dog walkers.

And had she?

Phidias explained that he had thought that, because she held a dog lead in her hand. But there was no dog visible.

So had she been looking for a dog that had run away?

Phidias said that had been his first impression. But the woman apparently could not or would not speak. And she had moved on without answering his questions.

A lost soul.

Phidias busied himself making mid-morning coffee for us both while I settled in to the administration. Then he came back out of the kitchenette and stood in the doorway, the coffee jug in his hand.

You know, Lucy, he said unexpectedly, dead or alive, and most probably of course dead, I believe the marshes hold the key to the disappearance of that old lady.

But how on earth could we find her?

He said, mysteriously: The phrase "lost at sea" keeps coming back to me.

So I asked him what he meant by that.

Would you like a biscuit? he asked.

No thank you, I said. I explained that I was trying to cut down, and he said that was just as well because he now realised we had none left.

The marshland, he went on, a fascinating region. Essentially, it forms the remains of an ancient sea.

I said I knew that, I had read it somewhere.

You can feel it when you're there, he said. It is a complex environment, one you can very easily drown in.

But where do you look?

He went back to the coffee-making. I could hear him in there, half-humming his jazz tune. He returned with two mugs of coffee.

Do you know Moorish Point? he asked me.

It's a tourist attraction, I said, in the hills beyond Deadhurst. I mentioned that I had been there more than once. You got a great view there, that was what visitors went for.

Exactly, he said. A vantage point.

And Phidias asked me questions about it. Mainly, how far you could see, and what you could see. I told him you could probably take in most of the Dead Level and the marshland to the east, including the Industrial Ponds. And the coastline on either side of Deadmans Beach. And he got quite excited at that.

Let's have a little outing! he exclaimed. Will you drive me up there?

I replied that I certainly could, if that was what he wanted.

I want to obtain a sense of the whole region, he said.

I said that was no problem.

Then he calmed down, and became his businesslike self again. What's in the diary for today? he asked me. I reminded him that I had made an appointment for him to interview Mrs Hastings this morning.

Mrs Hastings?

The owner of the Sanctuary Café.

He patted his hand on his forehead and flipped his palm in a gesture of apology or annoyance. He had forgotten.

I offered to drive him into Deadmans Beach, but he said he would walk or take the bus.

He is in the mind's eye corpse-like, dark-coated, hiding his belligerence and his malice beneath a coating of respectability. Borg was never to be trusted. He had an advanced law degree, after all. He was still for long periods of time. Then, wearing the aspect of a falcon, he would swoop or stoop unexpectedly out of nowhere in pursuit of his prey. Out of a clear sky. And his companion and hitman, very likely McKinley – it looked like McKinley – what of him? Ever the practical one, carrying out Borg's schemes to the nth degree, executing his associate's carefully crafted instructions. The two were last seen in the metropolis. They always looked like a pair of undertakers. People laughed at them, but only behind their backs. It was a time of extreme danger. That all this could have been left behind was perhaps never more than a fantasy. Their return was inevitable.

But there was no need to panic. All that had been reported was that two men were observed wandering around the Dead Level Business Park, evidently lost. Perhaps one peered into a window, that was all. They were attempting to find out whether anyone was around to answer their queries. That would have been it.

But in that case, why did they not respond when Gordon Prescott went out and challenged them? Why did they remain mute? Why did they make their escape without a word?

Surely these two, had they had continuing business with ourselves, would have pursued the usual routes? There were numerous avenues of communication they could have used.

Unless they wished to keep their communication private, untraceable. In which case, they would return.

It would be necessary to view those images again, to see if any more information could be extracted from them. Which was also, by coincidence, what needed to be done at the Sanctuary Café.

Then there was the option of involving the police, perhaps under the good auspices of Gordon Prescott. No, perhaps not. Too much tedious and unnecessary explaining would be entailed, the labyrinth of the back-story would need to be negotiated, and to what end, to what effect? A great deal of unpleasantness would still have to occur, and yet there would still be no solution. Better to hold firm, better to think, to engage the imagination.

But Mrs Hastings awaited.

•

No sooner had Phidias departed than I received a call from Mrs Darling at All Saints Primary.

The upshot of this was that George is in trouble again. He has been suspended.

I had to lock the office prematurely and drive to the school in Deadhurst. I parked in the usual place, had the usual problem at the security gate, got in, asked for Mrs Darling. The receptionist on duty was the curt one. Mrs Darling was nowhere to be found. She had been called away on some emergency, I was told. But *this* was an emergency, I snapped. So where was my son? Your son's name? George White, I said. Ah, yes. I was asked to calm down, not to worry. Was he OK? As far as she knew. He had been excluded from class, and he was in the "parents' waiting lounge". I was escorted to it.

And there he was, sitting at a table, drawing in his little notebook, the one Phidias had given him. He looked up when I entered. Hello, mum, he said.

Was there any supervision? A teaching assistant was "looking after" him, but she was flitting in and out, and had little time to talk. I asked George if he was all right, and he replied nonchalantly that he was, and that Mrs Darling had told him I was going to come and pick him up. So he had been waiting for me, and doing some drawing while he waited. He showed me his work. Mrs Darling was expected back imminently. I couldn't believe it.

The teaching assistant came back in, beaming broadly, and asked whether I was going to take him home, and whether there was anything else she could do.

So he has been sent home? I asked. Why?

There had been an "incident". Mrs Darling would explain, but it was best for everyone if George were to be removed from the school today. But if I were willing to wait for half an hour or so, George seemed quite happy, and so on and so forth.

The everyday business and buzz of the school was continuing in the background.

Mrs Darling was away for the best part of an hour.

So what was all that about, George?

Nothing, Mummy.

It can't be nothing.

It's nothing.

Nothing nothing nothing. That's all you can say. So you've been sent home from school for nothing? Is that it? No reason at all?

Yeah.

Mrs Darling said you were in a fight.

It wasn't my fault.

Well, then, if it wasn't I'll take it up with the school. But why don't you begin by telling me about it?

Nigel started it.

So it was all Nigel's fault?

Yes.

George, I know you don't like Nigel, but I've told you before the thing to do is just to keep away from him.

I tried. But he follows me around.

Does he?

He called me a Beacher. What does that mean?

Did he? That was wrong of him. It's a derogatory word.

What's doggetry?

It means it's a bad thing to say. He was disrespecting you because you don't live in Deadhurst village, you come from Deadmans Beach. You mustn't take any notice. Just ignore it.

Oh, I answered him back.

What did you say?

I called him a fucking wally.

George! I told you *never* to say that word!

What, wally?

You know quite well what I mean.

Sorry, mum.

Besides, it's only going to make things worse.

You say the f-word.

I do not.

You do.

Only if I'm very upset, and then it makes me feel bad and I'm sorry about it.

You said it to Daddy.

That's because I was very cross the other day, and I couldn't help it. But I shouldn't have. George, you must promise never to use that word at school again.

OK, mum.

So he called you a Beacher and you swore at him, you used the f-word, and then what happened?

He hit me.

And you hit him back?

Yes. And then he went crying to the teacher. He's a big baby, mum. He's a big baby wally.

And the teacher punished you?

Yeah, she didn't do anything to him, which is really unfair because he started it. And he was laughing at me behind her back. ·

OK, George, well you didn't do yourself any favours by swearing at him and hitting him back. But it sounds like Nigel needs telling off, so I will say that to Mrs Darling when I can get to talk to her. All right, pet?

It's really unfair.

I know, I know. George, we'll keep you out of school for the next couple of days while I take it up with Mrs Darling. Is that all right?

Yes, mum, I don't mind that.

OK, cool.

Mummy?

Can I come to work with you and play at Mr Peralta's office?

Well, I tell you what, Mr Peralta wants me to drive him up to Moorish Point in the next couple of days, so maybe you'd like to come along, if he allows it?

Oh, mum, that would be really great.

All right, George, but you have to behave.

I always behave.

•

Mrs Hastings, sole proprietor of the Sanctuary Café, Deadmans Beach, was a large woman who breathed heavily and appeared to bear a considerable share of the world's problems on her shoulders. In her official cubbyhole, she waved her chubby, mottled hands around, her fingernails of carmine hue, her chief accessory a pink nebuliser, which she made use of from time to time.

Yeah, I remember the old lady you're talking about, Edie we called her, she used to come in here regular.

How often?

Every few weeks, I reckon. Sometimes a bit more often.

Did you ever talk to her?

Oh yeah, we all did. Edie, we had a bit of banter with her. She come in regular for her cup of tea. But she was getting a bit batty, the poor old girl. One time she forgot her purse, didn't have any money to pay for her tea, she got in a right old state about it with my girl. So I had to intervene, I said, just don't you worry about it, Edie, it's on the house. It's on the house this time. Do you have your pass for the bus home? Oh, she said, yes, she had her pass, but she was so grateful, insisted she would definitely pay for that tea next time she was in. Definitely. Well, of course next time she'd forgotten all about it, but I didn't expect that.

But you don't remember, or your staff don't remember her particular visit on the fifteenth of March last year?

So what is this, then, another interrogation?

I'm sorry, Mrs Hastings, I'm not trying to upset you.

Because we had the police prying round at that time, and they was asking all kinds of questions. I tried to help them as best I could, but it's not good for business having the police round, you know. Not good for the image at all. Especially with the troubles we've been having.

I understand perfectly.

You know, we run a good, honest business here, trying to do the best we can.

You have a few challenges?

Challenges! Yeah, I'll say we have challenges. We've had vandalism, attempted burglary...

That's why you put in the CCTV camera?

Yeah, my husband sorted that. Because we had young hoodies hanging around. We have to keep especially vigilant, you know.

And these police officers who were asking you questions a year or so ago, how were they, do you remember?

Young ones, you know. A bloke and a girl.

What sort of questions were they asking?

I dunno. It is over a year ago, Mr Peralta, I can't remember.

But they were particularly interested in the CCTV?

Oh yeah, they asked about it immediately. They were talking about that date you mentioned. Had Edie been round that day? Well, I wasn't here, see? I looked it up in the diary. It would have been the girl that day, I was off. Because it wouldn't have been a particularly busy day. I asked the girl, I asked her, but she couldn't remember nothing. Strictly between you and me, she's a bit useless, that girl. But you can't get the staff here in Deadmans Beach. So then they asked, what about the security camera? Wanted to have a look, to see if the old lady had been picked up on it.

And she had?

Yeah, the police officers went through the tape, rewinding until they got to the time and date they wanted. And she come up after a while. They were very excited about that, I remember.

So they viewed the footage there and then?

Yeah, I had to put the tape on for them. It comes up on this screen here, see?

I see. It's live all the time, is it?

Yeah, twenty-four seven. Because of the problems we've had, you know. It's live now, as you can see. But it don't record unless, you know there's some ... I don't know, what's the word, it's –

Motion-activated?

Motion-activated, yeah, that's it. If there's some movement, it puts it on tape. Otherwise it don't.

Is it possible to view the original videotape again?

You're joking!

I beg your pardon?

I ain't got it no more, they took it.

The police didn't give it back?

They asked could they take away the tape, to digitise it, they said. You know, they was going to make a digital copy, to put on the computer. Promised they'd return it. Well, they never.

Why doesn't that surprise me?

So, excuse me, Mr Peralta, why are you investigating this all over again?

Because the old lady's nephew asked us to.

Because the police was rubbish?

Something like that.

Tell me about it.

You've had previous dealings with the police?

Are you implying something, Mr Peralta?

No, not at all. I have had many dealings with the police myself, in my line of work, and I can tell you it's frustrating at times. Mrs Hastings, can I ask you a favour?

Yeah, fire away.

I wonder if we could test out the security system, very briefly. What I propose to do is go out of the front door of the café, and then re-enter. Then, if I may, I would like to view the resulting video footage.

Well, it would've already picked you up coming in.

I am aware of that, but I would like to recreate the conditions exactly, in other words replicate the coming and going or the going and coming. So if it isn't too much of a nuisance –

Yeah, no, be my guest. For all the good it will do. I mean, I'm not trying to be funny, but it's all a bit of a waste of time, isn't it? That old girl's gone, she ain't gonna come back, is she? It's very sad, but there's probably some simple explanation, I'm not saying she's been done in, but she probably fell into the sea or, I don't know –

Nevertheless –

It's probably for the best.

For the best?

Well, I'm not being funny or anything, but when you get to that state she was getting to, it's probably a kindness that she finds peace. Just so long as she didn't suffer. There should be a way. When you get to that state. I believe that. Put them out of their misery, it's a kindness, innit? I mean, I've said to my husband many times, if I start losing my marbles, or worse, just shoot me.

A bit impractical? Not to say illegal, as far as present legislation goes?

Yeah, he says to me, how am I gonna do that? Give us a break. Then we have a good old laugh about it.

I'll bet you do.

What are you going to shoot me with, I says to him. Ha-ha-ha-ha-ha.

(She resorted to her pink nebuliser once more.)

All right, Mrs Hastings, now I shall exit the café, and we shall see what results on the video screen.

Let's have a look.

So we got to wind it back.

Ah, I see.

Yeah, it worked, there's you going out of the café, Mr Peralta. And you're going down the path to the main road, just like you did.

Excellent.

Large as life and twice as natural, ha-ha-ha-ha-ha.

Precisely.

It's a bit ropy, but we couldn't afford a fancy system. My husband says it's the best one we could get for the money.

And then it jumps to when I come back into shot again.

Yeah, here you come.

So I re-enter the café and it no longer senses any motion so it cuts out. Can you play it again?

Yeah, OK.

Thank you.

Here we go.

Hold on a second, there seems to be something wrong.

What's that?

The date stamp.

The what?

What's the date today, Mrs Hastings?

Nineteenth of May.

So why does the date running at the bottom of the picture show as sixteenth of June?

I dunno. I never noticed that before, that the date was wrong.

There's a discrepancy of ... it's twenty-eight days out.

If you say so.

Has the date been manually re-set?

Well, it ain't been touched for ages.

You're saying the system has been running continuously?

Yeah, since the café was temporarily closed.

Ah, of course, you were closed for a couple of months, I believe, from around November a year ago?

Yeah, you knew about that?

That is, around eighteen months ago? Was that the environmental health issue you had?

It was not about issues, we was closed for refurbishments.

Sorry, I understood there was a court case –

You don't want to believe everything you read in the papers. We was closed for refurbishments.

For refurbishments, yes.

We got a lot of malicious comments, it was all rubbish. And then with the police nosing round, that was the last straw. It's hard enough trying to run a business with all the bollocks you get, without having bad publicity on top, which is unwarranted. Completely unwarranted.

All right, Mrs Hastings, I do sympathise, and I really don't want to go into that, it's none of my concern. But can we establish that you were closed between November and January a year ago?

Yeah, we re-opened first of February.

And the security camera was perhaps offline for that period?

Yeah, it might have been.

So you re-opened first of February last year?

Ah, yeah, I remember now, my husband set the system up again. Because we had to take the camera down, because we was having work done to the door.

And is there a chance he might have mistakenly set the date as one/three instead of one/two? In other words, first of March instead of first of February?

It's possible. I dunno.

And if so, it's been twenty-eight days in advance ever since then?

It's possible. To be perfectly honest, Mr Peralta, I never noticed that until now. And the police certainly didn't. I sincerely hope we won't be in trouble over this, it's the last thing we need.

Not at all, it's not your fault at all. It was an honest mistake. But let's get this straight: when the video was recorded of Edith Watkins arriving and leaving the café, which purported to be in the hour or so before and after two on the afternoon of the fifteenth of March –

Yeah?

– it was actually the fifteenth of February. In other words a couple of weeks after you'd re-opened. And a whole month before she actually went missing.

Yeah, could be. I see what you're saying.

In which case we would need to have another look at that video-cassette, and see if there's anything for the actual fifteenth of March – which would be marked as, let's see, twelfth of April, I would think.

But –

Yes, I know what you're going to say, Mrs Hastings. The police still have the tape. And getting it back from them would be a huge hassle, perhaps impossible. But in any case, I would wager a large sum that even were we to retrieve it we would find there is no sign of Edith Watkins on it for the date in question.

•

I can't believe it! This letter arrives in the post from All Saints Primary School, official notepaper, signed by Mrs Darling, extremely sorry, bla bla bla, in view of the unfortunate incident on 19th May, bla bla bla, and also his poor attendance record – *poor attendance record!* he's missed, what, half a dozen days at most! – George White is, bla bla bla, excluded from school until the end of the summer term. We will review this in consultation with you, the parent, with a view to, bla bla bla, beginning of the autumn term in September.

How can they do this? It's a complete injustice. It was George who was the victim in this "unfortunate incident", and yet there is no mention of any sanction on the boy who bullied him, no mention of him at all.

I phoned Dave immediately, and he went up the wall. Wanted to go over to the school and have it out with Mrs Darling right away. I had to dissuade him. I managed to persuade him, I think, not to act hastily. We've already been fingered as bad parents, so it would not help at all. We have to think about this. I told Kitty, and she was aghast. She was adamant that this was not legal. She said it breached our rights, and George's rights. She said we have to challenge this legally, go to court if necessary, she could put me in touch with her lawyer friend. At this point, my head started spinning. I didn't want to deal with this, I *can't* deal with this.

The trip to Moorish Point has been postponed till next week, as we have a backlog of admin in the office to deal with, so I shall have to take George into work with me over the next couple of days, and see how we go from there. As for George himself, he's quite nonchalant, even maybe rather happy and relieved that he doesn't have to go to school. I don't blame him, but I don't know what the future holds for him. He doesn't lack things to do, he always finds projects – but I worry he needs some friends, it's not right, the way he is. I have to be there for him, but I don't really know what "there" means.

A glance at the contour lines on the Ordnance Survey map confirmed Moorish Point as the highest position in the region, reputedly commanding views over the entirety of the Dead Level and the marshlands, and indeed of the coastline and far out to sea on a clear day.

The day, however, was far from clear. A sea mist was coming in, and the fields around the business park were shrouded in it early in the morning. The prognosis was that it would clear later on, and it was advisable therefore to proceed on that basis.

Lucy arrived at nine-thirty as usual, in her car, with her son George in tow. Departure was at ten. The mist persisted, and the grey fields slipped by, revealing little detail. The boy chattered and asked numerous questions from the back seat. He appeared, as always, to be of high intelligence and some charm. At the second junction, we departed from the road to Moorshurst, turning left and taking a minor road which, as it approached the high ground beyond Deadhurst village, started to climb, and then to wind as it climbed more steeply. Lucy appeared perfectly familiar with the route and the territory. And here a dramatic landscape began to reveal itself in the gaps amid the swirling mist, as the road negotiated some steep gradients in its approach to high ground and occasionally plunged through forested declines – pine and birch chiefly featuring here – before resuming its upward trajectory. The view at the pinnacles would have been impressive in good light, but was still hampered by the mist across the downlands, which lent the landscape an air of the uncanny. Occasionally, the stragglers from a flock of sheep, no more than two or three individuals perhaps, turned to stare across the fence at our vehicle as it passed, evidently a different breed from those on the Dead Level, of darker wool and more impassive demeanour, with horns curled tightly against their skulls.

Few vehicles were encountered along the way. Lucy negotiated the bends with considerable expertise. The boy asked questions from time to time about what we were observing, and these were answered in the best way that could be managed. Lucy's conversation, however, kept reverting to the topic of his exclusion from school, and what strategies might be adopted to counter this. And so half an hour passed, and we were approaching Moorish Point.

The mist here had begun to drop away, and some rays of watery sunlight were now penetrating as the last of the evergreen thickets were left behind and we were through again for the final time into open highland. It sloped beneath us in every direction.

No other vehicles were present in the small car park at the top. A briefly worded information board and an exhortation to visitors to take their rubbish home with them were situated next to it. There was little evidence of the Iron Age fortress that was reputed to have occupied this space, but an abundance of rocks oddly shaped by erosion lay around. Remnants of mist still lingered, but shadows were beginning to be defined.

Lucy was wearing dark glasses. Her son jumped nimbly from rock to rock. From time to time he called out to her. The pale sunlight shone on his thin, light hair, and the resemblance between mother and son became strikingly evident.

A buzzard flew past, from right to left.

The hum of a light aircraft could be heard.

There's a lot of sky here.

Yes indeed, Lucy.

And a lot of landscape.

The landscape would seem to be the chief attraction.

I've always liked it because you can see everything from here.

When the mist permits, yes. But we carry our landscapes around with us, I suppose.

Yes, I suppose so, Phidias.

There is always a landscape very close at hand – too close for comfort sometimes.

Phidias, do you still think Edith Watkins is somewhere down there … in the marshlands?

I have the odd feeling that she may be.

Even though –

I know what you're going to say, Lucy, even though my conversation with the proprietor of the Sanctuary Café has completely demolished the thesis that she visited and departed from there on the fifteenth of March last year.

So she never got on that bus?

No.

You're sure about that?

As sure as I can be.

But you're saying she may be in the marshes? Or her, I don't know, her ghost?

The one thing I discovered was how treacherous a location it is. And the deeper one goes into it the more dangerous it is. Any departure from the path –

So we need to tell Mr Watkins about this.

We need to apprise him of the latest development, yes. I shall have to have a meeting with him in a week or so, when

I've had the chance to think about this a little more clearly.

Well, it's not really a *development*, is it? More like the opposite of one. It's like we're going backwards. Rather than finding new clues, it's like the clues we already had are being removed.

Yes, it is a little like that.

But we have to tell him.

The question is what are we going to tell him? We need to tread very carefully here.

Yes.

Because of the disturbing implications –

And then it's like ... there are new clues which are not really clues at all, which are just weird. I mean, that memorial bench, I swear I saw that, unless I'm totally insane, and now that seems to have vanished –

You are not insane, Lucy, I assure you –

Mummy!

Yes, George?

Can we see our house from here?

I don't know. It's a very long way off.

I've got good eyesight. Haven't I, Mummy?

George, you can borrow my binoculars if you're careful with them.

Oh yes, Mr Peralta!

Can you hold them? Put them to your eyes, hang on a moment –

I can see something.

There's the focus, you adjust it like this.

That's really cool, Mr Peralta.

This is a great vantage point, is it not, George?

What's that?

It means a place from which you can see clearly.

Observation, observation, observation!

Precisely, George.

Phidias, what did you mean, disturbing implications –

The question of the disappearance of the old lady was a

tragic enough one when there were some clues as to how that could have occurred. Now that the clues are, as you suggest, being removed, the tragedy is, if anything, compounded, even as the problem appears to deepen.

Do you think there was a crime?

It is at the front of the possibilities.

Was she murdered in the marshes?

It's possible.

You don't think ... the neighbour, Sharon. I just suddenly thought – she has now become just about the last person to see her alive.

So far as we can tell, but it may not be so. Let's say, the last person currently thought to have seen her alive.

You don't think she –?

You interviewed her, Lucy, what's your opinion?

I can't possibly believe she'd be capable – but she had the opportunity, and she did go away for three days immediately after she says she saw her – so she could've – but why?

My opinion, for what it's worth, is that it is a remote possibility. But of course there is no motivation there that we can see. A useful thing to do, anyway, to eliminate that entirely, would be to find out the name of that hotel in Paris she stayed at with her boyfriend, and then corroborate her stay there. The police may have done that. Yet there are other possibilities. We have to keep an open mind.

I'll do that. But *someone* killed her?

All we can say is that there is a very high probability she is dead. But we already knew that.

So we are looking at a body?

We could be literally looking at a body. Had we perfect vision. Telescopic and x-ray vision. The whole of the marshland is before us. The secret is there, in plain sight.

Somewhere – down there –

But the question of location is not an easy one. I mean, location itself is a problematical enough notion.

Why?

Time and space are perennially shifting. I mean to say, space-time.

You're losing me, Phidias.

I apologise. Did you know Trevor Tanner was a model railway enthusiast?

I did. You went to see his model railway, didn't you?

Yes, I did.

What's that got to do with it?

It occupies almost the whole of his house. And it is, insofar as it can be represented in that finite space, a model of this entire area, the one we see below us. Only, it isn't. It's a model of what it might be, or what it might have been. He supposes that a branch railway link between the main line and Deadmans Beach had actually been constructed, back in the nineteenth century. And so his is a model of an alternative, parallel world, the world that we would witness now had that development occurred.

Not the real world?

It raises the question of what is the real world.

The one we are in! The one we are looking at!

But we don't even know what that is. And there is no possibility of obtaining enough data to ascertain it with enough precision. Not to mention the existence of conflicting data.

Conflicting data?

You are certain, for instance, that you saw a memorial bench erected for Edith to commemorate a death which nobody seems certain has occurred, and which nobody has taken responsibility for.

That's what I thought I saw.

I have no reason to doubt you. Maybe there are alternative worlds whose apparitions interfere with ours. Worlds arising from different pathways taken.

That is too weird. And anyway, it seems to have disappeared from our world, if it ever was there.

Well, we have to do the best we can, Lucy. That is all we can do.

The whole of the marshland and the Dead Level were laid out as Lucy had previously described. Rough heathland immediately confronted us, dotted with tiny sheep, tumbling below for some miles into the valley, leading to the immense plain that was once the primeval shallow sea. And there, to the right, a patchwork of fields delineated by drainage ditches and tracks; to the left, the same dissolving into a more fluid and elusive landscape, punctuated by the grey shimmer that was the Industrial Ponds. The promontory on which Deadhurst was built was concealed by the contours of the nearer landscape and by bursts of thick, dark woodland.

It had all the appearance of a world – no more nor less than the world that we imagine. There, activities would be taking place that could not be computed or completely known, no matter how much information was put into the computation.

And it seemed, as Lucy surmised, that even those clues that had been given, which might have permitted more robust theories – or even educated guesses – were being removed one by one.

But with every minute that passed, the mist was dispersing, and the distant coast, beyond the marshes, was coming more clearly into view. The tiny conurbation that was Deadmans Beach could now be seen – it clung to the edge of the land, the small fleet of fishing boats just visible on the beach. The sea emerged from its veil: at the horizon, a thin strip of turquoise just below the variegated sky, and the rest of that watery mass an ever-changing brown-grey in colour.

10

Clarification is what we need above all. It was in pursuit of this – to speak the truth, vain pursuit – that Gordon Prescott was once more visited, and found in his screen-bedecked lair. He was rubbing his spectacles with a cloth and repositioning them on the bridge of his nose. He accepted the apology for intrusion with good grace, and offered to run the footage again.

No problem, Phidias, is what he said. And he turned to the technology at his disposal. Quickly, however, it became clear that the exercise was without point. Two dark, pixellated figures were observed. Their build, their gait, their demeanour were all within the expected parameters. But you could run the footage backwards and forwards, you could freeze the action at any point, and no further information would be obtainable. And so futility was the key signature.

It was at this point that Trevor entered. He waited in the doorway politely until Gordon beckoned him in. They conferred. They were in agreement. But instead of promptly with-drawing, Trevor said: Phidias, if you have a moment, perhaps we could have a word. In private, if you like.

In private?

If you like.

Well, you can talk to me here. If Gordon doesn't mind.

I don't mind at all.

It is a delicate subject.

Go ahead, I'm sure we can all take it.

Phidias, it concerns your *de facto* residence in Unit 13.

I do realise it is unofficial and temporary –

Quite so, quite so, and I'd like you to know that I person-ally have no problem with it, and I'm sure Gordon here like-wise –

But –

But it has been mentioned to me.

Mentioned.

Yes, there has been a mention. By a senior member of the management board.

What was said?

It was in the form of a question. A question put to me, fol-lowing an observation. He reminded me of the rules. I said I was well aware of the rules, of course.

As we all are, I accept that.

Quite so, quite so, Phidias. So I said I was well aware of the rules, and what was the issue? And he said Unit 13. What of Unit 13, I said. He said remind me of the client there. I said it was Peralta Associates, Private Investigators. Ah yes, of course, he said. Now it has been brought to my attention, those were the very words he used, it has been brought to my attention that the premises of Unit 13 may be in the process of being used for domestic residential purposes.

Brought to his attention? How so?

He didn't specify. Anyway, he went on, can I remind you that retail units may not be used for residential purposes?

Such use contravenes planning regulations and also our insurance policies. He was quite right to remind me of this, of course. He was well within his rights. You understand?

Perfectly, Trevor.

What I'm saying is –

I've been rumbled.

I wouldn't put it so –

I understand what you're saying.

A blind eye has been turned.

Yes, and I'm grateful.

A blind eye has been turned, as Gordon here is well aware, and we know there is no security risk, and the situation poses no problem personally for either of us, but –

The said situation cannot be allowed to continue for much longer.

Exactly so, Phidias. You took the words right out of my mouth. A blind eye has been turned, but it can't remain blind for much longer.

The eye must see again, and if it sees an irregular arrangement –

I appreciate your understanding, Phidias.

How long?

Beg pardon?

How long have I got to make alternative arrangements?

Oh, please don't feel rushed, we don't want to be unreasonable.

But within a finite amount of time?

Within a reasonable time-frame. Just so long as I can reassure this senior member of the management board. Just so long as I can assure him that the issue is being addressed. I mean, actively addressed.

The blind eye must open, and see clearly again.

Exactly so, exactly so. Take your time, we are reasonable people.

But I don't want to cause problems for you fellows.

We appreciate that, Phidias.

I'll get on to it. I must do that. I couldn't have reasonably hoped that this, shall we say, informal arrangement was a permanent solution. I would have been deluded had I done so. Perhaps, for a while, I was deluded. But a sense of reality has to set in eventually. In any case, I have been a little shaken by this report – these intruders –

Oh, I'm sure Gordon here can deal with security issues –

Absolutely so. But I accept that I will need to take certain measures – leave it with me, Trevor.

Good man, Phidias.

And thank you for your help, Gordon.

My pleasure.

On leaving Gordon Prescott's office – on the way to the self-storage unit – a tall young man, bespectacled and with a fringe of beard, was encountered. The shock of his appearance was principally created by the tinting of his spectacles in the pale sunshine, which lent him an air of otherworldliness.

Hey, Phidias! he called, his hand out in greeting, and all of a sudden he became familiar – another wave-form collapsing. He was of course one of the young men from the band Hedgemonicker.

Pete, isn't it? Good afternoon to you, sir.

How you doing, man?

Moderately well, although I am having to contemplate a change of plan right now, but I won't bore you with that. And yourself?

Not too bad.

Are you going in there?

The self-storage depot? Yeah.

Are you about to have another band rehearsal?

No, not this evening. I'm just dropping in to our unit to pick up some gear I need.

You were about to tour, as I recall?

Yes, that's right, we're off on a mini-tour next week. We're taking our folk metal music nationwide.

And remind me, you're next playing locally when?

Not till the autumn. Bonfire Night at the old Dick.

Ah, that's right. The Richard the Conqueror in Deadmans Beach. I shall make a note in my diary. I should have already done so.

It would be great to see you there. How are you getting on with your investigations?

We do our best.

You haven't found that old lady yet?

No, not at all, alas. I have actually been attempting to retrace her steps, or what we guess may have been her steps, but the picture is becoming less clear by the day.

Wasn't she lost in the marshes?

That is one theory, yes.

And you've been out there?

I reconnoitred some of the area beyond Thieves Bridge to get a sense of how it might have been –

Wow, yeah, did you go the other side of the Industrial Ponds?

Indeed I did.

That's well into what Geezer calls the Grey Area, then.

I recall that is what he called it.

And you were saying some interesting stuff about anomalies, I remember. Did you find any?

Anomalies? One or two puzzling and even distressing experiences.

See any of the weird people?

Well, you could say that. There was a woman who appeared to have lost her dog. But she didn't respond to my conversation. In fact, she didn't seem to register my presence in any way. And then I noticed, when I was trying to observe her characteristics, one quite unusual one: she had six fingers on each hand.

You are kidding me!

It is a rare but not unprecedented genetic abnormality –

No, Phidias, I mean, are you putting me on?

I would not dream of it.

You're seriously saying you saw Six-Fingered Sally?

Is she a well-known local personality?

Phidias, Six-Fingered Sally is a legend! Dating from maybe the early eighteenth century. I can't believe this! You didn't know?

I know nothing of this.

Six-Fingered Sally – I can't believe this – we wrote a song about her – this is really spooking me! And you say she was looking for her dog?

She was in modern dress, certainly not in eighteenth century garb, and had a dog lead in her hand. I thought she was with a dog-walking group I previously encountered. But you're saying this Six-Fingered Sally is a three-hundred-year-old legend?

We have a song … it's in the band's repertoire. Six-Fingered Sally. Or Six-Fingered Sal, or Sally Six Fingers, I forget what we decided to call it. And you say she was even looking for a dog! I'm speechless, Phidias, my back hairs are going up.

What was the legend?

She was a woman who was born partly disabled, I suppose, and she had this condition, that she had an extra finger on each hand. She is supposed to have had a brutal husband who beat her, and finally she killed him. With an axe, they say. So with that she ran off, with her dog, leaving the husband's bleeding body behind. The next day the dog came back. It kept howling and moaning. People took it out into the marshes to see if it would lead them to her, but it just stood and howled. And no more was ever heard of her, but over the years and even into recent times people claim to have seen a six-fingered woman wandering the marshes calling for her dog.

That is … extraordinary.

Jesus, Phidias, I can't believe this.

It has now shaken me, too. I assure you I am not trying to kid you, Pete.

I can't believe it.

This legend, then – is any significance ascribed to it?

What do you mean?

People who see this alleged apparition – does local super-stition apportion any meaning to the vision, if you like?

I can't say.

Does it portend anything? In superstitious terms?

Phidias ... I can't say.

The night was marked again by restlessness – restlessness within which twin pursuers figured. Heartbeat was raised. Twin figures were observed, on the shingle, in the distance of the dream. They were thieves. Everyone knew this, but few dared say it aloud for fear of reprisals. Fear of Borg in particu-lar, for he was the clever one, even, some said, an erudite man. But he wore his erudition like a Kalashnikov. And he would always achieve what he wanted, with dogged persua-sion. As for McKinley, he was always the enforcer. Always? By no means. He had not always been there. Borg's previous partner, Lopez, would have been remembered by many. There had been a smidgeon of humanity in Lopez. There had been occasions when an expression had flickered across the face of Lopez that could have been decipherable as pity or compas-sion. Not to say that Lopez couldn't take the tough decisions. But this redeeming quality of his, even though barely dis-cernible, had been too much for Borg, who had finally got rid of him. Borg had dispensed with Lopez as one releases a dead rodent from a trap into a dustbin, snapping the lid shut and thinking no more of it afterwards – and he had taken up McKinley instead. McKinley had no scruples. He would do whatever was necessary, and would ask no questions. He was totally loyal, we will concede him that. Given the nod, he would disappear into the darkness and do the necessary. It was believed he had been born into unspeakably insalubrious circumstances; he had had to fight his way out of them with implacable courage. That was the secret of his maleficence. And he took his chances, one hundred percent. There was no escaping McKinley.

So there would have to be a change of plan; it had always been on the cards, and the omens, if one were to lend credence to omens, were now conspiring to point in this direction. Eyes that had been tremblingly shut, in fitful oblivion, were now wide open. Once again, things could not continue as they had been, or as they had been imagined. It was necessary not to imperil oneself, but, more importantly, not to be the cause of putting others in peril. Specifically, employees – and their loved ones. Therefore the change of plan. As well that it was enforced by other circumstances, by the circumstance in particular of having to find other domiciliary arrangements. The plan would be put into operation forthwith.

•

I can't quite get my head around the doings of today. I am still trying to piece it all together.

Let's start from the beginning. That might be helpful. When I arrived at nine-thirty this morning, as usual, with George in tow, I found Phidias in a state of anxiety. He hadn't slept well, yet again. Apparently he's had a meeting with Trevor and Gordon, and he's been told he can't continue to reside at the Peralta Associates premises, so he's making emergency plans to live somewhere else. Well, that's what he told me at first, but then it emerged he's really spooked by the reports of these two guys snooping around. He is convinced they are people from his past, and that they are after him. But when I asked what it was all about, he clammed up. Said it was to do with money, that was all. That it would be safer if he was out of the way. So could he leave me in the office while he went scouting around on various errands this morning?

I said sure, I had plenty to do. And George was quite happy playing on his own. But do you need a lift, I asked. No, he said, he was only going in to Deadmans Beach and would either walk or take the bus.

At around eleven Phidias calls me from the Sanctuary Caravan Park. He's negotiating to buy a mobile home! But he wants me to look up some documents, and I had to remind him that his personal files, at his request, had been moved into Room 248 in the self-storage depot. I said I would nip over there, have a root around and call him back.

What to do about George? This is where I made the mistake. I should have taken him next door with me. It wouldn't have mattered if the office had been closed for half an hour. Nobody was expected anyway. But George was constructing some fantasy of his own with his building bricks and didn't want to be disturbed. So I said to him, I have to go next door for a short while. Just mind the shop, will you, there shouldn't be anybody, but if anybody does turn up, just ask them to sit down and tell them I'll be back. OK, Mummy, he says.

Big mistake.

I was in there, in Room 248, rummaging among the shelving trying to find the documents Phidias wanted, when suddenly there was this awful noise echoing down the corridors. An alarm siren. It went on and on, unbearable. And next thing there was the swift pitter-patter of footsteps and here came George running like mad along the corridor towards me (I was standing in the doorway of the storage unit), his face flushed, shouting, Mummy Mummy Mummy!

Hello?

Hello.

Oh, hello, young man. I didn't see you there.

My name's George.

I am pleased to meet you. My name is Borg and this is my associate, McKinley. We are looking for Mr Peralta.

He's not here.

Ah, I see. Is there anyone in charge here?

I'm in charge.

You are?

My mum put me in charge.

And who is your mum?

My mum's name is Lucy White, and I am George White.

Is that right? So where is Mr Peralta?

I don't know.

You don't know?

No, I don't.

He doesn't know. Well, this is rum state of affairs, is it not, McKinley? He doesn't know. Or he won't tell us.

I'm telling the truth!

Are you really?

Mum says you can sit down.

Thank you, we would rather stand, young man.

Well, you can sit if you like. There are chairs.

So where is your mother, then?

Why do you want to know?

We should like to speak to her.

I thought you wanted to speak to Mr Peralta.

Perhaps your mother would be able to tell us the where-abouts of Mr Peralta, if you are unable to. So where is she?

She's in Room 248.

Room 248, what's that?

It's where Mr Peralta has his library. It's where he keeps his things.

Ah, now, that would be of great interest to us. His things, McKinley!

Why do you want Mr Peralta's things?

We only want to retrieve what belongs to us. What belongs to Mr Peralta belongs to Mr Peralta. What belongs to us must be rendered up to us. We would like to persuade Mr Peralta to return what is due. So can you lead us to this Room 248, where we can have a word with your mother about our intentions?

It isn't here.

Where is it, then?

It's next door. But you aren't allowed to go there.

Next door, what do you mean, next door?

He means the self-storage depot, Borg.

Ah, you may be right, McKinley. Do you mean the self-storage depot, young man?

(No reply.)

Young man, is that what you mean?

(No reply.)

Well?

Yes, but you can't get in there. Because there's security. You have to sign the book and that.

Perhaps you could take us and we could see for ourselves?

I'm supposed to stay in charge here. Mummy said so.

Oh, Mummy said so, did she?

Yeah, she did.

I'm sure she wouldn't mind if you just showed us the way.

Yeah, but you can't get in because of the security.

So you said.

(Pause.)

You could go the back way.

Ah, now we're getting somewhere.

You could go round through the back yard and into the service lift. That's what it's called, the big lift with the cage door that comes across. The service lift. I know how to do that. You can get in the back, and then the service lift is there and you have to press 2 for the second floor. But you have to know the way.

Splendid, perhaps you could show us.

Then you don't have to sign the book. But I think it's not really allowed.

I'm sure the rules could be bent just on this particular occasion.

I don't think I could.

Is Mr Peralta with your mother? Is that why you're prevaricating?

What's prevari – What's that?

Is he?

No, he's not! I told you, I don't know where Mr Peralta is.

Very well, young man, if you can lead us to this Room Whatever It Is, your mother can enlighten us as to his whereabouts. It will only take a few minutes.

Room 248.

That's the one. Can you do that?

All right.

I couldn't get any sense out of George at first. He was babbling nineteen to the dozen, in a great state of excitement. Two blokes, he kept shouting, two blokes, they were after Mr Peralta. What blokes, I asked, what did they look like? And all the time that awful siren was going, whooo-whooo-whooo, so I could hardly hear a word of what *I* was saying let alone him. As far as I could make out, his words were: They had dark suits on, like those funeral people.

You mean, like undertakers?

Yes, he said, undertakers, that's what they looked like. One's tall and thin and the other is a bit shorter and he doesn't say a lot. Mummy, I don't like them very much.

It took a while for me to understand that these two gentlemen had been trapped in the lift, which had jammed, and that George had had something to do with this.

Eventually, I got some sense out of him. So we went down by the staircase to the ground floor. There was a bit of a kerfuffle going on. Gordon Prescott was there in his shirtsleeves, summoned, no doubt, by the alarm's going off. He was on his radio, calling someone who it turned out was a technician.

I really didn't like them, that's why I did it, George kept repeating. I didn't mean any harm, honest, mum.

I reassured him, without at that stage yet knowing what he had or hadn't done.

The service lift had been jammed, it turned out.

Can we get the alarm turned off? Gordon was pleading into his walkie talkie, exasperated.

The heavy lattice door had been pulled right across. Inside, as if through the bars of a cage, two men in dark suits could be seen. The floor of the lift within was above the level of the floor on our side. In other words, the lift was not quite aligned with our floor.

The two men stood, occasionally pacing. I could see their shadowy shapes and their white faces. They were like wild animals caged in a zoo. They were quite silent, but their faces were like thunder.

The alarm suddenly stopped – a blessed relief. We could hear ourselves speak without shouting.

Gordon acknowledged me. Do you happen to know how this occurred, Lucy? he asked.

I turned the question to George.

I didn't mean to do any harm, George kept repeating.

Nobody's blaming you, son, said Gordon in a kindly tone. But did you jam the gate mechanism?

Yes, said George.

The taller of the two men trapped inside the cage suddenly spoke up: The young man did it deliberately.

Gordon turned to him: Do you two gentlemen have business here?

We have business with Mr Phidias Peralta, the man said.

But you do not rent a storage facility in this building? said Gordon.

The man was silent.

I apologise for what has happened, said Gordon, but I have to say that you do not have security clearance to be in this facility.

That's as may be but it doesn't give the boy the right to jam the lift with us inside, said the man coldly.

The technician turned up with his bag of tricks.

Lift's been jammed, Bill, said Gordon.

How did that happen? said Bill.

This young gentleman apparently is responsible.

Bill grumbled, but set to work. After a while, he muttered: How did he do that? It's not supposed to be possible. He knelt down and opened his bag to extract tools.

I worked it out, said George. Now that he realised he wasn't going to be punished, he was beginning to look rather pleased with himself.

Haven't I seen you before? Gordon's question was addressed to the two trapped men, while Bill was trying to unjam the mechanism.

I don't believe we have met, said the taller man.

Gordon said: I have reason to think you have been recorded on the security camera previously, attempting to gain access to the premises.

The two men in the cage were silent. I think the manager of the storage facility and someone else had also arrived at this point, so there was quite a crowd of us by now.

I piped up: If you really have some business to transact with Phidias, I think you had better do it through the normal channels. I can make an appointment for you if you like.

The taller man, who looked like a hawk with his sharp features, said: We are former associates of Mr Peralta. Our business is personal.

So who shall I say wants an appointment? I asked him. And he replied: My name is Borg, and this is my partner Mr McKinley. Mr Peralta will know who we are.

But he wouldn't say any more.

Bill, looking up from his work, asked George: How the hell did you do this, son?

George said: I pulled the gate and then I got out before it was completely shut and then I pulled that lever and then I pulled it the other way. Then there was that noise.

I heard the smaller, squatter of the two men mutter something that sounded like "little bastard".

It's not supposed to happen, said Bill. I'm amazed. It would have taken terrific force.

Can you fix it, mate? asked Gordon anxiously.

Yeah, said Bill, I'll get it done in a minute.

It was actually well over a minute – even ten minutes – before the two strangers were freed. The floor of the lift came down with a bump and the gate was able to be opened. They emerged, poker-faced. They would not talk to me, or even look at me. George, meanwhile, skulked behind me, somewhat apprehensive. Gordon lectured them about the security arrangements of the Dead Level Business Park, and in particular those of Dead Level Self Storage. They nodded and scowled, and left the premises without further ado.

Gordon confirmed with me that these were the two individuals who had previously been identified on the security camera. Without the shadow of a doubt, he said.

I called Phidias to report on it but had to leave a voicemail message as he wasn't answering.

I am mortified about what I have done. Leaving George alone in the office! What was I thinking about? Anything could have happened. I am relieved that he came to no harm.

I have already been identified as a bad parent. I keep him

out of school. I am evidently unable to set a good example for him. Now I neglect his welfare. I leave a seven-year-old child alone in a publicly accessible office for nearly half an hour. I'm terrified the school will find out about this.

But I have to say I am also secretly rather proud. His account of what happened is still a little confusing and contradictory. He seems to have been confused himself when they appeared in the office, according to him, and started asking questions he barely understood. But it looks like he got a bad feeling from these two individuals, and he did his best to protect me. Yes, he went with his gut feeling. And what an inspired choice – to lock them in the lift – and what quick thinking and resourcefulness.

The caravan site would once have been scrubland, leading on to dunes. It had been raining overnight, and there were still saturated patches in the grass between pitches. Imagine owning your very own holiday home – that was the offer on the big hoarding. And did you know we are open 52 weeks a year?

This was a normal morning in the less picturesque hinterland of Deadmans Beach. A van with the logo "Transport Solutions Ltd" went by, then two young people on bicycles. A dismal row of shops, including a newsagent with plastic tubs in acid colours for sale outside, a bookmaker, a butcher and several boarded-up frontages, marked one horizon; on the other was a distant view of bungalows. There were signifiers of the seaside. There were slumbering things on wires. The Sanctuary Café was not visible from here. The entrance to the Sanctuary Caravan Park had seemed less than enticing, but needs must. People were going about their daily business. A man barked into a mobile phone: Hello, that's fine, I'm near enough. A young woman with piled-up hair and wearing sunglasses (despite the overcast conditions) pushed an unhappy child in a buggy. A dark man of Asian appearance wearing a white hoodie, white jogging pants and black trainers, his white ear buds tethered to the device with which he fiddled nervously, crossed the path of an obese man in a T-shirt and shorts with tattoos on his thick pale calves.

There were indubitably bargains to be had among the roster of mobile homes available for sale or rent. They could be inspected, and they were. One had been recently renovated. Another even retained the fuchsias in hanging baskets left by a previous tenant. There were too many flags for comfort.

The young saleswoman in the site office was exceedingly pleasant and reasonable. And so negotiations proceeded. But then we were interrupted by Lucy's disturbing voicemail message. The discussions were put on hold while this was attended to, which necessitated a return to the office.

It was not unexpected, unfortunately, that the twin pursuers would be back. But that they returned so quickly, and with such brazen impunity, was worrying. And that Lucy and her son were put into such potential danger was, frankly, unforgiveable. A recrudescence of this event should not be permitted.

It was not entirely clear what had happened, or what would have happened had the young lad not acted as he did. His own account was, as Lucy had warned, confusing and contradictory, but this was entirely understandable. Lucy was, equally understandably, consumed with guilt at having exposed him to the experience. It seemed that Borg and McKinley had entered the premises boldly, seeing that the office was open, expecting a confrontation and welcoming it. The lad implied that they had threatened him, but on questioning further he maintained they had been "nice at first". What it was about them that had changed his mind was one of the areas of unclarity. He likened them to funeral directors, which seemed quite apt, and said they were "polite". He was keen to assure us that he had been polite in his turn. In one version, he had claimed that his trapping them in the service lift had been an accident, that he had not meant to do this, but on being asked why in that case he had apparently deliberately stepped outside the lift before shutting the gate he changed his narrative, saying that he had "had an idea" about what to do. At times he was tearful, and wanting to be consoled by his mother, at others he was proud, even close to bragging about his part in the drama.

As to what had happened next, according to Lucy the two had quietly slipped away while Gordon was trying to talk to them. Gordon himself was evasive, but maintained he had "read the riot act" to them, following his identification of them with the two figures observed days before acting suspiciously, and told us he had obtained an assurance from them that they would not return. Lucy said she had heard no such assurance, but that on the contrary she had tried to get them to make an appointment with her, which they had ignored or declined. They had not of course specified what their business was. And so the episode had ended, as it began, in unclarity.

Lucy.

Yes, Phidias?

I can't stay here. It is not going to work. On a number of levels.

I know. What are you going to do?

This business unit is paid for until the end of the year, and the self-storage unit continues indefinitely as long as I want it. But I've now signed a contract on a small mobile home in the Sanctuary Caravan Park. The trouble is –

Are you all right with that, Phidias?

Perfectly. The trouble is I can't move in for a few days. It isn't ready yet. Meanwhile –

Do you still want me coming in?

Yes, of course, for the present. We have some ongoing business, not a great deal, I have to say. It may be in the fullness of time ... but there is one pressing need, I have an appointment with Kieran Watkins.

That's right, he's coming here tomorrow morning.

I will see him here then. He will want a full report on the case of his aunt. It will, of course, not be conclusive. Then it will be up to him whether he continues with our services or not.

He hasn't yet paid the deposit.

Has he not? I had better mention it.

After that –

We can transact all remaining business with our clients remotely. We shall continue to be in contact –

I can stay and run the office from here.

I don't know if that will be wise.

I'm not afraid of those two characters.

I don't want to put yourself or your child in danger. The twin pursuers are relentless.

Don't worry, I'm keeping George close. Or I can farm him out with Dave. Until we sort out his future schooling.

I understand completely. By the way –

Yes, Phidias?

While we're on the topic of the Watkins case, will you check out Sharon's, the next door neighbour's story? Check with the police, who should have contacted the airline and the hotel in Paris, as we discussed.

Yes, of course.

After my meeting with Mr Watkins I may need to make myself scarce for a short while, until I can move in to the caravan. Then we'll take it from there.

The interior of Dead Level Self Storage – the building being a windowless warehouse – offered no visual clues as to the state of the world outside. Subdued security lighting served no more than to illuminate the corridors sufficiently for practical purposes; and all corridors in this three-storey maze appeared identical, differentiated only by the room numbers stencilled on each metal door. A glance at the watch, however, was enough to glean the information that dusk would already have fallen on the environs of the Dead Level, that most of the day staff would have gone home by now, and that the business park outside would be as quiet as it was within the building.

Row upon row of books gleamed silently, packed into the Dexion metal shelving in Room 248. The library was no longer speaking. Perhaps it could no longer speak; it had done its job on earth. That contemplating the final abandonment of this comfort was even possible: that was a breakthrough.

It was a long time since the lift gate at the other end of the building, the one that had been jammed by a small boy and then unjammed with some difficulty, had last clanged shut, echoing through the premises; but if one were to listen intently for a while there were always minute creaks and bumps that would have passed unnoticed when the foreground noise was more prominent. And high above somewhere, a soft chittering, a susurrus, could just be discerned. It was only intermittent, and its return was always unpredictable.

After close listening, the explanation slowly became manifest. Earlier, sparrows had been observed from the outside entering and leaving the space below the eaves of the building. It would seem that some had built their nests there, and were now settling for the night. Which called to mind the account by Bede, in his history of the English people, of the advice from a chieftain to Edwin, King of Northumbria, comparing our all too brief popping into and out of existence to the flight of a sparrow, escaping out of the winter storms – the unknown – in through one door of the warm, brightly lit mead hall where the king sat at supper with his aldermen and thanes, only to exit immediately at another, vanishing out of sight once more, passing from unknown into unknown again.

The Dead Level Self Storage warehouse was no mead hall, but it too offered temporary refuge of a kind from pervading uncertainty and certain oblivion.

The chieftain was, of course, advocating adoption of the nostrums of Christianity as a bulwark against uncertainty and oblivion. However, for Lucretius the Epicurean, writing centuries earlier, these conditions, and in particular the notion of oblivion, had held no terrors. Oblivion attended us for eternities before our birth, and this did not trouble us, he argued, so why should we be any more troubled by the oblivion that will ensue once again upon the end of the brief fluttering of consciousness that we term life?

But the sparrows had now apparently ceased their activities. A very low and soft drumming, however, was just discernible. Coming from far above, it was evidence that the weather had deteriorated further; it had started raining again, the drizzle caressing the metal roof. It would be necessary to make a quick exit to avoid becoming soaked in the short passage between here and Unit 13, where a final night in the bunk beckoned.

.

11

From this point on, the Watkins case grew more and more troubling. Not because more evidence was coming to light – it was rather the reverse, as Lucy had remarked: even the slender evidence there was for the disappearance having itself been erased. But the elimination of even such fragile certainties as we had held cast a new shadow over that fateful occurrence of fifteen months previously.

It became obvious that the scheduled meeting with Kieran Watkins would be a difficult one. This was, in fact, the three-monthly catch-up, whereby we would review progress on his case, summarise the situation, decide on any future course of action. The drawback, of course, was that the case was not proceeding in a way Mr Watkins might have wanted. From certain standpoints, it might be seen to be not proceeding at all, or proceeding in a backward direction.

The veil had gathered further around the disappearance of Edith Watkins. The sole piece of evidence that she had made one last trip to the coast – the final one of her customary visits to the Deadmans Beach fishery and the Sanctuary Café – had been demolished, and in the absence of other eye-witness accounts there was nothing to show she had actually made such a trip at all. The testimony of her neighbour Sharon had indeed suggested that this intention was in her mind, but Sharon had also said forcefully that she had discouraged her from doing so, in view of her poor health and the high winds prevailing that day.

The mystery was compounded by Lucy's bizarre encounter with a memorial bench commemorating the old lady – an encounter that has not been repeated. And we had not been able to obtain any confirmation that anyone had commissioned such a memorial. Lucy's reliability as a witness could not be called into question, so such an anomalous occurrence could only add to the intractability of the case, and would otherwise need to be set aside.

So we were left with final, definite sightings of Edith Watkins on the morning of the 15th of March in or close to her home in Moorshurst – and nothing more.

This was the summary awaiting Kieran Watkins as his black 4x4 pulled up outside Unit 13. He was admitted by Lucy. He was affable, polite, dressed casually in a polo shirt and pressed jeans, his car keys still jangling in his hand as he entered the office. The difficulty of the meeting would be compounded by having to remind him he had not paid the agreed deposit and that furthermore another tranche of payment was now due. He agreed to Lucy's being present during the interview.

So, Phidias, you are confirming absolutely that that CCTV video did not show my aunt on the last day of her life?

That is correct. It was an old video, from a month previously. It had been incorrectly date-tagged.

Ah.

I'm sorry if this is disappointing, but that is a fact, I'm afraid.

Hmm.

How do you feel about that, Kieran? I hope this is not –

That explains it.

What do you mean?

I had a feeling – it doesn't matter –

You had a feeling about what? You had thought the video might not have been right?

I didn't mean that. I'm sorry, Phidias, as you can imagine, this has all been distressing for me. What led you to find out this video was not what it seemed?

Three things. First, the fifteenth of March had been windy, but there was no sign of wind on the clips we saw, indeed it seemed to be an exceptionally calm day. Secondly, as Lucy here astutely observed, your aunt appeared to be using the multicoloured walking stick that is still in its holder at home, her black walking stick being the one that is actually missing. But thirdly, and most conclusively, the date-stamp on the CCTV system at the Sanctuary Café is twenty-eight days out of synch, and we have established why that is. The event shown – your aunt arriving at and departing from the café – can therefore be definitively dated to the fifteenth of February previously.

Ah.

So, we have to be clear about this, Kieran –

Have you seen any video footage from the actual date in March, then?

Unfortunately, the video cassette it would be on is currently in the possession of the police, who took it away to digitise what they thought was the relevant passage. Lucy and I have been trying to retrieve it from them, but –

It doesn't matter.

We will try to obtain it, Kieran.

It doesn't matter, it won't show anything.

Well, that is actually what I surmise. In the complete absence of any corroborating eye-witness evidence, I am willing to bet there is nothing to show your aunt's presence at the café on the actual date. However, we will leave no stone unturned.

It's a waste of time.

Kieran, you are now implying that you had doubts about that video from the start. Why is that?

I don't know about doubts ... I had a feeling. It wasn't right. I'm sorry, that's all I can say.

Well, let's move on. Let's try to establish what we actually know about the final sightings of your aunt. We'll start with Sharon, the next door neighbour.

Yes.

You know her personally, of course.

Not well. I was on nodding acquaintance with her over a few years while visiting my aunt. Subsequently, after the ... event ... well, I got to know her a little better. She was very helpful to us.

So you have a good impression of her?

Oh, yes.

As you can appreciate, being one of the last people to see your aunt alive, she needed to be checked out. Lucy conducted an interview with her, and subsequently, at my request, checked out her alibi.

Her alibi?

Purely routine, naturally. Sharon said she had seen your aunt early in the morning before she herself departed for the airport for a three-day holiday in Paris with her boyfriend. She said your aunt had expressed an intention to go for one of her trips to Deadmans Beach, and that she had attempted to dissuade her. Lucy, can you update us on this?

Yes, of course, Phidias. Exactly as she said, she was in Paris for three days with her boyfriend. I confirmed that with DCI Green's team, who had contacted the hotel.

You see, the police do do their homework properly sometimes, Kieran. Sorry to interrupt, Lucy.

Also the flight – she and her companion had checked in and were on board. So she must have departed to meet her flight quite early that morning, the fifteenth. And I'd also contacted the owner of the corner shop opposite.

Just tell Kieran what he said.

Well, Mr Patel there remembers the occasion of Edith Watkins' disappearance quite well. And he is adamant she was in the shop that morning, he says around nine-thirty on the fifteenth, to buy her paper. He remembers particularly that she didn't look very well, confirming Sharon's assessment, incidentally, but she was definitely alive after Sharon had departed. And he had told the police that too. So he says.

Thanks, Lucy, very good work. Well done. So in actual fact, what we have established is that Sharon and Mr Patel now seem to have become established as the last persons to see her alive. Early to mid-morning on the fifteenth. So far as we know.

So far as we know?

So far as we know, Kieran. Can you tell us definitively when you last saw her?

Well, it would have been the week previously, I mean, when I called round for my usual routine visit.

To keep an eye on her?

Yes, and to have a cup of tea and a chat.

You did that regularly?

Recently I had been doing that, yes. I told you.

And you're sure about that?

Of course I am.

You definitely did not see her on the fifteenth or after?

No, I told you.

I recall you told me you and your wife wanted to have your aunt round for Sunday lunch, but she had not responded to your phone message, so you'd decided to drive over to Moorshurst on the eighteenth and drop in to see how she was.

Yes, that's what happened.

But the eighteenth was not a Sunday. It was, let me recall, a Thursday.

No, no, that's right, Sunday had passed.

I see. So it was just increasing concern that made you take the sudden decision to drive over?

Yes.

Sharon told Lucy that she had phoned you when she returned from France and found the milk bottles on the doorstep.

Did she?

She did, didn't she, Lucy?

That's right.

You don't recall that?

I can't remember. She may have done. Anyway, I met her when I was there. I've explained all this.

Quite so, Kieran. I just wanted to be absolutely clear what happened. Because you didn't mention this. Anyway, you're absolutely sure you had not seen your aunt since your last regular visit a week before her disappearance?

Over a week before. The Monday of the week before, I believe.

The Monday before the Sunday you were proposing to invite her over to your home in Deadhurst for lunch?

Yes.

Did you mention this proposed invitation when you saw her then?

I may have done. But I followed it up with a phone call, on the Saturday I think, because I knew she was apt to forget. But she didn't answer, and I had to leave a message, which she didn't return.

So Sunday came and went?

Yes, I'm afraid we let it go by. What of it, Phidias? We know she was still alive then.

You didn't think to drop in and see her the following day, Monday the fifteenth?

I'm beginning to be uncomfortable with this questioning. No, I didn't. There was a lot else on my mind. It hung over for a few days more.

You're sure about that?

Of course I'm sure. I did try ringing again, but there was no reply.

It's quite natural to feel guilt that you didn't act more quickly, I understand.

That's not it, I just –

So, Kieran, what else was on your mind?

I had business issues. There were some things to sort out with my company.

Your company is or was in trouble?

Phidias, I really resent this. My business affairs have nothing to do with this. I hired you in good faith –

I do apologise. Let's move on.

To be quite frank, you don't seem to be making any more progress with this than the police did. In fact, we seem to be going backwards.

That point has already been made. I am not sure it is valid, however. Showing evidence to be in error isn't going backwards.

Then you come up with strange stories about a memorial bench to my aunt which doesn't exist –

We have no explanation for that. But you do believe, do you not, that your aunt is no longer alive?

That seems obvious, doesn't it?

What do *you* think happened?

That's what I paid you to find out.

With respect, you haven't paid us yet, but that is a matter we will attend to shortly.

I'm sorry, I will sort that out.

Kieran, I have some ideas as to what might have happened, but I'd like to hear your point of view.

OK, well, we've established she was alive until mid-morning on the fifteenth of March at least. Everybody thought she went to Deadmans Beach, but you're now saying that's not the case. Maybe she intended to go. She got on the bus, but she never made it. Maybe she was confused, and got off before the bus even reached Deadmans Beach, wandered off into the marshes, got lost – well, you get the picture.

That is a very plausible theory.

Is it yours?

It's one I have entertained.

Phidias, I'm going to have to reconsider this. We're getting nowhere.

It's your decision. I am willing for us to continue until we reach a conclusion. But I understand your position, Kieran.

I wanted some ...

Closure?

That was it.

If it is achievable, about which there is some doubt, I am not sure you will find that that is what you really want.

What a strange thing to say. I'm sorry, but I will really have to reconsider.

As I said – it's your decision.

What did you make of that, Lucy?

He's not a happy bunny, is he?

One might say so. But aside from that – I am feeling troubled.

What's troubling you?

Everything's pointing in one direction. And it is not a direction one wants to go in.

Phidias, you've got me there. I don't have a sense of direction. I don't have any sense of direction at all. I mean, that's exactly what's upsetting me.

I understand completely. But if there is one thing more upsetting than an absence of direction it is the certainty of the closing down of all but one direction, and of its being towards a darker place.

Oh God, that sounds scary.

I'm sorry, I didn't mean to frighten you. There are some themes going through my head. The phrase "lost at sea" keeps resonating for some reason. I don't mean that she has been. The chief detail I recall includes staining on the kitchen as well as bathroom floor, the lock picked on that roll-top desk, what else, yes, the mysterious business of the walking stick that you picked up on. And the fact that more than one person has commented on her seeming unwell in the last weeks before she vanished.

What does all that add up to?

I am not sure, but I have some ideas.

Do you think she was the victim of an intruder?

I doubt it.

So where do we go from here?

Lucy, I need to share some topics with you, I need to recapitulate everything that has been going on in my head. It may be of advantage to do so.

Phidias.

Yes?

Are you going to be all right?

Yes, of course.

You said something about making yourself scarce.

For a couple of days.

I'll need to contact you.

I'll be on the end of a phone.

Just so you –

Until I can move into the caravan.

I'll keep the office open.

Good girl. Make sure your son is safe.

Of course. My husband is helping.

That's good to know.

What you said ... it's really bothered me. I found it really disturbing.

I know. I wish it were otherwise.

How are we going to –

I'll map out a strategy. Don't worry about it.

Is that it for now, then?

That's it. I'll see you, Lucy.

•

So Dave came round here, for this "what are we going to do about George?" meeting. George himself had been successfully packed off to bed. Dave seemed distracted. I made him a cup of coffee and showed him the report from All Saints Primary, which is an outrageous document. Absolutely outrageous.

Suspended from school after "a fight with another child", it says. No mention of this other child's (Nigel's) part in the matter. As far as we know, he is still attending school and hasn't been sanctioned.

Previous incidents of indiscipline and fighting. What incidents? No evidence about numbers or circumstances. Very vague here.

That stupid business about allegedly climbing the flagpole, which is not what he did, and I thought that had been sorted.

Apparently told another child, Rosie, very loudly in class that God did not exist, making her cry. I know that Rosie, a nasty, conniving little madam.

A total of fourteen days of unexplained absence from school this year. Nowhere near that many, and I always let the school know when he was off.

Dave agreed with all this. I mean, he was totally with me.

That's a rare experience I am grateful for. So are we going to challenge this? he said.

I said I didn't have the stomach for it. What did he suggest?

He was silent.

The easy option, I pointed out, is just to keep him off school for the rest of the term. Then he starts again in September.

And then what, said Dave. And I shrugged my shoulders at that. Then what?

It starts all over again.

That's right.

Maybe he would be better off at Deadmans Beach Junior School after all, I suggested.

Oh yeah, Luce, otherwise known as Chav Primary. Do us a favour.

I know, but –

You said over our dead bodies.

I know. I know.

There's so many kids there who are completely out to lunch. I mean, I'm sorry, but they are mental, some of them.

Well, yes. On the other hand, George might get on better with them.

Are you saying our son's a nutcase?

Not at all. Of course not, Dave. But he's been fingered as a Beacher. So he might as well be with the other Beachers.

That is a point of view. But.

But?

Lucy, you spent so much energy getting him into All Saints, and avoiding having to send him to Deadmans Beach Junior. So much energy. I have to hand it to you, you went the extra mile, the extra twenty-six miles, whatever, and we did it, thanks to you –

But he doesn't fit in there.

No.

We've got to face it.

What did George tell you?

He doesn't really want to go back to All Saints.

What does he want?

Dave, he's only seven. He doesn't know what he wants.

And so the conversation went on, returning again and again, deep into the evening, to the same intractable knot.

Finally, in an attempt to break this knot, I suggested: Would you like a glass of wine, Dave?

Like the old days? he said. I think he seemed surprised and pleased.

I said I had a nice bottle of Shiraz, just opened. I took down two glasses from the cupboard in the kitchen. We went into the living room. From then on, I think I began to relax. I had been so tense. It wasn't just the George business, but I couldn't get the Phidias business out of my head either. That's to say, not only what was going on with Phidias himself, but what he had confided to me about the Watkins case, and all that that implied. I didn't say anything about that to Dave, of course. It wasn't his concern, and it wouldn't have been right. But the peculiar predicament Phidias was in, his evasiveness and his evident distress, all of that, I had to unburden it to Dave, and he listened patiently. I mentioned what Phidias had told me – that he might have to "make himself scarce for a short while" until he could move into his caravan. And that I didn't know what he meant by that, and how disturbing I found it.

I told him all about the episode in Dead Level Self Storage. I hadn't dared broach it before – I mean, about my leaving George on his own in the Peralta Associates office, and what happened then – and he listened in intense silence. I described the two visitors, and how George had handled them. He was particularly taken by the way our son had trapped them in the service lift. I can't believe he did that, he kept saying. That's insane, he said more than once, nodding and beaming eagerly. But George is OK?

He's perfectly fine, I assured him.

He wanted to know about the two visitors – the twin pursuers, as Phidias had called them. Did I know who they were? This Borg – and –

McKinley.

They were soberly dressed, then, he enquired. Yes, I told him, they didn't look on the face of it like ruffians. I said that Phidias had told me one of them, Borg in fact, was a lawyer – maybe even a barrister, I couldn't remember exactly what Phidias had said. But a dangerous and unprincipled man too.

Not a contradiction in terms, observed Dave. But what's their beef with Phidias?

I replied that Phidias couldn't or wouldn't say. But I had the impression he had got into deep waters with them – financially, perhaps – and was in the kind of difficulties he couldn't extricate himself from.

But if this guy is a lawyer, and has some claim on Phidias, why doesn't he just pursue him in the courts? asked Dave. Why is he turning up with a thug to intimidate him?

I couldn't answer this. I could only surmise the obvious – that there were extra-legal aspects to this dispute – even that there was crime involved –

Dave interrupted me: So who is this guy, anyway?

Borg?

No, your boss, Phidias Peralta.

Well, you know, he's a private eye.

I know that, said Dave, but where does he come from?

I had to confess how little I knew about Phidias. Yes, of course, I'd asked him, but his answers had always been vague and general. He'd worked in London as a private investigator, I knew. He had had "associates" and an assistant to one of them had disappeared in mysterious circumstances. He didn't like to talk about this too much. He had had problems. He had considered retirement, but decided instead to leave London and to relocate his business down here. Yes, of course, I'd searched online. There hadn't been anything. Zilch.

Zilch, said Dave, really zilch? I can't believe that. These days.

And then Dave said, I thought maybe you had something going with him.

Something going?

Yeah, you know, a thing, he said.

With Phidias?

You seemed to be so wrapped up in his doings and – not that it bothers me –

I had to interrupt then. He gave me a job, I pointed out. And he's been really helpful and kind. I've learned a lot already. I've learned so much, even in this short time. And he's been kind to George too.

I just thought there was a thing, said Dave, I'm sorry.

I didn't know how to respond to this. There is no "thing", I emphasised. I told him the idea was absurd.

That's all right then, he said. We'll leave aside the enigma that is Phidias Peralta.

Except that I'm worried about him, I explained. He seemed like a man on the run, is what I was trying to say. But what he was running from, and where he was running to, well, those were not such easy questions to answer.

There was a sudden silence. The wine bottle had been drained. Dave looked at his watch.

It's getting late, he said, I really ought to be going.

I was concerned about his driving. He tried to shrug that off, saying half a bottle of wine was nothing. He stood up – he looked lost, though.

Do you want to stay the night? I finally asked.

He put his hand on my shoulder and looked searchingly into my eyes. Would that be OK?

I said it would. He looked overcome with emotion.

Yeah, all right, he said. I'll sleep on the sofa.

You don't have to, I said.

So that's what happened, that's what he did, he stayed the night with me, and George was surprised and insanely happy to find him there in the morning, and enlisted his help in feeding the fish, and I had to do a lot of work afterwards when Dave had gone to impress upon the young man that this was not a precedent, this did not necessarily mean anything.

•

Is this it, then?

This is it.

Something terrible happened. A cascade of consciousness, a disorder of consciousness.

They were visible everywhere now, the memories, rising out of their sediments, radiating outside the electromagnetic spectrum, but their description could not be notated...

... a couple of scarecrows. But the light was very poor.

(unreadable)

They were visible everywhere now, the twin pursuers, even when they were not physically present. For they were not.

Not, assuredly, at this time. Nor had they been heard from, not since the boy had briefly trapped them, at any rate. Yet their images were imprinted on the retina, in vivid monochrome, silver and black, the principal hue of dreams. The head said they were gone, but the heart beheld them still.

The night-long disc jockey had continued to play the soothing sound he called jazz. Very occasionally, it actually was. And this is Miles Davis, he said. Flamingo Sketches. *Flamingo*? And rain pattered against the window. It all seemed to have taken place a long time ago.

This had been the final night.

A strategy would now have to be mapped out. Semblances would have to be teased out into actualities. All possibilities were, had been present, but the time had come for the wave function to collapse, for the smeared-out cloud of probabilities to gain focus. And from then on only one way was indicated, and that was the path that needed to be followed, the alternative multitudinous paths that snaked elsewhere into and between other possibilities being abandoned, and then forgotten for all time.

The tranquility of the Dead Level Business Park passed all understanding. Clouds drifted above it. Vans were parked. The day was wearing on. It was perfect, but like a dream that can only imperfectly be recalled. From nowhere, a stray plastic bag, resembling a small animal, caught whatever breeze there was, filled and fluttered. Then slid across and collapsed at the kerb. An empty beer can had been dropped some time ago in the middle of the road, at the entrance way, and shone there, occasionally catching the same breeze and rolling slightly hither and thither on the tarmac. A silver car turned into the entrance, its tyres just missing it but causing air movement, whereupon the can rolled a little more. The tinkling sound it made as it did so was just audible. The car moved towards its parking place, out of sight. There was silence for a period of maybe five to ten minutes. At the end of this time, a driver in overalls emerged from the doorway of one of the business units to the left, walked purposefully over to his parked van, got in. The sound of the engine revving up swelled into the air. Presently, the van, a dirty white in colour, moved slowly towards the entrance. Its front offside tyre clipped the beer can, which lay now partly flattened near the middle of the entry road as the van disappeared in the direction of the Barbican Gate. A sparrow descended with the intention of pecking at some small object in the gutter, but soon flew off again. The partly flattened beer can was no longer moving in the breeze. The low hum of another approaching vehicle could now be heard, and presently it was visible, a dark saloon car that paused briefly on the road outside before turning left into the entranceway. Both its offside tyres caught the beer can full on, and when it passed it could be seen that the can was now completely flattened: an apparently two-dimensional oblong of wrinkled, inert, silvery metal stuck to the tarmac. The dark saloon car disappeared from view.

Two or three more minutes passed without any notable occurrences taking place.

Then two dark figures emerged from around the corner. They were apparently engrossed in conversation.

It was time to go.

The small velvet bag containing two dice was extracted from a left-hand pocket. The dice were rolled on the low brick wall next to the bus stop.

The dice showed eight (three and five).

Therefore stop number eight would be the destination.

The bus arrived, about five minutes later than timetabled.

According to the map, stop number eight on the road to Moorshurst served the village of Hole, and this was indeed the name showing on the bus stop indicator as the bus pulled up.

But no such village, nor in fact habitation of any kind, was visible on alighting.

The intermittent sound of the traffic on the main road soon faded into the distance. A broken path was indicated, and was followed. There was a pond, a duck, a coot. There were dandelions. There was endless sky encircling. Mounds of bare earth were visible, in shades of maroon, brown, rouge; then, a kissing gate having been traversed, a broken hedge marked the first path. A half-dilapidated notice forbade caravanning or camping. Trees thinned out. In addition to the dandelions, here, gorse was present in clumps. But it was clear that the village was missing. There was a hole where Hole should have been.

Further on along this entangled path, the road having now been completely left behind, the first marker was characterised by rusted steel and perished rubber: the abandoned remains of a bicycle, part interred in mud, part overrun by vegetation. It appeared to have been an old-fashioned gentleman's three-speed bike, in so far as it was possible to tell.

The second was another noticeboard, fallen this time, embedded horizontally in the wild grass, its post having been sheared off. It had been considerably weathered, but the message, though half submerged, was still legible:

FUN DOG SHOW

&

PLOUGHING MATCH

The lettering was much faded, and the date advertised was approximately seven years previously.

Now it was possible to discern the remains of habitation: for example, a rectangular patch of bumpy and weed-infested concrete bounded by the base of a perimeter wall, a ground-plan in situ; further off, the remains of brickwork, rendered uneven by weather; a strand or two of barbed wire, at one point interrupted by a pale suspended object, which on closer examination turned out to be a single latex glove. In a hollow, meanwhile, nestled the crumpled ghost of a plastic water bottle.

The vista beyond was of fields, with little in the way of distinguishing features. It may be that paths and ditches were etched into them, but they were not directly visible from the present vantage point. There were what appeared to be water meadows, there was young wheat, but a long way off. No livestock were visible.

Early afternoon, but the light was heavy.

Attached to two strands of barbed wire was a third notice:

A WARNING FOR VISITORS
These hazards are present in this area:
• beware underwater obstacles
• caution: uneven surfaces
• caution: slippery surface
• danger: sudden drop

And sure enough, the footing immediately gave way at this point, and the danger warned of in the final bullet point was palpably demonstrated. Here, a hidden waterway, clearly one of the side-branches of the Old Canal, was made manifest. Its trajectory was suddenly obvious, although it had hitherto been hidden from view. A muddy path tracked it, and it was necessary to follow this. The ditch, swollen with apparently stagnant water of a brown-green hue, was, it could now be observed, fringed thickly if unevenly with reeds. The reeds were beginning to wither and flatten.

Following this would lead one into the heart of what had been indicated on the map as a disused defence training zone. To confirm orientation, a compass would have been handy. In its absence, the familiar line of wind turbines – always on the eastern horizon, always apparently at the same distance – would have served as a marker. But the wind turbines seemed, unaccountably, to have vanished. It may have been that they were obscured by the bank on the opposite side of the ditch. Easy to check, it might have been thought. A plank bridge was observed a little way further on, and this was negotiated, with difficulty and care, for it was slippery. Upon gaining the opposite side, it was then necessary to climb the bank, and again care needed to be taken when trying to gain footholds in the muddy soil. At last, the top of the bank was reached. But the horizon beyond showed only as undulating slopes beneath a grey sky, and provided no view of any wind turbines.

Instead, in the foreground, another sign was revealed: a weather-battered hoarding stood clear of the skyline on its rotten wooden framework. Its terrible familiarity was inexplicable. The same sans-serif lettering, in the same faded tan colouring, shadowed to the bottom and left in a slightly deeper colour, against a creamy background. But surely we were in an entirely different location? Nevertheless, there it was. In block capitals, it said:

DÉJÀ VU

12

Now the weather began to deteriorate more than somewhat, the breeze strengthening in sudden gusts, damp and chill. Location was increasingly indeterminate. We were in open country. Not even the pretence of a hedge here.

The grass at this point was increasingly coarse and tussocky. There was a quick shadow. A hawk of some species had quit the scene: a raptor, anyway. Or a rapier. That was its appearance. It had the appearance of a weapon that snatched and lunged, and then was no more. Was it possibly the marsh harrier (*Circus aeruginosus*)? But no, it would have returned and patrolled the area, as that species does.

It was increasingly hard to determine where the path led; it seemed to multiply and offer various possibilities. But if one was selected, it then led to a dead end, that is to say, a quagmire or an impassable object, and on returning to the branching point it appeared that the options had now changed. There was no longer a path, or it took a different direction. That, at any rate, was the impression given.

One technique might have been to maintain a running commentary, noting verbally the characteristics visible at each position. But here, in the oceanic tumble of the marshland, words were again beginning to lose their shape; there was no metric by which to judge them. The body chamber resounded with meaningless sounds.

The barbed wire offered a guideline of sorts. It was incomplete; it had been breached or trampled down at many points, but it would appear to delineate the extent of the abandoned army training zone. So that on one side of this marker could sometimes be discerned underfoot the remains of concrete or tarmac pathways and access routes now overwhelmed by undergrowth; and sometimes there was a ramp, or the ruin of a concrete structure, a container perhaps for refuse bins, or a small outhouse. Attention was diverted for a while by the rusting hulk of a vehicle resting in a depression – clearly the carapace of a tractor that had been abandoned many years previously, and which had no further hope of being retrieved, now that access to it had been made impossible by encroaching vegetation. After this, few further markers of what we are pleased to term civilisation were evident; the final one being a notice in red capitals on a white ground, again affixed to the barbed wire, proclaiming

DANGER

but the nature of the danger was not specified in any way; perhaps the part of the notice, or a second notice, giving details, was now missing.

And beyond this, even the undergrowth failed, except for patches of gorse which now increasingly interrupted a vista coming into view, a vast ground composed principally of shingle.

On our earlier trip, a field of closely packed daisies resembling a shingle beach had been observed. But daisies would have shrivelled and died some time ago. In fact, this apparent meadow was composed of real shingle that spread seemingly endlessly to the southern horizon, an inland beach left behind by a sea that had retreated millennia ago; the fossil of a shore inhabited solely by herring gulls which sat on it in groups at various points, or came and went as they pleased – but there were not many even of them. At least, this offered dryer conditions underfoot, and there seemed to be one trodden path across it. So this was followed.

This location was permeated by a hissing sound, uncannily like that of waves; but this was impossible, as we were a considerable distance from the sea. Aside from this could be heard the regular crunch of footsteps, and the contrapuntal rhythmic sound created by breathing. Occasionally, the gulls called, and the noise of this echoed from horizon to horizon. The enormous sky forebode. Predominantly grey in various streaked shades, it alternately darkened and lightened as the cumulonimbus clouds thickened or dispersed slowly, driven by the prevailing wind. There was just a hint of steady light in the location where the sun might be supposed to be descending, and this alone gave what sense of orientation might be possible. The pebbles comprising this shingle expanse were extremely various in coloration, size and shape, ranging from white through ochre shades to slate-grey and black, and fragments of shell were at intervals interposed. Then an occasional object caught the interest: a small, pale and possibly almost intact skeleton lying in a hollow, for instance, but of what creature it was impossible to tell. Was it fish or fowl? The skeleton of a vertebrate, at any rate, it seemed at first, yet closer inspection gave more equivocal results. Perhaps the remains of this creature had been invaded and part consumed by other organisms of other phyla as they rotted, and these too had perished and left their own remains entangled within the first, resulting in a grotesque and impenetrable jumble.

After what seemed a very long time the far limit of this island of shingle was reached, and the marshland here resumed, now without any visible trace of human habitation or action.

And there was no question of even an equivocal path. All directions were simultaneously offered, without any indication as to which might be preferable. The sky was an overall grey. Vegetation had returned but was nowhere of any great height. Grasses mingled with shrubs at random, whispering softly in an undulating terrain whose contours showed little variation of pattern. That is to say, the terrain sank and rose, sank and rose, but gave no sense of any overarching structure. Feet were sodden, breath was coming short. Somewhere, a string quartet was playing; but of course that was absurd. The sky was cavernous. The earth was soaked. Water was present everywhere, and drowning was an option. There was buzzing. Somewhere, thoughts were coming to an end. Geometry was being redefined in a continual process. A bird of an unknown species flew overhead and disappeared into the gulf of the distance. But it was hard to distinguish distance from interior, for all mental geography was affected at this point, and all viewpoints were indistinguishable. Perspective started to break down, as vanishing points multiplied. And now the earth and the sky were beginning to change places. It was increasingly necessary to hold to the principle that rule and method were of greater importance than knowledge of facts, and that this would see us through.

But that cathedral vault formerly identified as the sky: it was slowly exploding. For the clouds were parting to the west, and the rays of the setting sun were coming through in a golden haze that had no definite shape to it. As though through stained glass. That was the illusion. But it gave some orientation at least. Shadows were then thrust across the world. And they lengthened imperceptibly.

Walking continued.

And the light fell upon the middle distance and revealed something: a structure. In all that huge vacancy and indeterminacy it was identifiably a human structure. The only one.

It was hard to make out at first, situated as it was in the midst of difficult terrain: boggy in parts, dominated by mud that was flat and shining with a silvery hue in the declining light. Patches of mud around the structure were etched by the countless imprints of birds' feet and interrupted by clumps of reedy plants. It was difficult to tell whether there was a safe way through. Nearer to the object, darker strands indicated, possibly, vegetation rooted in firmer ground. An approach route could therefore be contemplated with care.

The structure had the initial appearance of a sarcophagus. Why such a concept should spring to mind was difficult to say. It was cradled by a raised bed nestling between the mudflats. But there was indeed a way through.

The approach necessitated a change of angle, and it soon became apparent that the structure was in fact a boat. A traditional clinker-built boat of perhaps six or seven metres in length. Or, to be more accurate, the wreck of one. It was a hull, essentially, marooned miles from any present sea, stripped of all traces of paint, having arrived at the same colour as the surrounding mud that embedded it not quite to the waterline; its prow upstanding but all traces of mast or superstructure long vanished, listing slightly to starboard. And it clearly had been there, in its present position, for many years.

But there was someone on board.

No, this was not possible, it was an illusion. A figure of the imagination, which had been overtaxed in this wilderness. The vessel had long been abandoned.

There was movement.

The approach continued.

Hello! Is anybody there?

Now there surely could be no doubt. There was a small, dark figure crouched in the centre of the hull. Or was there? It seemed to come and go.

Hello! Is anybody there?

There was no reply.

It had a definite shape. Could it be distinguished as a human shape? In a maroon coat, wearing a dark hat?

Hello?

We had approached the gunwales of the vessel without mishap. The figure in profile seated amidships was staring in front of it, that is to say to the right, in the direction of the prow and of the blurred light that was the setting sun.

So the figure was looking westward.

It was not completely possible to say whether the boat was boarded at this point. It was not completely possible to say whether the human figure that appeared to inhabit it reacted to the boarding party or not. It was not completely possible to say she was an elderly woman in a dark red coat and a black hat, clutching a dark bag and a black walking stick. That her face was pinched and pale.

It was not, by this time, completely possible to assert anything in particular.

She turned, and said, in a clear voice, a first glimmer of recognition appearing in her faraway face: Good evening.

There was a pause that seemed to lapse into eternity.

Are you Edith Watkins?

I … think so. Who am I speaking to?

My name is Phidias Peralta. I'm a private investigator.

I'm very pleased to meet you.

And I'm delighted to have found you.

(Another lapse.)

I'm sorry, what did you say your name was?

Phidias. Phidias Peralta. May I call you Edith?

You can call me anything you like. And you're a –

Private investigator.

And are you investigating something now?

I have been investigating your disappearance.

Oh. Did I disappear?

Apparently you did.

Oh dear, I don't think I remember that. That's awful. But my memory is getting very bad, you know.

You disappeared on the fifteenth of March last year.

And what's the date today?

We're now into September, over a year on.

Well, now, if I had disappeared, I'm sure I would have remembered that at least.

Something happened on that date last year, Edith. Do you remember what that was?

I don't think so, dear.

Never mind. Would you like to go home, Edith?

I'm surprised you know my name. I must confess I don't recognise you at all, but there you are, my memory's not what it was, Mr, er –

Peralta. Phidias Peralta.

That's a beautiful name. But anyway, you must think me very inhospitable.

Not at all.

I'd offer to make you a cup of tea, but I rather suspect we have no milk.

Don't worry about that, Edith. Actually, coffee is my tipple, but I fear there isn't a decent cup of Americano to be had nearby.

In fact, there's not much of anything here.

Do you know where you are?

Not really. And you're a –?

A private detective.

You're not with the police?

No.

So you're all by yourself?

I have an assistant at present.

And who is he?

It's a she. Her name is Lucy White.

That is a lovely name. She's not here with you, by any chance?

No, she's not, she's back in the office. Edith, what is this place? Do you know what this place is?

Well, I thought I was at home. Now I'm not so sure.

And home is 104 Meeting Place Avenue, Moorshurst?

No ... no ... I live in Needless.

That's the village where you were born, isn't it?

That's right, dear. There are two villages called Needless, there's Needless Within and Needless Without. We live in Needless Without.

When you say "we", you mean your family?

Yes, my mother and father and my brother and I. Where are we now?

We could be anywhere, Edith. We could be there.

Oh dear, I think I'm getting a little confused. Who are we?

That's a very good question. But we shall get to that in a minute. How about starting by describing your home in Needless Without to me?

Oh, it's only a little cottage. But there's a lot of land attached. By the way, can I make you a cup of tea, dear?

I'm all right, Edith.

Oh, wait a minute. No milk.

That's OK. Don't worry.

Silly me.

Your father was a market gardener?

That's right, he still is. Shall we go out into the garden?

Yes, Edith, why don't we? What can we see there?

In the garden?

Yes, what can we see around us?

Oh, my goodness. Here's the vegetable garden. You can see the runner bean frames here. And those are the cold frames over there, and on the right is the compost heap, it's like a mountain. But it's all …

Is it all as it was?

No, it's so overgrown now …

Don't distress yourself, Edith.

I can't bear to see it like this. My father was always so meticulous in his way of working. Oh, I can hear the chickens. Can you hear them?

Where are they?

Over there. You see the old galvanised iron shed? Right next to that, there are the chicken coops. The fence goes a long way down into the ground. I mean, my father had to plant the posts and the wire mesh a long way down. He said that was because of the foxes. My brother and I used to go in there to collect the eggs. That was such fun. And look, the old sundial is still there on the wall. My father used to joke about winding it up. It was the same joke every time. Of course, the stables are next door. You can hear the horses snorting, listen. But my goodness, it's all … and then, along there are the rabbit hutches. Can you see them? Rows and rows of them. We had pet rabbits, my brother and I, but my mother said they had to be separate from the other rabbits. Because if you give rabbits names you'll never be able to slaughter them. Oh dear … look at the state of it all …

It was a long time ago, I suppose.

Such a long time ago. It's so overgrown. There are dandelions and nettles everywhere. And the hollyhocks have all run wild. And look, there's no glass in the greenhouse now, and you can't see the path any more. It's a jungle. My father would have hated to see it like that.

Did you have a happy childhood, Edith?

Oh, yes. We used to play in the woods with the other children. I went to the village school, and I loved that. Then, as I grew up, I wasn't so happy any more.

Why was that?

I was searching for something. But I didn't know what it was.

Did you find it?

I didn't know what I was looking for until I met Derek's family.

Derek was your – your childhood sweetheart –

Oh yes, he was the love of my life, I suppose. His family were so different. They lived in the other Needless, Needless Within. They had a big house. And it was full of books!

Books?

Books and books. In tall bookcases. And all the way up the stairs. I loved their smell. I'd pick one out and pretty soon I'd get absorbed in it, but nobody minded. Derek would be reading another one. Then we'd talk about it, about the books we'd read. Derek's father was a teacher, I was a little afraid of him at first, with his glittering glasses and his shock of hair. But he was really rather funny when you got to know him, when he got to like you, which he did. He could be hilarious, quite unexpectedly. The only thing is, I'd be afraid I'd wet myself laughing. I'd be afraid I'd let myself down. And Derek's mother would play the piano. She played rather well, you know. Beethoven and Brahms and all that. I'd never heard any of that music before. And she said I was a clever girl. I'll always remember that. She said, Edith, you're such a clever girl. You should go to college. But my father wouldn't hear of that.

He didn't allow it?

He ruled the roost. So until I was twenty-one I was stuck.

And Derek?

Oh, I was in love with him, and he with me. We planned to get married, just as soon as we could. But then the war came, and he was called up. Oh, I don't want to talk about this any more, it might upset me. Where are they all now?

Indeed.

Sometimes I wonder if they ever existed. That's a horrid thought.

It is not a thought to dwell on.

Do we exist?

Ah, now, that is the question.

Derek and I used to argue about it. What if we were fictional characters, he'd say.

Interesting that you should mention that, Edith. Do you know Giles?

Giles? I can't say that I do.

He's one of the fishermen at Deadmans Beach, or rather, an ex-fisherman, because he's retired now.

Do you know them? I love talking to the fishermen!

Anyway, Giles ... he has long, snowy-white hair –

Yes, I know. Is he the one that wears make-up?

Yes.

I know who you're talking about. I don't know him very well.

He is a very religious man. He talks about God as the author of all things. And according to him, it is God's job to believe in us.

Oh, how splendid!

If the author believes in us, then we exist.

But if not?

Then we vanish, I suppose. But how, in that case, would anything exist?

That's so very interesting. Oh, you have to meet Derek. You would find him such fun.

Does anything exist? And why does it exist? That question used to exercise me, above all else, as a child, and I failed to understand why it didn't seem to exercise anybody else.

I was the same, dear. Just the same.

I didn't realise at the time, of course, that I was merely rediscovering Leibniz's question. Why is there something rather than nothing? I would lie awake in bed – this is the only back-story I am going to permit – in the flat above Main Street, and there were rainbow colours playing through the window shutters onto the ceiling, bars of colour, red, orange, yellow, violet. They originated from the neon signage on the ice-cream parlour, Tony's ice-cream parlour, in the street below opposite. There was a murmur of night conversations faintly wafting up from the street. And I could also hear the music from the ice-cream parlour's jukebox, endlessly repeating hits by Del Shannon or the Everly Brothers with their twanging guitars and melancholy vocal harmonies –

Oh, I remember those hits!

– which sounded exceptionally mournful, almost like keening, or like yearning for some lost world – but I would be lying there awake, worrying why all this existed, worrying that it might not, that the world, and myself in it, might be a figment of the imagination. But whose imagination? And worrying why nobody else seemed at all bothered by the question. And it was only much later that I read philosophy, and the answers to the question of why anything exists, if there were any answers, seemed to come down to either God or statistics, and since I'd by then rejected God it came down to statistics, that is to say, *something* is far more probable than nothing. Well, that is one approach.

Do you know, dear, I stopped believing in God when I was a teenager. It was after all those discussions with Derek and his family in their house in Needless Within. I didn't dare tell my own family, though.

Still, Giles has evidently come to a conclusion that works for him. We exist because an author-god has invented us and believes in us. But when you look at the world around us, in which we figure as characters, what a mediocre author-god this must be. A world-building deity, capriciously arranging things in patterns, allowing mistakes and anomalies to occur through neglect or carelessness –

Oh, you do have the gift of the gab, Mr, er –

Peralta. But you can call me Phidias.

Phidias. That's an unusual name. But rather lovely. Is it Greek? I shall remember that. Phidias.

I'm sorry to go on, Edith, I didn't mean to.

You must be Greek. After all, you said you are a philosopher!

I am more of a failed poet.

Come now, you are being very modest.

Not falsely so. We aim high, but we fall short. Anyway, there shall be no more of my back-story. It is of little relevance. Let us return to you. Edith, do your remember when you moved into Meeting Place Avenue?

That's right, I did, didn't I? After my brother died. I moved to Moorshurst. Of course I did. It's all coming back.

It was your nephew, your brother's son, who helped you move, was it not?

I'm trying to remember why that happened.

You were living in London.

Was I? Yes, I suppose I was. I was working there.

And maybe it was because your nephew's family was the only family you had left, so you wanted to be nearer to them?

I can't think why.

Anyway, did he –

I'm sorry, what did you ask me, dear?

About your nephew.

Oh, Kieran. Of course.

Did you get on with him?

He was very kind to me.

But did you get on with him?

To be quite frank, if I may be quite frank. To be quite frank ... I never did much care for him. I'm sorry, that's an awful thing to say about your own kith and kin. My brother's own son.

You can be frank with me.

I used to pity his wife, what was her name?

Anna, I believe.

Anna, that's right, of course. I used to pity her having to put up with him.

Why so?

Well, he's such a bully. Always wanting his own way. I couldn't stand that. Maybe that's why I never married. Well, Derek was different, but he.... But you know, I shouldn't be so mean. He could be very nice to me when he wanted.

Kieran?

That's right, my nephew. Kieran is his name.

How was that?

I beg your pardon?

In what way was he nice to you?

Well, he started visiting me every week, I think. He would make me tea. I always used to make *him* a cup of tea before, on the rare occasions when he visited, but then things changed, he came more often, he wouldn't let me make the tea, he insisted on doing it himself. Aunt Edith, would you like a cuppa? Aunt Edith, would you like this, would you like that? To the point where I started thinking, what does he want from me? I know that sounds awful.

So his behaviour had changed?

I beg your pardon?

He had never done this before, visited you weekly and made you tea?

Oh, goodness, no, he never used to take much notice of me, and I confess I never took much notice of him. In fact, we used to be at loggerheads quite a bit. Perhaps that was my fault. I liked his son, Robin's his name, you know, a lovely little lad. My great-nephew. Very bright. Doesn't take after his dad much. But yes, Kieran started paying a lot of attention to me.

Perhaps he was beginning to be concerned about your state of health –

Well, there's nothing in the least wrong with my health –

– and whether you were managing on your own all right.

Oh yes, he wanted to put me in a home.

He told us he had suggested your moving to sheltered accommodation. But you didn't like that idea.

No, I did not. Not one bit.

I understand.

Do you know, I don't think he was really concerned about me. The thing he most worries about is his own respectability. That, and making money. He is such a strait-laced man, my nephew. He likes to be seen to do the right thing in the eyes of the world. But maybe there's more to it than that.

And do you remember the last time you saw him?

No, I can't say that I do.

You don't recall what happened in March last year?

Not really.

You say you were in good health?

I think … I wasn't feeling quite the ticket, but –

You used to go for a walk regularly, along the seafront?

That's right, I did.

Do you remember the last time you did that?

Oh … it was ever such a long time ago.

And you took the bus?

Yes, the bus, that's right. I have a bus pass. Because I'm quite an old lady now, you know.

Do you remember the last time you took the bus?

I'm trying. But you know, my memory's not what it was.

Memory is, in the end, all we have. Without memory, there is nothing – so far as human beings are concerned. The narrative is all that exists for us, so far as it remains in place, but once it is lost, the events it narrates pass into the oblivion that is *what was* – and *what will be* is then lost to us as well.

The marshland was designated as a wilderness. That is to say, humans were not the dominant species here. Invertebrates proliferated, living between the herbaceous plants and tall grasses that were found throughout the region, in the ponds and reed beds, in feral ditches that multiplied and divided uncountably and seemingly without end. There was no past or future here. There was only the eternal conflict between sufficiency and insufficiency. Unknown objects were seen. They represented latent possibilities. Animals that had once bred in captivity had escaped and mutated over many generations, making their economies wherever they would. They were no longer recognisable. Food was somehow sourced, wherever it could be. Voles plopped, the kingfisher showed his metal. His blue metal. A melismatic cry might be heard, uttered by an unknown creature, then all would fall silent again, save for the hissing of the reeds, through which the scent of loaded water vapour could be detected. Loaded, that is, with certain chemicals; for, while humans were not present, their signature could be detected from a considerable distance.

An elderly woman with white hair moved from her living room into the hallway after the front doorbell rang. She moved slowly. Through the pebbled glass panel in the front door she could see a dark human shape waiting. She reached the door and opened it.

What happened before that? What happened before the narrative began? It was not completely possible to say. Before the narrative began there was no narrative. There may have been occurrences. We can speculate about them but we cannot say with any degree of certainty. Then the narrative began. It consisted in the specific language acts used to describe it, and in a sense it *was* those language acts, encoding memories. The observer always interferes, indeed shapes what happens, simply by virtue of observing.

In another version of the story, the elderly woman dies peacefully in her bed, surrounded by her grieving family. They fund a memorial bench on the seashore, where she loved to walk, in her memory. In yet another version ... but enough.

And after the narrative ended? After the narrative – which is the coherence lent to events by the functions of observation and memory? By the function of language? What happened next? After the narrative ended there was no more narrative. So it stopped making sense. Many things could be said, and they were said, they had been said. But after the final page was turned there was no more to say.

•

I'm doing my nut because I have no idea where Phidias is and what has happened to him.

He's been gone for three days.

The last thing he said to me was to reiterate that thing about needing to make himself scarce. And he added, just for a couple of days. Until he could move into that caravan he's rented, here in Deadmans Beach. But he said he would be on the end of a phone, and so far I've sent several texts and left several voicemail messages and have had no reply. I also phoned the caravan park, but the person I spoke to said she had not seen Mr Peralta since he signed the contract three or four days ago. She confirmed the caravan was now ready to move into any time, and the keys were waiting. I had a cold feeling about it. This is not like him.

That is why I finally decided to report his disappearance to the police.

I phoned Moorshurst police station and asked to speak to Detective Chief Inspector Green. Instead, I got some junior officer who apologised that DCI Green was not available, asked me a load of questions and tried to fob me off, saying there was probably a simple explanation, he would probably turn up soon, not to worry. I insisted that this was serious, and he finally said they would send an officer round to the Peralta Associates office at Unit 13, Dead Level Business Park, but to be patient, they were very busy, and so on.

I checked with both Trevor and Gordon, but neither had seen any sign of Phidias. Gordon added that he often used to see the light on in the unit late at night, indicating that Phidias was in, but that it had been dark for the past few days, as far as he could recall. He'd assumed Phidias had at last found a place to live.

Eventually, someone turned up. A young, uniformed policeman with a flushed face and pale blue eyes who revealed spiky hair when he removed his headgear as he sat down in the office. He quietened the radio that chattered at his breast and took a notebook and pen out of one of his voluminous pockets.

Painstakingly, he asked me exactly the same questions I had already been asked on the phone, and laboured to write down each of my answers. He was really a very nice boy.

I told him Phidias's name and my relationship to him (employee). I said I didn't know of any close family or other close acquaintances. I described the recent events, including the visit from those two strangers (he asked me to describe them), and the fact that Phidias had recently found a place to live which was ready to move into but had not turned up there. I explained the business we were in. I mentioned DCI Green of course, no reaction from him. I tried to recall the exact time I'd taken my leave of Phidias three days ago, and what had been said then.

The policeman frowned at his notebook as he completed an entry, then looked up again at me.

Has he left a note? he asked, staring at me meaningfully.

A note?

Yes, he said, anything that might be construed (and he apologised clumsily for this), might be construed as a suicide note, for example.

Suicide? No, nothing like that. The thought appalled me.

The policeman reflected for a bit. Then he spoke again. He wanted a recent photograph of Phidias. I should have known he'd want this, it was obvious, yet I hadn't given it any thought. I had to say there were none that I knew of, but I would go through his things.

Can you give me a description? he asked.

I tried to collect my thoughts. But nothing came out. Patiently, he said again:

Can you describe him, madam?

By this time, I was really floundering. Why, I don't know. Phidias had praised my powers of observation. But my mind went blank. I started to splutter. Feebly, I made an effort, but to no avail. A few words came out:

Well, he's ... he's indescribable.

And then, an hour after the policeman had departed, suddenly Phidias's email dropped into my inbox with that bright, familiar "ping".

I stared at the heading in initial amazement, then, just for a moment, enormous relief. And then I looked at the date it had been sent, and my relief crumpled like a deflating balloon, and the apprehension, the cold fear you could even say, began to return. Because the date and time was over three days ago, in fact barely a couple of hours after my last face-to-face conversation with Phidias. For some inexplicable reason, the message had taken all that time to reach me.

The header was "Where we are now and what you could do". Which was strange. Frantically, I opened the message. This is what it said:

Dear Lucy,

I apologise for what must have seemed my strange behaviour over recent days. The truth is that I have been reliving past traumas, which have nothing whatsoever to do with you, so I am truly sorry if I have troubled you unnecessarily.

As I said, I will need to remove myself for a day or two until I am satisfied that the coast is clear and there is a safe space for me to return to. I also feel the need to distance myself in order to deflect attention and any possible danger to you, but I hasten to assure you that this is in any case only a remote possibility. I should say that in the past few months I have developed an enormous respect and affection for you and your remarkable young son, and I would always wish to see you thrive.

So please don't worry yourself unduly on your own behalf. As for me, you may see me soon, or you may not. In the latter event, some things will need to be put in place, whether we like it or not, so I will try both to make myself absolutely clear and also to suggest courses of action that would cause the least nuisance.

The rent on the office at Unit 13, Dead Level Business Park, is of course paid for up to the end of the year, so it can be kept going as an address of convenience for the present. If I have not returned by the end of the year, the lease should be terminated, all furniture disposed of and all valuables stored together with the books in Room 248 in Dead Level Self Storage, where they can be left for another year, in the absence of any further instructions for now. If there are no further instructions, the library can then safely be discarded in whatever way seems most convenient.

If by chance I do not return to occupy the mobile home at the Sanctuary Caravan Park, the agreement I signed will eventually lapse, and so that should not concern us further.

Regarding the business, please keep things ticking over

until the end of the year, but obviously do not take on any new cases. As you know, business has not exactly been plentiful, and there is some doubt in any case whether the operation would in fact be viable in the long term. In the absence of any further instructions from me, it can therefore be wound up at that point. The few remaining cases, with one exception, are drawing to their conclusions and I am confident you can deal with these very adequately.

The exception is, of course, the Watkins case. Again, I expect this to conclude, in that I fear Mr Watkins is disinclined to continue the investigation, and in that event it would be normal to send a final bill (by the way, has he paid anything yet? I forgot to check with you), tie up the loose ends and file the case as closed. However, there are, as you know, very troubling aspects to this one, and I am really sorry if my continued absence were to cause you problems that might potentially be overwhelming. So I am in a quandary as to what to tell you to do in the event that I do not return, or do not return within a reasonable time.

I can only make some suggestions, but must stress that you do not have to follow them. It is not, strictly, your business, and you should not feel burdened by responsibility here. The police, after all, should have handled this a little better than they did – a lot better than they did – and it should be their responsibility to make efforts to seek to conclude this case.

As you know, the existing leads, or apparent leads, as to the circumstances of Edith Watkins' disappearance seem to have dissolved along the way. As I discussed with you, however, while in one sense the enigma might appear to have been compounded, in other ways things are, paradoxically, clearer. I am now of the opinion that Edith is no longer living, and that her body may be found – or, more accurately, may never be found – somewhere in the marshland beyond Deadhurst, Deadmans Beach and Moorshurst: a huge, desolate and even dangerous region, and therefore a daunting prospect for any search party. I say this because the only alternative I can think of, that it has been lost at sea, doesn't seem likely, in that sooner or later, certainly by now, it would have been washed ashore and found.

So this remains the likeliest probability. But as to how she got there, well, once again I need to remind you of our previous discussion. It is still possible that she alighted from the bus at the wrong stop, perhaps on her way to Deadmans Beach rather than on her way back from there, lost her way and died in the marsh. However, putting all such evidence together as we can muster, we are led inevitably to the remaining, and very disturbing possibility we have already discussed.

My intention had been to put this to the client and consider his reaction, but I would not blame you if you did not wish to pursue this. It isn't pleasant. So if that is the case, all I can suggest is that you hand the result of our inquiries back to DCI Green at Moorshurst Police and leave it with him. I am not optimistic that this would lead to a satisfactory conclusion. It seems clear the police have more or less washed their hands of the case and would be extremely reluctant to reopen it – whatever they may say – but at least you and I would have discharged our responsibilities to the best of our abilities and with a clear conscience.

I hope none of this will be necessary and that I will be back to take care of business, but it is as well to have all contingency plans in hand.

I am now about to catch the bus, wherever it will take me.

Yours truly,

Phidias

•

A coin is tossed in an empty room. It clatters to the floor. Tails.

There is no-one in the room.

•

Edith? Edith? Are you still there?

Hello?

Edith, keep talking to me.

Who is this?

You memory is failing, Edith. I am Phidias Peralta, and I am a private investigator. We were having a conversation.

I remember you. Of course I do. Do you know, I don't feel quite the ticket.

You're not feeling well?

I'll be all right in a minute. I'm sorry, I'm being so rude. Would you like a cup of tea?

I'm all right for now, Edith. What's that on the side of your head?

I think I had a fall. That's what they say when you get to my age, "She had a fall."

Is that blood?

I ... I do believe it is. Look at that. Oh dear.

It seems as though you've had some kind of a head injury.

Head injury?

It looks bad.

It's nothing. I shall be all right.

Your face has gone a strange colour.

Oh dear.

Something terrible happened.

I think so.

But we don't know what it was.

(No reply.)

(An eternity of sorts.)

Do you know where you are now?

I'm at home, of course.

Have you been out?

I ... don't know.

Did you go out for a bus ride and a walk?

Yes, that's right, I think I went to Deadmans Beach. I like going there. Or at least, I meant to go. I can't remember whether I did. I wasn't feeling very well.

It was a very windy day.

Yes, it's windy.

We lost track of you, Edith.

What do you mean? I'm here. I think I may go for my walk now. I'm feeling a lot better.

Your colour has started to come back. Do you know what date it is?

It's ... I do believe it's March. The middle of March? You see, I'm not so ga-ga as they say! Anyway, I'm going for my walk. Would you like to join me, dear? I'm so enjoying our conversation.

Are you sure it's March, Edith?

It's a windy day. I remember now. Sharon said so. March winds, you see. What time is it?

It's early evening.

Is it really? Too late for a walk, then.

But eighteen months have elapsed since then, since you disappeared.

I disappeared?

Yes.

What on earth are you talking about, dear? I don't mean to be rude, but ... here I am. I'm not invisible, you know.

By no means. At any rate, you are visible to me.

And I can see you, dear. Where are we now?

A good question, Edith. We appear to be in a boat.

So we are!

We could be at sea.

Lost at sea.

Do you think it might be called the *Dead Level Boys*?

I haven't a clue what it's called, dear.

I imagine it to be a fishing boat. But it could stand for any kind of boat, I suppose.

I went on a fishing expedition once.

I know you did. Tell me about it.

I wanted to see what it was like, to be out at sea. I thought about ...

(A further lapse.)

Edith? Are you still there?

Of course I am!

You come and go. What were you thinking about?

I was thinking about Derek. He was lost at sea, you know. That's what they said, "Lost at sea". That's all we ever knew.

He was a naval officer during the second world war?

That's right. He was the captain of a minesweeper. I was so proud of him.

And what happened?

She went down in the North Sea. Torpedoed, they said. But nobody knew really, what had happened. We never found out.

How did you receive the news?

Apparently two policemen, or two people from the War Ministry, I can't remember, turned up on the doorstep of his parents' house. And then his father came over to our house at Needless Without to tell me, and when I saw him at the front door I knew immediately. He didn't have to say anything. I knew my Derek was gone. But you know, I've always wanted to feel what that was like, to be lost at sea. For years and years. The nearest I got was on that fishing boat, once we were out there on the open sea, under the sky. Bobbing along in the middle of that huge expanse of water. Oh dear.

Are you all right?

Perfectly, dear. I wanted to join him, you know. I so wanted to join my Derek. Ah, that was stupid.

Not stupid at all.

It would have been a fearful problem for the fishermen. I couldn't do that. It would have been so selfish. That was old Gallop, you know, Doc Gallop, that was his boat.

I did that trip too. I met his son.

Did you? A nice boy. Very quiet. He used to help launch the boat from the seashore. What's his name, I forget?

Darren.

Darren, that's it. Young Darren. And so you also went out on a fishing trip with Doc Gallop?

No, with Darren.

Ah, yes.

He has his own boat now.

Of course. And is his father still fishing?

Old Doc passed away a few years ago.

So he did. I'm so forgetful. I was very grateful to the fishing people, they were ever so good to me. I wanted to help them in any way I could.

Did you speak with Darren about that? He's president of the Fishermen's Association these days.

Of course he is. That's right. I'm glad you reminded me. I wanted to leave my money to them. The, that's right, yes, the Fishermen's Association.

And did you? Did you write a will?

Yes, I did, it's all coming back to me now. Well, I didn't go to a lawyer, or anything like that. They're all such crooks, you know. Yes, I wrote out a will. Anybody can do that. You can buy a form from the stationer's. My family have no need of my money, anyway, I'm sure they're well provided for. But the fishing community, they have such a lot of problems these days.

You are certain you did that, Edith? You left all of your estate to the Fishermen's Association? You're sure of that?

As sure as I can be of anything, my dear. But then, my memory's not what it was. Where are we now?

The light's getting worse, so it's hard to tell. We are, at a rough guess, in the middle of nowhere.

That's a good place to be.

As good a place as anywhere.

Well, I suppose I must be getting home. And you, Mr, er –

I have some problems back home, Edith. But my assistant will, I hope, be dealing with them.

Oh, I'm sorry to hear that. What kind of problems? Though it's none of my business, I do apologise –

My nemesis is pursuing me. Or should I say, my nemeses – if that's the correct plural – for there are two of them.

Is that so?

Two men who wish me ill.

That sounds alarming.

A misunderstanding, nothing more. But a misunderstanding in which large sums of money figure. And the people I am dealing with have little sense of, shall we say, subtlety, or human understanding –

I know people like that!

– they lack insight, shall we say.

What are you going to do?

I don't know. It did not seem they were capable of tracking me down, but perhaps it was foolish or complacent to think so. In hindsight, it was very foolish.

I sometimes feel I become more foolish the longer I live.

We are supposed to acquire wisdom.

Oh, phooey!

Perhaps "phooey" is the best word to sum it all up. Yet a few decades on this earth should be sufficient for us to acquire at least some learning. If the fool would persist in his folly he would become wise. A poet said that.

Children learn extremely quickly, don't you think? But then we lose the ability later in life.

What would you say is the greatest lesson you have learned, Edith?

If I've learned anything, I've forgotten it. I'm pretty well ga-ga now, you know.

Ah, come now, you are in your prime.

My dear, I am an old lady now. Haven't you noticed?

So you are, you've had eighty-nine years on this earth, or is it ninety – it's unclear still. So let me still press you. What do you think you've learned in that time, what can you tell us?

Life is short.

Yes, that about sums it up I suppose, Edith.

Doesn't it just? You're trundling along, you're hopping along quite happily and the years go by and everything seems to be lovely. And then one day suddenly it's all over. And you think –

Yes?

– where's it all gone?

And what's it been about?

Exactly so, dear, what has it all been about? It doesn't seem like much time has passed, and yet it's eighty or ninety years, as you say. And there hasn't even been the time to – well –

Anything else?

I beg your pardon?

Anything else you've learned, Edith, anything you can tell me?

You have to be kind.

Yes?

Kindness is important. Don't you think so, Mr, er? Oh, I am so sorry, I must be completely losing my memory.

Peralta. Just call me Phidias. So ... you have to be kind. Even when there is so much unkindness, and worse, around?

Oh, particularly so. Don't you think?

I believe you may be right.

There is ... I know there is unpleasantness.

And irrationality.

Yes, that too.

In my case ... I have to accept ... I am dedicated to rational explanations, Edith, but I have had to learn, especially in my line of business, to give up my anxiety and accept that humans often act irrationally. But that most of them ... most of them are harmless. Or at least, intend to be harmless.

Harmlessness is good.

Another poet said that. More or less. But what do we do about those who are not harmless? Those who mean us ill?

Let's not say anything about them.

But we must. They must be held to account.

That person I was talking about, who I was fond of – oh my, I can't believe this, I've even forgotten *his* name now –

Derek?

Yes, Derek, of course! How on earth did you know his name? Oh, I *am* getting forgetful! He was lost at sea, you know. Well, he used to say much the same. I remember him saying that. In fact, now I think about it, he once used the exact words you just did. Isn't that extraordinary? He said "They must be held to account." I think he was talking about the Nazis. But what can you do? Life is so short.

Yes it is.

I think you were harmed, Edith.

Was I?

But I can't see your wound now. Has it healed?

Did I have a wound?

It looked like a blow to the head.

Maybe that's just – maybe it never –

Perhaps we imagined it. But it's getting too dark to see. How are you feeling, Edith?

(Fading.)

Edith? Are you there?

(No answer.)

Edith?

Hello? Is that you, Derek?

No, it's not. This is Phidias Peralta. How are you feeling, Edith?

I think ... I'm quite well, I think.

You said earlier you were not feeling too good.

We had a conversation, didn't we? I am all the better for it.

Excellent.

Where are we now?

Who can say? Perhaps we are in the mystery room.

What on earth do you mean by that?

There are 169 storage rooms advertised in the Dead Level Self-Storage facility. But only 168 can be located. My assistant's admirable young son suggests the superfluous room, which has no actual location, is a mystery room.

That's where we are?

Maybe. Or maybe we are in the middle of nowhere. Nowhere is a good place to be in the middle of.

But who are we?

We are characters in a story which takes place in the middle of nowhere.

It does look oddly like that.

The middle of nowhere being a synonym for the world of the imagination.

Or it could be just nowhere.

It could be everywhere.

Are we alive?

We may or may not be. In an indeterminate state. Like Schrödinger's cat.

Oh, I used to have a cat. Her name was Tammy.

What happened to her?

She disappeared one day.

She may be around here, then.

Oh, good. I should so like to see Tammy again.

Schrödinger's cat was both alive and dead.

How awful!

It was only an imaginary cat.

Even so.

A thought experiment is what he called it.

I would look for Tammy if I could. But it is getting rather dark. So perhaps another day. I do wish I knew for certain where we were.

Absolute certainty is not attainable, and not even as desirable as one might think.

I'm pretty sure, Mr, er ... I'm pretty sure that we are not in the real world. We seem to have left that behind. And do you know, I'm not altogether sorry about that.

Is that so, Edith?

Yes. The world seemed to be populated by idiots. Don't you find? Then I feel quite awful about feeling that way.

No need to feel awful. I myself share that opinion from time to time.

Oh, good.

Have you met any people here?

Where?

Where you are. Wherever we are.

Oh, a few. There are some strange characters, you know.

I met a woman, who I afterwards learned was named Six-Fingered Sally.

No, I don't believe I've come across her. But I met the lady with the tail.

Is that so?

Very nice lady, very well turned out. But she had a tail coming out of the bottom of her skirt. It looked like a cat's tail. It twitched. She didn't have a great deal to say for herself, but she had a nice smile. Oh, I say, maybe she wasn't a lady, maybe that was Tammy in disguise. It's just occurred to me. I didn't think of that. Or the cat belonging to that gentleman you mentioned, Schruh-, Schruh- ...

Schrödinger.

That's the fellow.

Well, Edith, I don't know about you, but I have reached the end of my road.

Oh, I don't want to keep you, my dear. I did imagine you would have things to do. Problems to clear up. Didn't you say you were a detective, or something? I have a feeling you did.

My assistant can take care of them. She is perfectly capable of doing so. A delightfully accomplished young woman. Lucy White is her name. And she has a remarkable son, the young man I previously mentioned, who I am sure will do very well.

That's good. As for me, there is nothing left that I want to do.

If we are characters in a story we are at liberty to do anything.

Anything? That would be fun!

Anything the author allows us to do.

Oh, bugger the author!

Edith, I am full of admiration for your spirit.

Do you know, I could have sworn you were Derek. Did I tell you about Derek?

You did.

I feel Derek is very close.

He may be. It's time for you to take some rest, Edith.

I'm so grateful to you.

It's time to rest. Let us take our leave. The light is fading. The time has come.

Indeed it has. It's been so delightful speaking with you, Mr –

Peralta.

Mr Peralta.

But just call me Phidias.

Phidias.

13

As Phidias had predicted, Kieran Watkins has decided he wants to close the inquiry into the disappearance of his aunt. On the phone, he sounded testy and nervy, and also annoyed when I told him Phidias wasn't available, and that I had no idea when he might be available. He persisted for a while, he insisted on speaking to Phidias, and it was all I could do to convince him that I would be able to meet his needs and sort everything out.

We could have done it all on the phone, or by post, but I took it into my head to insist on meeting him. I must have a self-destructive streak, I guess. Phidias did say, in that last email, that I didn't have to do any of this, but I just feel I do. As a pretext, I told Mr Watkins I needed to return that framed photograph of his aunt he had lent us, and didn't want to entrust it to the post, as I was sure it must be precious to him, and so on, and so on, and he bought into that. But he said he didn't have time to visit the office, so I countered that by saying I could easily pop over to his house in Deadhurst, and he grudgingly – I think – agreed to meet me there. In a week's time. He was away in London until then. That's the best we could do.

Why do I take on this kind of responsibility when there are so many other things on my mind? Phidias's disappearance being, of course, the major worry. But also – September is upon us, and the start of the new school year, yet George's future schooling is still a cause of uncertainty. He's provisionally enrolled into Deadmans Beach Junior now – they have plenty of places – but we haven't yet cut the ties with All Saints in Deadhurst, and technically they are still expecting him back. Yet he doesn't want to go back there, I'm pretty sure, although he's still evasive whenever I broach the topic. We're going to have to make a decision now.

But the Watkins business.

It's no wonder that I feel such dread and apprehension.

•

There was never an elderly woman. It was a trick of the light, as they say. Light is so tricky. Especially as the sun goes down. And it now turns out its speed may not after all be absolutely uniform. Observations from the farthest regions of the universe, and therefore from the earliest times, may be found to confirm this. But the facts are these. The hull of a clinker-built boat lay in a wilderness of mud interspersed with islands of sedge, far from any sea. It listed to starboard but did not move. It was empty. Nothing moved. Nothing had moved for a very long time.

On the far horizon, something did. Twin pinpricks of light were visible. There was movement of a subtle kind, movement of a distant object, dark but unfathomable, with bright eyes.

There was also sound: a hum, almost imperceptible at first. Gradually, it became easier to detect this sound and to assess its quality. The object itself was obscured by the faint mist that lingered at the edges, but it gradually began to gain definition.

In the late evening sky also, starkly delineated against pale grey, a dark V-shape was manifested now, gliding slowly from side to side with that distinct motion associated with the marsh harrier. It could be observed to patrol the terrain with great care and attention, soaring, gliding, dipping, moving on. The grey colouring, the black marking at the wing tips, all of this was now visible, identifying the bird as a male. And it continued its patrol for a while. But after some moments, suddenly it dropped, possibly onto a prey item it had spotted, plunging to the ground some distance from our observation point and disappearing from sight.

Now the vehicle that approached from the horizon, for this is what it was, could be observed more clearly, even through the increasing gloom. It was black. Not the four-wheel-drive model that might have been expected, but a saloon car, wholly unsuited to this terrain. Its headlights had been switched on. It was of a substantial size, and there was an elegance about its lines that spoke of big money. It had clearly found a path to follow in this wilderness, but not a particularly satisfactory one to judge from the bumping motions within its trajectory. The hum of the engine was unmistakable.

It came to a stop about fifty to a hundred metres distant, so far as could be estimated, possibly having attained the nearest approach to our position obtainable; the engine died and the headlights were extinguished. There was a pause of a few moments. Then doors were opened, and two male figures emerged: the shorter one from the driver's side, the other from the front seat passenger's. A satisfying double sound, midway between a thud and a cushioned clunk, haloed by a slight reverberation, signalled the closing of both doors. The pair of figures, dark-suited, sober-tied, silent, stood for a moment on either side of their vehicle looking in this direction. Then, slowly, they started to pick their way forward.

It was evident they were having difficulty finding a suitable trajectory through the worst of the boggy areas, but to their credit they did not evade the problems and continued their approach with some determination. As they neared, it became obvious that their shoes and the bottoms of their trousers as far as the knees were becoming soaked and caked with unwelcome mud.

They stopped while still ten metres away and looked at each other, then again in our direction. The twilight obscured their faces. The taller of the two spoke. The voice was familiar.

Mr Peralta?

It was necessary and also only polite to return the greeting.

Good evening, gentlemen. What can I do for you?

•

The fact is, Phidias has been missing for a month now. With each passing day, it becomes less likely that we shall see him again. I don't know what to do.

I told Kieran Watkins this when we were settled in his living room. He seemed nonplussed.

That's a bit strange, he said.

More than a bit.

When you report a missing person, you don't expect the investigating detective to disappear as well, he added.

He said it in a way that suggested he regarded all this as further evidence of the unsatisfactory service he had been having from us, and would be putting in a complaint.

It's not usual, I agreed.

This was going to be hard.

Increasingly, I grow uncomfortable whenever I visit the beautiful village of Deadhurst. I suppose that's magnified by the experience we've had of George's school there. But this visit, and the reason for it – well, that increased my unease and unhappiness. I kept telling myself I wasn't committed to anything. If it seemed too difficult, all I needed to do was hand over the photograph of Edith Watkins I'd come to return, and depart.

I passed the school on the way, but deliberately parked in a tree-lined street well away from it, close to the Watkins address. The trees were already, I noticed, being touched by the beginning of autumn. Only a few leaves had been shed onto the street so far, but the colour of those remaining on the branches was beginning to change, the hue was travelling from deep green to lighter, towards the yellow.

The Watkins house is really quite lovely. Local aged brick, rosy in colour. White window frames. It's set back a little from the road. Immaculate shrubbery, a few fruit trees. I could have driven in through the open gate, there would have been plenty of space in the driveway, but I hadn't known that. Never mind. The only vehicle parked on the wide expanse of gravel was the familiar black Range Rover, an enormous emblem, like a royal standard, showing Kieran Watkins to be in residence. It gleamed silently.

But actually the first thing I noticed was an estate agent's board on a wooden pole beside the entranceway, proclaiming FOR SALE.

And it was one of the first things I commented on after he had greeted me at the front door and shown me to that comfortable living room with the leather armchairs.

Yes, he said shortly, I'm putting the property on the market.

He said property, not home.

It's a beautiful house, I commented, it must be worth quite a bit.

I hope so, he said. I am hoping to downsize, to move to a

smaller property. Whether in the village or not remains to be seen.

You are? But not with your wife?

You may have heard that my wife and I have decided to split up.

We heard from your son Robin that you were no longer living together. I'm sorry.

Yes, that's right, Anna's been living with her sister for the past year. We've now come to … an arrangement. We just needed to sort out the finances.

So there have been some financial issues? I inquired, and then bit my lip. And he became edgy again.

If you are referring to the question of your invoice, Lucy, I'm sorry this has taken so long, but do rest assured all of that will be sorted very shortly.

I said innocently: I didn't mean that. Business has been bad for everybody recently, I suppose.

Well, he said, my affairs, the affairs of my company, are not yours to worry about.

He tried to change the subject, offering a hot drink, but I declined.

Here's the photo of your aunt safely returned to you – still in its frame, I said.

Oh, thank you, I'm much obliged.

I'm really sorry we have made so little progress finding her.

Well, that's not your fault at all, Lucy.

Though I have to tell you that we have a theory.

A theory?

Yes, Mr Watkins, a possible, even probable scenario. What I'm trying to say is that we are attempting closure here. Even though closure is not always necessarily welcome.

What on earth do you mean?

Sorry, just channelling Phidias for a moment.

I think you should say more.

Right, I will. But first, can I ask you a question?

Go ahead.

Why did you bring this case to Peralta Associates?

Why? I should have thought that was obvious.

(Silence.)

Lucy, I should have thought it was obvious. I don't understand your question. I wanted my aunt found.

But you were certain she was dead?

I ... well, this seems the most obvious hypothesis, doesn't it? I hardly think she is now likely to emerge alive and well, having had a nice holiday somewhere –

So you wanted, sorry to put it bluntly, Mr Watkins, you wanted her body found?

Well, er ...

But at the same time you *didn't* want her body found? You were in some quandary here, I suppose, in a horrible double bind?

Well, nobody wants their worst suspicions confirmed, do they, but –

There were possibly bad consequences to follow from her body being found?

I didn't say that.

Mr Watkins, why were you so certain your aunt was dead?

I really don't like this line of questioning, if I may say so. It was a gut feeling –

It was more than that, wasn't it?

I have no idea what you are talking about, Lucy.

I am pursuing closure, and I think you know what I mean. Let me put something else to you. When you first saw that CCTV clip the police unearthed of your aunt leaving the café, allegedly on the day she disappeared, the fifteenth of March, you were with your son, weren't you?

That's right, I was.

And he reported that you seemed very shocked by it.

Did he? I suppose I was.

He told Phidias that you went very pale when you saw it, in fact Robin's exact words as noted by Phidias were that you went as white as a sheet.

Is that what he said?

It hit you like a thunderbolt.

Yes.

And when we later discovered that video was not in fact shot on that day, but a month earlier, you said to Phidias: That explains it.

Did I? I don't remember.

Was that because you knew for a fact – for a fact – that your aunt Edith was already dead before the time when that footage was mistakenly claimed to have been shot?

That's ... outrageous.

Mr Watkins, I must ask you this, it's very important – have you told us the complete truth?

As far as I know.

I don't think so, Mr Watkins. I think there's something you've been hiding from us.

I've hidden nothing.

You knew she was dead. That's why that video was such a shock. You knew your aunt hadn't been to Deadmans Beach. She died in her home. You knew she died on that very date, the fifteenth of March, some time from the late morning onward. In fact, you witnessed her death.

(Silence.)

Didn't you?

(Silence.)

It was an accident.

(Silence.)

She had a fall, didn't she?

Yes. It was an accident.

Tell me about it.

She had a fall ... about a year before, in the bathroom –

No, no, we knew about that, this is why you had all those disability aids installed in her house, I'm talking about the fifteenth of March last year, she had a second fall, you witnessed that fall, didn't you?

Wait a minute, you're getting ahead of yourself –

It was a fatal fall this time wasn't it? Was it in the kitchen it happened?

Yes ... no, listen, I'm sorry, I can't say anything, I have to end this conversation –

Because there's some evidence for that, some traces of staining –

You have no evidence.

– similar to the staining on the bathroom floor upstairs from the previous time.

You have no evidence.

So it was an accident?

I never said ... I never said that.

You just did. It was an accident, you said. Why didn't you immediately call the emergency services?

I didn't ... I said her death must have been accidental, I was only surmising.

Most people would have immediately called 999, but you didn't. Why was that?

(Silence.)

Was that because you knew a post-mortem was inevitable and you were apprehensive about the results of that?

This is absolutely outrageous.

Well, why didn't you?

I cannot comment on –

You had a big, big dilemma.

What on earth –

Let's recap a bit, Mr Watkins. You visited her that day, the day of her disappearance, contrary to what you told us before, which was that you waited a full three or four days after she failed to reply to your Sunday lunch invitation and then found the house empty on the eighteenth. No, you visited her on the fifteenth, and there she was. You insisted on making her a cup of tea, as had become the custom. I'm going out on a limb here a bit, I have to say, but perhaps this time you made a mistake. You were in the kitchen making the tea, and suddenly she was there in front of you, instead of remaining in her armchair in the front room as she normally did. And she saw you.

She what?

Mr Watkins, I would actually describe your complexion now as white as a sheet. You don't look at all well.

I'm ... I'm speechless.

She saw what you were doing.

What was I doing?

She saw what you were putting in her tea, what you had been putting in that tea you were making for her weekly, you'd been doing it for quite a long time by then. Which would explain why she was getting progressively more unwell. What was it?

What was what?

The substance you'd been introducing into her tea. You're the chemist, you're the expert.

Let me remind you that I founded a company making additives for preserving foods or enhancing their flavour. It's not a pharmaceutical company, we don't make drugs or poisons.

Nevertheless, you're a qualified chemist, you know what you're doing. Maybe it wasn't a poison that would have killed her directly, but something to make her unwell over a period of time, compromise her immune system or whatever, so she would be more likely to succumb to any passing infection. Does that sound familiar? Anyway, you had the means.

I'm sorry, but this is preposterous.

She immediately saw what you were doing, and put two and two together, and she was outraged. I mean, she may have been on the road to dementia, but she wasn't stupid. She accosted you –

I did not murder my aunt.

Maybe not. Maybe you resisted her, pushed her back. That would have been a contributory factor to the fall, though. Anyway, I'm speculating. I'm prepared to believe you did not deliberately kill her.

I did not murder my aunt.

OK, so her actual death may have been an accident. However, attempted murder over a long period –

Come on, that's ridiculous.

I don't know that that charge would stick, I have to admit. You've very likely got rid of all the evidence a long time ago. Anyway, she fell. Perhaps she hit her head?

What if she did?

Did she die immediately?

(No reply.)

As I said – you had a big dilemma. You could have called an ambulance. Why didn't you?

I refuse to answer such questions. If you have any allegations to make, the proper thing to do is go to the police. Let's see if they believe you. But you have no evidence for these outrageous charges. I'm sorry, but I'm going to have to ask you to –

Well, I would suggest you took fright and just left the house and left her there. But then, thinking it over, this course of action made matters worse. You thought and thought, and you came to a decision. Whatever you'd been feeding her would still be in her system. The post-mortem would have shown it. This wasn't what you'd planned. So you had to get rid of her body. You devised a scenario where she would unaccountably disappear. That was believable, because everybody knew she was going ga-ga. So you returned that evening, under cover of darkness. You knew Sharon, the next door neighbour, was away, perhaps because your aunt had just told you, so there was little risk. Does all this sound familiar?

(No reply.)

Mr Watkins? You seem a little overcome with emotion, are you all right?

I was ... I never disrespected her.

Well, you removed her body, and you put it in the boot of that big Range Rover of yours. She was a very small woman, she hardly weighed anything. She didn't weigh much in your arms, did she?

I ...

You're really not looking at all well, you're perspiring quite a bit –

I was always respectful to my aunt.

You kept your head. You didn't forget to take her coat and hat and handbag, and also her walking stick. Not her favourite flower-patterned walking stick, but the black one, but you weren't to know that was not the one she preferred. Can't get everything right. Did you actually put the coat on her? That would have been difficult. You did all that, anyway, and then you drove out to the marshes in the middle of the night and dumped her. I suppose it was very handy having that four-wheel drive car of yours. And once you're out in the marshes – you're trembling, Mr Watkins.

I have nothing to say.

By the way, I'm assuming you didn't share this with your wife, did you? But maybe she found out, or she suspected.

Maybe that's the real reason for your separation. And also why you've avoided having us interview her.

Please leave Anna out of this.

You'll have to correct me if some of these details are wrong. Phidias and I discussed the evidence, and I will admit there's a bit of guessing about some of this, so I apologise if we've made mistakes, but I think we've got the bare bones of it right, haven't we? I mean, if we haven't, please do say, please give me the full, true story in your own words. Please tell me what really happened.

I have nothing to say.

The question is – let's say for the sake of argument what you said was right, your aunt's actual death was an accident – all the same, you'd been trying to hasten her death, and there'd be the post-mortem and all that, which is the likeliest explanation why you didn't just call the emergency services. The question is, why were you trying to kill her?

I didn't kill her.

You tried to. So what was the motivation? Let's be charitable to start off with. It was kinder to hasten her death, wasn't it? She had dementia, she refused care, things were going wrong, what kind of a life was left to her in the final years? It's always a horrendous prospect, isn't it? Better if she was put out of her misery. It's a kindness, isn't it, that's what people say. Plus of course, a disaster was waiting to happen. She'd already had one fall. Then you'd get the social services intervening, and so on. And they'd say she can't be supported at home, she's at risk, she needs to go into residential care, and that costs an absolute fortune, so down the plughole goes all the money. We've seen that happen so many times. So there's a less kind side to it, isn't there? Her house has to be sold to pay for nursing home costs. That's the prospect ahead, isn't it? There goes the inheritance, just when it was needed.

I wasn't motivated by ... I didn't kill her. I've always tried to do the right thing.

Especially needed now your firm has hit the buffers, and you have big financial problems. Anyway, you're the next of kin, but wait a minute, there was that row you had with your aunt.

About care?

No, about her deciding to leave all her inheritance to the Fishermen's Association. So what do you do, having disposed of the body, or maybe even before you disposed of the body and cleaned up the blood from her fall as best you could, we're not clear on the exact sequence of events here – you break into her roll-top desk where she's always kept all her papers. You can't find the key, bit of a panic, so you force the lock. That bit of evidence is there, I mean the forced lock. You find the piece of paper she's written her will on. That's gone now, isn't it? There's no will now. You inherit by default, as next of kin. Except you don't, of course. Because her death has not been established for certain.

Lucy ... Ms White ... I think this has gone on long enough. I must ask you to leave my house.

I'll be gone very soon, Mr Watkins. But first – you have yet another dilemma. You want your aunt to be presumed dead so that you can inherit her estate, right? But you don't want her body found, at least not for a while, because it might implicate you. And you're pressing the police to declare her dead, but of course they won't, because there isn't the evidence. You've got the law a bit wrong there. I must admit I had the law wrong too, until Phidias put me right. There has to be pretty incontrovertible evidence someone is dead before they can declare that – for example, evidence they were on an aircraft that plunged into the sea. Not just a disappearance. So now, your motivation for hiring Phidias Associates is a bit obscure. On the one level, you're being told by family and friends the police are making no headway, it's outrageous how they've practically dropped the case, and you're always wanting to be seen to do the right thing, that's the way you are, Mr Watkins, and people say, your wife and your son say, perhaps you should hire a private detective, so that's what you do. On another level, since the police do seem to have washed their hands of it, and no progress is to be made, maybe that is your only hope of establishing your aunt's death once and for all. So you're ambivalent about involving us. But I don't know what you were expecting, the discovery of a body out on the marshes so decomposed that any evidence of poisoning has long gone. And tyre marks washed away. Actually, I think your motivation was more vague than that, but only you can enlighten us.

OK, as I said, I must now ask you to leave. I consider this harassment. I will have no hesitation in calling the police if you refuse.

Will you tell us where you dumped the body?

(No reply.)

Where did you dump the body?

(No reply.)

It's out in the marshland somewhere, isn't it?
Dump is an unduly harsh term.
What you did was harsh.

(Silence.)

There's the door. Please leave, Lucy.

Your best hope is declared death in absentia. That's what it's called. It takes seven years, usually. That's the legal proce-dure when there's no evidence for a disappeared person's death. After that period, then the person is presumed officially dead, and the inheritors can apply for probate. That may be too late to solve your current financial problems. But – one more time – I appeal to you to put yourself out of your misery, and tell the truth about everything. Including where you drove to dump the body.

There's the door.

In the meantime, I'm going to take the evidence to the police, and we'll see what happens.

You have no evidence.

It's all right, I'm leaving now. Seven years, Mr Watkins.

Your bill will be paid, Ms White, don't worry about that.

That doesn't matter now. Actually, a year and a half have already gone by, so you have five and a half years to go before you inherit your aunt's estate. Unless you can be persuaded to end the misery first by telling the truth. Five and a half years, Mr Watkins. On your own. Five and a half years.

•

As a poet once said: at last it octobers. The nights are drawing in, the clocks will go back soon. Brief summer is already a memory, and the cold wind is blowing in from the sea in the east.

We report from the room that has no computable location. If it had a window, one could look over and one would see the boat. And much else.

In Deadmans Beach they are making preparations for Bonfire Night. The town has the honour of starting the bonfire season, which will have its various manifestations over the following few weekends in each town and village and settlement of the region. At the shoreline end of the playing fields, beside the community hut and just on the ridge above the beach, a small mountain has been constructed out of pallets, and is now being readied for tonight's bonfire. Men in acid-lemon high-vis jackets and white hard hats circle it, shouting instructions. Their shouts echo.

Visitors are already starting to come into town in increasing numbers. Each year the festivities attract more and more, which can only be a good thing for the economy of this multiply deprived coastal town.

The Richard the Lionheart Inn is decked out for the occasion, and the drink is already being liberally dispensed. Outside the pub, a list is displayed of the bands recently featured and yet to appear:

> September 23rd – The Gulls
> September 30th – Deadmen Walking
> October 7th (Bonfire Night) – Hedgemonicker
> October 14th – Owl & the Pussycat
> October 21st – All of the Above
> October 28th – tbc
> December 23rd – The Old Dick Xmas Party

In the centre of town, where traffic has been cordoned off, a line of impromptu huts has been erected, offering for purchase hot and cold comestibles, plastic masks, firecrackers and light sabres; and also a merry-go-round has been installed for the children, the rides offered being as follows: a ship named Tina Marie; a donkey and a duck; a bus with the designated destination of "Toytown"; a horse; a blue vintage car; a paddle steamer; a deer with the neck of a giraffe; a cockerel; a red racing car. A bell signals the start of the ride; vintage swing band music plays.

A sand sculptor has set up his business on the pavement a short distance from the pub. Clad in a dark blue anorak and a porkpie hat, he kneels, sculpting meticulously a figure that arises from the very paving stones. A number of young women dressed as pirates move past, giggling. Someone leads a miniature reindeer out of a side street. A guitar chord, E minor, rings out from the pub, where the soundcheck has begun. The clouds to the west start to take on the hue of flamingos.

Oi! Seen this? He's made a dog out of sand!

And real dogs yap, swing music plays, motorbikes start to rev.

Unknown objects become icons and emblems. It is past sunset now, and the empty building is dark. But the street lights come on. There is glowing elsewhere. There is a smell of cordite.

This is the work of the collective imagination.

Have you seen her?
Have you seen her?
Sally Six Fingers, have you seen her?

Her little dog knows her,
She goes flying with the crows
Upon the marshes where the light glows –

Yeah, Six Fingered Sally,
I caught her creeping down the alley....

•

I feel sick.

•

I'm sick with sadness and disgust. I can't stop thinking about it. He was shaking like a leaf at one point. That man – I can't even bring myself to say his name. He went all white. I managed, amazingly, to keep my own composure until I got back in the car, and then I started shaking too as I sat there at the steering wheel, I couldn't help it. He's guilty as sin. I could see it in his eyes. I didn't know what to do. I sat staring out of the windscreen, staring at a dead leaf that had floated down from a tree and lodged in the gap behind the windscreen wiper. Eventually, I pulled myself together, put the car in gear and drove home.

But I recorded it all.

I don't know exactly how Phidias would have handled the situation. But we did discuss the case. He was very definitive. And he said he was intending to confront ... that man. Well, I tried to channel Phidias throughout the whole business. I don't know if I handled it right. So anyway, what I'd done was I took Phidias's little digital recorder with me, he'd shown me how to use it, and I kept it in my handbag. I turned it on while I was waiting at the front door, and I kept it on. I kept praying as we were talking that that little red light was on inside my handbag. It had been. And when I played it back at home, there it all was. Clear as a bell. The whole interview.

So this morning I went into the office, switched on the computer and found the connecting cable. I uploaded the recording to the computer, the way Phidias had shown me. Now I had a sound file, and I played it all back through the computer speakers, and the whole conversation was there. I wrote an email to Detective Chief Inspector Green, and I attached the sound file to it. I don't know if that was the right procedure, maybe email is too insecure, but I didn't know what else to do. Actually, having sent the email, which I took a long time composing, I thought it might have been better to phone him, so I did that as well, and got through to his voicemail. I left a message for him.

Enough. By mid-afternoon I was done. So off I went back to Deadmans Beach to pick George up from his new school. I had forgotten it was the day of the bonfire. He was buzzing with excitement. It seemed that was all they had talked about in school, and he couldn't wait. I had of course told him he could stay up for the bonfire procession and the fireworks.

We had also arranged to meet up with Dave in town, so George was doubly excited.

And this was what happened.

As every year, the procession assembled at the shoreline, close to the fishing beach. Darkness was falling, firebrands were lit. There seemed more people than ever, representing Bonfire Societies in all the towns around, each delegation dressed in their particular uniform, each holding their emblem and guarding it carefully as they milled around. George loved it. Well, then we spotted Dave. And Dave and I gave each other a kiss on the cheek. George jumped up and down, holding a sparkler. The smells of charcoal and cordite wafted over, mingling with those of hamburgers and hot dogs cooking. We could hear the noise of the band starting up in the Richard the Lionheart over the way, the unmistakable sound of that band we've heard rehearse so often in Dead Level Self Storage, Hedgemonicker they're called. I thought of Phidias. And blow me down, I then caught sight of the effigy that always heads the procession, the figure they are going to burn on the bonfire at the end of the night. They were just assembling, ready to march off, holding the huge figure aloft. For a crazy instant, I thought it was him. I thought the bonfire effigy was Phidias! Why, I don't know. A moment later it looked nothing like him: it was grotesque, it wore a hat, which I had never seen him in. But just for that moment, if that young policeman had returned to remind me of his question to me, please describe Mr Peralta, I would have pointed to that giant scarecrow they were holding up, wobbling as it went, as the parade moved off, and said: That's him, that's what he looks like.

Dave glanced at me with a puzzled expression on his face, and said: You all right, Luce?

I nodded, speechless. The illusion had passed.

He said: We'll catch the parade again when it comes back, then.

That's what we always did. They marched off, circling the town, and an hour or so later, after George had had a go on the merry-go-round – though maybe he is too old for that now – they would return to the shore, via the playing fields, and we would rejoin them as they congregated around the little mountain of wood that was the bonfire, and set the effigy on top of it, and someone would set light to the whole edifice, and the flames would start to lick, and once the bonfire was going, roaring into the night, the fireworks would begin, which George always adored.

So past us, following the effigy, marched the Bonfire Societies. Each group held up its placard with its own insignia, each topped by a trio of firebrands. They were headed by a fire eater, a lithe and somewhat gorgeous young man, naked from the waist up, his torso glowing green and yellow. He pranced from side to side, goading the crowds of spectators. In his right hand he held a brand that had been lit, in his left a bottle. Then with a grand gesture, he directed the flame to his mouth, gulped and blew a great fountain of fire into the sky. People cheered, and he did it again. And again.

A firecracker burst suddenly, and young women screamed in delight. The darkness was lit by blazing torches, and the light played on the faces of the people and made them awesome.

As the procession was passing, I became aware of a man trying to attract my attention. He was rather stockily built, wearing a hoodie with the hood down and a beanie on his head.

Excuse me, he said, are you Lucy White?

Yes, I said.

He offered his hand. Darren Gallop, he said, of the Fishermen's Association.

Dave, meanwhile, was distracted trying to answer some of George's multiple questions.

I asked Darren how he recognised me.

Seen you driving Mr Peralta around, he said. And he told me about you.

I said I was pleased to meet him, having heard so much about him in turn from Phidias, and he said he wanted to express his sympathy. If that was the right expression. Had I heard anything from Phidias, he wanted to know.

I had to tell him I hadn't.

You know I took him out on the boat.

I said I did know.

Only, he said, people will think anyone our family takes out on a fishing trip eventually disappears.

I know, it's weird, I said. He smiled.

Actually, I had a message for him. You could tell him. If he comes back. I hope he comes back.

I said I hoped so too.

He said: It's about Giles. He talked at some length with Giles.

That's the guy with the long white hair? I said. Who used to be a fisherman?

That's him, said Darren. Well, he died.

I said: Phidias told me he was planning his own funeral. I'm sorry to hear that.

We're all sorry, Darren said. But yes, he had it all sorted.

I mentioned the other thing Phidias had told me: that Giles was planning on being buried at sea. Had that happened? And Darren gave me what I can only describe as a surreptitious wink.

Yeah, he said, we had the church funeral, with what we call the light coffin. And then the real one. We used the *Jumpy Mary*.

And the vicar −?

Oh, the padre was in on it, said Darren, you bet. He came with us on the boat. We had a lovely ceremony, about three miles out. Just a select few, the *Jumpy Mary* can't take a lot. The landlord of the old Dick, where he liked to drink, some of his drinking companions, including Dodie, you know Dodie? No? Anyway. Very appropriate. The padre read out some prayers, and all that. Then we slid him out. Into the waves, that's where he belonged.

Was this at night?

At dawn.

So your padre was happy with that?

Oh yes. Giles was very religious, you know. Though he had some odd ideas, but yes, very religious. The padre knows that. Though he don't say nothing. All the way back home, we was very quiet, in remembrance of Giles, though we had a little drink too, and the padre joined in with that. Then a bit of a south-westerly came up. Well, quite a bit of one. The padre was sick as a dog. But there you are. No, I just wanted Phidias to know.

I said if Phidias reappeared I would relate this story to him, and would also give him Darren's good wishes, which he was most insistent about. Then I remembered something: I had one question.

Shoot, said Darren Gallop.

You know that business about Edith Watkins?

Little Edie, right.

Did she definitely say to you she was leaving all her possessions in her will to the Fishermen's Association?

Yeah, said Darren.

You are sure about that?

Yeah, repeated Darren. She said it more than once.

And you thought she had her faculties when she said it?

Oh yes, this was a while ago. I know she went a bit doolally at the end, but she was compos mentis then, yeah.

You know no will was ever found?

That's what they say.

I told him that I thought the Fishermen's Association had been cheated.

It don't matter, he said.

George was tugging at my elbow. He wanted us to move over to where the bonfire was, to await the return of the procession. Dave and Darren acknowledged each other. From the Richard the Lionheart, the sound of Hedgemonicker's set suddenly boomed, maybe as the door opened with people thronging in and out. I could hear the clanging of the guitar and also the voices seemed more impassioned. Then it muffled again.

I said I thought the Fishermen's Association being cheated of its inheritance was just one of the many sadnesses of this despicable business.

Darren repeated: It don't matter. That's the way it happened. That's the way it goes. OK, nice to meet you.

With a wave, he disappeared into the night.

We moved on.

The bonfire started to blaze. The effigy was all lit up for a while, then began to sag. Then the fireworks.

Hello, is that Lucy White?

Speaking.

Hello, Lucy, this is DCI Oliver Green here, from Moorshurst Police.

Oh, thank you so much for getting back to me, I really wanted to –

I am sorry we've made no progress in finding your employer, Mr Peralta. We just have no leads. I wanted to express my sympathy on behalf of the force, and to assure you we'll keep trying. You've no doubt been in regular contact with my colleagues.

Yes, I have, but –

We're trying to trace these two males you describe, Mr Borg and Mr McKinley. We're having difficulty, and it may be these are assumed names. If so, that makes our job doubly difficult.

I understand.

We'll stay in touch and let you know as soon as we have anything of moment to report. In the meantime –

Did you get my email, Chief Inspector?

Your email? Yes, I was about to come to that –

And the attachment? Did you get the sound file?

Indeed I did, and I listened to it most carefully.

What did you think?

Very interesting. We need to proceed cautiously here, however.

Did you hear what Kieran Watkins said?

I assure you I listened to every word.

He as good as admits his guilt!

Unfortunately, "as good as" isn't good enough.

What do you mean? He agrees that he saw his aunt fall in her own home on the fifteenth of March, and that this was fatal. Which contradicts what he said previously, that he didn't go over to her house until three days later, when she'd, quote unquote, disappeared. Then he has no answer to my question, if he was there, why he didn't call the emergency services –

Wait a minute. Yes, he implicitly agrees with that statement when he says "It was an accident". Then, moments later, he seems to retract that. There's a degree of confusion there, I must say, but it doesn't amount to a full-on confession. Any half-decent lawyer would successfully argue that he was taken aback and confused by your line of questioning, and said things he hadn't meant to say.

But you didn't see his body language –

Precisely. The recording is all the evidence we have. You have the advantage of being able to assess his demeanour as he said what he said, and no doubt you would testify to that in a court of law, but in the end it would be just your word against his in that respect.

But if the recording of my interview isn't enough in itself to convict him, surely it's enough to –

To trigger a further investigation on our part?

That's right.

I have given a lot of thought to that, and I will continue to do so, but I'm not yet convinced.

You could examine his Range Rover for any signs of —

Lucy, if this happened at all it happened over eighteen months ago. There is little chance that any traces, such as blood from a corpse or mud on the tyres from any particular part of the marshland, would remain now.

There is evidence of old bloodstains on the kitchen floor, similar to the bathroom upstairs where she had her previous fall.

Well, I must admit we missed that, but in itself that doesn't prove anything.

And you also missed, but Phidias picked up, the forced lock on Edith Watkins' roll-top desk.

Which could have happened any time.

And you could take a statement from Darren Gallop, president of the Fishermen's Association, that she had told him definitively she'd made out a will to benefit them, yet no will had been found.

Well, we have no reason to doubt Mr Gallop's word, but, again, any competent lawyer could argue that Ms Watkins was already suffering from dementia when she told him that and liable to assert things that were not true.

So you're not going to take this forward.

I didn't say that. Your recording is of great interest, as is your and Mr Peralta's theory as to what happened in this case, and we shall take it very seriously indeed, and certainly have a word with Mr Watkins, but more than that for now I cannot say.

Will you ask him to say where he was on the morning and evening of the fifteenth?

I have no doubt we will. If he has an alibi, that is the end of the matter. If he does not, that still doesn't, of itself, establish any guilt.

What if he admits he saw her die and disposed of her body?

Well, that in itself would be a criminal offence. If so, we would require him to lead us to the place where he disposed of it.

Why don't you just search the marshes anyway?

Lucy, that is wholly impractical. I don't need to remind you of the extent of the marshland beyond Moorshurst. We do not have the resources to search the whole territory. A corpse could be disposed of anywhere. We would need some guidance.

And if he did admit to witnessing her death and disposing of her body, would you then question him as to why he did that?

Obviously if that were to happen there would be some motivation there we would investigate, but I have to say the one you came up with was perhaps the most speculative part of your entire theory. It would be very hard to prove. Please believe that we will indeed question Mr Watkins in the light of your interview, and will let you know the result of that.

I can't believe it. One thing after another. Trevor Tanner rings me up from the Dead Level Business Park: there's been a burglary in Unit 13. So I have to drop everything and drive there.

Lucy, I'm terribly sorry about this. It's Trevor, hovering outside our office. The door is ajar. Was it broken into? No, whoever it was just walked in. They must have had a key. What does that mean?

The computer is gone, likewise the digital recorder I'd left on the desk next to it. One or two of the desk drawers have been half pulled out. They have all been emptied of their contents.

All Trevor can repeat is: really, really sorry. He pats my hand.

Was anyone seen?

And this is the irony: after all the discussions we've had about security surveillance, it appears that the CCTV camera covering this part of the site has failed. It hasn't come up with any pictures. Gordon Prescott, who turns up at that point, can't explain it. Just blank. Nothing. He's trying to find out what's wrong with his beloved kit.

Other items of value have gone. Whoever it was knew what they were doing.

The police have already been called, Gordon assures me, and Trevor nods his head frantically.

When they turn up, it's a pair of officers, and one of them is the same boy who took my statement about Phidias's disappearance. He nods at me like an old friend. He wonders whether the intruders may have been the individuals I reported previously, the "two males" – Mr Borg and Mr McKinley? If so, they already have a description. They are already searching for them. Any sign of a vehicle? But it happened during the night. A mess of tyre tracks in the parking lot, impossible to decipher. And they more than likely parked in the road anyway.

In the middle of all this, I get a call on my mobile. DCI Oliver Green again. It's nothing to do with the burglary. He doesn't know about it yet, of course. I'm thinking he's going to tell me he's pulled Kieran Watkins in for questioning. But he says:

I have to tell you, Lucy, that Mr Watkins contacted me to complain about you.

What?

Before you start getting worried about this, Lucy, he said, I managed to dissuade him from making a formal complaint.

A formal complaint? About what?

Harassment, he says.

I did not harass him. I was very polite at all times while I was talking to him.

I'm sure you were, he replies, in fact I know you were, and as I said I managed to talk him out of it.

And did you question him about everything we discussed?

We will think about interviewing Mr Watkins, he says, but we shall need to do an assessment of the case beforehand.

So when did Kieran Watkins phone you?

And DCI Green said he didn't phone.

He didn't?

No, he sought me out at the golf club, said DCI Green.

At the golf club?

I was speechless for a moment. So you're golfing chums, chief inspector?

He sounded embarrassed: No, not at all, I scarcely know the gentleman, we just both happen to be members of Moorshurst Golf Club. He, er, accosted me in the bar. I assure you –

You're not going to interview him, are you? I said.

I assure you –

It's not going to happen, is it?

Again, he said: Lucy, I assure you –

But I just rang off.

I'm sitting there in the office, at the empty desk. The police officers have gone, leaving me with a "crime number", and so have Trevor and Gordon. A pale shaft of light is coming in through the window. There's the furniture we bought. Through the doorway is the cubicle where Phidias slept, and beside it the shower cubicle. It's all very quiet and peaceful.

I no longer have the evidence, I realise. With the computer and digital recorder gone, I have no record to hand of that confession. If it was a confession. Surely – sudden thought – surely Kieran Watkins didn't do the burglary ... no, that's daft, it couldn't have been him, he wouldn't have known ... unless ... but the police have the recording now. If they want to do anything with it. It's up to them. It's not up to me.

The kitchenette over there. The fridge. Now the sun is really coming out. It's streaming through. Phidias used to stand there making his coffee. But the coffee-maker has also gone, I now realise. Another item for the list.

Was it Phidias who broke in?

Gordon said before he went that we could discuss whether the business park's insurance would cover the theft. Said it was better to talk it over with him rather than with Trevor, who is "all over the place", according to him. This on account of Trevor having decided to take early retirement at the end of the year. To spend more time with his model railway, said Gordon with a smile. I think Gordon is in line for promotion to site manager.

It probably doesn't matter, I told him. It's of no great consequence now.

So I'm sitting there for a while, wondering if I shall see Phidias again, and coming to the conclusion that it is unlikely. I have to admit I started coming over all emotional. I can't share this. Because I really have no-one to share it with.

Also, I missed a period. And now the next one is late. Kitty is the only person I've told about that, but Dave will have to know. Everything is getting more and more complicated.

Now George needs picking up from school.

Tried a different tack this morning. Tried to access Peralta Associates' email account from my home computer, which I've never done before. I need to find the email I sent to DCI Green with the attached sound file of the confession. Got in a muddle. Got a message that the account I was trying to access was not available. Or there was no such account. Something like that. So I gave up.

But before George was due to be picked up from Deadmans Beach Junior, I had another notion. I drove to the Dead Level Business Park. I wanted to check out Room 248 in the self-storage depot, I wasn't quite clear why. Something nagged at me. And this is where it started to get weird all over again.

I parked, and went into reception. The monosyllabic boy was in there. I signed the book and went upstairs with my key.

So there was Room 248. I opened the padlock with my key. And found an empty room.

I couldn't comprehend this for a while. Was this the right

room? I checked the number stencilled on the door. Of course it was, my key would not have opened any other room. But the Dexion metal shelving Phidias had put together, and the rows and rows of his books that had crammed it, had vanished. So too the comfy chair and standard lamp he had set up there. The room was completely empty.

I felt cold and clammy. Just like the time I found that mysterious memorial bench, I felt I was going out of my mind. I went downstairs again and questioned the boy at the desk. Had anyone come in during the past few days and cleaned out the contents of Room 248? He didn't know. He couldn't say. I looked through the signatures in the book over the past week – a crazy thought occurred to me that I would see Phidias's, that he had somehow come back from the dead and retrieved his books. After all, he was the only other person with a key to that room. But there was no signature I could recognise.

Where had the books gone? I immediately heard George's voice in my head: Maybe they've been taken to the mystery room?

Which reminded me: school would be out, I was already late to pick my son up. I abandoned the quest. I have no job, no employer and no trace of him. There are no answers.

George informed me that he'd found a second sailfin molly dead in the aquarium.

Oh dear, I said, which one is it? My mind was elsewhere.

Orpheus, he said. He was floating.

I said I expected Eurydice would be pining, and did he want to bury Orpheus in the garden alongside Bruiser?

No, he said, I've got rid of him.

Of his own accord he'd fished out the little corpse with the net and deposited it in the waste bin. I commended him for his initiative, but he must have heard the surprise in my voice.

Well, I suppose mollies die all the time, don't they? he said, by way of elucidation.

I suppose they do.

Mummy, he said.

Yes?

Can we buy some more mollies some time soon?

Of course we can, George.

Mummy.

What now?

Is Mr Peralta coming back?

Mr Peralta? I don't think so, my love.

That's a shame. I liked him.

I know you did.

Where is he now?

I don't know, dear.

Is he in the mystery room?

The what?

You remember, Mummy, we couldn't find it.

Well, I don't know. It seems as if we knew Mr Peralta for quite a while, doesn't it, and yet it's not actually that long. Goodness me, how long has it been?

How long is what, Mummy?

Since I started this job working for Mr Peralta. It was in March, wasn't it?

About 16 million seconds.

Good grief, have you been counting?

Not all the time.

Part of the time?

Well, actually, I just worked it out.

OK, let's see, there's Christmas coming up next, I suppose, how long is it till school breaks up for Christmas?

Hmm. Only about six million seconds.

Blimey, George. Did you just work *that* out?

Yes.

So are you looking forward to the end of term?

Yeah.

But you are getting on all right at your new school, aren't you?

Yeah, all right.

Because you never say. You never tell me anything. Come on, tell me truthfully, love, how are you getting on at Deadmans Beach Junior?

All right.

Have you made any friends?

Yeah, sort of.

And you're doing interesting things, you're learning stuff?

Yeah.

So what did you do today?

We played football.

Yes, of course you did. Did you enjoy that?

Yeah. I touched the ball three times.

And what do you think of your classmates?

Some of them are all right. Some of them are a bit stupid. Well, most of them.

That's a bit depressing, George.

Yeah.

What makes you think they're stupid?

Well ... none of them know who the Beatles were. And they don't know anything about climate change.

Maybe there's a job for you to do there, to enlighten them, George.

Well, they're not interested. But I am looking forward to Christmas, Mummy.

That's good. So what do you want Santa Claus to bring you?

There's no Santa Claus.

Oh, so we've reached that stage, have we?

It's just you, isn't it, Mummy?

No comment.

You and Daddy. In the middle of the night.

I'm not saying anything.

But Mummy.

Yes?

Is Daddy coming back?

That's a difficult question.

What's difficult about it?

We need to think about it very carefully.

You see, Mummy, you say I don't tell you anything, but you don't tell me anything either –

Give us a break, George, your dad and I are trying to work things out.

– and you're supposed to be a role model.

A role model? Where on earth do you get this fancy language from? I'm trying, George, I'm trying. We're both trying.

I wish Daddy was back.

It's not that easy, George.

It *is* easy.

I promise you we're trying.

(Silence.)

George? We're doing our best.

Hmm.

George, speak to me, please.

Why should I?

Give us a kiss now.

(Silence.)

Come on, George, don't be silly, give Mummy a kiss.

Don't want to.

Come on, just a cuddle, just a wee hug.

All right.

•

The sum of human knowledge is far from complete. Sometimes it seems as though it is becoming less and less complete
as time goes by. Out on the Dead Level fields, sheep will be
packed into their winter fleece again, aligned horizontally.
Here there are no back-stories, there is no closure; there are
only latent possibilities. The marsh frogs sing their five-fold
song. So things go slipping into the future. Things lose their
exactness. Another poet said that.

On the tree line encircling the village of Deadhurst, beyond
the Old Canal, a grey heron may clearly be observed visiting
its nest to feed a large, late fledgling. To the right of this,
smoke pours out from between trees on the distant hills. Also
a pylon projects above the tree line. Along the canal, a juvenile
mute swan ducks its head gracefully as it swims under a thick
drainage pipe, encrusted with corrosion, that crosses the
water within its trajectory. On the nearside of the canal graze
a herd of beautiful and tranquil cattle, the adults mostly
cream coloured, the young ones ranging from earth- to choco-
late-brown. It is restful to contemplate gorgeous kine. In the
meadow through which they range, several tiny brilliant red
and black butterfly-like creatures of unknown species, and
much smaller than any known, flit from flower to flower, taking advantage of a spell of late sunshine before winter sets in.
Upon the wires and between the hedgerows, starlings are
grouped in pre-migration patterns. On the sloping field to the
east a woman followed by two sheepdogs can be seen opening
a farm gate and marching through briskly to mount a quad
bike hauling a trailer. One dog jumps into the trailer to take a
ride; the other runs alongside as she drives off rapidly across
the field in the direction of the line of wind turbines whose
blades rotate slowly on the horizon. There is a sudden flash of
sunlight on the meres, which are dotted with fowl.

Music is playing a considerable distance away. The old,
well-loved and banal chord changes.

The mystery of banality resides in this: how it points to the absence at the heart of presence. You can only show what is not, and not what is. Only when you have shown everything that is not will what is be revealed.

In Deadmans Beach, on the day after the bonfire procession, a lorry passes slowly along the high street attended by three young men in hi-vis jackets collecting warning cones. An elderly woman is accompanied on her walk by her West Highland terrier. She carries a small plastic bag containing its morning production, which she drops into the bin provided for that purpose. Intermittent conversations are audible. Outside the sub-post office and general store, where on offer are piles of bags of potting compost, fat balls packed into green netting, four-litre plastic flasks of blue de-icer and "remarkable food for your freezer", a woman asks a man: Have you still got your gallbladder? The reply is indecipherable. An elderly white man in glasses wearing an African wool cap and a multicoloured woollen jumper glances upwards as a cloud masks the sun. What you doing for Christmas, anything nice? We're going to *them* this year. It's nice to get away. Isn't it just?

The Catch-22 fish & chip shop and the Go Sing Chinese takeaway are both closed. In the Sanctuary Café, a man with a flamboyant moustache attempts to interest the dour girl who serves the tables: You don't often see a setting full moon, he is saying. The girl is clearly not paying attention. She continues to remove the used crockery and cutlery with a great clattering. A fresh notice has recently been posted next to the till, setting out the conditions for the café's Christmas dinner: 7pm sit down; you will get a three-course meal with a bottle of wine to share between two people; bookings only, and bookings must be made no later than 15th December; payment required at time of booking. Outside, the double-decker bus to Moorshurst, the 201, draws up at the stop, pauses, then moves off again. Deadmans Beach parish church advertises a sale of secondhand books, mostly battered paperbacks – thrillers, romances, "literary" novels – with some encyclopaedias and DVDs inter-spersed. Another sign outside claims: God says I know the plans for you. Just up the road, a dilapidated shopfront adver-tises Mortgages, Business Premises, Below Valuation Proper-ties. But By Appointment Only – please leave all post next door at No 51A, urges a typewritten message appended.

Near the school, a concrete public toilet block, decorated with graffiti, shows a notice headed ANTI-SOCIAL BEHAV-IOUR:

> There have been complaints of anti-social behaviour occurring in these facilities.
> The exterior entrances to these toilets are under surveillance.
> Persons who frequently enter this building may be reported to the ASBO Panel.

But another notice adds: Sorry these toilets are closed for the winter. Please use the disabled cubicle. (It appears, how-ever, that the thus-named cubicle is literally disabled in that it cannot be locked.)

A woman is heard to comment as she goes past with her partner: You see them toilets, once the pride of Deadmans Beach – look at them now!

Music can be heard more distinctly now. There is consider-able reverberation on the guitar, the percussion is busy and redolent of the qualities of wood and stretched skin, the bass sound resembles somewhat that of a North African instru-ment. The vocals can be distinguished clearly. There are vocal harmonies using intervals that could be described as plaintive – the intervals associated culturally with plaint and hurt:

> Yeah, Six Fingered Sally,
> I caught her creeping down, creeping down....

The music dies away suddenly. It may be it was only a memory, or an after-echo. Branches in the hedge marking the boundary between the bungalow township and the playing fields are clad in lichen. There is a roar, and a bulbous helicopter of unknown design, closely resembling a giant bee, flies overhead noisily and is soon gone. A solitary gull wheels over the football pitch, which has been marked out, yet lacks goalposts. Beyond the Marine Treatment Works, in the distance, a solitary dark figure and dog can be observed on the shingle; then nothing save rocks covered in kelp exposed by the tide, and a grey line of breakers edged with foam.

On the shoreline, where the wind is high, three gigantic tractor/bulldozers shunt back and forth, constantly moving vast quantities of shingle. It is not possible to see through the tinted glass of their cabs, mounted high on the vehicles, and there is no other obvious sign of human agency. All evidence of last night's bonfire has now been obliterated. Further along the shore is to be found the small fleet of fishing boats, drawn high up on the shingle, safe from the rough waters, slumbering peacefully.

Onward come the great breakers, rolling in sequence, one after the other, with hundreds of points of white light flashing at their crests, sometimes merging into white sheets that charge the shore and crash at the breaking point. Three or four crests are always in the process of forming, replacing those that have decayed and burst into formless foam, while further off new rollers can also be observed building, sometimes breaking before ever reaching the beach. A multitude of hues mingle: the predominating indigo of that shadow before which swirls a filigree of froth, but streaked with dark grey and brown, and the rainbow brilliance of the crest, and beyond that yellow, ochre and purple, even apparent flesh-tones where the pale, half-shrouded sun is glancing off the bulk of the water as it advances from the horizon. Or seems to advance, for this is an illusion: the mass of the water is in fact scarcely moving; it is the pure energy of the wave formation moving through it that creates that impression, just as the colours themselves are caused by vibrations of various frequencies reflected at different angles from a disturbed air/water interface. So the illusion replicates itself all the way down to the molecular level until emptiness is found, and the only record of movement is that produced by the mind – this report, for example – though the mind produces only illusions. Glittering, flashing, sparkling, the great mass of water appears always to be disintegrating or at the point of disintegrating, turning white lacework filaments on a dark green background into pure white. We name this the sea – and truly it is something great and terrible and wonderful to be lost at.

Also available from grand**IOTA**

APROPOS JIMMY INKLING
Brian Marley
In a Westminster café-cum-courtroom, Jimmy Inkling is on trial, perhaps for his life. Unless, of course, he's dead already. But will that be enough to prevent him from eliminating those who give evidence against him?

978-1-874400-73-8   318pp

WILD METRICS
Ken Edwards
1970s London: short-life communal living, the beginnings of the alt-poetry scene, not forgetting sex, drugs and rock'n'roll. Forty years on: where have the wild metrics of those days taken us? This prose extravaganza dives into the inscrutable forking paths of memory, questions what poetry is, and concludes that the author cannot know what he is doing.

978-1-874400-74-5   244pp

BRONTE WILDE
Fanny Howe
This early novel, briefly in print in the 1970s, has been revised by the author and is now published in this form for the first time. It is also her first novel to be published in the UK. It is the tragic tale of a dispossessed young woman in thrall to a childhood friend, set against the background of the emerging counter-culture of the early 1960s.

978-1-874400-75-2   158pp

Production of this book has been made possible with the help of the following individuals and organisations who subscribed in advance:

Peter Bamfield
Chris Beckett
Charles Bernstein
Lillian Blakey
Andrew Brewerton
Ian Brinton
Jasper Brinton
Peter Brown
Norma Cole
Claire Crowther
Beverly Dahlen
Rachel DuPlessis
Ian Durant
Elaine Edwards
Allen Fisher/Spanner
Jim Goar
Paul A Green
Paul Griffiths
Charles Hadfield
John Hall
Andrew Hamilton
Randolph Healy
Rob Holloway
Anthony Howell
Peter Hughes
Romana Huk
Pierre Joris
Richard Makin
Colleen McCallion

Aodhan McCardle
Michael Mann
Shelby Matthews
Askold Melnyczuk
Mark Mendoza
Peter Middleton
Joe Milazzo
David Miller
John Muckle
John Olson
Irene Payne
Sean Pemberton
Simon Perril
Lou Rowan
Sad Press
Michael Schmidt
Maurice Scully
Hazel Smith
Valerie Soar
Harriet Tarlo
Pam Thompson
Keith Tuma
Keith Washington
Susan Wheeler
June Wilkes
John Wilkinson
Tyrone Williams

4 x anon

www.grandiota.co.uk